D0383772

DIANA PALMER

The prolific author of more than one hundred books, Diana Palmer got her start as a newspaper reporter. A multi-*New York Times* and *USA TODAY* bestselling author and voted one of the top ten romance writers in America, she has a gift for telling the most sensual tales with charm and humor. Diana lives with her family in Cornelia, Georgia.

DONNA ALWARD

A busy wife and mother of three (two daughters and the family dog), Donna Alward believes hers is the best job in the world: a combination of stay-at-home mom and romance novelist. An avid reader since childhood, Donna always made up her own stories. She completed her arts degree in English literature in 1994, but it wasn't until 2001 that she penned her first full-length novel and found herself hooked on writing romance. In 2006 she sold her first manuscript, and now writes warm, emotional stories for Harlequin® Romance.

In her new home office in Nova Scotia, Donna loves being back on the east coast of Canada after nearly twelve years in Alberta, where her career began, writing about cowboys and the West. Donna's debut romance, *Hired by the Cowboy,* was awarded the Bookseller's Best Award in 2008 for Best Traditional Romance.

With the Atlantic Ocean only minutes from her doorstep, Donna has found a fresh take on life and promises even more great romances in the near future!

Donna loves to hear from readers. You can contact her through her website, www.donnaalward.com, her page at www.myspace.com/dalward or through her publisher.

New York Times Bestselling Author

DIANA PALMER

Diamond in the Rough

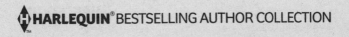
HARLEQUIN® BESTSELLING AUTHOR COLLECTION

Recycling programs
for this product may
not exist in your area.

ISBN-13: 978-0-373-18070-7

Copyright © 2013 by Harlequin Books S.A.

The publisher acknowledges the copyright holders of the individual works
as follows:

DIAMOND IN THE ROUGH
First North American Publication 2009
Copyright © 2009 by Diana Palmer

FALLING FOR MR. DARK & DANGEROUS
First North American Publication 2008
Copyright © 2008 by Donna Alward

For questions and comments about the quality of this book,
please contact us at CustomerService@Harlequin.com.

Printed in U.S.A.

CONTENTS

Dear Friends,

It has been several years since I wrote two books dealing with a little town called Medicine Ridge in Montana. One of those books was *Circle of Gold,* which was the story of Gil Callister and his daughters' governess Kasie Mayfield, whom he later married. Gil had a brother, John, who featured largely in the book, but whose story was never told.

I was given the opportunity to revisit the Callisters and tell what happened to John. While my heart is still with the Long, Tall Texans of Jacobsville, Texas, (and there will be many more stories about them in years to come), I do like those Men of Medicine Ridge in Montana. So John's story may not be the last one I tell.

I have spent many happy days roaming around Montana, and I can tell you that it has some of the nicest people on earth. It also has some of the most beautiful scenery anywhere. I hope that I've managed to capture some of the magic and elegance of this historic state in the books I write about it. If you've never been to Montana, it's a great place to vacation. I can vouch for that!

I hope you enjoy John Callister's story. Thank you all for your years of loyalty, and your friendship.

Love from your fan,

Diana Palmer

DIAMOND IN THE ROUGH

New York Times Bestselling Author

Diana Palmer

For my friend Nancy C.,
who came all the way from Indiana just to meet me.
Thanks for the beautiful cowboy quilt, Nancy—
I'll never forget you!

And thanks to all of you on my bulletin board at
my website, including Nancy and Amy, who spent
hours of their precious free time making me a
compendium of all the families in Jacobsville,
Texas! Now, guys, maybe I can make fewer mistakes
when I write about them! Love you all.

Chapter 1

The little town, Hollister, wasn't much bigger than Medicine Ridge, Montana, where John Callister and his brother Gil had a huge ranch. But they'd decided that it wasn't wise to confine their whole livelihood to one area. They needed to branch out a little, maybe try something different. On the main ranch, they ran a purebred bull and breeding operation with state-of-the-art science. John and Gil had decided to try something new here in Hollister, Montana; a ranch which would deal specifically in young purebred sale bulls, using the latest technology to breed for specific traits like low calving weight, lean conformation, and high weight gain ratio, among others. In addition, they were going to try new growth programs that combined specific organic grasses with mixed protein and grains to improve their production.

In the depressed economy, tailor-made beef cattle

would cater to the discerning organic beef consumer. Gil and John didn't run beef cattle, but their champion bulls were bred to appeal to ranchers who did. It was a highly competitive field, especially with production costs going sky-high. Cattlemen could no longer depend on random breeding programs left up to nature. These days, progeny resulted from tailored genetics. It was a high-tech sort of agriculture. Gil and John had pioneered some of the newer computer-based programs that yielded high on profits coupled with less wasteful producer strategies.

For example, Gil had heard about a program that used methane gas from cattle waste to produce energy to run ranch equipment. The initial expense for the hardware had been high, but it was already producing results. Much of the electricity used to light the barns and power the ranch equipment was due to the new technology. Any surplus energy could be sold back to the electric company. The brothers had also installed solar panels to heat water in the main house and run hydraulic equipment in the breeding barn and the stockyard. One of the larger agricultural magazines had featured an article about their latest innovations. Gil's photo, and that of his daughters and his new wife, had graced the pages of the trade publication. John had been at a cattle show and missed the photo shoot. He didn't mind. He'd never been one to court publicity. Nor was Gil. But they wouldn't miss a chance to advertise their genetically superior cattle.

John usually traveled to show the cattle. But he was getting tired of spending his life on the road. Now that Gil had married Kasie, the brothers' former assistant, and the small girls from Gil's first marriage, Bess and Jenny, were in school, John was feeling lonelier than ever, and more restless. Not that he'd had a yen for

Kasie, but Gil's remarriage made him aware of the passing of time. He wasn't getting any younger; he was in his thirties. The traveling was beginning to wear on him. Although he dated infrequently, he'd never found a woman he wanted to keep. He was also feeling like a fifth wheel at the family ranch.

So he'd volunteered to come up to Hollister to rebuild this small, dilapidated cattle ranch that he and Gil had purchased and see if an injection of capital and new blood stock and high-tech innovation could bring it from bankruptcy to a higher status in the world of purebred cattle.

The house, which John had only seen from aerial photos, was a wreck. No maintenance had been done on it for years by its elderly owner. He'd had to let most of his full-time cowboys go when the market fell, and he wasn't able to keep up with the demands of the job with the part-timers he retained. Fences got broken, cattle escaped, the well went dry, the barn burned down and, finally, the owner decided to cut his losses. He'd offered the ranch for sale, as-is, and the Callister brothers had bought it from him. The old man had gone back East to live with a daughter.

Now John had a firsthand look at the monumental task facing him. He'd have to hire new cowboys, build a barn as well as a stable, spend a few thousand making the house livable, sink a well, restring the fences, buy equipment, set up the methane-based power production plant... He groaned at the thought of it. The ranch in Medicine Ridge was state-of-the-art. This was medieval, by comparison. It was going to take longer than a month or two. This was a job that would take many months. And all that work had to be done before any cattle could be brought onto the place. What had seemed like a pleasant hobby in the beginning now looked like it would become a career.

There were two horses in a corral with a lean-to for protection from the weather, all that remained of the old man's Appaloosas. The remuda, or string of working ranch horses, had been sold off long ago. The remaining part-time cowboys told John that they'd brought their own mounts with them to work, while there was still a herd of cattle on the place. But the old man had sold off all his stock and let the part-timers go before he sold the ranch. Lucky, John thought, that he'd been able to track them down and offer them full-time jobs again. They were eager for the work. The men all lived within a radius of a few miles. If John had to wait on replacing the ranch's horses, the men could bring their own to work temporarily while John restocked the place.

He planned to rebuild and restock quickly. Something would have to be done about a barn. A place for newborn calves and sick cattle was his first priority. That, and the house. He was sleeping on the floor in a sleeping bag, heating water on a camp stove for shaving and bathing in the creek. Thank God, he thought, that it was spring and not winter. Food was purchased in the town's only café, where he had two meals a day. He ate sandwiches for lunch, purchased from a cooler in the convenience store/gas station at the edge of town. It was rough living for a man who was used to five-star hotels and the best food money could buy. But it was his choice, he reminded himself.

He drove into town in a mid-level priced pickup truck. No use advertising that he was wealthy. Prices would skyrocket, since he wasn't on friendly terms with anyone here. He'd only met the cowboys. The people in town didn't even know his name yet.

The obvious place to start, he reasoned, was the feed store. It sold ranch supplies including tack. The owner might know where he could find a reputable builder.

He pulled up at the front door and strode in. The place was dusty and not well-kept. There seemed to be only one employee, a slight girl with short, wavy dark hair and a pert figure, wearing a knit pullover with worn jeans and boots.

She was sorting bridles but she looked up when he approached. Like many old-time cowboys, he was sporting boots with spurs that jingled when he walked. He was also wearing an old Colt 45 in a holster slung low on his hip under the open denim shirt he was wearing with jeans and a black T-shirt. It was wild country, this part of Montana, and he wasn't going out on the range without some way of protecting himself from potential predators.

The girl stared at him in an odd, fixed way. He didn't realize that he had the looks that would have been expected in a motion picture star. His blond hair, under the wide-brimmed cowboy hat, had a sheen like gold, and his handsome face was very attractive. He had the tall, elegant body of a rider, lean and fit and muscular without exaggerated lines.

"What the hell are you doing?" came a gruff, angry voice from the back. "I told you to go bring in those new sacks of feed before the rain ruins them, not play with the tack! Get your lazy butt moving, girl!"

The girl flushed, looking frightened. "Yes, sir," she said at once, and jumped up to do what he'd told her to.

John didn't like the way the man spoke to her. She was very young, probably still in her teens. No man should speak that way to a child.

He approached the man with a deadpan expression, only his blue eyes sparkling with temper.

The man, overweight and half-bald, older than John, turned as he approached. "Something I can do for you?" he asked in a bored tone, as if he didn't care whether he got the business or not.

"You the owner?" John asked him.

The man glared. "The manager. Tarleton. Bill Tarleton."

John tilted his hat back. "I need to find someone who can build a barn."

The manager's eyebrows arched. His eyes slid over John's worn jeans and boots and inexpensive clothing. He laughed. His expression was an insult. "You own a ranch around here?" he asked in disbelief.

John fought back his temper. "My boss does," he said, in an impulsive moment. "He's hiring. He just bought the Bradbury place out on Chambers Road."

"That old place?" Tarleton made a face. "Hell, it's a wreck! Bradbury just sat on his butt and let the place go to hell. Nobody understood why. He had some good cattle years ago, cattlemen came from as far away as Oklahoma and Kansas to buy his stock."

"He got old," John said.

"I guess. A barn, you say." He pursed his lips. "Well, Jackson Hewett has a construction business. He builds houses. Fancy houses, some of them. I reckon he could build a barn. He lives just outside town, over by the old train station. He's in the local telephone directory."

"I'm obliged," John said.

"Your boss…he'll be needing feed and tack, I guess?" Tarleton added.

John nodded.

"If I don't have it on hand, I can order it."

"I'll keep that in mind. I need something right now, though—a good tool kit."

"Sassy!" he yelled. "The man wants a tool kit! Bring one of the boxes from that new line we started stocking!"

"Yes, sir!" There was the sound of scrambling boots.

"She ain't much help," the manager grumbled. "Misses work sometimes. Got a mother with cancer and a little sister, six, that the mother adopted. I guess she'll end up alone, just her and the kid."

"Does the mother get government help?" John asked, curious.

"Not much," Tarleton scoffed. "They say she never did much except sit with sick folk, even before she got the cancer. Sassy's bringing in the only money they got. The old man took off years ago with another woman. Just left. At least they got a house. Ain't much of one, but it's a roof over their heads. The mother got it in the divorce settlement."

John felt a pang when he noticed the girl tugging a heavy toolbox. She looked as if she was barely able to lift a bridle.

"Here, I'll take that," John said, trying to sound nonchalant. He took it from her hands and set it on the counter, popping it open. His eyebrows lifted as he examined the tools. "Nice."

"Expensive, too, but it's worth it," Tarleton told him.

"Boss wants to set up an account in his own name, but I'll pay cash for this," John said, pulling out his wallet. "He gave me pocket money for essentials."

Tarleton's eyes got bigger as John started peeling off twenty-dollar bills. "Okay. What name do I put on the account?"

"Callister," John told him without batting an eyelash. "Gil Callister."

"Hey, I've heard of him," Tartleton said at once, giving John a bad moment. "He's got a huge ranch down in Medicine Ridge."

"That's the one," John said. "Ever seen him?"

"Who, me?" The older man laughed. "I don't run in those circles, no, sir. We're just country folk here, not millionaires."

John felt a little less worried. It would be to his advantage if the locals didn't know who he really was. Not yet, anyway. Since he was having to give up cattle shows for the foreseeable future, there wasn't much chance that his face would be gracing any trade papers. It might be nice, he pondered, to be accepted as an ordinary man for once. His wealth seemed to draw opportunists, especially feminine ones. He could enjoy playing the part of a cowboy for a change.

"No problem with opening an account here, then, if we put some money down first as a credit?" John asked.

"No problem at all." Tarleton grinned. "I'll start that account right now. You tell Mr. Callister anything he needs, I can get for him!"

"I'll tell him."

"And your name...?" the manager asked.

"John," he replied. "John Taggert."

Taggert was his middle name. His maternal grandfather, a pioneer in South Dakota, had that name.

"Taggert." The manager shook his head. "Never heard that one."

John smiled. "It's not famous."

The girl was still standing beside the counter. John handed her the bills to pay for the toolbox. She worked the cash register and counted out his change.

"Thanks," John said, smiling at her.

She smiled back at him, shyly. Her green eyes were warm and soft. "You're welcome."

"Get back to work," Tarleton told her.

"Yes, sir." She turned and went back to the bags on the loading platform.

John frowned. "Isn't she too slight to be hefting bags that size?"

"It goes with the job," Tarleton said defensively. "I had a strong teenage boy working for me, but his parents moved to Billings and he had to go along. She was all I could get. She swore she could do the job. So I'm letting her."

"I guess she's stronger than she looks," John remarked, but he didn't like it.

Tarleton nodded absently. He was putting Gil Callister's name in his ledger.

"I'll be back," John told him as he picked up the toolbox.

Tarleton nodded again.

John glanced at the girl, who was straining over a heavy bag, and walked out of the store with a scowl on his face.

He paused. He didn't know why. He glanced back into the store and saw the manager standing on the loading platform, watching the girl lift the feed sacks. It wasn't the look a manager should be giving an employee. John's eyes narrowed. He was going to do something about that.

One of the older cowboys, Chad Dean by name, was waiting for him at the house when he brought in the toolbox.

"Say, that's a nice one," he told the other man. "Your boss must be stinking rich."

"He is," John mused. "Pays good, too."

The cowboy chuckled. "That would be nice, getting a paycheck that I could feed my kids on. I couldn't move my family to another town without giving up land that belonged to my grandfather, so I toughed it out. It's been rough, what with food prices and gas going through the roof."

"You'll get your regular check plus travel expenses," John told him. "We'll pay for the gas if we have to send you anywhere to pick up things."

"That's damned considerate."

"If you work hard, your wages will go up."

"We'll all work hard," Dean promised solemnly. "We're just happy to have jobs."

John pursed his lips. "Do you know a girl named Sassy? Works for Tarleton in the feed store?"

"Yeah," Dean replied tersely. "He's married, and he makes passes at Sassy. She needs that job. Her mama's dying. There's a six-year-old kid lives with them, too, and Sassy has to take care of her. I don't know how in hell she manages on what she gets paid. All that, and having to put up with Tarleton's harassment, too. My wife told her she should call the law and report him. She won't. She says she can't afford to lose the position. Town's so small, she'd never get hired again. Tarleton would make sure of it, just for spite, if she quit."

John nodded. His eyes narrowed thoughtfully. "I expect things will get easier for her," he predicted.

"Do you? Wish I did. She's a sweet kid. Always doing things for other people." He smiled. "My son had his appendix out. It was Sassy who saw what it was, long before we did. He was in the feed store when he got sick. She called the doctor. He looked over my Mark and agreed it was appendicitis. Doc drove the boy over to Billings to the hospital. Sassy went to see him. God knows how she got there. Her old beat-up vehicle would never make it as far as Billings. Hitched a ride with Carl Parks, I expect. He's in his seventies, but he watches out for Sassy and her mother. Good old fellow."

John nodded. "Sounds like it." He hesitated. "How old is the girl?"

"Eighteen or nineteen, I guess. Just out of high school."

"I figured that." John was disappointed. He didn't understand why. "Okay, here's what we're going to do about those fences temporarily..."

In the next two days, John did some amateur detective work. He phoned a private detective who worked for the Callisters on business deals and put him on the Tarleton man. It didn't take him long to report back.

The feed store manager had been allowed to resign from a job in Billings for unknown reasons, but the detective found one other employee who said it was sexual harassment of an employee. He wasn't charged with anything. He'd moved here, to Hollister, with his family when the owner of the feed store, a man named Jake McGuire, advertised in a trade paper for someone to manage it for him. Apparently Tarleton had been the only applicant and McGuire was desperate. Tarleton got the job.

"This McGuire," John asked over his cell phone, "how old is he?"

"In his thirties," came the reply. "Everyone I spoke to about him said that he's a decent sort."

"In other words, he doesn't have a clue that Tarleton's hassling the girl."

"That would be my guess."

John's eyes twinkled. "Do you suppose McGuire would like to sell that business?"

There was a chuckle. "He's losing money hand over fist on that place. Two of the people I spoke to said he'd almost give it away to get rid of it."

"Thanks," John said. "That answers my question. Can you get me McGuire's telephone number?"

"Already did. Here it is."

John wrote it down. The next morning, he put in a call to McGuire Enterprises in Billings.

"I'm looking to buy a business in a town called Hollister," John said after he'd introduced himself. "Someone said you might know the owner of the local feed store."

"The feed store?" McGuire replied. "You want to buy it?" He sounded astonished.

"I might," John said. "If the price is right."

There was a pause. "Okay, here's the deal. That business was started by my father over forty years ago. I inherited it when he died. I don't really want to sell it."

"It's going bankrupt," John replied.

There was another pause. "Yeah, I know," came the disgusted reply. "I had to put in a new manager there, and he didn't come cheap. I had to move him and his wife from Billings down here." He sighed. "I'm between a rock and a hard place. I own several businesses, and I don't have the time to manage them myself. That particular one has sentimental value. The manager just went to work. There's a chance he can pull it out of the red."

"There's a better chance that he's going to get you involved in a major lawsuit."

"What? What for?"

"For one thing, he was let go from his last job for sexual harassment, or that's what we turned up on a background check. He's up to his old tricks in Hollister, this time with a young girl just out of high school that he hired to work for him."

"Good Lord! He came with excellent references!"

"He might have them," John said. "But it wouldn't surprise me if that wasn't the first time he lost a job for the same reason. He was giving the girl the eye when I was in there. There's local gossip that the girl may sue if your manager doesn't lay off her. There goes your bottom line," he added dryly.

"Well, that's what you get when you're desperate for personnel," McGuire said wearily. "I couldn't find anybody else who'd take the job. I can't fire him without proper cause, and I just paid to move him there! What a hell of a mess!"

"You don't want to sell the business. Okay. How about leasing it to us? We'll fire Tarleton on the grounds that we're leasing the business, put in a manager of our own, and you'll make money. We'll have you in the black in two months."

"And just who is 'we'?" McGuire wanted to know.

"My brother and I. We're ranchers."

"But why would you want to lease a feed store in the middle of nowhere?"

"Because we just bought the Bradbury place. We're going to rebuild the house, add a stable and a barn, and we're going to raise purebred young bulls on the place. The feed store is going to do a lot of business when we start adding personnel to the outfit."

"Old man Bradbury and my father were best friends," McGuire reminisced. "He was a fine rancher, a nice gentleman. His health failed and the business failed with him. It's nice to know it will be a working ranch again."

"It's good land. We'll make it pay."

"What did you say your name was?"

"Callister," John told him. "My brother and I have a sizable spread over in Medicine Ridge."

"Those Callisters? My God, your holdings are worth millions!"

"At least." John chuckled.

There was a soft whistle. "Well, if you're going to keep me in orders, I suppose I'd be willing to lease the place to you."

"And the manager?"

"I just moved him there." McGuire groaned again.

"We'll pay to move him back to Billings and give him two weeks' severance pay," John said. "I will not agree to let him stay on," he added firmly.

"He may sue."

"Let him," John replied tersely. "If he tries it, I'll make it my life's work to see that any skeleton in his past is brought into the light of day. You can tell him that."

"I'll tell him."

"If you'll give me your attorney's name and number, I'll have our legal department contact him," John said. "I think we'll get along."

There was a deep chuckle. "So do I."

"There's one other matter."

"Yes?"

John hesitated. "I'm going to be working on the place myself, but I don't want anyone local to know who I am. I'll be known as the ranch foreman—Taggert by name. Got that?"

There was a chuckle. "Keeping it low-key, I see. Sure. I won't blow your cover."

"Especially to Tarleton and his employee," John emphasized.

"No problem. I'll tell him your boss phoned me."

"I'm much obliged."

"Before we settle this deal, do you have someone in mind who can take over the business in two weeks if I put Tarleton on notice?"

"Indeed I do," John replied. "He's a retired corporate executive who's bored stiff with retirement. Mind like a steel trap. He could make money in the desert."

"Sounds like just the man for the job."

"I'll have him up here in two weeks."

"That's a deal, then."

"We'll talk again when the paperwork goes through."

"Yes."

John hung up. He felt better about the girl. Not that he expected Tarleton to quit the job without a fight. He hoped the threat of uncovering any past sins would work the magic. The thought of Sassy being bothered by that would-be Casanova was disturbing.

He phoned the architect and asked him to come over to the ranch the following day to discuss drawing up plans for a stable and a barn. He hired an electrician to rewire the house and do the work in the new construction. He employed six new cowboys and an engineer. He set up payroll for everyone he'd hired through the corporation's main offices in Medicine Ridge, and went about getting fences repaired and wells drilled. He also phoned Gil and had him send down a team of engineers to start construction on solar panels to help provide electricity for the operation.

Once those plans were underway, he made a trip into Hollister to see how things were going at the feed store. His detective had managed to dig up three other harassment charges against Tarleton from places he'd lived before he moved to Montana in the first place. There were no convictions, sadly. But the charges might be enough. Armed with that information, he wasn't uncomfortable having words with the man, if it was necessary.

And it seemed that it would be. The minute he walked in the door, he knew there was going to be trouble. Tarleton was talking to a customer, but he gave John a glare that spoke volumes. He finished his business with the customer and waited until he left. Then he walked up to John belligerently.

"What the hell did your employer tell my boss?" he demanded furiously. "He said he was leasing the store, but only on the condition that I didn't go with the deal!"

"Not my problem," John said, and his pale eyes glittered. "It was my boss's decision."

"Well, he's got no reason to fire me!" Tarleton said, his round face flushing. "I'll sue the hell out of him, and your damned boss, too!"

John stepped closer to the man and leaned down, emphasizing his advantage in height. "You're welcome. My boss will go to the local district attorney in Billings and turn over the court documents from your last sexual harassment charge."

Tarleton's face went from red to white in seconds. He froze in place. "He'll…what?" he asked weakly.

John's chiseled lips pulled up into a cold smile. "And I'll encourage your hired girl over there—" he indicated her with a jerk of his head "—to come clean about the way you've treated her as well. I think she could be persuaded to bring charges."

Tarleton's arrogance vanished. He looked hunted.

"Take my advice," John said quietly. "Get out while you still have time. My boss won't hesitate a second. He has two daughters of his own." His eyes narrowed menacingly. "One of our ranch hands back home tried to wrestle a temporary maid down in the hay out in our barn. He's serving three to five for sexual assault." John smiled. "We have a firm of attorneys on retainer."

"We?" Tarleton stammered.

"I'm a managerial employee of the ranch. The ranch is a corporation," John replied smoothly.

Tarleton's teeth clenched. "So I guess I'm fired."

"I guess you volunteered to resign," John corrected. "That gets you moved back to Billings at the ranch's expense, and gives you severance pay. It also spares you lawsuits and other...difficulties."

The older man weighed his options. John could see his mind working. Tarleton gave John an arrogant look. "What the hell," he said coldly. "I didn't want to live in this damned fly trap anyway!"

He turned on his heel and walked away. The girl, Sassy, was watching the byplay with open curiosity. John raised an eyebrow. She flushed and went back to work at once.

Chapter 2

Cassandra Peale told herself that the intense conversation the new foreman of the Bradbury place was having with her boss didn't concern her. The foreman had made that clear with a lifted eyebrow and a haughty look. But there had been an obvious argument and both men had glanced at her while they were having it. She was worried. She couldn't afford to lose her job. Not when her mother, dying of lung cancer, and her mother's ward, Selene, who was only six, depended on what she brought home so desperately.

She gnawed on a fingernail. They were mostly all chewed off. Her mother was sixty-three, Cassandra, who everyone called Sassy, having been born very late in life. They'd had a ranch until her father had become infatuated with a young waitress at the local cafeteria. He'd left his family and run away with the woman, taking most of their savings with him. Without money to pay bills, Sassy's mother had been forced to sell the cattle and most of the land and let the cowboys go. One of them, little Selene's father, had gotten drunk out of desperation and ran his truck off into the river. They'd found him the next morning, dead, leaving Selene completely alone in the world.

My life, Sassy thought, *is a soap opera. It even has a villain.* She glanced covertly at Mr. Tarleton. All he needed was a black mustache and a gun. He'd made her working life hell. He knew she couldn't afford to quit. He was always bumping into her "accidentally," trying to handle her. She was sickened by his advances. She'd never even had a boyfriend. The school she'd gone to, in this tiny town, had been a one-room schoolhouse with all ages included and one teacher. There had only been two boys her own age and three girls including Sassy. The other girls were pretty. So Sassy had never been asked out at all. Once, when she was in her senior year of high school, a teacher's visiting nephew had been kind to her, but her mother had been violently opposed to letting her go on a date with a man she didn't know well. It hadn't mattered. Sassy had never felt those things her romance novels spoke of in such enticing and heart-pattering terms. She'd never even been kissed in a grown-up way. Her only sexual experience—if you could call it that—was being physically harassed by that repulsive would-be Romeo standing behind the counter.

She finished dusting the shelves and wished fate would present her with a nice, handsome boss who was single and found her fascinating. She'd have gladly settled for the Bradbury place's new ramrod. But he didn't look as if he found anything about her that attracted him. In fact, he was ignoring her. Story of my life, she thought as she put aside the dust cloth. It was just as well. She had two dependents and no spare time. Where would she fit a man into her desperate life?

"Missed a spot."

She whirled. She flushed as she looked way up into dancing blue eyes. "W…what?"

John chuckled. The women in his world were sophisticated and full of easy wisdom. This little violet was as unaffected by the modern world as the store she worked in. He was entranced by her.

"I said you missed a spot." He leaned closer. "It was a joke."

"Oh." She laughed shyly, glancing at the shelf. "I might have missed several, I guess. I can't reach high and there's no ladder."

He smiled. "There's always a soapbox."

"No, no," she returned with a smile. "If I get on one of those, I have to give a political speech."

He groaned. "Don't say those words," he said. "If I have to hear one more speech about the economy, I'm having my ears plugged."

"It does get a little irritating, doesn't it?" she asked. "We don't watch the news as much since the television got hit by lightning. The color's gone whacky. I have to think it's a happy benefit of a sad accident."

His eyebrows arched. "Why don't you get a new TV?"

She glowered at him. "Because the hardware store doesn't have a fifty-cent one," she said.

It took a minute for that to sink in. John, who thought nothing of laying down his gold card for the newest wide-screened TV, hadn't realized that even a small set was beyond the means of many lower-income people.

He grimaced. "Sorry," he said. "I guess I've gotten too used to just picking up anything I like in stores."

"They don't arrest you for that?" she asked with a straight face, but her twinkling eyes gave her away.

He laughed. "Not so far. I meant," he added, thinking fast, "that my boss pays me a princely salary for my organizational skills."

"He must, if you can afford a new TV." She sighed. "I don't suppose he needs a professional duster?"

"We could ask him."

She shook her head. "I'd rather work here, in a job I do know." She glanced with apprehension at her boss, who was glaring toward the two of them. "I'd better get back to work before he fires me."

"He can't."

She blinked. "He can't what?"

"Fire you," he said quietly. "He's being replaced in two weeks by a new manager."

Her heart stopped. She felt sick. "Oh, dear."

"You won't convince me that you'll miss him," John said curtly.

She bit a fingernail that was already almost gone. "It's not that. A new manager might not want me to work here anymore…"

"He will."

She frowned. "How can you know that?"

He pursed his lips. "Because the new manager works for my boss, and my boss said not to change employees."

Her face started to relax. "Really?"

"Really."

She glanced again at Tarleton and felt uncomfortable at the furious glare he gave her. "Oh, dear, did somebody say something to your boss about him…about him being forward with me?" she asked worriedly.

"They might have," he said noncommittally.

"He'll get even," she said under her breath. "He's that

sort. He told a lie on a customer who was rude to him, about the man's wife. She almost lost her job over it."

John felt his blood rise. "All you have to do is get through the next two weeks," he told her. "If you have a problem with him, any problem, you can call me. I don't care when or what time." He started to pull out his wallet and give her his business card, until he realized that she thought he was pretending to be hired help, not the big boss. "Have you got a pen and paper?" he asked instead.

"In fact, I do," she replied. She moved behind the counter, tore a piece of brown paper off a roll, and picked up a marking pencil. She handed them to him.

He wrote down the number and handed it back to her. "Don't be afraid of him," he added curtly. "He's in enough trouble without making more for himself with you."

"What sort of trouble is he in?" she wanted to know.

"I can't tell you. It's confidential. Let's just say that he'd better keep his nose clean. Now. I need a few more things." He brought out a list and handed it to her. She smiled and went off to fill the order for him.

He took the opportunity to have a last word with Tarleton.

"I hear you have a penchant for getting even with people who cross you," John said. His eyes narrowed and began to glitter. "For the record, if you touch that girl, or if you even try to cause problems for her of any sort, you'll have to deal with me. I don't threaten people with lawsuits. I get even." The way he said it, added to his even, unblinking glare, had backed down braver men than this middle-aged molester.

Tarleton tried to put on a brave front, but the man's demeanor was unsettling. Taggert was younger than

Tarleton and powerfully muscled for all his slimness. He didn't look like a man who ever walked away from a fight.

"I wouldn't touch her in a blind fit," the older man said haughtily. "I just want to work out my notice and get the hell back to Billings, where people are more civilized."

"Good idea," John replied. "Follow it."

He turned on his heel and went back to Sassy.

She looked even more nervous now. "What did you say to him?" she asked uneasily, because Tarleton looked at her as if he'd like her served up on a spit.

"Nothing of any consequence," he said easily, and he gave her a tender smile. "Got my order ready?"

"Most of it," she said, obviously trying to get her mind back to business. "But we don't carry any of this grass seed you want. It would be special order." She leaned forward. "The hardware store can get it for you at a lower price, but I think we will be faster."

He grinned. "The price won't matter to my boss," he assured her. "But speed will. He's experimenting with all sorts of forage grasses. He's looking for better ways to increase weight without resorting to artificial means. He thinks the older grasses have more nutritional benefit than the hybrids being sowed today."

"He's likely right," she replied. "Organic methods are gaining in popularity. You wouldn't believe how many organic gardeners we have locally."

"That reminds me. I need some insecticidal soap for the beans we're planting."

She hesitated.

He cocked his head. His eyes twinkled. "You want to tell me something, but you're not sure that you should."

She laughed. "I guess so. One of our organic gar-

deners gave up on it for beans. She says it works nicely
for tomatoes and cucumbers, but you need something
with a little more kick for beans and corn. She learned
that the hard way." She grimaced. "So did I. I lost my
first corn planting to corn borers and my beans to bean
beetles. I was determined not to go the harsh pesticide
route."

"Okay. Sell me something harsh, then." He chuckled.

She blushed faintly before she pulled a sack of powerful but environmentally safe insecticide off the shelf
and put it on the counter.

Tarleton was watching the byplay with cold, angry
eyes. So she liked that interfering cowboy, did she? It
made him furious. He was certain that the new foreman
of the Bradbury ranch had talked to someone about him
and passed the information on to McGuire, who owned
this feed store. The cowboy was arrogant for a man who
worked for wages, even for a big outfit like the Callisters'. He was losing his job for the second time in six
months and it would look bad on his record. His wife
was already sick of the moving. She might leave him. It
was a bad day for him when John Taggert walked into
his store. He hoped the man fell in a well and drowned,
he really did.

His small eyes lingered on Sassy's trim figure. She
really made him hot. She wasn't the sort to put up much
of a fight, and that man Taggert couldn't watch her day
and night. Tarleton smiled coldly to himself. If he was
losing his job anyway, he didn't have much to lose.
Might as well get something out of the experience.
Something sweet.

Sassy went home worn-out at the end of the week.
Tarleton had found more work than ever before for her

to do, mostly involving physical labor. He was rearranging all the shelves with the heaviest items like chicken mash and hog feed and horse feed and dog food in twenty-five and fifty-pound bags. Sassy could press fifty pounds, but she was slight and not overly muscular. It was uncomfortable. She wished she could complain to someone, but if she did, it would only make things worse. Tarleton was getting even because he'd been fired. He watched her even more than he had before, and it was in a way that made her very uncomfortable.

Her mother was lying on the sofa watching television when Sassy got home. Little Selene was playing with some cut-outs. Her soft gray eyes lit up and she jumped up and ran to Sassy, to be picked up and kissed.

"How's my girl?" Sassy asked, kissing the soft little cheek.

"I been playing with Dora the Explorer, Sassy!" the little blonde girl told her. "Pippa gave them to me at school!"

Pippa was the daughter of a teacher and her husband, a sweet child who always shared her playthings with Selene. It wasn't a local secret that Sassy could barely afford to dress the child out of the local thrift shop, much less buy her toys.

"That was sweet of her," Sassy said with genuine delight.

"She says I can keep these ones," the child added.

Sassy put her down. "Show them to me."

Her mother smiled wearily up at her. "Pippa's mother is a darling."

Sassy bent and kissed her mother's brow. "So is mine."

Mrs. Peale patted her cheek. "Bad day?" she added.

Sassy only smiled. She didn't trouble her parent with

her daily woes. The older woman had enough worries of her own. The cancer was temporarily in remission, but the doctor had warned that it wouldn't last. Despite all the hype about new treatments and cures, cancer was a formidable adversary. Especially when the victim was Mrs. Peale's age.

"I've had worse," Sassy told her. "What about pancakes and bacon for supper?" she asked.

"Sassy, we had pancakes last night," Selene complained as she showed her cut-outs to the woman.

"I know, baby," Sassy said, bending to kiss her gently. "We have what we can afford. It isn't much."

Selene grimaced. "I'm sorry. I like pancakes," she added apologetically.

"I wish we could have something better," Sassy said. "If there was a better-paying job going, you can bet I'd be applying for it."

Mrs. Peale looked sad. "I'd hoped we could send you to college. At least to a vocational school. Instead we've caused you to land in a dead-end job."

Sassy struck a pose. "I'll have you know I'm expecting a prince any day," she informed them. "He'll come riding up on a white horse with an enormous bouquet of orchids, brandishing a wedding ring."

"If ever a girl deserved one," Mrs. Peale said softly, "it's you, my baby."

Sassy grinned. "When I find him, we'll get you one of those super hospital beds with a dozen controls so you can sit up properly when you want to. And we'll get Selene the prettiest dresses and shoes in the world. And then, we'll buy a new television set, one that doesn't have green people," she added, wincing at the color on the old console TV.

Pipe dreams. But dreams were all she had. She looked

at her companions, her family, and decided that she'd much rather have them than a lot of money. But a little money, she sighed mentally, certainly would help their situation. Prince Charming existed, sadly, only in fairy tales.

The architect had his plans ready for the big barn. John approved them and told the man to get to work. Within a few days, building materials started arriving, carried in by enormous trucks: lumber, steel, sand, concrete blocks, bricks, and mortar and other construction equipment. The project was worth several million dollars, and it created a stir locally, because it meant jobs for many people who were having to commute to Billings to get work. They piled onto the old Bradbury place to fill out job applications.

John grinned at the enthusiasm of the new workers. He'd started the job with misgivings, wondering if it was sane to expect to find dozens of laborers in such a small, economically depressed area. But he'd been pleasantly surprised. He had new men from surrounding counties lining up for available jobs, experienced workers at that. He began to be optimistic.

He was doing a lot of business with the local feed store, but his presence was required on-site while the construction was in the early stages. He'd learned the hard way that it wasn't wise to leave someone in charge without making sure they understood what was required during every step.

He felt a little guilty that he hadn't been back to check that Sassy hadn't had problems with Tarleton, who only had two days left before he was being replaced. The new manager, Buck Mannheim, was already in town, renting a room from a local widow while he familiarized himself with the business. Tarleton, he told John, wasn't making it easy for him to do that. The man was resentful, surly, and he was making Sassy do some incredibly hard and unnecessary tasks at the store. Buck would have put a stop to it, but he felt he had no real authority until Tartleton's two weeks were officially up. He didn't want them to get sued.

As if that weasel would dare sue them, John thought angrily. But he didn't feel right putting Buck in the line of fire. The older man had come up here as a favor to Gil to run the business, not to go toe-to-toe with a belligerent soon-to-be-ex-employee.

"I'll handle this," John told the older man. "I need to stop by the post office anyway and get some more stamps."

"I don't understand why any man would treat a child so brutally," Buck said. "She's such a nice girl."

"She's not a girl, Buck," John replied.

"She's just nineteen," Buck replied, smiling. "I have a granddaughter that age."

John felt uncomfortable. "She seems older."

"She's got some mileage on her. A lot of responsibility. She needs help. That child her mother adopted goes to school in pitiful clothes. I know that most of the money they have is spent for utilities." He shook his head. "Hell of a shame. Her mother's little check is all used up for medicine that she has to take to stay alive."

John felt guilty that he hadn't looked into that situation. He hadn't planned to get himself involved with his employees' problems, and Sassy wasn't technically even that, but it seemed there was nobody else in a position to help. He frowned. "You said Sassy's mother was divorced? Where's her husband? Couldn't he help? Even if Sassy's not young enough for child support, she's still his child. She shouldn't have to be the breadwinner."

"He ran off with a young woman. Just walked out the door and left. He's never so much as called or written in the years he's been gone, since the divorce," Buck said knowledgeably. "From what I hear, he was a good husband and father. He couldn't fight his infatuation for the waitress." He shrugged. "That's life."

"I hope the waitress hangs him out to dry," John muttered darkly. "Sassy should never have been landed with so much responsibility at her age."

"She handles it well, though," Buck said admiringly. "She's the nicest young woman I've met in a long time. She earns her paycheck."

"She shouldn't be having to press weights to do that," John replied. "I got too wrapped up in my barn to keep an eye on her. I'll make up for it today."

"Good for you. She could use a friend."

John walked in and noticed immediately how quiet it was. The front of the store was deserted. It was mid morning and there were no customers. He scowled, wondering why Sassy wasn't at the counter.

He heard odd sounds coming from the tack room. He walked toward it until he heard a muffled scream. Then he ran.

The door was locked from the inside. John didn't need ESP to know why. He stood back, shot a hard kick with his heavy work boots right at the door handle, and the door almost splintered as it flew open.

Tarleton had backed Sassy into an aisle of cattle feed sacks. He had her in a tight embrace and he was trying his best to kiss her. His hands were on her body. She was fighting for her life, panting and struggling against the fat man's body.

"You sorry, son of a…!" John muttered as he caught the man by his collar and literally threw him off Sassy.

She was gasping for air. Her blouse was torn and her shoulders ached. The stupid man had probably meant to do a lot more than just kiss her, if he'd locked the door, but thanks to John he'd barely gotten to first base. She almost gagged at the memory of his fat, wet mouth on her lips. She dragged her hand over it.

"You okay?" John asked her curtly.

"Yes, thanks to you," she said heavily. She glared at the man behind him.

He turned back toward Tarleton, who was flushed at being caught red-handed. He backed away from the homicidal maniac who started toward him with an expression that could have stopped traffic.

"Don't you…touch me…!" Tarleton protested.

John caught him by the shirtfront, drew back his huge fist, and knocked the man backward out into the feed store. He went after him, blue eyes sparking like live electricity, his big fists clenched, his jaw set rigidly.

"What the…?" came a shocked exclamation from the front of the store.

A man in a business suit was standing there, eyebrows arching.

"Mr….McGuire!" Tarleton exclaimed as he sat up on the floor holding his jaw. "He attacked me! Call the police!"

John glanced at McGuire with blazing eyes. "There's a nineteen-year-old girl in the tack room with her shirt torn off. Do you need me to draw you a picture?" he demanded.

McGuire's gray eyes suddenly took on the same

sheen as John's. He moved forward with an odd, gliding step and stopped just in front of Tarleton. He whipped out his cell phone and pressed in a number.

"Get over here," he said into the receiver. "Tarleton just assaulted Sassy! That's right. No, I won't let him leave!" He hung up. "You should have cut your losses and gone back to Billings," he told the white-faced man on the floor, nursing his jaw. "Now, you're going to jail."

"She teased me into doing it!" Tarleton cried. "It's her fault."

John glanced at McGuire. "And I'm a green elf." He turned on his heel and went back to the tack room to see about Sassy.

She was crying, leaning against an expensive saddle, trying to pull the ripped bits of her blouse closed. Her ratty little faded bra was visible where it was torn. It was embarrassing for her to have John see it.

John stripped off the cotton shirt he was wearing over his black undershirt. He eased her hands away from her tattered blouse and guided her arms into the shirt, still warm from his body. He buttoned it up to the very top. Then he framed her wet face in his big hands and lifted it to his eyes. He winced. Her pretty little mouth was bruised. Her hair was mussed. Her eyes were red and swollen.

"Me and my damned barn," he muttered. "I'm sorry."

"For…what?" she sobbed. "It's not your fault."

"It is. I should have expected something like this."

The bell on the door jangled and heavy footsteps echoed on wood. There was conversation, punctuated by Tarleton's protests.

A tall, lean man in a police uniform and a cowboy hat knocked at the tack door and walked in. John turned, letting him see Sassy's condition.

The newcomer's thin mouth set in hard lines and his black eyes flashed fire. "You all right, Sassy?" he asked in a deep, bass voice.

"Yes, sir, Chief Graves," she said brokenly. "He assaulted me!" she accused, glaring at Tarleton. "He came up behind me while I was putting up stock and grabbed me. He kissed me and tore my blouse…" Her voice broke. "He tried to…to…!" She couldn't choke the word out.

Graves looked as formidable as John. "He won't ever touch you again. I promise. I need you to come down to my office when you feel a little better and give me a statement. Will you do that?"

"Yes, sir."

He glanced at John. "You hit him?" he asked, jerking his head toward the man still sitting on the floor outside the room.

"Damned straight I did," John returned belligerently. His blue eyes were still flashing with bad temper.

Chief Graves glanced at Sassy and winced.

The police chief turned and went back out into the other room. He caught Tarleton by his arm, jerked him to his feet, and handcuffed him while he read him his rights.

"You let me go!" Tarleton shouted. "I'm going back to Billings in two days. She lied! I never touched her that way! I just kissed her! She teased me! She set me up! She lured me into the back! And I want that damned cowboy arrested for assault! He hit me!"

Nobody was paying him the least bit of attention. In fact, the police chief looked as if he'd like to hit Tarleton himself. The would-be Romeo shut up.

"I'm never hiring anybody else as long as I live," McGuire told the police chief. "Not after this."

"Sometimes snakes don't look like snakes," Graves told him. "We all make mistakes. Come along, Mr. Tarleton. We've got a nice new jail cell for you to live in while we get ready to put you on trial."

"She's lying!" Tarleton raged, red-faced.

Sassy came out with John just behind her. The ordeal she'd endured was so evident that the men in the room grimaced at just the sight of her. Tarleton stopped shouting. He looked sick.

"Do you mind if I say something to him, Chief Graves?" Sassy asked in a hoarse tone.

"Not at all," the lawman replied.

She walked right up to Tarleton, with her green eyes glittering with fury, drew back her hand, and slapped him across the mouth as hard as she could. Then she turned on her heel and walked right back to the counter, picked up a sack of seed corn that she'd left there when the assault began, and went back to work.

The three men glanced from her to Tarleton. Their faces wore identical expressions.

"I'll get a good lawyer!" Tarleton said belligerently.

"You'll need one," John promised him, in a tone so full of menace that the man backed up a step.

"I'll sue you for assault!" he said from a safe distance.

"The corporation's attorneys will enjoy the exercise," John told him coolly. "One of them graduated from Harvard and spent ten years as a prosecutor specializing in sexual assault cases."

Tarleton looked sick.

Graves took him outside. John turned to McGuire.

The man in the suit rammed his hands into his pockets and grimaced. "I'll never be able to make that up to her," he said heavily.

"You might tell her that you recommended raising her salary," John replied.

"It's the least I can do," he agreed. "That new employee of yours—Buck Mannheim. He's sharp. I learned things I didn't know just from spending a half hour talking to him. He'll be an asset."

John nodded. "He retired too soon. Sixty-five is no great age these days." He glanced toward the back, where Sassy was moving things around. "She needs to see a doctor."

"Did Tarleton...?" McGuire asked with real concern.

John shook his head. "But he would have. If I'd walked in just ten minutes later..." His face paled as he considered what would have happened. "Damn that man! And damn me! I should have realized he'd do something stupid to get even with her!"

"I should have realized, too," McGuire added. "Don't beat yourself to death. There's enough guilt to share. Dr. Bates is next to the post office. He has a clinic. He'll see her. He's been her family physician since she was a child."

"I'll take her right over there."

Sassy looked up when John approached her. She looked terrible, but she wasn't crying anymore. "Is he going to fire me?" she asked John.

"What in hell for? Almost getting raped?" he exclaimed. "Of course not. In fact, he's mentioned getting you a raise. But right now, he wants you to go to the doctor and get checked out."

"I'm okay," she protested. "And I have a lot of work to do."

"It can wait."

"I don't want to see Dr. Bates," she said.

He shrugged. "We're both pretty determined about

this. I don't really think you'd like the way I deal with mutiny."

She stuck her hands on her slender hips. "Oh, yeah? Let's see how you deal with it."

He smiled gently. Before she could say another word, he picked her up very carefully in his arms and walked out the front door with her.

Chapter 3

"You can't do this!" Sassy raged as he walked across the street with her, to the amusement of an early morning shopper in front of the small grocery store there.

"You won't go voluntarily," he said philosophically. He looked down at her and smiled gently. "You're very pretty."

She stopped arguing. "W...what?"

"Pretty," he repeated. "You've got grit, too." He chuckled. "I wish you'd half-closed that hand you hit Tarleton with, though." The smile faded. "That piece of work should be thrown into the county detention center wearing a sign telling what he tried to do. They'd pick him up in a shoebox."

Her small hands clung to his neck. "I didn't see it coming," she said, still in shock. "He pushed me into the tack room and locked the door. Before I could save myself, he pushed me back into the feed sacks and started kissing me and trying to get inside my blouse. I never thought I'd get away. I was fighting for all I was worth…" She swallowed hard. "Men are so strong. Even pudgy men like him."

"*I* should have seen it coming," he said, staring ahead with a set face. "A man like that doesn't go quietly. This could have been a worse tragedy than it already is."

"You saved me."

He looked down into her wide, green eyes. "Yes. I saved you."

She managed a wan smile. "Funny. I was just talking to Selene—my mother's little ward—about how Prince Charming would come and rescue me one day." She studied his handsome face. "You do look a little like a prince."

His eyebrow jerked. "I'm too tall. Princes are short and stubby, mostly."

"Not in movies."

"Ah, but that's not real life."

"I'll bet you don't know a single prince."

She'd have been amazed. He and his brother had rubbed elbows with crowned heads of Europe any number of times. But he couldn't admit that, of course.

"You could be right," he agreed easily.

He paused to open the door with one hand with Sassy propped on his knee. He walked into the doctor's waiting room with Sassy still in his arms and went up to the receptionist behind her glass panel. "We have something of an emergency," he said in a low tone. "She's been the victim of an assault."

"Sassy?" the receptionist, a girl Sassy had gone to school with, exclaimed. She took one look at the other girl's face and went running to open the door for John. "Bring her right in here. I'll get Dr. Bates!"

* * *

The doctor was a crusty old fellow, but he had a kind heart and it showed. He asked John to wait outside while he examined his patient. John stood in the hall, staring at anatomy charts that lined the painted concrete block wall. In no time the sliding door opened and he motioned John back into the cubicle.

"Except for some understandable emotional upset, and a few light bruises, she's not too hurt." The doctor glowered. "I would like to see her assailant spend a few months or, better yet, a few years, in jail, however."

"So would I," John told him, looking glittery and full of outrage. "In fact, I'm going to work on that."

The doctor nodded. "Good man." He turned to Sassy, who was quiet and pale now that her ordeal was over and reaction was starting to set in. "I'm going to inject you with a tranquilizer. I want you to go home and lie down for the rest of the day." He held up a hand when she protested. "Selene's in school and your mother will cope. It's not a choice, Sassy," he added as he leaned out of the cubicle and motioned to a nurse.

While he was giving the nurse orders, John stuck his hands in his jeans pockets and looked down at Sassy. She had grit and style, for a woman raised in the back of beyond. He admired her. She was pretty, too, although she didn't seem to realize it. The only real obstacle was her age. His face closed up as he faced the fact that she was years too young for him, even without their social separation. It was a pity. He'd been looking all his adult life for a woman he could like as well as desire. This sweet little firecracker was unique in his female acquaintances. He admired her.

His pale eyes narrowed on Sassy's petite form. She had a very sexy body. He loved those small, pert breasts under the cotton shirt. He thought how bruised they probably were from Tarleton's fingers and he wanted to hurt the man all over again. He knew she was untouched. Tarleton had stolen her first intimacy from her, soiled it, demeaned it. He wished he'd wiped the floor with the man before the police chief came.

Sassy saw his expression and felt uneasy. Did he think she was responsible for the attack? She winced. He didn't know her at all. Maybe he thought she had led Tarleton on. Maybe he thought she'd deserved what happened to her.

She lowered her eyes in shame. The doctor came back in with a syringe, rolled up her sleeve, swiped her upper arm with alcohol on a cotton ball, and injected her. Sassy didn't even flinch. She rolled down her sleeve.

"Go home before that takes effect, or you'll be lying down in the road." The doctor chuckled. He glanced at John. "Can you…?"

"Of course," John said. He smiled at Sassy, allaying her fears about his attitude. "Come on, sprout. I'll drive you."

"There's new stock that has to be put up in the store," she began to protest.

"It will still be waiting for you in the morning. If Buck needs help, I'll send some of my men into town to help him."

"But it's not your responsibility…"

"My boss has leased the feed store," he reminded her. "That makes it my responsibility."

"All right, then." She turned her head and smiled at the doctor. "Thanks."

He smiled back. "Don't you let this take over your life," he lectured her. "If you have any problems, you come back. I know a psychologist who works for the school system. She also takes private patients. I'll send you to her."

"I'll be okay."

John nodded at the doctor and followed Sassy out the door.

On the way home, Sassy sat beside him in the cab of the big pickup truck, fascinated by all the high-tech gadgets. "This is really nice," she remarked, smoothing over the leather dash. "I've never seen so many buttons and switches in a truck before."

He smiled lazily, steering with his left hand while he toyed with a loaded key ring in one of the big cup holders. "We use computers for roundup and GPS to move cattle and men around."

"What about your phone?" she asked, looking for it.

He indicated the second cup holder, where his cell phone was sitting. "The car is Bluetooth enabled," he explained. "So the phone is hands free. I can shorthand the call by saying the first or last name of the person I want to call. The phone does the rest. I can access the internet and my email through it, as well."

"Wow," she said softly. "It's like the *Starship Enterprise*, isn't it?"

He could have told her that his brand-new Jaguar XF was more in that line, with controls that rose out of the console when the push-button ignition was activated, backup cameras, heated seats and steering wheel, and a supercharged V8 engine. But he wasn't supposed to be able to afford that sort of luxury, so he kept his mouth shut.

"This must be a very expensive truck," she murmured.

He grinned. "Just mid-range. Our bosses don't skimp on tools," he told her. "That includes working equipment for assistant feed store managers as well."

She looked at him through green eyes that were becoming drowsy. "Are we getting a new assistant manager to go with Mr. Mannheim?" she asked.

"Sure. You," he added, glancing at her warmly. "That goes with a rise in salary, by the way."

Her breath caught. "Do you mean it?"

"Of course."

"Wow," she said softly, foreseeing better used appliances for the little house and some new clothes for Selene. "I can't believe it!"

"You will." He frowned. "Don't fall over in your seat."

She laughed breathily. "I think the shot's taking effect." She moved and grimaced, absently touching her small breasts. "A few bruises are coming out, too. He really was rough."

His face hardened. "I hate knowing he manhandled you," he said through his teeth. "I wish I'd come to the store sooner."

"You saved me, just the same," she replied. She smiled. "My hero."

He chuckled. "Not me, lady," he mused. "I'm just a working cowboy."

"There's nothing wrong with honest labor and hard work," she told him. "I could never wrap my mind around some rich, fancy man with a string of women following him around. I like cowboys just fine."

The words stung. He was living a lie, and he shouldn't have started out with her on the wrong foot. She was an honest person. She'd never trust him again if she realized how he was fooling her. He should tell her who he really was. He glanced in her direction. She was asleep. Her head was resting against the glass, her chest softly pulsing as she breathed.

Well, there would be another time, he assured himself. She'd had enough shocks for one day.

He pulled up in her driveway, went around and lifted her out of the truck in his arms. He paused at the foot of the steps to look down at her sleeping face. He curled her close against his chest, loving her soft weight, loving the sweet face pressed against his shirt pocket. He carried her up the steps easily, knocked perfunctorily at the door, and opened it.

Her mother, Mrs. Peale, was sitting in a chair in her bathrobe, watching the news. She cried out when she saw her daughter.

"What happened to her?" she exclaimed, starting to rise.

"She's all right," he said at once. "The doctor sedated her. Can I put her down somewhere, and I'll explain."

"Yes. Her bedroom…is this way." She got to her feet, panting with the effort.

"Mrs. Peale, you just point the way and sit back down," he said gently. "You don't need to strain yourself."

Her kind face beamed in a smile. "You're a nice young man. It's the first door on the left. Her bedroom."

"I'll be right back."

He carried Sassy into the bare little room and pulled back the worn blue chenille coverlet that was on the twin bed where she slept. Everything was spotless, if old. He lifted Sassy's head onto the pillow, tugged off her boots, and drew the coverlet over her, patting it down at her waist.

She breathed regularly. His eyes went from her disheveled, wavy dark hair to the slight rise of her firm breasts under the shirt he'd loaned her, down her narrow waist and slender hips and long legs. She was attractive. But it was more than a physical attractiveness. She was like a warm fireplace on a cold day. He smiled at his own imagery, took one last look at her pretty, sleeping face, went out, and pulled the door gently closed behind him.

Mrs. Peale was watching for him, worried. "What happened to her?" she asked at once.

He sat down on the sofa next to her chair. "Yes. She's had a rough day…"

"That Tarleton man!" Mrs. Peale exclaimed furiously. "It was him, wasn't it?"

His eyebrows arched at her unexpected perception. "Yes," he agreed slowly. "But how would you know…?"

"He's been creeping around her ever since McGuire hired him," she said in her soft, raspy voice. She paused to get her breath. Her green eyes, so much like Sassy's, were sparking with temper. "She came home crying one day because he touched her in a way he shouldn't have, and she couldn't stop him. He thought it was funny."

John's usually placid face was drawn with anger as he listened.

Mrs. Peale noticed that, and the caring way he'd brought her daughter home. "Forgive me for being blunt, but who are you?" she asked gently.

He smiled. "Sorry. I'm John…Taggert," he added, almost caught off guard enough to tell the truth. "My boss bought the old Bradbury place, and I'm his foreman."

"That place." She seemed surprised. "You know, it's haunted."

His eyebrows arched. "Excuse me?"

"I'm sorry. I shouldn't have said that…!" she began quickly.

"No. Please. I'd like to know," he said, reassuring her. "I collect folk tales."

She laughed breathily. "I guess it could be called that. You see, it began a long time ago when Hart Bradbury married his second cousin, Miss Blanche Henley. Her father hated the Bradburys and opposed the marriage, but Blanche ran away with Hart and got married to him anyway. Her father swore vengeance. One day, not long afterward, Hart came home from a long day gathering in strays, and found Blanche apparently in the arms of another man. He threw her out of his house and made her go back home to her father."

"Don't tell me," John interrupted with a smile. "Her father set her up."

"That's exactly what he did, with one of his men. Blanche was inconsolable. She sat in her room and cried. She did no cooking and no housework and she stopped going anywhere. Her father was surprised, because he thought she'd take up her old responsibilities with no hesitation. When she didn't, he was stuck with no help in the house and a daughter who embarrassed him in front of his friends. He told her to go back to her husband if he'd have her.

"So she did. But Hart met her at the door and told her he'd never live with her again. She'd gone from him to another man, or so he thought. Blanche gave up. She walked right out the side porch onto that bridge beside the old barn, and threw herself off the top. Hart heard her scream and ran after her, but she hit her head on a boulder when she went down, and her body washed up on the shore. Hart knew then that she was innocent. He sent word to her father that she'd killed herself. Her father went rushing over to Hart's place. Hart was waiting for him, with a double-barreled shotgun. He gave the old man one barrel and saved the other for himself." She grimaced. "It was almost ninety years ago, but nobody's forgotten."

"But they call the ranch the Bradbury place, don't they?" John asked, puzzled.

Mrs. Peale smiled. "Hart had three brothers. One of them took over the property. That was the great-uncle of the Bradbury you bought the ranch from."

"Talk about tragedies that stick in the mind," John mused. "I'm glad I'm not superstitious."

"How is it that you ended up bringing my daughter home?" she wondered aloud.

"I walked into the tack room in time to save her from Tarleton," he replied simply. "She didn't want to go to the doctor, so I carried her across the street and into his office." He sighed. "I suppose gossips will feed on that story for a week."

Mrs. Peale laughed. She had to stop suddenly, because her weak lungs wouldn't permit much of it. "Sassy is very stubborn."

He nodded. "I noticed." He smiled. "But she's got grit."

"Will she be all right?" she asked, worried.

"The doctor said that, apart from some bruises, she will. Of course there's the trauma of the attack itself."

"We'll deal with that…if we have to," the old woman said quietly. She bit her lower lip. "Do you know about me?" she asked suddenly.

"Yes, I do," he replied.

Her thin face was drawn. "Sassy has nobody. My husband ran off and left me with Sassy still in school. I took in Selene when her father died while he was working for us, just after Sassy's father left. We have no living family. When I'm gone," she added slowly, "she won't have anybody at all."

"She'll be all right," John assured her quietly. "We've promoted her to assistant manager of the feed store. It comes with a raise in salary. And if she ever needs help, she'll get it. I promise."

She turned her head like a bird watching him. "You have an honest face," she said after a minute. "Thank you, Mr. Taggert."

He smiled. "She's sweet."

"Sweet and unworldly," she said heavily. "This is a good place to raise children, but it doesn't give them much sense of modern society. She's a babe in the woods, in some ways."

"She'll be fine," he assured her. "Sassy may be naïve, but she has an excellent self-image and she's a strong woman. If you could have seen her swinging on Tarleton," he added on a chuckle, with admiration in his pale eyes.

"She hit him?" she exclaimed.

"She did," he replied. "I wish they'd given her five minutes alone with him. It might have cured him of ever wanting to force himself on another woman. Not," he added darkly, "that he's going to have the opportunity for a very long time. The police chief has him in jail pending arraignment. He'll be brought up on assault charges and, I assure you, he won't be running around town again."

"Mr. McGuire should never have hired him," she muttered.

"I can assure you that he knows that."

She bit her lip. "What if he gets a good lawyer and they turn him loose?"

"In that case," John chuckled, "we'll search and find enough evidence on crimes in his past to hang him out to dry. Whatever happens, he won't be a threat to Sassy ever again."

Mrs. Peale beamed. "Thank you for bringing her home."

"Do you have a telephone here?" he asked suddenly.

She hesitated. "Yes, of course."

He wondered at the hesitation, but not just then. "If you need anything, anything at all, you can call me." He pulled a pencil and pad out of his pocket, one he'd bought in town to list supplies, and wrote the ranch number on it. He handed it to Mrs. Peale. "Somebody will be around all the time."

"That's very kind of you," she said quietly.

"We help each other out back home," he told her. "That's what neighbors are for."

"Where is back home, Mr. Taggert?" she asked curiously.

"The Callisters we work for live at Medicine Ridge," he told her.

"Those people!" She caught her breath. "My goodness, everybody knows who they are. In fact, we had a man who used to work for them here in town."

John held his breath. "You did?"

"Of course, he moved on about a year ago," she added, and didn't see John relax. "He said they were the best bosses on earth and that he'd never have left if his wife hadn't insisted she had to be near her mother. Her mother was like me," she added sadly, "going downhill by the day. You can't blame a woman for feeling like that. I stayed with my own mother when she was dying." She looked up. "Are your parents still living?"

He smiled. "Yes, they are. I don't know them very

well yet, but all of us are just beginning to get comfortable with each other."

"You were estranged?"

He nodded. "But not anymore. Can I do anything for you before I leave?"

"No, but thank you."

"I'll lock the door on my way out."

She smiled at him.

"I'll be out this way again," he said. "Tell Sassy she doesn't have to come in tomorrow unless she just wants to."

"She'll want to," Mrs. Peale said confidently. "In spite of that terrible man, she really likes her work."

"I like mine, too," John told her. He winked. "Good night."

"Good night, Mr. Taggert."

He drove back to the Bradbury place deep in thought. He wished he could make sure that Tarleton didn't get out of jail anytime soon. He was still worried. The man was vindictive. He'd assaulted Sassy for reporting his behavior. God knew what he'd do to her if he managed to get out of that jail. He'd have to talk to Chief Graves and see if there was some way to get his bond set sky-high.

The work at the ranch was coming along quickly. The framework for the barn was already up. Wiring and plumbing were in the early stages. A crew was starting to remodel the house. John had one bedroom as a priority. He was sick of using a sleeping bag on the floor.

He phoned Gil that night. "How are things going at home?" he asked.

Gil chuckled. "Bess brought a snake to the dinner table. You've never seen women run so fast!"

"I'll bet Kasie didn't run," he mused.

"Kasie ticked it under the chin and told Bess it was the prettiest garter snake she'd ever seen."

"Your new wife is a delight," John murmured.

"And you can stop right there," Gil muttered. "She's my wife. Don't you forget that."

John burst out laughing. "You can't possibly still be jealous of her now!"

"I can, too."

"I could bring her truckloads of flowers and hands full of diamonds, and she'd still pick you," John pointed out. "Love trumps material possessions. I'm just her brother-in-law now."

"Well, okay," Gil said after a minute. "How are the improvements coming along?"

"Slowly." John sighed. "I'm still using a sleeping bag on the hard floor. I've given them orders to finish my bedroom first. Meanwhile, I'm getting the barn put up. Oh, and I've leased us a feed store."

There was a pause. "Should I ask why?"

"The manager tried to assault a young woman who's working for the store. He's in jail."

"And you leased the store because…?"

John sighed. "The girl's mother is dying of lung cancer," he said heavily. "There's a young girl they took in when her father died…she's six. Sassy is the only one bringing in any money. I thought if she could be promoted to assistant manager, she might be able to pay her bills and buy a few new clothes for the little girl."

"Sassy, hmmm?"

John flushed at that knowing tone. "Listen, she's just a girl who works there."

"What does she look like?"

"She's slight. She has wavy, dark hair and green eyes

and she's pretty when she smiles. When I pulled Tarleton off her, she walked up and slapped him as hard as she could. She's got grit."

"Tarleton would be the manager?"

"Yes," John said through his teeth. "The owner of the store, McGuire, hired him long distance and moved him here with his wife. Tarleton's lost at least one job for sexual harassment."

"Then why the hell did McGuire hire him?"

"He didn't know about the charges—there was never a conviction. He said he was desperate. Nobody wanted to work in this outback town."

"So who are we going to get to replace him?"

"Buck Mannheim."

"Good choice," Gil said. "Buck was dying of boredom after he retired. The store will be a challenge for him."

"He's a good manager. Sassy likes him already, and she knows every piece of merchandise on the place and the ordering system like the back of her hand. She keeps the place stocked."

"Is she all right?"

"A little bruised," John said. "I took her to the doctor and then drove her home. She slept all the way there."

"She didn't fuss about having the big boss carting her around?" Gil asked amusedly.

"Well, she doesn't know that I am the big boss," John returned.

"She what?"

John scowled. "Why does she have to know who I am?"

"You'll get in trouble if you start playing with the truth."

"I'm not playing with it. I'm just sidestepping it for

a little while. I like having people take me at face value for a change. It's nice to be something more than a walking checkbook."

Gil cleared his throat. "Okay. It's your life. Let's just hope your decision doesn't come back to bite you down the line."

"It won't," John said confidently. "I mean, it isn't as if I'm planning anything permanent here. By the time I'm ready to come back to Medicine Ridge, it won't matter, anyway."

Gil changed the subject. But John wondered if there might not be some truth in what his big brother was saying. He hoped there wasn't. Surely it wasn't a bad thing to try to live a normal life for once. After all, he asked himself, how could it hurt?

Chapter 4

Sassy settled in as assistant manager of the feed store. Buck picked at her gently, teased her, and made her feel so much at home that it was like belonging to a family. During her second week back at work, she asked permission to bring Selene with her to work on the regular Saturday morning shift. Her mother had had a bad couple of days, she explained, and she wasn't well enough to watch Selene. Buck said it was all right.

But when John walked into the store and found a six-year-old child putting up stock, he wasn't pleased.

"This is a dangerous place for a kid," he told Sassy gently. "Even a bridle bit falling from the wall could injure her."

Sassy stopped and stared at him. "I hadn't thought about that."

"And there are the pesticides," he added. "Not that I think she'd put any in her mouth, but if she dropped one of those bags, it could fly up in her face." He frowned. "We had a little girl on the ranch back in Medicine Ridge who had to be transported to the emergency room when a bag of garden insecticide tore and she inhaled some of it."

"Oh, dear," Sassy said, worried.

"I don't mind her being here," John assured her. "But find her something to do at the counter. Don't let her wander around. Okay?"

She cocked her head at him. "You know a lot about kids."

He smiled. "I have nieces about Selene's age," he told her. "They can be a handful."

"You love them."

"Indeed I do," he replied, his eyes following Selene as she climbed up into a chair at the counter, wearing old but clean jeans and a T-shirt. "I've missed out on a family," he added quietly. "I never seemed to have time to slow down and think about permanent things."

"Why not?" she asked curiously.

His pale eyes searched hers quietly. "Pressure of work, I suppose," he said vaguely. "I wanted to make my mark in the world. Ambition and family life don't exactly mesh."

"Oh, I get it," she said, and smiled up at him. "You wanted to be something more than just a working cowboy."

His eyebrow jerked. "Something like that," he lied. The mark he meant was to have, with his brother, a purebred breeding herd that was known all over the world—a true benchmark of beef production that had its roots in Montana. The Callisters had attained that reputation, but John had sacrificed for it, spending his life on the move, going from one cattle show to another with the ranch's prize animals. The more awards their breeding bulls won, the more they could charge for their progeny.

"You're a foreman now," she said. "Could you get higher up than that?"

"Sure," he said, warming to the subject. He grinned. "We have several foremen, who handle everything from grain production to cattle production to AI," he added. "Above that, there's ranch management."

Her eyebrows drew together. "AI?" she queried. "What's that?"

If she'd been older and more sophisticated, he might have teased her with the answer. As it was, he took the question at face value. "It's artificial breeding," he said gently. "We hire a man who comes out with the product and inseminates our cows and heifers."

She looked uncomfortable. "Oh."

He smiled. "It's part of ranch protocol," he said, his tone soft. "The old-fashioned way is hit or miss. In these hard times, we have to have a more reliable way of insuring progeny."

She smiled back shyly. "Thanks for not explaining it in a crude way," she said. "We had a rancher come in here a month ago who wanted a diaper for his female dog, who was in heat." She flushed a little. "He thought it was funny when I got uncomfortable at the way he talked about it."

His thumb hooked into his belt as he studied her. The comment made him want to find the rancher and have a long talk with him. "That sort of thing isn't tolerated on our spread," he said shortly. "We even have dress requirements for men and women. There's no sexual harassment, even in language."

She looked fascinated. "Really?"

"Really." He searched her eyes. "Sassy, you don't have to put up with any man talking to you in a way that embarrasses you. If a customer uses crude language, you go get Buck. If you can't find him, you call me."

"I never thought…I mean, it seemed to go with the job," she stammered. "Mr. Tarleton was worse than some of the customers. He used to try to guess the size of my…of my…well—" she shrugged, averting her eyes "—you know."

"Sadly, I do," he replied tersely. "Listen, you have to start standing up for yourself more. I know you're young, but you don't have to take being talked down to by men. Not in this job."

She rubbed an elbow and looked up at him like a curious little cat. "I was going to quit," she recalled, and laughed a little nervously. "I'd already talked to Mama about it. I thought even if I had to drive to Billings and back every day, I'd do it." She grimaced. "That was just before gas hit over four dollars a gallon." She sighed. "You'd have to be a millionaire to make that drive daily, now."

"I know," he said with heartfelt emotion. He and Gil had started giving their personnel a gas ration allowance in addition to their wages. "Which reminds me," he added with a smile, "we're adding gas mileage to the checks now. You won't have to worry about going bankrupt at the pump."

"That's so nice of you!"

He pursed his lips. "Of course. I am nice. It's one of my more sterling qualities. I mean, along with being debonair, a great conversationalist, and good at poker." He watched her reaction, smiling wickedly when she didn't quite get it. "Did I mention that dogs love me, too?"

She did get it then, and laughed shyly. "You're joking."

"Trying to."

She grinned at him. It made her green eyes light up, her face radiant. "You must have a lot of responsibility, considering how much work they're doing out at your ranch."

"Yes, I do," he admitted. "Most of it involves organization."

"That sounds very stressful," she replied, frowning. "I mean, a big ranch would have an awful lot of people to organize. I would think that you'd have almost no free time at all."

He didn't have much free time. But he couldn't tell her why. Actually the little bit of time he'd already spent here, even working, was something like a holiday, considering the load he carried when he was at home. He and Gil between them were overworked. They delegated responsibility where they could, but some decisions could only be made by the boss. "Well, it's still sort of a goal of mine," he hedged. "A man has to have a little ambition to be interesting." He studied her with pursed lips. "What sort of job goals do you have?"

She blinked, thinking. "I don't have any, really. I mean, I want to take care of Mama as long as I can. And I want to raise Selene and make sure she has a good education, and to save enough to help her go to college."

He frowned. Her goals were peripheral. They involved helping other people, not in advancing herself. He'd never considered the future welfare of anyone except himself—well, himself and Gil and the girls and, now, Kasie. But Sassy was very young to be so generous, even in her thoughts.

Young. She was nineteen. His frown deepened as he

studied her youthful, faintly flushed little face. He found her very attractive. She had a big heart, a nice smile, a pretty figure, and she was smart, in a common-sense sort of way. But that age hit him right in the gut every time he considered her part in his life. He didn't dare become involved with her.

"What's wrong?" she asked perceptively.

He shifted from one big, booted foot to the other. "I just had a stray thought," he told her. He glanced at Selene. "You've got a lot of responsibilities for a woman your age," he added quietly.

She laughed softly. "Don't I know it!"

His eyes narrowed. "I guess it cramps your social life. With men, I mean," he added, hating himself because he was curious about the men in her life.

She laughed. "There are only a couple of men around town who don't have wives or girlfriends, and I turn them off. One of them came right out and said I had too much baggage, even for a date."

His eyebrows arched. "And what did you say to that?"

"That I loved my mother and Selene and any man who got interested in me would have to take them on as well. That didn't go over big," she added with twinkling eyes. "So I've decided that I'm going to be like the Lone Ranger."

He blinked. "Masked and mysterious?"

"No!" she chuckled. "I mean, just me. Well, just me and my so-called dependents." She glanced toward Selene, who was quietly matching up seed packages from a box that had just arrived. Her eyes softened. "She's very smart. I can never sort things the way she can. She's patient and quiet, she never makes a fuss. I think she might grow up to be a scientist. She already has that sort of introspective personality, and she's careful in what she does."

"She thinks before she acts," he translated.

"Exactly. I tend to go rushing in without thinking about the consequences," she added with a laugh. "Not Selene. She's more analytical."

"Being impulsive isn't necessarily a bad thing," he remarked.

"It can be," she said. "But I'm working on that. Maybe in a few years, I'll learn to look before I leap." She glanced up at him. "How are things going out at the Bradbury place?"

"We've got the barn well underway already," he said. "The framework's done. Now we're up to our ears in roofers and plumbers and electricians."

"We only have a couple of each of those here in town," she pointed out, "and they're generally booked a week or two ahead except for emergencies."

He smiled. "We had to import some construction people from Billings," he told her. "It's a big job. Simultaneously, they're trying to make improvements to the house and plan a stable. We've got fencing to replace, wells to bore, agricultural equipment to buy… it's a monumental job."

"Your boss," she said slowly, "must be filthy rich, if he can afford to do all that right now when we've got gas prices through the roof!"

"He is," he confided. "But the ranch will be self-sufficient when we're through. We're using solar panels and windmills for part of our power generation."

"We had a city lawyer buy land here about six years ago," she recalled. "He put in solar panels to heat his house and all sorts of fancy, energy-saving devices." She winced. "Poor guy."

"Poor guy?" he prompted when she didn't continue.

"He saw all these nature specials and thought grizzly bears were cute and cuddly," she said. "One came up into his backyard and he went out with a bag full of bread to feed to it."

"Oh, boy," he said slowly.

She nodded. "The bear ate all the bread and when he ran out, it started eating him. He did manage to get away finally by playing dead, but he lost the use of an arm and one eye." She shook her head. "He was a sad sight."

"Don't tell me," he said. "He was from back East."

She nodded. "Some big city. He'd never seen a real bear before, except in zoos and nature specials. He saw an old documentary on this guy who lived with bears and he thought anybody could make friends with them."

"Reminds me of a story I heard about a lady from D.C. who moved to Arizona. She saw a rattlesnake crawling across the road, so the story goes, and thought it was fascinating. She got out of her car and walked over to pet it."

"What happened to her?"

"An uncountable number of shots of antivenin," he said, "and two weeks in the hospital."

"Ouch."

"You know all those warning labels they have on food these days? They ought to put warning labels on animals." He held both hands up, as if holding a sign. "Warning: Most wild reptiles are not cute and cuddly and they will bite and can kill you. Or: Grizzly bears will eat bread, fruit, and some people."

She laughed at his expression. "I ran from a grizzly bear once and managed to get away."

"Fast, are you?"

"He was old and slow, and I was close to town. But I had great incentive," she agreed.

"I've never had to outrun anything," he recalled. "I did once pet a moose who came up to serenade one of our milk cows. He was friendly."

"Isn't that unusual?"

"It is. Most wild animals that will let you close enough to pet them are rabid. But this moose wasn't sick. He just had no fear of humans. I think maybe he was raised as a pet by people who were smart enough not to tell anybody."

"Because...?" she prompted.

"Well, it's against the law to make a pet of a wild animal in most places in the country," he explained. He smiled. "That moose loved corn."

"What happened to him?"

"He started charging other cattle to keep his favorite cow to himself, so we had to move him up farther into the mountains. He hasn't come back so far."

She grinned. "What if he does? Will you let him stay?"

He pursed his lips. "Sure! I plan to spray-paint him red, cut off his antlers, and tell people he's a French bull."

She burst out laughing at the absurd comment.

Selene came running up with a pad and pencil. "'Scuse me," she said politely to John. She turned to her sister. "There's a man on the telephone who wants you to order something for him."

Sassy chuckled. "I'll go right now and take it down. Selene, this is John Taggert. He's a ranch foreman."

Selene looked up at him and grinned. She was missing one front tooth, but she was cute. "When I grow up, I'm going to be a fighter pilot!"

His eyebrows arched. "You are?"

"Yup! This lady came by to see my mama. She's a nurse. Her daughter was a fighter pilot and now she flies big airplanes overseas!"

"Some role model," John remarked to Sassy, awed.

She laughed. "It's a brave new world."

"It is." He went down on one knee in front of Selene, so that her eyes could look into his. "And what sort of plane would you like to fly?" he teased, not taking her seriously.

She put a small hand on his broad shoulder. Her blue eyes were very wide and intent. "I like those F-22 Raptors," she said breathlessly. "Did you know they can supercruise?"

He was fascinated. He wasn't sure he even knew what sort of military airplane that was. His breath exhaled. "No," he confessed. "I didn't."

"There was this program on TV about how they're built. I think Raptors are just beautiful," she said with a dreamy expression.

"I hope you get to fly one," he told her.

She smiled. "I got to grow up, first, though," she told him. She gasped. "Sassy!" she exclaimed. "That man's still on the phone!"

Sassy made a face. "I'm going, I'm going!"

"You coming back to see us again?" Selene asked John when he stood up.

He chuckled. "Thought I might."

"Okay!" She grinned and ran back to the counter, where Sassy was just picking up the phone.

John went to find Buck. It was a new world, indeed.

Tarleton was taken before the circuit judge for his arraignment and formally charged with the assault on

Sassy. He pleaded not guilty. He had a city lawyer who gave the local district attorney a haughty glance and requested that his client, who was blameless, be let out on his own recognizance in lieu of bail. The prosecutor argued that Tarleton was a flight risk.

The judge, after reviewing the charges, did agree to set bail. But he set it at fifty thousand dollars, drawing furious protests from the attorney and his client. With no ability to raise such an amount, even using a bail bondsman, Tarleton would have to wait it out in the county detention facility. It wasn't a prospect he viewed with pleasure.

Sassy heard about it and felt guilty. Mr. Tarleton, for all his flaws, had a wife who was surely not guilty of anything more than bad judgment in her choice of a husband. It seemed unfair that she would have to suffer along with the defendant.

She said so, to John, when he turned up at the store the end of the next week.

"His poor wife." She sighed. "It's so unkind to make her go through it with him."

"Would you rather let him walk?" he asked quietly. "Set him free, so that he could do it to another young woman—perhaps with more tragic results?"

She flushed. "No. Of course not."

He reached out and touched her cheek with the tips of his fingers. "You have a big heart, Sassy," he said, his voice very deep and soft. "Plenty of other people don't, and they will use your own compassion against you."

She looked up curiously, tingling and breathless from just the faint contact of his fingers with her skin. "I guess some people are like that," she conceded. "But most people are kind and don't want to hurt others."

He laughed coldly. "Do you think so?"

His expression was saying things that she could read quite accurately. "Somebody hurt *you*," she guessed. Her eyes held his. They had an odd, blank look in them. "A woman. It was a long time ago. You never talk about it. But you hold it inside, deep inside, and use it to keep the world at a distance."

He scowled. "You don't know me," he said, defensive.

"I shouldn't," she agreed. Her green eyes seemed darker, more piercing. "But I do."

"Don't tell me," he murmured with faint sarcasm, "you can read minds."

She shook her head. "I can read wrinkles."

"Excuse me?"

"Your frown lines are deeper than your smile lines," she told him, not wanting to confess that her family had the "second sight," in case he thought she was peculiar. "It's a public smile. You leave it at the front door when you go home."

His eyes narrowed on her face. He didn't speak. She was incredibly perceptive for a woman her age.

She drew in a long breath. "Go ahead, say it. I need to mind my own business. I do try to, but it bothers me to see other people so unhappy."

"I am not unhappy," he said belligerently. "I'm very happy!"

"If you say so."

He glowered at her. "Just because a woman threw me over, I'm not damaged goods."

"How did she throw you over?"

He hadn't talked about it for years, not even to Gil. In one sense he resented this young woman, this stranger, prying into his life. In another, it made him want to talk about it, to stop the festering wound of it from growing even larger inside him.

"She got engaged to me while she was living with a man down in Colorado."

She didn't speak. She just watched him, like a curious little cat, waiting.

He grimaced. "I was so crazy about her that I never suspected a thing. She'd go away for weekends with her girlfriend and I'd watch movies and do book work at home while she was away. One weekend I had nothing to do, so I drove over to Red Lodge, where she'd said she was checked into a motel so that she could go fly-fishing with her girlfriend." He sighed. "Red Lodge isn't so big that you can't find people in it, and it does a big business in tourism. Turned out, her friend was male, filthy rich, and they had a room together. She had the most surprised look on her face when they came downstairs and found me sitting in the lobby."

"What did she say?" she asked.

"Nothing. Not one thing. She bit her lip and pretended that she didn't know the man. He was furious, and I felt like a fool. I went back home. She called and tried to talk to me, but I hung up on her. Some things don't take a lot of explaining."

He didn't add that he'd also hired a private detective, much too late, to find out what he could about the woman. It hadn't been the first time she'd kept a string of wealthy admirers, and she'd taken one man for a quarter of a million dollars before he found her out. She'd been after John's money, all along; not himself. He wasn't as forthcoming as the millionaire she'd gone fly-fishing with, so she'd been working on the millionaire while she left John simmering on a back burner. As a result, she'd lost both men, which did serve her right. But the experience had made him bitter and suspicious of all women. He still thought they only wanted him for his money.

"The other guy, was he rich?" Sassy asked.

John's lips made a thin line. "Filthy rich."

She touched the front of his shirt with a shy, hesitant little hand. "I'm sorry about that," she told him. "But in a way, you're lucky that you aren't rich," she added.

"Why?"

"Well, you never have to worry if women like you for yourself or your wallet," she said innocently.

"There isn't much to like," he said absently, concentrating on the way she was touching him. She didn't even seem to be aware of it, but his body was rippling inside with the pleasure it gave him.

"You're kidding, right?" she asked. Her eyes laughed up into his. "You're very handsome. You stand up for people who can't take care of themselves. You like children. And dogs like you," she added mischievously, recalling one of his earlier quips. "Besides that, you must like animals, since you work around cattle."

While she was talking, the hand on his chest had been joined by her other one, and they were flat on the broad, hard muscles, idly caressing. His body was beginning to respond to her touch in a profound way. His blue eyes became glittery with suppressed desire.

He caught her hands abruptly and moved them. "Don't do that," he said curtly, without thinking how it was going to affect her. He was in danger of losing control of himself. He wanted to reach for her, slam her against him all the way up and down, and kiss that pretty mouth until he made it swell and moan under his lips.

She jerked back, appalled at her own boldness. "I'm

sorry," she said at once, flushing. "I really am. I'm not used to men. I mean, I've never done that…excuse me!"

She turned and all but ran back down the aisle to the counter. When she got there, she jerked up the phone and called a customer to tell him his order was in. She'd already phoned him, and he hadn't answered, so she called again. It gave her something to do, so that John thought she was getting busy.

He muttered under his breath. Now he'd done it. He hadn't meant to make her feel brassy with that comment, but she was starting to get to him. He wanted her. She had warmth and compassion and an exciting little body, and she was getting under his skin. He needed a break.

He turned on his heel and walked out of the store. He should have gone back and apologized for being so abrupt, but he knew he'd never be able to explain himself without telling her the truth. He couldn't do that. She was years too young for him. He had to get out of town for a while.

He left Bradbury's former ranch foreman, Carl Baker, in charge of the place while he packed and went home to Medicine Ridge for the weekend.

It was a warm, happy homecoming. His big brother, Gil, met him at the door with a bear hug.

"Come on in," he said, chuckling. "We've missed you."

"Uncle John!"

Bess and Jenny, Gil's daughters by his first wife, came running down the hall to be picked up and cuddled and kissed.

"Oh, Uncle John, we missed you so much!" Bess, the eldest, cried, hugging him tightly around the neck.

"Yes, we did," Jenny seconded, kissing his bronzed cheek. "You can't stay away so long!"

"Did you bring us a present?" Bess asked.

He grinned. "Don't I always?" He laughed. "In the bag, next to my suitcase," he said, putting them down.

They ran to the bag, found the wrapped presents and literally tore the ribbons off to delve inside. There were two stuffed animals with bar codes that led children to websites where they could dress their pets and have adventures with them online in a safe environment.

"Web puppies!" Bess exclaimed, clutching a black Labrador

Jenny had a Collie. She cuddled it close. "We seen these on TV!"

"Can we use the computer, Daddy?" Bess pleaded. "Please?"

"The computer?" Kasie, Gil's new wife, asked, grinning. "What are you babies up to, now?" she added, pausing to hug John before she pressed against Gil's side with warm affection.

"It's a web puppy, Kasie!" Bess exclaimed, showing hers. "Uncle John bought them for us."

"I got a Collie, just like Lassie." Jenny beamed.

"We got to use the computer," Bess insisted.

Kasie chuckled. "Come on, then. You staying for a while?" she asked John.

"For the weekend," John replied, smiling at the girls. "I needed a break."

"I guess you did," Gil replied. "You've taken on a big task up there. Sure you don't need more help? We could spare Green."

"I'm doing fine. Just a little complication."

Kasie led the girls off into Gil's office, where the

computer lived. When they were out of earshot, Gil turned to John.

"What sort of complication?" he asked his younger brother.

John sighed. "There's a girl."

Gil's pale eyes sparkled. "It's about time."

John shook his head. "You don't understand. She's nineteen."

Gil only smiled. "Kasie was twenty-one. Barely. And I'm older than you are. Age doesn't have a lot to do with it."

John felt something of a load lift from his heart. "She's unworldly."

Gil chuckled. "Even better. Come have coffee and pie and tell me all about it!"

Chapter 5

Sassy put on a cheerful face for the rest of the day, pretending for all she was worth that having John Taggert push her away didn't bother her at all. It was devastating, though. She was shy with most men, but John had drawn her out of her shell and made her feel feminine and charming. Then she'd gone all googly over him and edged closer as if she couldn't wait to have him put his arms around her and kiss her. Even the memory of her behavior made her blush. She'd never been so forward with anyone.

Of course, she knew she wasn't pretty or desirable. He was a good deal older than she was, too, and probably liked beautiful and sophisticated women who knew their way around. He might not be a ranch boss, but he drove a nice truck and obviously made a good salary. In addition to all that, he was very handsome and charming. He'd be a woman magnet in any big city.

He'd saved her from Bill Tarleton, gotten her a raise and a promotion, and generally been kinder to her than she deserved. He probably had the shock of his life when she moved close to him as if she had the right, as if he belonged to her. The shame of it wore on her until she was pale and almost in tears when she left the shop that afternoon.

"Something bothering you, Sassy?" Buck Mannheim asked as they were closing up.

She glanced at him and forced a smile. "No, sir. Nothing at all. It's just been a long day."

"It's that Tarleton thing, isn't it?" he asked quietly. "You're upset that you'll have to testify."

She was glad to have an excuse for the way she looked. The assault did wear on her, but it was John Taggert's behavior, not her former boss's, that had her upset. "I guess it is a little worrying," she confessed.

He sighed. "Sassy, it's a sad fact of life that there are men like him in the world. But if you don't testify, he could get away with it. The reason you had trouble with him is that some other poor girl didn't want to have to face him in front of a jury. She let him walk. If he'd been convicted of sexual harassment, instead of just charged with it, he'd probably be in jail now. It might have stopped him from coming on to you."

She had to agree. "I suppose that's true. It's just... well, you know, Mr. Mannheim, some men think a woman leads them on if she just looks at them."

"I know. But that isn't the case here. John... Taggert—" he caught himself in the nick of time from letting John's real surname out "—will certainly testify to what he saw. He'll be there to back you up."

Which didn't make her feel any better, because John would probably think she worked at leading men on, considering how he'd had to push her away from him for being forward. She couldn't say that to Mr. Mannheim. It was too embarrassing.

"You just go on home, have a nice dinner, and stop worrying," he said with a smile. "Everything is going to be all right."

She let out a breath and smiled. "You remind me of my grandfather. He always used to tell me that things worked out, if we just sat back and gave them a chance. He was the most patient person I ever knew."

"I'm not patient." Buck chuckled. "But I do agree with your grandfather. Time heals."

"Don't I wish," she mused. "Good night, Mr. Mannheim. See you in the morning."

"I'll be here."

She got into the battered old truck her grandfather had willed her on his death, and drove home with black smoke pouring out behind her. The vehicle was an embarrassment, but it was all she had. Just putting gas in it and keeping the engine from blowing up was exorbitant. She was grateful for the gas allowance that she'd gotten with her promotion. It would help financially.

She parked at the side of the rickety old house and studied it for a minute before she walked up onto the porch. It needed so much repair. The roof leaked, there was a missing board on the porch, the steps were starting to sag, at least two windows were rotting out...the list went on and on. She recalled what John had said about the improvements that were being made on the Bradbury place, and it wasn't in nearly as bad a shape as this place. She despaired about what she was going to do when winter came. Last winter, she'd barely been able to afford to fill one third of the propane tank they used to heat the house. There were small space heaters in both bedrooms and a stove with a blower in the living room. They'd had to ration carefully, so they'd used a lot of quilts during the coldest months, and tried their best to save on fuel costs. It looked as though this year the fuel price would be twice as much.

She didn't dare think about the obstacles that lay ahead, especially her mother's worsening health. If the doctor prescribed more medicine, they'd be over their heads in no time. She already owed the local pharmacy half her next week's paycheck, because she'd had to supplement the cost of her mother's extra pills.

Well, she had to stop thinking about that, she decided. People were more important than money. It was just that she was the only person making any money. Now she was going to be involved in a court case, and it was just possible that John's boss might hear about it and not want such a scandalous person working in his store. Worse, John might tell him about how forward she'd been in the feed store today. She couldn't forget how angry he'd been when he walked out.

Just as she started up the steps, the sky opened up and it began to rain buckets. There was no time to lose. There were three big holes in the ceiling. One was right over the television set. She couldn't afford to replace the enormous tube television, which was her mother's only source of pleasure. It was almost twenty years old, and the color wasn't good, but it had lasted them since Sassy was a baby.

"Hi!" she called on her way down the hall.

"It's raining, dear!" her mother called from the bedroom.

"I know! I'm on it!"

She made a dash for the little plastic tub under the sink, ran into the living room, and made it just in the nick of time to prevent drips from overwhelming the TV set. It was too big and heavy to move by herself. Her mother couldn't do any lifting at all, and Selene was too small. Sassy couldn't budge it, so the only alternative was to protect it. She put the tub on the flat top and breathed a sigh of relief.

"Don't forget the leak in the kitchen!" Mrs. Peale called again. Her voice was very hoarse and thin.

Sassy grimaced. She sounded as if she was getting a bad case of bronchitis, and she wondered how she'd ever get her mother willingly loaded into the truck if she had to take her to town to Dr. Bates. Maybe the dear old soul would make a house call, if he had to. He was a good man. He knew how stubborn Sassy's mother was, too.

She finished protecting the house with all sorts of buckets and pots. The drips on metal and plastic made a sort of soothing rhythm.

She peeked into her mother's bedroom. "Bad day?" she asked gently.

Her mother, pale and listless, nodded. "Hurts to cough."

Sassy felt even worse. "I'll call Dr. Bates…"

"No!" Her mother paused to cough again. "I've got antibiotic, Sassy, and I've used my breathing machine today already," she said gently. "I just need some cough syrup. It's on the kitchen counter." She managed a smile. "Try not to worry so much, darling," she coaxed. "Life just happens. We can't stop it."

Sassy bit her lower lip and nodded as tears threatened.

"Now, now." Mrs. Peale held out her thin arms. Sassy ran to the bed and into them, careful not to press on her mother's frail chest. She cried and cried.

"I'm not going to die yet," Mrs. Peale promised. "I have to see Selene through high school first!"

It was a standing joke. Usually they both laughed, but Sassy had been through the mill for the past week. Her life was growing more complicated by the hour.

"We had a visitor today," her mother said. "Guess who it was?"

Sassy wiped at her eyes and sat up, smiling through the tears. "Who?"

"Remember Brad Danner's son Caleb, that you had a crush on when you were fifteen?" she teased.

Memory produced a vague portrait of a tall, lanky boy with black eyes and black hair who'd never seemed to notice her at all. "Yes."

"He came by to see you," Mrs. Peale told her. "He's been in the Army, serving overseas. He stopped by to visit and wanted to say hello to you." She grinned. "I told him to come to supper."

Sassy caught her breath. "Supper?" She sat very still. "But we've only got stew, and just barely enough for us," she began.

Mrs. Peale chuckled hoarsely. "He said we needed some take-out, so he's bringing a bucket of chicken with biscuits and honey and cottage fries all the way from Billings. We can heat it back up in the oven if it's cold when he gets here."

"Real chicken?" Sassy asked, her eyes betraying her hunger for protein. Mostly the Peales ate stews and casseroles, with very little meat because it was so expensive. "And biscuits with honey?"

"I guess I looked like I was starving," Mrs. Peale said wistfully. "I didn't have the heart to refuse. He was so persuasive." She smiled sheepishly.

"You wicked woman," Sassy teased. "What did you do?"

"Well, I was very hungry. He was talking about what he'd gotten himself and his aunt for supper last night, and I did mention that I'd forgotten what a chicken tasted like. He volunteered to come to dinner and bring it with him. What could I say?"

Sassy bent and hugged her mother warmly. "At least you'll get one good meal this week," she mused. "So will Selene." She sat up, frowning. "Where is Selene?"

"She's in her room, doing homework," Mrs. Peale replied. "She studies so hard. We have to find a way to let her go to college if she wants to."

"We'll work it out," Sassy promised. "Her grades will probably be so high that she'll get scholarships all over the place. She's a good student."

"Just like you were."

"I goofed off more than Selene does."

"You should put on a nice pair of jeans and a clean shirt," she told her daughter. "You can borrow some of my makeup. Caleb is a handsome young man, and he isn't going with anybody."

"You didn't ask?" Sassy burst out, horrified.

"I asked in a very polite way."

"Mother!"

"You should never turn down a prospective suitor," she chuckled. The smile faded. "I know you like Mr. Taggert, Sassy, but there's something about him…"

Her heart sank. Her mother was oddly accurate with her "feelings." "You don't think he's a criminal or something?"

"Silly girl. Of course not. I just mean that he seems out of place," Mrs. Peale continued. "He's intelligent and sophisticated, and he doesn't act like the cowboys who work around here, haven't you noticed? He's the sort of man who would look at home in elegant surroundings. He's immaculate and educated."

"He told me that he wanted to be a ranch manager one day," Sassy confided. "He probably works at building the right image, to impress people."

"That could be. But I think there's more to him than shows."

"You and your intuition," Sassy chided.

"You have it, too," the older woman reminded her. "It's that old Scotch-Irish second sight. My grandmother had it as well. She could see far ahead." She frowned. "She made a prediction that never made sense. It still doesn't."

"What sort?"

"She said I would be poor, but my daughter would live like royalty." She laughed. "I'm sorry, darling, but that doesn't seem likely."

"Everyone's entitled to a few misses," Sassy agreed.

"Anyway, go dress up. I told Caleb that we eat at six."

Sassy grinned at her. "I'll dress up, but it won't help. I'll still look like me, not some beauty queen."

"Looks fade. Character doesn't," her mother reminded her.

She sighed. "You don't find many young men in search of women with character."

"This may be the first. Hurry!"

Caleb was rugged-looking, tall and muscular and very polite. He smiled at Sassy and his dark eyes were intent on her face while he sat at the table with the two women and the little girl. He was serving in an Army unit overseas, where he was a corporal, he told them. He was a communications specialist, although he was good at fixing motors as well. The Army hadn't needed a mechanic when he enlisted, but they did need communications people, so he'd trained for that.

"Is it very bad over there, where you were?" Mrs. Peale asked, having struggled to the table with Caleb's help over Sassy's objections.

"Yes, it has been," Caleb said. "But we're making progress."

"Do you have to shoot people?" Selene asked.

"Selene!" Sassy exclaimed.

Caleb chuckled. "We try very hard not to," he told her. "But sometimes the warlords shoot at us. We're stationed high up in the mountains, where terrorists like to camp. We come under fire from time to time."

"It must be frightening," Sassy said.

"It is," Caleb said honestly. "But we do the jobs we're given, and try not to think about the danger." He glanced at Selene and smiled. "There are lots of kids around our camp. We get packages from home and they beg for candy and cookies from us. They don't get many sweets."

"Is there lots of little girls?" Selene asked.

"Now, we don't see many little girls," he told her. "Their customs are very different from ours. The girls mostly stay with their mothers. The boys tag along after their fathers."

"I'd like to tag along with my father," Selene said sadly. "But he went away."

"Away?"

Sassy mouthed "he died," and Caleb nodded quickly.

"Do have some more coffee, Caleb," Mrs. Peale offered.

"Thank you. It's very good."

Sassy had rationed out enough for a pot of the delicious beverage. It was expensive, and they rarely drank it. But Mrs. Peale said that Caleb loved coffee and he had, after all, contributed the meal. Sassy felt that a cup of good coffee wasn't that much of a sacrifice, under the circumstances.

After dinner, they gathered around the television to watch the news. Caleb looked at his watch and said he had to get back to Billings, because his aunt wanted to go to a late movie, and he'd promised to take her.

"But I'd like to come back again before I return to duty, if I may," he told them. "I had a good time tonight."

"So did we," Sassy said at once. "Please do."

"We'll make you a nice macaroni and cheese casserole next time, our treat," Mrs. Peale offered.

He hesitated. "Would you mind if I contributed the cheese for it?" he asked. "I'm partial to a particular brand."

They saw right through him, but they pretended not to. It had to be obvious that they were managing at a subsistence level.

"That would be very kind of you," Mrs. Peale said with genuine gratitude.

He smiled. "It would be my pleasure. Sassy, would you walk me out?"

"Sure!"

She jumped up and walked out to his truck with him. He turned to her before he climbed up into the cab.

"My aunt has a cousin who lives here. She says your mother is in very bad shape," he said.

She nodded. "Lung cancer."

He grimaced. "If there's anything I can do, anything at all," he began. "Your mother was so good to my cousin when she lost her husband in the blizzard a few years ago. None of us have forgotten."

"You're very kind. But we're managing." She grinned. "Thanks for the chicken, I'd forgotten what they tasted like," she added, mimicking her mother's words.

He laughed at her honesty. "You always did have a great sense of humor."

"It's easier to laugh than to cry," she told him.

"So they say. I'll come by tomorrow afternoon, if I may, and tell you when I'm free. My aunt has committed me to no end of social obligations."

"You could phone me," she said.

He grinned. "I'd rather drive over. Humor me. I'll escape tea with one of aunt's friends who has an eligible daughter."

She chuckled. "Avoiding matrimony, are you?"

"Apparently," he agreed. He pursed his lips. "Are you attached?"

She sighed. "No. Sorry." Her eyes widened. "Are you?"

He grimaced. "I'm trying not to be." He shrugged. "She's my best friend's girl."

She relaxed. He wasn't hunting for a woman. "I have one of those situations, too. Except that he doesn't have a girlfriend, that I know of."

"And he doesn't like you?"

"Apparently not."

"Well, if that doesn't take the cake. Two fellow sufferers, and we meet by accident."

"That's life."

"It is." He studied her warmly. "You know, I was so shy in high school that I never got up the nerve to ask you out. I wanted to. You were always so cheerful, always smiling. You made me feel good inside."

That was surprising. She remembered him as a standoffish young man who seemed never to notice her.

"I was shy, too," she confessed. "I just learned to bluff."

"The Army taught me how to do that," he said, smiling. "This man you're interested in—somebody local?"

She sighed. "Actually, he's sort of the foreman of a ranch. The men he works for bought the old Bradbury place…"

"That wreck?" he exclaimed. "Whatever for?"

"They're going to run purebred calves out there, once they build a new barn and stable and remodel the house and run new fences. It's going to be quite a job."

"A very expensive job. Who are his bosses?"

"The Callister brothers. They live in Medicine Ridge."

He nodded. "Yes. I've heard of them. Hardworking men. One of their ranch hands was in my unit when I first shipped out. He said it was the best place he'd ever worked." He laughed. "He said the brothers got right out in the pasture at branding time and helped. They weren't the sort to sit in parlors and sip expensive alcohol."

"Imagine, to be that rich and still go out to work cattle," she said with a wistful smile.

"I can't imagine it," he told her. "But I'd love to be able to. I'm getting my college degree in the military. When I come out, I'm going to apprentice at a mechanic's shop in Billings and, hopefully, work my way up to partnership one day. I love fixing motors."

She gave him a wry look. "I wish you'd love fixing mine," she said. "It's pouring black smoke."

"How old is it?" he asked curiously.

"About twenty years…"

"Rings and valves," he said at once. "It's probably going to need rebuilding. At today's prices, you'd come out better to sell it for scrap and buy a new one."

"Pipe dreams." She laughed. "We live up to the last penny I bring home. I could never make a car payment."

"Have you thought about moving to Billings, where you could get a better job?"

"I'd have to take Mama and Selene with me," she said simply, "and we'd have to rent a place to live. At least we still have the house, such as it is."

He frowned. "You landed in a fine mess," he said sympathetically.

"I did, indeed. But I love my family," she added, "I'd rather have what I have than be a millionaire."

His dark eyes met her green ones evenly. "You're a nice girl, Sassy. I wish I'd known you better before I met my best friend's girl."

"I wish I'd known you better before John Taggert came to town." She sighed. "As it is, I'll be very happy to have you for a friend." She grinned. "We can cry on each other's shoulders. I'll even write to you when you go back overseas if you'll give me your address."

His face lit up. "I'd like that. It will help throw my buddy off the trail. He caught me staring at his girlfriend's photo a little too long."

"I'll send you a picture of me," she volunteered. "You can tell him she reminded you of me."

His eyebrows lifted. "That won't be far-fetched. She's dark haired and has light eyes. You'd do that for me?"

"Of course I would," she said easily. "What are friends for?"

He smiled. "Maybe I can do you a good turn one day."

"Maybe you can."

He climbed into the truck. "Tell your family I said good-night. I'll drive over tomorrow."

She smiled up at him. "I'll look forward to it."

He threw up a hand and pulled out into the road. She watched him go, remembering that there were still a few pieces of chicken left. She'd have to rush inside and put them up quickly before Selene grew reckless and ate too much. If they stretched out that bucket of chicken, they could eat on it for most of the week. It was a godsend, considering their normal grocery budget. God bless Caleb, she thought warmly. He really did have a big heart.

John Callister had spent a pleasant weekend with his brother and Kasie and the girls. Mrs. Charters had made him his favorite foods, and even Miss Parsons, Gil's former governess who was now his bookkeeper, seemed to enjoy his visit. There was a new assistant since Gil had married Kasie. He was a male assistant, Arnold Sims, who seemed nice and was almost as efficient as Kasie had been. He was an older man, and he and Miss Parsons spent their days off together.

It was nice to get away from the constant headache of construction and back to the bosom of his family. But he had to return to Hollister, and mend fences with Sassy. He should have found a kinder way to keep her at arm's length while he found his footing in their changing relationship. Her face had gone pale when he'd jerked back from her. She probably thought he found her offensive. He hated leaving her with that false impression, but his sudden desire for her had shocked and disturbed him. He hadn't been confident enough to go back and face her until he could hide his feelings.

There had to be some way to make it up to her. He'd think of a way when he got back to Hollister, he assured himself. He could explain it away without too much difficulty. Sassy had a kind heart. He knew she wouldn't hold grudges.

But when he walked into the store Monday afternoon, he got a shock. Sassy was leaning over the counter, smiling broadly at a very handsome young man in jeans and a chambray shirt. And if he wasn't mistaken, the young man was holding her hand.

He felt something inside him explode with pain and resentment. She'd put her hands on his chest and looked up at him with melting green eyes, and he'd wanted her to the point of madness. Now she was doing the same thing to another man, a younger man. Was she just a heartless flirt?

He walked up to the counter, noting idly that the younger man didn't seem to be disturbed by him, or even interested in him.

"Hi, Sassy," he said coolly. "Did you get in that special feed mix I asked you to order?"

"I'll check, Mr. Taggert," she said politely and with a quiet smile. She walked into the back to check the invoice of the latest shipment that had just come that morning, very proud that she'd been able to disguise her quick breathing and shaky legs. John Taggert had a shattering effect on her emotions. But he didn't want her, and she'd better remember it. What a blessing that Caleb had come to the store today. Perhaps John would believe that she had other interests and wasn't chasing after him.

"Nice day," John said to the young man. "I'm John Taggert. I'll be ramrodding the old Bradbury ranch."

The boy smiled and extended a hand. "I'm Caleb Danner. Sassy and I went to school together."

John shook the hand. "Nice to meet you."

"Same here."

John looked around at the shelves with seeming nonchalance. "You work around here?" he asked carelessly.

"No. I'm in the Army Rangers," the boy replied, surprising his companion. "I'm stationed overseas, but I've been home on leave for a couple of weeks. I'm staying with my aunt in Billings."

John's pale eyes met the boy's dark ones. "That's a substantial drive from here."

"Yes, I know," Caleb replied easily. "But I promised Sassy a movie and I'm free tonight. I came to see if she'd go with me."

Chapter 6

The boy was an Army Ranger, he said, and he was dating Sassy. John felt uncomfortable trying to pump the younger man for information. He wondered if Caleb was seriously interested in Sassy, but he had no right to ask.

She was poring over bills of lading. He watched her with muted curiosity and a little jealousy. It disturbed him that this younger man had popped up right out of the ground, so to speak, under his own nose.

It took her a minute to find the order and calm her nerves. But she managed to do both. She looked up as John approached the counter. He looked very sexy in those well-fitting jeans and the blue-checked Western-cut shirt he was wearing with his black boots and wide-brimmed hat. She shouldn't notice that, she told herself firmly. He wouldn't like having her interested in him; he'd already made that clear. She had to be businesslike.

"The feed was backordered," she said politely. "But

it should be here by Friday, if that's all right. If it isn't," she added quickly when he began to look irritated, "I can ask Mr. Mannheim to phone them..."

"No need," he said abruptly. "We can wait. We aren't moving livestock onto the place until we have the fences mended and the barn finished. I just want to have the feed on hand when they arrive."

"We'll have it by next week. No problem."

He nodded. He tried to avoid looking at her directly. She was wearing jeans with a neat little white peasant blouse that had embroidery on it, and she looked very pretty with her dark hair crisp and clean, and her green eyes shimmering with pleasure. Her face was flushed and she was obviously unsettled. The boy at the counter probably had something to do with that, he thought irritably. She seemed pretty wrapped up in him already.

"That's fine," he said abruptly. "I'll check back with you next week, or I'll have one of the boys come in."

"Yes, sir," she replied politely.

He nodded at Caleb and stalked out of the store without another glance at Sassy.

Caleb pursed his lips and noted Sassy's heightened color. "So that's him," he mused.

She drew in a steadying breath. "That's him."

"Talk about biting off more than you can chew," he murmured dryly.

"What do you mean?"

"Nothing," he returned, thinking privately that Taggert looked like a man who'd forgotten more about women than Sassy would ever learn about men. Taggert seemed sophisticated, for a cattleman, and was obviously used to giving orders. Sassy was too young for that fire-eater, too unsophisticated, too everything. Besides all that, the ranch foreman had spoken to her politely, but in a manner that was decidedly impersonal. Caleb didn't want to upset Sassy by putting all that into words. Still, he felt sympathy for her. She was as likely to land that big fish as he was to find himself out on the town with his best friend's girl.

"How about that movie?" he asked quickly, changing the subject. "The local theater has three new ones showing…"

They went to Hollister's only in-town movie theater, a small building in town that did a pretty good business catering to families. There was a drive-in movie on the outskirts of town, in a cow pasture, but Caleb wasn't keen on that, so they went into town.

The movie they chose was a cartoon movie about a robot, and it was hilarious. Sassy had worried about leaving her mother and Selene alone, but Mrs. Peale refused to let her sacrifice a night out. Sassy did leave her prepaid cell phone with her mother, though, in case of an emergency. Caleb had one of his own, so they could use it if they were in any difficulties.

Caleb drove her back home. He had a nice truck; it wasn't new, but it was well-maintained. He was sending home the payments to his aunt, who was making them for him.

"I only have a year to go," he told her. "Yesterday, I got a firm offer of a partnership in Billings at a cousin's car dealership. He has a shop that does mechanical work. I'd be in charge of that, and do bodywork as well. I went by to see him on a whim, and he offered me the job, just like that." His dark eyes twinkled. "It's what I've wanted to do my whole life."

"I hope you make it," she told him with genuine feeling.

He bent and kissed her cheek. "You're a nice girl, Sassy," he said softly. "I wish…"

"Me, too," she said, reading the thought in his face. "But life makes other plans, sometimes."

"Doesn't it?" he chuckled.

"When do you report back to duty?" she asked.

"Not for a week, but my aunt has every minute scheduled. She had plans for tonight, too, but I out- foxed her," he said, grinning.

"I enjoyed the movie. And the chicken," she told him.

"I enjoyed the macaroni and cheese we had tonight," he replied. He was somber for a minute. "If you ever need help, I hope you'll ask me. I'd do what I can for you."

She smiled up at him. "I know that. Thanks, Caleb. I'd make the same offer. But—" she sighed "—I have no clue what I'd ever be able to help you with."

"I'll send you my address," he said, having already jotted hers down on a piece of paper. "You can send me that photo, to throw my buddy off the track."

She laughed. "Okay. I'll definitely do that."

"I'll phone you before I leave. Take care."

"You, too. So long."

He got into his truck and drove away.

Sassy walked slowly up the porch and into the house, her mind still on the funny movie.

She was halfway into the living room when she re- alized that one of the muffled voices she'd been hear- ing was male.

As she entered the room, John Taggert looked up from the sofa, where he was sitting with her mother. Her mother, she noted, was grinning like a Cheshire cat.

"Mr. Taggert came by to see how I was doing. Wasn't that sweet of him?" she asked her daughter.

"It really was," Sassy replied politely.

"Had a good time?" John asked her. He wasn't smiling.

"Yes," she said. "It was a cartoon movie."

"Just right for children," he replied, and there was something in his blue eyes that made her heart jump.

"We're all children at heart. I'm sure that's what you meant, wasn't it, Mr. Taggert?" Mrs. Peale asked sweetly.

He caught himself. "Of course," he replied, smiling at the older woman. "I enjoy them myself. We take the girls to movies all the time."

"Girls?" Mrs. Peale asked, frowning.

"My nieces," he explained. "They love cartoons. My brother and his wife take them mostly, but I fill in when I'm needed."

"You like children?"

He smiled. "I love them."

Mrs. Peale opened her mouth.

Sassy knew what was coming, so she jumped in. "Caleb's going to phone us before he goes back overseas," she told her mother.

"That's nice of him." Mrs. Peale beamed. "Such a kind young man."

"Kind." Sassy nodded.

"Would you like something to drink, Mr. Taggert?" Mrs. Peale asked politely. "Sassy could make some coffee…?"

John glanced at his watch. "I've got to go. Thanks anyway. I just wanted to make sure you were all right," he told Mrs. Peale, and he smiled at her. "Sassy's…boyfriend mentioned that he was taking her to a movie, and I thought about you out here all alone."

Sassy gave him a glare hot enough to scald. "I left

Mama my cell phone in case anything happened," she said curtly.

"Yes, she did," Mrs. Peale added quickly. "She takes very good care of me. I insisted that she go with Caleb. Sassy hasn't had a night out in two or three years."

John shifted, as if that statement made him uneasy.

"She doesn't like to leave me at all," Mrs. Peale continued. "But it's not fair to her. So much responsibility, and at her age."

"I never mind it," Sassy interrupted. "I love you."

"I know that, sweetheart, but you should get to know nice young men," she added. "You'll marry one day and have children. You can't spend your whole life like this, with a sick old woman and a child…"

"Please," Sassy said, hurting. "I don't want to think about getting married for years yet."

Mrs. Peale's face mirrored her sorrow. "You should never have had to handle this all alone," she said regretfully. "If only your father had…well, that's not something we could help."

"I'll walk Mr. Taggert to the door," Sassy offered. She looked as if she'd like to drag him out it, before her mother could embarrass her even more.

"Am I leaving?" he asked Sassy.

"Apparently," she replied, standing aside and nodding toward the front door.

"In that case, I'll say good night." He smiled at Mrs. Peale. "I hope you know that you can call on me if you ever needed help. I'm not in the Army, but I do have skills that don't involve an intimate knowledge of guns—"

"This way, Mr. Taggert," Sassy interrupted emphatically, catching him firmly by the sleeve.

He grinned at Mrs. Peale, whose eyes were twinkling now. "Good night."

"Good night, Mr. Taggert. Thank you for stopping by."

"You're very welcome."

He followed Sassy out onto the front porch. She closed the door.

His eyebrows arched. "Why did you close the door?" he asked. His voice deepened with amusement. "Are you going to kiss me good night and you don't want your mother to see?"

She flushed. "I wouldn't kiss you for all the tea in China! There's no telling where you've been!"

"Actually," he said, twirling his wide-brimmed hat in his big hands, "I've been in Medicine Ridge, reporting to my bosses."

"That's nice. Do drive safely on your way back to your ranch."

He stopped twirling the hat and studied her stiff posture. He felt between a rock and a hard place.

"The Army Ranger seems like a good sort of boy," he remarked. "Responsible. Not very mature yet, but he'll grow up."

She wanted to bite him. "He's in the Army Rangers," she reminded him. "He's been in combat overseas."

His eyebrows lifted. "Is that a requirement for your dates, that they've learned to dodge bullets?"

"I never said I wanted a man who could dodge bullets!" she threw at him.

"It might be a handy skill for a man—dodging things, I mean, if you're the sort of woman who likes to throw pots and pans at men."

"I have never thrown a pot at a man," she said emphatically. "However, if you'd like to step into our kitchen, I could make an exception for you!"

He grinned. He could have bet that she didn't talk like that to the soldier boy. She had spirit and she didn't take guff from anyone, but it took a lot to get under her skin. It delighted him that he could make her mad.

"What sort of pot did you have in mind throwing at me?" he taunted.

"Something made of cast iron," she muttered. "Although I expect you'd dent it."

"My head is not that hard," he retorted.

He stepped in, close to her, and watched her reaction with detached amusement. He made her nervous. It showed.

He put his hat back on, and pushed it to the back of his head. One long arm went around Sassy's waist and drew her to him. A big, lean hand spread on her cheek, coaxing it back to his shoulder.

"You've got grit," he murmured deeply as his gaze fell to her soft mouth. "You don't back away from trouble, or responsibility. I like that."

"You...shouldn't hold me like this," she protested weakly.

"Why not? You're soft and sweet and I like the way you smell." His head began to bend. "I think I'll like the way you taste, too," he breathed.

He didn't need a program to know how innocent she was. He loved the way her hands gripped him, almost in fear, as his firm mouth smoothed over the parted, shocked warmth of her lips.

"Nothing heavy," he whispered as his mouth played with hers. "It's far too soon for that. Relax. Just relax, Sassy. It's like dancing, slow and sweet..."

His mouth covered hers gently, brushing her lips

apart, teasing them to permit the slow invasion. Her hands relaxed their death grip on his arms as the slow rhythm began to increase her heartbeat and make her breathing sound jerky and rough. He was very good at this, she thought dizzily. He knew exactly how to make her shiver with anticipation as he drew out the intimate torture of his mouth on her lips. He teased them, playing with her lower lip, nibbling and rubbing, until she went on tiptoe with a frustrated moan, seeking something far rougher and more passionate than this exquisite whisper of motion.

He nipped her lower lip. "You want more, don't you, honey?" he whispered roughly. "So do I. Hold tight."

Her hands slid up to his broad shoulders as his mouth began to burrow hungrily into hers. She let her lips open with a shiver, closing her eyes and reaching up to be swallowed whole by his arms.

It was so sweet that she moaned with the ardent passion he aroused in her. She'd never felt her body swell and shudder like this when a man held her. She'd never been kissed so thoroughly, so expertly. Her arms tightened convulsively around his neck as he riveted her to the length of his powerful body, as if he, too, had lost control of himself.

A minute later, he came to his senses. She was just nineteen. She worked for him, even though she didn't know it. They were worlds apart in every way. What the hell was he doing?

He pulled away from her abruptly, his blue eyes shimmering with emotion, his grasp a little bruising as he tried to get his breath back under control. His jealousy of the soldier had pushed him right into a situation he'd left town to avoid. Now, here he was, faced with the consequences.

She hung there, watching him with clouded, dreamy eyes in a face flushed with pleasure from the hungry exchange.

"That was a mistake," he said curtly, putting her firmly at arm's length and letting her go.

"Are you sure?" she asked, dazed.

"Yes, I'm sure," he said, his voice sharp with anger.

"Then why did you do it?" she asked reasonably.

He had to think about a suitable answer, and his brain wasn't working very well. He'd pushed her away at their last meeting and felt guilt. Now he'd compounded the error and he couldn't think of a good way to get out of it.

"God knows," he said heavily. "Maybe it's the full moon."

She gave him a wry look. "It's not a full moon. It's a crescent moon."

"A moon is a moon," he said doggedly.

"That's your story and you're sticking to it," she agreed.

He stared down at her with conflict eating him alive. "You're nineteen, Sassy," he said finally. "I'm thirty-one."

She blinked. "Is that supposed to mean something?"

"It means you're years too young for me. And not only in age."

She raised her eyebrows. "It isn't exactly easy to get experience when you're living in a tiny town and supporting a family."

He ground his teeth. "That isn't the point..."

She held up a hand. "You had too much coffee today and the caffeine caused you to leap on unsuspecting women."

He glowered. "I did not drink too much coffee."

"Then it must be either my exceptional beauty or my

overwhelming charm," she decided. She waited, arms folded, for him to come up with an alternate theory.

He pulled his hat low over his eyes. "It's been a long, dry spell."

"Well, if that isn't the nicest compliment I ever had," she muttered. "You were lonely and I was the only eligible woman handy!"

"You were," he shot back.

"A likely story! There's Mrs. Harmon, who lives a mile down the road."

"Mrs. Harmon?"

"Yes. Her husband has been dead fifteen years. She's fifty, but she wears tight skirts and a lot of makeup and in dim light, she isn't half bad."

He glowered even more. "I am not that desperate."

"You just said you were."

"I did not!"

"Making passes at nineteen-year-old girls," she scoffed. "I never!"

He threw up his hands. "It wasn't a pass!"

She pursed her lips and gave him a sarcastic look.

He shrugged. "Maybe it was a small pass." He stuck his hands in his pockets. "I have a conscience. You'd wear on it."

So that was why he'd pushed her away in the store, before he left town. Her heart lifted. He didn't find her unattractive. He just thought she was too young.

"I'll be twenty next month," she told him.

It didn't help. "I'll be thirty-two in two months."

"Well, for a month we'll be almost the same age," she said pertly.

He laughed shortly. "Twelve years is a lot, at your age."

"In the great scheme of things, it isn't," she pointed out.

He didn't answer her.

"Thanks for stopping by to check on my mother," she said. "It was kind."

He lifted a shoulder. "I wanted to see if the soldier was hot for you."

"Excuse me?!"

"He didn't even kiss you good night," he said.

"That's because he's in love with his best friend's girl."

His expression brightened. "He is?"

"I'm somebody to talk about her with," she told him. "Which is why I don't get out much, unless a man wants to tell me about his love life and ask for advice." She studied him. "I don't guess you've got relationship problems?"

"In fact, I do. I'm trying not to have one with an inappropriate woman," he said, tongue-in-cheek.

That took a minute to register. She laughed. "Oh. I see."

He moved closer and toyed with a strand of her short hair. "I guess it wouldn't hurt to take you out once in a while. Nothing serious," he added firmly. "I am not in the market for a mistress."

"Good thing," she returned, "because I have no intention of becoming one."

He grinned. "Now, that's encouraging. I'm glad to know that you have enough willpower to keep us on the straight and narrow."

"I have my mother," she replied, "who would shoot you in the foot with a rusty gun if she even thought you were leading me into a life of sin. She's very religious. She raised me to be that way."

"In her condition," he said solemnly, "I'm not surprised that she's religious. She's a courageous soul."

"I love her a lot," she confessed. "I wish I could do more to help her."

"Loving her is probably what helps her the most," he said. He bent and brushed a soft kiss against her mouth. "I'll see you tomorrow."

She smiled. "Okay."

He started to walk down the steps, paused, and turned back to her. "You're sure it's not serious with the soldier?"

She smiled more broadly. "Very sure."

He cocked his hat at a jaunty angle and grinned at her. "Okay."

She watched him walk out to his vehicle, climb in, and drive away. She waved, but she noticed that he didn't look back. For some reason, that bothered her.

John spent a rough night remembering how sweet Sassy was to kiss. He'd been fighting the attraction for weeks now, and he was losing. She was too young for him. He knew it. But on the other hand, she was independent. She was strong. She was used to responsibility. She'd had years of being the head of her family, the breadwinner. She might be young, but she was more mature than most women her age.

He could see how much care she took for her mother and her mother's little ward. She never shirked her duties, and she worked hard for her paycheck.

The bottom line was that he was far too attracted to her to walk away. He was taking a chance. But he'd taken chances before in his life, with women who were much inferior to this little firecracker. It wouldn't hurt to go slow and see where the path led. After all, he could walk away whenever he liked, he told himself.

The big problem was going to be the distance between them socially. Sassy didn't know that he came from great wealth, that his parents were related to most of the royal houses of Europe, that he and his brother had built a world-famous ranch that bred equally famous breeding bulls. He was used to five-star hotels and restaurants, stretch limousines in every city he visited. He traveled first-class. He was worldly and sophisticated. Sassy was much more used to small-town life. She wouldn't understand his world. Probably, she wouldn't be able to adjust to it.

But he was creating hurdles that didn't exist yet. It wasn't as if he was in love with her and aching to rush her to the altar, he told himself. He was going to take her out a few times. Maybe kiss her once in a while. It was nothing he couldn't handle. She'd just be companionship while he was getting this new ranching enterprise off the ground. When he had to leave, he'd tell her the truth.

It sounded simple. It was simple, he assured himself. She was just another girl, another casual relationship. He was going to enjoy it while it lasted.

He went to sleep, finally, having resolved all the problems in his mind.

The next day, he went back to the feed store with another list, this one of household goods that he was going to need. He was looking forward to seeing Sassy again. The memory of that kiss had prompted some unusually spicy dreams about her.

But when he got there, he found Buck Mannheim handling the counter and looking worried.

He waited while the older man finished a sale. The customer left and John approached the counter.

"Where's Sassy?" he asked.

Buck looked concerned. "She phoned me at home.

Her mother had a bad turn. They had to send an ambulance for her and take her up to Billings to the nearest hospital. Sassy was crying…"

He was talking to thin air. John was already out the door.

He found Sassy and little Selene in the emergency waiting room, huddled together and upset.

He walked into the room and they both ran to him, to be scooped up and held close, comforted.

He felt odd. It was the first time he could remember being important to anyone outside his own family circle. He felt needed.

His arms contracted around them. "Tell me what happened," he asked at Sassy's ear.

She drew away a little, wiping at her eyes with the hem of her blouse. It was obvious that she hadn't slept. "She knocked over her water carafe, or I wouldn't even have known anything was wrong. I ran in to see what had happened and I found her gasping for breath. It was so bad that I just ran to the phone and called Dr. Bates. He sent for the ambulance and called the oncologist on staff here. They've been with her for two hours. Nobody's told me anything."

He eased them down into chairs. "Stay here," he said softly. "I'll find out what's going on."

She was doubtful that a cowboy, even a foreman, would be able to elicit more information than the patient's own family, but she smiled. "Thanks."

He turned and walked down the hall.

Chapter 7

John had money and power, and he knew how to use both. Within two minutes, he'd been ushered into the office of the hospital administrator. He explained who he was, why he was there, and asked for information. Even in Billings, the Callister empire was known. Five minutes later, he was speaking to the physician in charge of Sassy's mother's case. He accepted responsibility for the bill and asked if anything more could be done than was being done.

"Sadly, yes," the physician said curtly. "We're bound by the family's financial constraints. Mrs. Peale does have insurance, but she told us that they simply could not afford anything other than symptomatic relief for her. If she would consent, Mrs. Peale could have surgery to remove the cancerous lung and then radiation and chemotherapy to insure her recovery. In fact, she'd have a very good prognosis…"

"If money's all that's holding things up, I'll gladly

be responsible for the bill. I don't care how much it is. So what are you waiting for?" John asked.

The physician smiled. "You'll speak to the financial officer?"

"Immediately," he replied.

"Then I'll speak to the patient."

"They don't know who I am," John told him. "That's the only condition, that you don't tell them. They think I'm the foreman of a ranch."

The older man frowned. "Is there a reason?"

"Originally, it was to insure that costs didn't escalate locally because the name was known," he said. "But by then, it was too late to change things. They're my friends," he added. "I don't want them to look at me differently."

"You think they would?"

"People see fame and money and power. They don't see people. Not at first."

The other man nodded. "I think I understand. I'll get the process underway. It's a very kind thing you're doing," he added. "Mrs. Peale would have died. Very soon, too."

"I know that. She's a good person."

"And very important to her little family, from what I've seen."

"Yes."

He clapped John on the shoulder. "We'll do everything possible."

"Thanks."

When he wrapped up things in the financial office, he strolled back down to the emergency room. Sassy was pacing the floor. Selene had curled up into a chair with her cheek pillowed on her arm. She was sound asleep.

Sassy met him, her eyes wide and fascinated. "What did you *do?*" she exclaimed. "They're going to operate on Mama! The doctor says they can save her life, that she can have radiation and chemotherapy, that there's a grant for poor people...she can live!"

Her voice broke into tears. John pulled her close and rocked her in his strong, warm arms, his mouth against her temple. "It's all right, honey," he said softly. "Don't cry."

"I'm just so happy," she choked at his chest. "So happy! I never knew there were such things as grants for this sort of thing, or I'd have done anything to find one! I thought...I thought we'd have to watch her die..."

"Never while there was a breath in my body," he whispered. His arms contracted. A wave of feeling rippled through him. He'd helped people in various ways all his life, but it was the first time he'd been able to make this sort of difference for someone he cared about. He'd grown fond of Mrs. Peale. But he'd thought that her case was hopeless. He thanked God that the emergency had forced Sassy to bring her mother here. What a wonderful near-tragedy. A link in a chain that would lead to a better life for all three of them.

She drew back, wiping her eyes again and laughing. "Sorry. I seem to spend my life crying. I'm just so grateful. What did you do?" she asked again.

He grinned. "I just asked wasn't there something they could figure out to do to help her. The doctor said he'd check, and he came up with the grant."

She shook her head. "It happened so fast. They've got some crackerjack surgeon who's teaching new techniques in cancer intervention here, and he's the one they're getting to operate on Mama. What's more, they're going to do it tomorrow. They already asked her, and she just almost jumped out of the bed she was so excited." She wiped away more tears. "We brought her up here to die," she explained. "And it was the most wonderful, scary experience we ever had. She's going to live, maybe long enough to see Selene graduate from college!"

He smiled down at her. "You know, I wouldn't be surprised at all if that's not the case. Feel better?"

She nodded. Her eyes adored him. "Thank you."

He chuckled. "Glad I could help." He glanced down at Selene, who was radiant. "Hear that? You'll have to go to college."

She grinned. "I want to be a doctor, now."

"There are scholarships that will help that dream come true, at the right time," he assured her.

Sassy pulled the young girl close. "We'll find lots," she promised.

"Thank you for helping save our mama," Selene told John solemnly. "We love her very much."

"She loves you very much," John replied. "That must be pretty nice, at your age."

He was saying something without saying it.

Sassy sent Selene to the vending machines for apple juice. While she was gone, Sassy turned to John. "What was your mother like when you were little?"

His face hardened. "I didn't have a mother when I was little," he replied curtly. "My brother and I were raised by our uncle."

She was shocked. "Were your parents still alive?"

"Yes. But they didn't want us."

"How horrible!"

He averted his eyes. "We had a rough upbringing.

Until our uncle took us in, we were in—" he started to say boarding school, but that was a dead giveaway "—in a bad situation at home," he amended. "Our uncle took us with him and we grew up without a mother's influence."

"You still don't have anything to do with her? Or your father?"

"We started seeing them again last year," he said after a minute. "It's been hard. We built up resentments and barriers. But we're all working on it. Years too late," he added on a cold laugh.

"I'm sorry," she told him. "Mama's been there for me all my life. She's kissed my cuts and bruises, loved me, fought battles for me... I don't know what I would have done without her."

He drew in a long breath and looked down into warm green eyes. "I would have loved having a mother like her," he said honestly. "She's the most optimistic person I ever knew. In her condition, that says a lot."

"I thought we'd be planning her funeral when we came in here," Sassy said, still shell-shocked.

He touched her soft cheek gently. "I can understand that."

"How did you know where we were?" she asked suddenly.

"I went into the feed store with a list and found Buck holding down the fort," he said. "He said you were up here."

"And you came right away," she said, amazed.

He put both big hands on her small waist and held her in front of him. His blue eyes were solemn. "I never planned to get mixed up with you," he told her honestly. "Or your family. But I seem to be part of it."

She smiled. "Yes. You are a part of our family."

His hands contracted. "I just want to make the point that my interest isn't brotherly," he added.

The look in his eyes made her heartbeat accelerate. "Really?"

He smiled. "Really."

She felt as if she could fly. The expression on her face made him wish that they were in a more private place. He looked down to her full mouth and contemplated something shocking and potentially embarrassing.

Before he could act on what was certainly a crazy impulse, the doctor who'd admitted Mrs. Peale came walking up to them with a taller, darker man. He introduced himself and his companion.

"Miss Peale, this is Dr. Barton Crowley," he told Sassy. "He's going to operate on your mother first thing in the morning."

Sassy shook his hand warmly. "I'm so glad to meet you. We're just overwhelmed. We thought we'd brought Mama up here to die. It's a miracle! We never even knew there were grants for surgery!"

John shot a warning look at the doctor and the surgeon, who nodded curtly. The hospital administrator had already told them about the financial arrangements.

"We can always find a way to handle critical situations here," the doctor said with a smile. He nodded toward Dr. Crowley. "He's been teaching us new surgical techniques. It really was a miracle that he was here when you arrived. He works at Johns Hopkins, you see," he added.

Sassy didn't know what that meant.

John leaned down. "It's one of the more famous hospitals back East," he told her.

She laughed nervously. "Sorry," she told Dr. Crowley, who smiled. "I don't get out much."

"She works at our local feed store," John told them, beaming down at her. "She's the family's only support. She takes care of her mother and their six-year-old ward as well. She's quite a girl."

"Stop that," Sassy muttered shyly. "I'm not some paragon of virtue. I love my family."

His eyebrows arched and his eyes twinkled. "All of it?" he asked amusedly.

She flushed when she recalled naming him part of the family. She forced her attention back to the surgeon. "You really think you can help Mama? Our local doctor said the cancer was very advanced."

"It is, but preliminary tests indicate that it's confined to one lobe of her lung. If we can excise it, then follow up with chemotherapy and radiation, there's a good chance that we can at least prolong her life. We might save it altogether."

"Please do whatever you can," Sassy pleaded gently. "She means so much to us."

"She was very excited when I spoke with her," Dr. Crowley said with a smile. "She was concerned about her daughters, she told me, much more than with her own condition. A most unique lady."

"Yes, she is," Sassy agreed. "She's always putting other people's needs in front of her own. She raised me with hardly any help at all, and it was rough."

"From what I see, young woman," the surgeon replied, "she did a very good job."

"Thanks," she said, a little embarrassed.

"Well, we'll get her into surgery first thing. When we see the extent of the cancerous tissue, we'll speak again. Try to get some rest."

"We will."

He and the doctor shook hands with John and walked back down the hall.

"I wish I'd packed a blanket or something," Sassy mused, eyeing the straight, lightly padded chairs in the distant waiting room. "I can sleep sitting up, but it gets cold in hospitals."

"Sitting up?" He didn't understand.

"Listen, you know how we're fixed," she said. "We can't afford a motel room. I always sleep in the waiting room when Mama's in the hospital." She nodded toward Selene, who was now asleep in the corner. "We both do it. Except Selene fits in these chairs a little better, because she's so small."

He was shocked. It was a firsthand look at how the rest of the world had to live. He hadn't realized that Sassy would have to stay at the hospital.

"Don't look like that," she said. "You make me uncomfortable. I don't mind being poor. I've got so many blessings that it's hard to count them."

"Blessings." He frowned, as if he wondered what they could possibly be.

"I have a mother who sacrificed to raise me, who loves me with her whole heart. I have a little sort-of sister who thinks I'm Joan of Arc. I have a roof over my head, food to eat, and, thanks to you, a really good job with no harassment tied to it. I even have a vehicle that gets me to and from work most of the time."

"I wouldn't call that vehicle a blessing," he observed.

"Neither would I, if I could afford that fancy truck you drive," she chided, grinning. "The point is, I have things that a lot of other people don't. I'm happy," she added, curious about his expression.

She had nothing. Literally nothing. But she could count her blessings as if they made her richer than a princess. He had everything, but his life was empty. All the wealth and power he commanded hadn't made him happy. He was alone. He had Gil and his family, and his parents. But in a very personal sense, he was by himself.

"You're thinking that you don't really have a family of your own," Sassy guessed from his glum expression. "But you do. You have me, and Mama, and Selene. We're your family." She hesitated, because he looked hunted. She flushed. "I know we're not much to brag about…"

His arm shot out and pulled her to him. "Don't run yourself down. I've never counted my friends by their bank books. Character is far more important."

She relaxed. But only a little. He was very close, and her heart was racing.

"You suit me just the way you are," he said gently. He bent and kissed her, tenderly, before he let her go and walked toward Selene.

"What are you doing?" she exclaimed when he lifted the sleeping child in his arms and started toward the exit.

"I'm taking baby sister here to a modest guest room for the night. You can come, too."

She blinked. "John, I can't afford—"

"If I hear that one more time," he interrupted, "I'm going to say bad words. You don't want me to say bad words in front of the child. Do you?"

She was asleep and wouldn't hear them, but he was making a point and being noble. She gave in, smiling. "Okay. But you have to dock my wages for it or I'll stay here and Selene can just hear you spout bad words."

He smiled over Selene's head on his chest. "Okay, honey."

The word brought a soft blush into Sassy's cheeks and he chuckled softly. He led the way out the door to his truck.

John's idea of a modest guest room was horrifying to Sassy when he stopped by the desk of Billings's best hotel to check in Sassy and Selene.

The child stirred sleepily in John's strong arms. She opened her eyes, yawning. "Mama?" she exclaimed, worried.

"She's fine," John assured her. "Go back to sleep, baby. Curl up in this chair until I get the formalities done, okay?" He placed her gently into a big, cushy armchair near the desk.

"Okay, John," Selene said, smiling as she closed her eyes and nodded off again.

"You'd better stay with her while I do this," John told Sassy, not wanting her to hear the clerk when he gave her his real name to pay for the room.

"Okay, John," she echoed her little sister, with a grin.

He winked at her and went back to the desk. The smile faded as he spoke to the male clerk.

"Their mother is in the hospital, about to have cancer surgery. They were going to sleep in the waiting room. I want a room for them, near mine, if it's possible."

The clerk, a kindly young man, smiled sympathetically. "There's one adjoining yours, Mr. Callister," he said politely. "It's a double. Would that do?"

"Yes."

The clerk made the arrangements, took John's credit card, processed the transaction, handed back the card, and then went to program the card-key for the new guests. He was back in no time, very efficient.

"I hope their mother does all right," he told John.

"So do I. But she's in very good hands."

He went back to Selene, lifted her gently, and motioned to Sassy, who was examining the glass coffee table beside the chairs.

She paused at a pillar as they walked into the elevator. "Gosh, this looks like real marble," she murmured, and then had to run to make it before the elevator doors closed. "John, this place looks expensive..."

"I'll make sure to tell Buck to dock your salary over several months, okay?" he asked gently, and he smiled.

She was apprehensive. It was going to be a big chunk of her income. But he'd already been so nice that she felt guilty for even making a fuss. "Sure, that's fine."

He led them down the hall and gave Sassy the card-key to insert in the lock. She stared at it.

"Why are you giving me a credit card?" she asked in all honesty.

He gaped at her. "It's the door key."

She cocked an eyebrow. "Right." She looked up at him as if she expected men with white nets to appear.

He laughed when he realized she hadn't a clue about modern technology. "Give it here."

He balanced Selene on one lifted knee, inserted the card, jerked it back out so the green light on the lock blinked, and then opened the door.

Sassy's jaw dropped.

"It's a card-key," he repeated, leading the way in.

Sassy closed the door behind them, turning on the lights as she went. The room was a revelation. There was a huge new double bed—two of them, in fact. There were paintings on the wall. There was a round table with two chairs. There was a telephone. There was a huge glass window, curtained, that looked out over Billings. There was even a huge television.

"This is a palace," Sassy murmured, spellbound as she looked around. She peered into the bathroom and actually gasped. "There's a hair dryer right here in the room!" she exclaimed.

John had put Selene down gently on one of the double beds. He felt two inches high. Sassy's life had been spent in a small rural town in abject poverty. She knew nothing of high living. Even this hotel, nice but not the five-star accommodation he'd frequented in his travels both in this country and overseas, was opulent to her. Considering where, and how, she and her family lived, this must have seemed like kingly extravagance.

He walked back to the bathroom and leaned against the door facing while she explored tiny wrapped packets of soap and little bottles of shampoo and soap.

"Wow," she whispered.

She touched the thick white towels, so plush that she wanted to wrap up in one. She compared them to her thin, tatty, worn towels at home and was shocked at the contrast. She glanced at John shyly.

"Sorry," she said. "I'm not used to this sort of place."

"It's just a hotel, Sassy," he said softly. "If you've never stayed in one, I imagine it's surprising at first."

"How did you know?" she asked.

"Know what?"

"That I'd never stayed in a hotel?"

He cleared his throat. "Well, it shows. Sort of."

She flushed. "You mean, I'm acting like an idiot."

"I mean nothing of the sort." He shouldered away from the door facing, caught her by the waist, pulled her close, and bent to kiss the breath out of her.

She held on tight, relieved about her mother, but worried about the surgery, and grateful for John's intervention.

"You've made miracles for us," she said when he let her go.

He searched her shimmering green eyes. "You've made one for me," he replied, and he wasn't kidding.

"I have? How?"

His hands contracted on her small waist. "Let's just say, you've taught me about the value of small blessings. I tend to take things for granted, I guess." His eyes narrowed. "You appreciate the most basic things in life. You're so…optimistic, Sassy," he added. "You make me feel humble."

"Oh, that's rich," she chuckled. "A backwoods hick like me making a sophisticated gentleman like you feel humble."

"I'm not kidding," he replied. "You don't have a lot of material things. But you're happy without them." He shrugged. "I've got a lot more than you have, and I'm…" He searched for the word, frowning. "I'm…empty," he said finally, meeting her quiet eyes.

"But you're the kindest man I've ever known," she argued. "You do things for people without even thinking twice what problems you may cause yourself in the process. You're a good person."

Her wide-eyed fascination made him tingle inside. In recent years, women had wanted him because he was rich and powerful. Here was one who wanted him because he was kind. It was an eye-opener.

"You look strange," she remarked.

"I was thinking," he said.

"About what?"

"About how late it is, and how much you're going to need some sleep. We'll get an early start tomorrow," he told her.

The horror came back, full force. The joy drained out of her face, to be replaced with fear and uncertainty.

He drew her close and rocked her in his arms, bending his head over hers. "That surgeon is rather famous," he said conversationally. "He's one of the best oncologists in the country, and it's a blessing that he ended up here just when your mother needed him. You have to believe that she's going to be all right."

"I'm trying to," she said. "It's just hard. We've had so many trips to the hospital," she confessed, and sounded weary.

John had never had to go through this with his family. Well, there was Gil's first wife who died in a riding accident. That had been traumatic. But since then, John had never worried about losing a relative to disease. He had, he decided, been very lucky.

"I'll be right there with you," he promised her. "All the time."

She drew back and looked up at him with fascinated eyes. "You will? You mean it? Won't you get in trouble with your boss?"

"I won't," he said. "But it wouldn't matter if I did. I'm not leaving you. Not for anything."

She colored and smiled at him.

"After all," he teased, "I'm a member of the family."

She smiled even more.

"Kissing kin," he added, and bent to brush a whisper of a kiss over her soft mouth. He forced himself to step away from her. "Go to bed."

"Okay. Thanks, John. Thanks for everything."

He didn't answer her. He just winked.

The surgery took several hours. Sassy bit her fingernails off into the quick. Selene sat very close to her, holding her hand.

"I don't want Mama to die," she said.

Sassy pulled her close. "She won't die," she promised. "She's going to get better. I promise." She prayed it wasn't going to be a lie.

John had gone to check with the surgical desk. He came back grinning.

"Tell me!" Sassy exclaimed.

"They were able to get all the cancerous tissue," he said. "It was confined to a lobe of her lung, as he suspected. They're cautiously optimistic that your mother will recover and begin to lead a full life again."

"Oh, my goodness!" Sassy exclaimed, hugging Selene close. "She'll get better!"

Selene hugged her back. "I'm so happy!"

"So am I."

Sassy let her go, got up, and went to hug John close, laying her cheek against his broad, warm chest. He enveloped her in his arms. She felt right at home there.

"Thank you," she murmured.

"For what?"

She looked up at him. "For everything."

He smiled at her, his eyes crinkling.

"What happens now?" she asked.

"Your mother recovers enough to go home, then we bring her back up here for the treatments. Dr. Crowley said that would take a few weeks, but except for some nausea and weakness, she should manage it very well."

"You'll come with us?" she asked, amazed.

He glowered at her. "Of course I will," he said indignantly. "I'm part of the family. You said so."

She drew in a long, contented breath. She was tired and worried but she felt newborn. "You're the nicest man I've ever known," she said.

He cocked an eyebrow. "Nicer than the Army guy?"

She smiled. "Even nicer than Caleb."

He looked over her head and glowered even more. "Speak of the devil!"

A tall, dark-haired man in an Army uniform was striding down the hall toward them.

Chapter 8

Sassy turned and, sure enough, Caleb was walking toward them in his Army uniform, complete with combat boots and beret. He looked very handsome.

"Caleb," Sassy said warmly, going to meet him. "How did you know we were here?"

He hugged her gently. "I have a cousin who works here. She remembered that I'd been down to see you in Hollister, and that your last name was Peale. How is your mother?"

"She just came out of surgery. Her prognosis is good. John found us a grant to pay for it all, isn't that incredible? I didn't know they had programs like that!"

Caleb knew they didn't. He looked at John and, despite the older man's foreboding expression, he smiled at him. He was quick enough to realize that John had intervened for Sassy's mother and didn't want anybody to know. "Yes, they do have grants, don't they? Nice of you to do that for them," he added, his dark eyes saying things to John that Sassy didn't see.

John relaxed a little. The boy might be competition, but his heart was in the right place. Sassy had said he was a friend, but Caleb here must care about her, to come right to the hospital when he knew about her mother. "They're a great bunch of people," he said simply.

"Yes, they are," Caleb agreed. He turned to smile down at Sassy while John fumed silently.

"Thank you for coming to see us," Sassy told the younger man.

"I wish I could stay," he told her, "but I'm on my way to the rimrocks right now. I'm due back at my assignment."

"The rimrocks?" Sassy asked, frowning.

"It's where the airport is," Caleb told her, grinning. "That's what we call it locally."

"I hope you have a safe flight back," she told him. "And a safe tour of duty."

"Now, that makes two of us," he agreed. "Don't forget to send me that photograph."

"I won't. So long, Caleb."

"So long." He bent and kissed her cheek, smiled ruefully at John, and walked back down the hall.

"What photograph?" John asked belligerently.

"It's not for him," she said, delighted that he looked jealous. "It's to throw his best friend off the track."

John was unconvinced. But just as he started to argue, the surgeon came into the waiting room, smiling wearily.

He shook hands with John and turned to Sassy. "Your mother is doing very well. She's in recovery right now, and then she'll go to the intensive care unit. Just for a couple of days," he added quickly when Sassy went pale and looked faint. "It's normal procedure. We want her watched day and night until she's stabilized."

"Can Selene and I see her?" Sassy asked. "And John?" she added, nodding to the man at her side.

The surgeon hesitated. "Have you ever seen anyone just out of surgery, young woman?" he asked gently.

"Well, there was Great-Uncle Jack, but I only got a glimpse of him...why?"

The surgeon looked apprehensive. "Post-surgical patients are flour-white. They have tubes running out of them, they're connected to machines...it can be alarming if you aren't prepared for it."

"Mama's going to live, thanks to you," Sassy said, smiling. "She'll look beautiful. I don't mind the machines. They're helping her live. Right?"

The surgeon smiled back. Her optimism was contagious. "Right. I'll let you in to see her for five minutes, no longer," he said, "as soon as we move her into intensive care. It will be a little while," he added.

"We're not going anywhere," she replied easily.

He chuckled. "I'll send a nurse for you, when it's time."

"Thank you," Sassy said. "From the bottom of my heart."

The surgeon shifted. "It's what I do," he replied. "The most rewarding job in the world."

"I've never saved anybody's life, but I expect it would be a great job," she told him.

After he left, John gave her a wry look.

"I saved a man's life, once," he told her.

"You did? How?" she asked, waiting.

"I threw a baseball bat at him, and missed."

"Oh, you," she teased. She went close to him, wrapped

her arms around him, and laid her head on his broad chest. "You're just wonderful."

His hand smoothed over her dark hair. Over her head, Selene was smiling at him with the same kind of happy, affectionate expression that he imagined was on Sassy's face. Despite the fear and apprehension of the ordeal, it was one of the best days of his life. He'd never felt so necessary.

Sassy was allowed into the intensive care unit just long enough to look at her mother and stand beside her. John was with her, the surgeon's whispered request getting him past the fiercely protective nurse in charge of the unit. Sassy was uneasy, despite her assurances, and she clung to John's hand as if she were afraid of falling without its warm support.

She stared at the still, white form in the hospital bed. Machines beeped. A breathing machine made odd noises as it pumped oxygen into Mrs. Peale's unconscious body. The shapeless, faded hospital gown was unfamiliar, like all the monitors and tubes that seemed to extrude from every inch of her mother's flesh. Mrs. Peale was white as a sheet. Her chest rose and fell very slowly. Her heartbeat was visible as the gown fluttered over her ample bosom.

"She's alive," John whispered. "She's going to get well and go home and be a different woman. You have to see the future, through the present."

Sassy looked up at him with tears in her eyes. "It's just…I love her so much."

He smiled tenderly and bent to kiss her forehead. "She loves you, too, honey. She's going to get well."

She drew in a shaky breath and got control of her emotions. She wiped at the tears. "Yes." She moved closer to the bed, bending over her mother. She remembered that when she was a little girl she'd had a debilitating virus that had almost dehydrated her. Mrs. Peale had perched on her bed, feeding her ice chips around the clock to keep fluids in her. She'd fetched wet cloths and whispered that she loved Sassy, that everything was going to be all right. That loving touch had chased the fear and misery and sickness right out of the room. Mrs. Peale seemed to glow with it.

"It's going to be all right, Mama," she whispered, kissing the pale, cool brow. "We love you very much. We're going home, very soon."

Mrs. Peale didn't answer her, but her hand on its confining board jumped, almost imperceptibly.

John squeezed Sassy's hand. "Did you see that?" he asked, smiling. "She heard you."

Sassy squeezed back. "Of course she did."

Three days later, Mrs. Peale was propped up in bed eating Jell-O. She was weak and sore and still in a lot of pain, but she was smiling gamely.

"Didn't I tell you?" John chided Sassy. "She's too tough to let a little thing like major surgery get her down."

Mrs. Peale smiled at him. "You've been so kind to us, John," she said. Her voice was still a little hoarse from the breathing tubes, but she sounded cheerful just the same. "Sassy told me all about the palace you're keeping her and Selene in."

"Some palace," he chuckled. "It's just a place to sleep." He stuck his hands into his jeans and his eyes twinkled. "But being kind goes with the job. I'm part of the family. She—" he pointed at Sassy "—said so."

"I did," Sassy confessed.

Mrs. Peale gave him a wry look. "But not too close a member…?"

"Definitely not," he agreed at once, chuckling. He looked at Sassy in a way that made her blush. Then he compounded the embarrassment by laughing.

In the weeks that followed, John divided his time between Mrs. Peale's treatments in Billings and the growing responsibility for the new ranch that was just beginning to shape up. The barn was up, shiny and attractive with bricked aisles and spotless stalls with metal gates. The corral had white fences interlaced with hidden electrical fencing that complemented the cosmetic look of the wood. The pastures had been sowed with old prairie grasses, with which John was experimenting. The price of corn had gone through the roof, with the biofuel revolution. Ranchers were scrambling for new means of sustaining their herds, so native grasses were being utilized, along with concentrated pelleted feeds and vitamin supplements. John had also hired a nearby farmer to plant grains for him and keep them during the growing season. His contractor was building a huge new concrete feed silo to house the grains when they were harvested at the end of summer. It was a monumental job, getting the place renovated. John had delegated as much authority as he could, but there were still management decisions that had to be made by him.

Meanwhile, Bill Tarleton's trial went on the docket and pretrial investigations were going on by both the county district attorney and the public defender's office for the judicial circuit where Hollister was located. Sassy was interviewed by both sides. The questions made her very nervous and uneasy. The public defender seemed to think she'd enticed Mr. Tarleton to approach her in a sexual manner. It hurt her feelings.

She told John about it when he stopped by after supper one Friday evening to check on Mrs. Peale. He hadn't been into the feed store the entire week because of obligations out at the ranch.

"He'll make me sound like some cheap tart in court," she moaned. "It will make my mother and Selene look bad, too."

"Telling the truth won't make anyone look bad, dear," Mrs. Peale protested. She was sitting up in the living room knitting. A knitted cap covered her head. Her hair had already started to fall out from the radiation therapy she was receiving, but she hadn't let it get her down. She'd made a dozen caps in different colors and styles and seemed to be enjoying the project.

"You should listen to your mother," John agreed, smiling. "You don't want him to get away with it, Sassy. It wasn't your fault."

"That lawyer made it sound like it was. The assistant district attorney who questioned me asked what sort of clothes I wore to work, and I told him jeans and T-shirts, and not any low-cut ones, either. He smiled and said that it shouldn't have mattered if I'd worn a bikini. He said Mr. Tarleton had no business making me uncomfortable in my workplace, regardless of my clothing."

"I like that assistant district attorney," John said. "He's a firecracker. One day he'll end up in the state attorney general's office. They say he's got a perfect record of convictions in the two years he's prosecuted cases for this judicial circuit."

"I hope he makes Mr. Tarleton as uncomfortable as that public defender made me," Sassy said with feeling. She rubbed her bare arms, as if it chilled her, thinking about the trial. "I don't know how I'll manage, sitting in front of a jury and telling what happened."

"You just remember that the people in that jury will most likely be people who've known you all your life," Mrs. Peale interrupted.

"That's the other thing." Sassy sighed. "The D.A.'s victim assistance person said the defending attorney is trying to get the trial moved to Billings, on account of Mr. Tarleton can't get a fair trial here."

John frowned. That did put another face on things. But he'd testify, as would Sassy. Hopefully Tarleton would get what he deserved. John knew for a fact that if he hadn't intervened, it would have been much more than a minor assault. Sassy knew it, too.

"It was a bad day for Hollister when that man came to town," Mrs. Peale said curtly. "Sassy came home every day upset and miserable."

"You should have called the owner and complained," John told Sassy.

She grimaced. "I didn't dare. He didn't know me that well. I was afraid he'd think I was telling tales on Mr. Tarleton because I wanted his job."

"It's been done," John had to admit. "But you're not like that, Sassy. He'd have investigated and found that out."

She sighed. "It's water under the bridge now," she replied sadly. "I know it's the right thing to do, taking him to court. But what if he gets off and comes after me, or Mama or Selene for revenge?" she added, worried.

"If he does," John said, and his blue eyes glittered dangerously, "it will be the worst decision of his life. I promise you. As for getting off, if by some miracle he does, you'll file a civil suit against him for damages and I'll bankroll you."

"I knew you were a nice man from the first time I laid eyes on you," Mrs. Peale chuckled.

Sassy was smiling at him with her whole face. She felt warm and protected and secure. She blushed when he looked back, with such an intent, piercing expression that her heart turned over.

"Why does life have to be so complicated?" Sassy asked after a minute.

John shrugged. "Beats me, honey," he said, getting to his feet and obviously unaware of the endearment that brought another soft blush to Sassy's face. "But it does seem to get more that way by the day." He checked his watch and grimaced. "I have to get back to the ranch. I've got an important call coming through. But I'll stop by tomorrow. We might take in a movie, if you're game."

Sassy grinned. "I'd love to." She looked at her mother and hesitated.

"I have a phone," her mother pointed out. "And Selene's here."

"You went out with the Army guy and didn't make a fuss," John muttered.

Mrs. Peale beamed. That was jealousy. Sassy seemed to realize it, too, because her eyes lit up.

"I'm not making a fuss," Sassy assured him. "And I love going to the movies."

John relented a little and grinned self-consciously. "Okay. I'll be along about six. That Chinese restaurant that just opened has good food—suppose I bring some along and we'll have supper before we go?"

They hesitated to accept. He'd done so much for them already...

"It's Chinese food, not precious jewels," he said. "Would you like to go out and look at my truck again?

I make a handsome salary and I don't drink, smoke, gamble or run around with predatory women!"

Now Mrs. Peale and Sassy both looked sheepish and grinned.

"Okay," Sassy said. "But when I get rich and famous one day for my stock-clerking abilities, I'm paying you back for all of it."

He laughed. "That's a deal."

The Chinese food was a huge assortment of dishes, many of which could be stored in the refrigerator and provide meals for the weekend for the women and the child. They knew what he'd done, but they didn't complain again. He was bighearted and he wanted to help them. It seemed petty to argue.

After they ate, he helped Sassy up into the cab of the big pickup truck, got in himself, and drove off down the road. It was still light outside, but the sun was setting in brilliant colors. It was like a symphony of reds and oranges and yellows, against the silhouetted mountains in the distance.

"It's so beautiful here," Sassy said, watching the sunset. "I'd never want to live anyplace else."

He glanced at her. He was homesick for Medicine Ridge from time to time, but he liked Hollister, too. It was a small, homey place with nice people and plenty of wide-open country. The elbow room was delightful. You could drive for miles and not meet another car or even see a house.

"Are we going to the theater in town?" she asked John.

He grinned like a boy. "We are not," he told her. "I found a drive-in theater just outside the city limits. The owner started it up about a month ago. He said he'd gone to them when he was young and thought it was time to bring them back. I don't know that he'll be able to stay open long, but I thought we'd check it out, anyway."

"Wow," she exclaimed. "I've read about them in novels."

"Me, too, but I've never been to one. Our uncle used to talk about them."

"Is it in a town?" she asked.

"No. It's in the middle of a cow pasture. Cattle graze nearby."

She laughed delightedly. "You're watching a movie with the windows open and a cow sticks its head into the car with you," she guessed.

"I wouldn't be surprised."

"I like cows," she said with a sigh. "I wouldn't mind."

"He runs beef cattle. Steers."

She looked at him. "Steers?"

"It's a bull with missing equipment," he told her, tongue-in-cheek.

"Then what's a cow?"

"It's a cow, if it's had calves. If it hasn't, it's a heifer."

"You know a lot about cattle."

"I've worked around them all my life," he said comfortably. "I love animals. We're going to have horses out at the ranch, too. You can come riding and bring Selene, any time you want."

"You'd have to teach Selene," she said. "She's never been on a horse and you'd have to coach me. It's been a long time since I've been riding."

He glanced at her with warm eyes. "I'd love that."

She laughed. "Me, too."

The drive-in was in a cleared pasture about a quarter of a mile off the main highway. There was a marquee, which listed the movie playing, this time a science-fiction one about a space freighter and its courageous crew which was fighting a technological empire that ran the inner planets of the solar system where it operated. They drove through a tree-lined dirt road down to the cleared pasture. There was room for about twenty cars, and six were already occupying one of three slight inclines that faced a huge blank screen. Each space had a pole, which contained two speakers, one for cars on either side of it. At the ticket stand, which was a drive-through affair manned by a teenager who looked like the owner John had already met, most likely his son, John paid for their tickets.

He pulled the truck up into an unoccupied space and cut off the engine, looking around amusedly. "The only thing missing is a concession stand with drinks and pizza and a rest room," he mused. "Maybe he'll add that, later, if the drive-in catches on."

"It's nice out here, without all that," she mused, looking around.

"Yes, it is." He powered down both windows and brought the speaker in on his side of the truck. He turned up the volume just as the screen lit up with welcome messages and previews of coming attractions.

"This is great!" Sassy laughed.

"It is, isn't it?"

He tossed his hat into the small backseat of the double-cabbed truck, unfastened his seat belt, and stretched out. As an afterthought, he unfastened Sassy's belt and drew her into the space beside him, with his long arm behind her back and his cheek resting on her soft hair.

"Isn't that better?" he murmured, smiling.

One small hand went to press against his shirtfront as she curled closer with a sigh. "It's much better."

The first part of the movie was hilarious. But before it ended, they weren't watching anymore. John had looked down at Sassy's animated face in the flickering light from the movie screen and longing had grown in him like a hot tide. It had been a while since he'd felt Sassy's soft mouth under his lips and he was hungry for it. Since he'd known her, he hadn't had the slightest interest in other women. It was only Sassy.

He tugged on her hair so that she lifted her face to his. "Is this all you'll ever want, Sassy?" he asked gently. "Living in a small, rural town and working in a feed store? Will you miss knowing what it's like to go to college or work in a big city and meet sophisticated people?" he asked solemnly.

Her soft eyes searched his. "Why would I want to do that?" she asked with genuine interest.

"You're very young," he said grimly. "This is all you know."

"Mr. Barber, who runs the Ford dealership here, was born in Hollister and has never been outside the county in his whole life," she told him. "He's been married to Miss Jane since he was eighteen and she was sixteen. They have five sons."

He frowned. "Are you saying something?"

"I'm telling you that this is how people live here," she said simply. "We don't have extravagant tastes. We're country people. We're family. We get married. We have kids. We grow old watching our grandchildren grow up. Then we die. We're buried here. We have beautiful country where we can walk in the forest or ride through fields full of growing crops, or pass through pastures where cattle and horses graze. We have clear, unpolluted streams and blue skies. We sit on the porch after dark and listen to the crickets in the summer and watch lightning bugs flash green in the trees. If someone gets sick, neighbors come over to help. If someone dies, they bring food and comfort. Nobody in trouble is ever ignored. We have everything we need and want and love, right here in Hollister." She cocked her head. "What can a city offer us that would match that?"

He stared at her without speaking. He'd never heard it put exactly that way. He loved Medicine Ridge. But he'd been in college back East, and he'd traveled all over the world. He had choices. Sassy had never had the chance to make one. On the other hand, she sounded very mature as she recounted the reasons she was happy where she lived. There were people in John's acquaintance who'd never known who they were or where they belonged.

"What are you thinking?" she asked.

"That you're an old soul in a young body," he said.

She laughed. "My mother says that all the time."

"She's right. You have a profound grasp of life. So you're happy living here. What if you had a scholarship and you could go to college and study anything you liked?"

"Who'd take care of Mama and Selene?" she asked softly.

"Most women would be more focused on their career than family responsibilities at your age."

"Maybe, but my family is important to me, and I'm happy to put them first." She settled closer to John. "Everybody's so busy these days. When do parents have time to get to know their kids? I've read that some kids have to text-message their parents and make appointments to meet. And they wonder why kids are so screwed up."

He sighed. "I guess my brother and I were protected

from a lot of that. Our uncle kept us close on the ranch. We played sports, but we were confined to one, and we had chores every day that had to be done. We didn't have cell phones or cars, and we mostly stayed at home until he thought we were old enough to drive. We always ate together and most nights we played board games or went outside with the telescopes to learn about the stars. He wasn't big on school activities, either. He said they were a corrupting influence, because we had city kids in our school with what he called outrageous ideas of morality."

She laughed. "That's what Mama called some of the kids at my school." She grimaced. "I guess I've been very sheltered. I do have a cell phone, but I don't know how to do half of what it's capable of."

"I'll teach you," he told her, smiling.

"I guess your phone does all kinds of stuff."

"The regular. Internet, movies, music, sports, email," he told her.

"Wow. I just use mine for calls and text."

He laughed. She was so out of touch. But he loved her that way. The smile faded as he looked down into her soft, melting eyes. He dropped his gaze to her mouth, faintly pink, barely parted.

"I suppose the future doesn't come with guarantees," he said to himself. He bent slowly. "I've been sitting here for five minutes remembering how your soft lips felt under my mouth, Sassy," he whispered as his parted lips met hers. "I ache like a boy for you."

As he spoke, he drew her across the seat, across his lap, and kissed her with slow, building hunger. His big hand deftly moved buttons out of buttonholes and slid right inside her bra with a mastery that left her breathless and too excited to protest.

He caressed the hard tip with slow, teasing movements while he fed on her mouth, teasing it, too, with slow, brief contacts that eventually made her moan and arch up toward him.

Her skin felt hot. She ached to have him take off her blouse and everything under it and look at her. She wanted to feel his lips swallowing that hard-tipped softness. It was madness. She could hear her own heartbeat, feel the growing desire that built inside her untried body. She'd never wanted a man before. Now she wanted him with a reckless abandon that blasted every sane reason for protest right out of her melting body.

John lifted his head, frustrated, and glanced around him in the darkness. The scene on the screen was subdued and so was the lighting. Nobody could see them. He bent his head again and, unobtrusively, suddenly stripped Sassy's blouse and bra up to her chin. His blazing eyes found her breasts, adored them. He shivered with need.

She arched faintly, encouraging him. He bent to her breasts and slowly drew one of them right inside his mouth, pulling at it gently as his tongue explored the hardness and drew a harsh moan from her lips.

The sound galvanized him. His mouth became rough. The arm behind her was like steel. His free hand slid down her bare belly and right into the opening of her jeans. He was so aroused that he didn't even realize where they were.

At least, he didn't realize it until something wet and rubbery slid over his bent head through the passenger window.

It took him a minute to realize it wasn't, couldn't be, Sassy's mouth. It was very wet. He forced his own head up and looked toward Sassy's window. A very large bovine head was inside the open window of the truck. It was licking him.

Chapter 9

"Sassy?" he asked, his voice hoarse with lingering passion.

She opened her eyes. "What?"

"Look out your window."

She turned her head and met the steer's eyes. "Aaaah!" she exclaimed.

He burst out laughing. He smoothed down her blouse and bra and sat up, his hand going gingerly to his hair. "Good Lord! I wondered why my hair felt so wet."

She fumbled her bra back on, embarrassed and amused at the same time. The little steer had moved back from the window, but it was still curious. It let out a loud "MOOOO." Muffled laughter came from a nearby car.

"Well, so much for my great idea that this was a good place to make out," John chuckled, straightening his shirt with a sigh. "I guess it wasn't a bad thing to get interrupted," he added, with a rueful smile at Sassy's red face. "Things were getting a little intense."

He didn't seem to be embarrassed at all, but Sassy had never gone so far with a man before and she felt fragile. She was uneasy that she hadn't denied him such intimate access to her body. And she couldn't forget where his other hand had been moving when the steer came along.

"Don't," John said softly when he read her expression. His fingers caught hers and linked into them. "It was perfectly natural."

"I guess you…do that all the time," she stammered.

He shrugged. "I used to. But since I met you, I haven't wanted to do it with anyone else."

If it was a line, it sounded sincere. She looked at him with growing hope. "Really?"

His fingers tightened on hers. "We've been through a lot of intense situations together in a little bit of time. Tarleton's assault. Your mother's close call. The cancer treatments." He looked into her eyes. "You said that I was like part of your family and that's how I feel, too. I'm at home when I'm with you." He looked down at their linked hands. "I want it to go on," he said hesitantly. "I want us to be together. I want you in my life from now on." He drew in a long breath. "I ache to have you."

She was uncomfortable with the way he said it, not understanding that he'd never tried to make a commitment to another woman in his life; not even when he was intimate with other women.

"You want to sleep with me," she said bluntly.

He smoothed his thumb over her cold fingers. "I want to do everything with you," he replied. "You're too young," he added quietly. "But, then, my brother just married a woman ten years his junior and they're ecstatically happy. It can work. I guess it depends on the woman, and we've already agreed that you're mature for your age."

"You aren't exactly over the hill, John," she replied, still curious about what he was suggesting. "And you're very attractive." She gave him a gamine look. "Even small hoofed animals are drawn to you."

He glared at her.

"Don't look at me," she laughed. "It was you that the little steer was kissing."

He touched his wet hair and winced. "God knows where his mouth has been."

She laughed again. "Well, at least he has good taste."

"Thanks. I think." He pulled a red work rag from the console and dried his hair where the steer had licked it. He was watching Sassy. "You don't understand what I'm saying, do you?"

"Not really," she confessed

"I suppose I'm making a hash of it," he muttered. "But I've never done this before."

"Asked someone to live with you, you mean," she said haltingly.

He met her eyes evenly. "Asked someone to marry me, Sassy."

She just stared. For a minute, she wasn't sure she wasn't dreaming. But his gaze was intent, intimate. He was waiting.

She let out the breath she'd been holding. She started to speak and then stopped, confused. "I…"

"If you've noticed any bad habits that disturb you, I'll try to change them," he mused, smiling, because she wasn't refusing.

"Oh, no, it's not that. I...I have a lot of baggage," she began nervously.

Then he remembered what she told him some time back, that her infrequent dates had said they didn't want to get involved with a woman who had so much responsibility for her family.

He grinned. "I love your baggage," he said. "Your mother and adopted sister are like part of my family already." He shrugged. "So I'll have more dependents." He gave her a wicked look. "Income tax time won't be so threatening."

She laughed out loud. He wasn't intimidated. He didn't mind. She threw her arms around him and kissed him so fervently that he forgot what they'd been talking about and just kissed her back until they had to come up for air.

"But I'll still work," she promised breathlessly, her eyes sparkling like fireworks. "I'm not going to sit down and make you support all three of us. I'll carry my part of the load!" She laughed, unaware of his sudden stillness, of the guilty look on his face. "It will be fun, making our way together. Hard times are what bring people close, you know, even more than the good times."

"Sassy, there are some things we're going to have to talk about," he said slowly.

"A lot of things," she agreed dreamily, laying her cheek against his broad, warm chest. "I never dreamed you might want to marry me. I'll try to be the best wife in the world. I'll cook and clean and work my fingers to the bone. I like horses and cattle. I'll help you with chores on the ranch, too."

She was cutting his heart open and she didn't know it. He'd lied to her. He hadn't thought of the consequences. He should have been honest with her from the beginning. But he realized then that she'd never have come near him if he'd walked into that feed store in his real persona. The young woman who worshipped the lowly cattle foreman would draw back and stand in awe of the wealthy cattle baron who could walk into a store and buy anything he fancied without even looking at a price tag. It was a sickening thought. She was going to feel betrayed, at best. At worst, she might think he was playing some game with her.

He smoothed his hand over her soft hair. "Well, it can wait another day," he murmured as he kissed her forehead. "There's plenty of time for serious discussions." He tilted her mouth up to his. "Tonight, we're just engaged and celebrating. Come here."

By the time they got back to her house, they were both disheveled and their mouths were swollen. Sassy had never been so happy in her life.

John had consoled himself that he still had time to tell Sassy the truth. He had no way of knowing that Bill Tarleton and his attorney had just gone before the district circuit judge in the courthouse in Billings for a hearing on a motion to dismiss all charges against him. The reason behind the motion, the attorney stated, was that the eyewitness who was to testify against Tarleton was romantically involved with the so-called victim and was, in fact, no common cowboy, but a wealthy cattleman from Medicine Ridge. The defense argued that this new information changed the nature of the accusation from a crime to an act of jealousy. It was a rich man victimizing a poor man because he was jealous of the man's attentions to his girlfriend.

The state attorney, who was also present at the hearing, argued that the new information made no difference to the primary charge, which was one of sexual assault and battery. A local doctor would testify to the young lady's physical condition after the assault. The public defender argued that he'd seen the doctor's report and it only mentioned reddish marks and bruising, on the young lady's arms, nothing more. That could not be construed as injury sustained in the course of a sexual assault, so only the alleged assault charge was even remotely applicable.

The judge took the case under advisement and promised a decision within the week. Meanwhile, the assistant district attorney handling the case in circuit court showed up at Sassy's home the following Monday evening, soon after Sassy had put Selene to bed, to discuss the case. His name was James Addy.

"Mr. Tarleton is alleging that Mr. Callister inflated the charges out of jealousy because of the attention Mr. Tarleton was paying you," Addy said in a businesslike tone, opening his briefcase on the dining room table while Sassy sat gaping at him.

"Mr. Callister? Who is that?" she asked, confused. "John Taggert rescued me. Mr. Tarleton kissed me and was trying to force me down on the floor. I screamed for help and Mr. Taggert, who came into the store at that moment, came to my assistance. I don't know any Mr. Callister."

The attorney stared at her. "You don't know who John Callister is?" he asked, aghast. "He and his brother Gil own the Medicine Ridge Ranch. It's world famous as a breeding bull enterprise. Aside from that, they have massive land holdings not only in Montana, but in adjoining states, including real estate and mining interests. Their parents own the Sportsman Enterprises chain of magazines. The family is one of the wealthiest in the country."

"Yes," Sassy said, trying to wrap her mind around the strange monolog, "I've heard of them. But what do they have to do with John Taggert, except that they're his bosses?" she asked innocently.

The attorney finally got it. She didn't know who her suitor actually was. A glance around the room was enough to tell him her financial status. It was unlikely that a millionaire would be seriously interested in such a poor woman. Apparently Callister had been playing some game with her. He frowned. It was a cruel game.

"The man's full name is John Taggert Callister," he said in a gentler tone. "He's Gil Callister's younger brother."

Sassy's face lost color. She'd been dreaming of a shared life with John, of working to build something good together, along with her family. He was a millionaire. That sort of man moved in high society, had money to burn. He was up here overhauling a new ranch for the conglomerate. Sassy had been handy and she amused him, so he was playing with her. It hadn't been serious, not even when he asked her to marry him! She felt sick to her stomach. She didn't know what to do now. And how was she going to tell her mother and Selene the truth?

She folded her arms around her chest and sat like a stone, her green eyes staring at the attorney, pleading with him to tell her it was all a lie, a joke.

He couldn't. He grimaced. "I'm very sorry," he said genuinely. "I thought you knew the truth."

"Not until now," she said in a subdued tone. She closed her eyes. The pain was lancing, enveloping. Her life was falling apart around her.

He drew in a long breath, searching for the right words. "Miss Peale, I hate to have to ask you this. But was there an actual assault?"

She blinked. What had he asked? She met his eyes. "Mr. Tarleton kissed me and tried to handle me and I resisted him. He was angry. He got a hard grip on me and was trying to force me down on the floor when Mr. Taggert—" She stopped and swallowed, hard. "Mr. Callister, that is, came to help me. He pulled Mr. Tarleton off me. Then he called law enforcement."

The lawyer was looking worried. "You were taken to a doctor. What were his findings?"

"Well, I had some bruises and I was sore. He ripped my blouse. I guess there wasn't a lot of physical evidence. But it did scare me. I was upset and crying."

"Miss Peale, was there an actual *sexual* assault?"

She began to understand what he meant. "Oh! Well... no," she stammered. "He kissed me and he tried to fondle me, but he didn't try to take any of my other clothes off, if that's what you mean."

"That's what I mean." He sat back in his chair. "We can't prosecute for sexual assault and battery on the basis of an unwanted kiss. We can charge him with sexual assault for any sexual contact which is unwanted. However, the law provides that if he's convicted, the maximum sentence is six months in jail or a fine not to exceed $500. If in the course of sexual contact the perpetrator inflicts bodily injury, he can get from four years to life in prison. In this case, however, you would be required to show that injury resulted from the attempted kiss. Quite frankly," he added, "I don't think a jury, even under the circumstances, would consider unwanted touching and bruising to be worth giving a man a life sentence."

She sighed. "Yes. It does seem a bit drastic, even to me. Is it true that he doesn't have any prior convictions?" she asked curiously.

He shook his head. "We found out that he was arrested on a sexual harassment charge in another city, but he was cleared, so there was no conviction."

She was tired of the whole thing. Tired of remembering Tarleton's unwanted advances, tired of being tied to the memory as long as the court case dragged on. If she insisted on prosecuting him for an attack, she couldn't produce any real proof. His attorney would take her apart on the witness stand, and she'd be humiliated yet again.

But as bad as that thought was, it was worse to think about going into court and asking them to put a man, even Tarleton, in prison for the rest of his life because he'd tried to kiss her. The lawyer was right. Tarleton might have intended a sexual assault, but all he managed was a kiss and some bruising. That was uncomfortable, and disgusting, but hardly a major crime. Still, she hated letting him get off so lightly.

She almost protested. It had been a little more than bruising. The man had intended much more, and he'd done it to some other poor girl who'd been too shamed to force him to go to trial. Sassy had guts. She could do this.

But then she had a sudden, frightening thought. If John Taggert Callister was called to appear for the prosecution, she realized suddenly, it would become a media event. He was famous. His presence at the trial would draw the media. There would be news crews, cameras, reporters. There might even be national exposure. Her mother would suffer for it. So would Selene. For herself, she would have taken the chance. For her mother, still undergoing cancer treatments and unsuited to stress of any kind right now, she could not.

Her shoulders lifted. "Mr. Addy, the trial will come with a media blitz if Mr.…Mr. Callister is called to testify for me, won't it? My mother and Selene could be talked about on those horrible entertainment news programs if it came out that I was poor and John was rich and there was an attempted sexual assault in the mix. Think how twisted they could make it sound. It would be the sort of sordid subject some people in the news media love to get their hands on these days. Just John's name would guarantee that people would be interested in what happened. They could make a circus out of it."

He hesitated. "That shouldn't be a consideration…"

"My mother has lung cancer," she replied starkly. "She's just been through major surgery and is now undergoing radiation and chemo for it. She can't take any more stress than she's already got. If there's even a chance that this trial could bring that sort of publicity, I can't take it. So what can I do?"

Mr. Addy considered the question. "I think we can plea bargain him to a charge of sexual assault with the lighter sentence. I know, it's not perfect," he told her. "He'd likely get the fine and some jail time, even if he gets probation. And it would at least go on the record as a conviction and any future transgression on his part would land him in very hot water. He has a public defender, but he seems anxious to avoid spending a long time in jail waiting for the trial. I think he'll agree to the lesser charge. Especially considering who the witness is. When he has time to think about the consequences of trying to drag John Callister's good name through the mud, and consider what sort of attorneys the Callisters would produce for a trial, I believe he'll jump at the plea bargain."

She considered that, and then the trauma of a jury trial with all the media present. This way, at least Tarleton would now have a criminal record, and it might be enough to deter him from any future assaults on other women. "Okay," she said. "As long as he doesn't get away with it."

"Oh, he won't get away with it, Miss Peale," he said solemnly. "I promise you that." He pondered for a minute. "However, if you'd rather stand firm on the original charge, I'll prosecute him, despite the obstacles. Is this plea bargain what you really want?"

She sighed sadly. "Not really. I'd love to hang him out to dry. But I have to consider my mother. It's the only possible way to make him pay for what he tried to do without hurting my family. If it goes to a jury trial, even with the media all around, he might walk away a free man because of the publicity. You said they were already trying to twist it so that it looks like John was just jealous and making a fuss because he could, because he was rich and powerful. I know the Callisters can afford the best attorneys, but it wouldn't be right to put them in that situation, either. Mr. Callister has two little nieces…" She grimaced. "You know, the legal system isn't altogether fair sometimes."

He smiled. "I agree. But it's still the best system on earth," he replied.

"I hope I'm doing the right thing," she said on a sigh. "If he gets out and hurts some other woman because I backed down, I'll never get over it."

He gave her a long look. "You aren't backing down, Miss Peale. You're compromising. It may look as if he's getting away with it. But he isn't."

She liked him. She smiled. "Okay, then."

He closed his briefcase and got to his feet. He held out his hand and shook hers. "He'll have a criminal record," he promised her. "If he ever tries to do it again, in Montana, I can promise you that he'll spend a lot of time looking at the world through vertical bars." He meant every word.

"Thanks, Mr. Addy."

"I'll let you know how things work out. Good evening."

Sassy watched him go with quiet, thoughtful eyes. She was compromising on the case, but on behalf of a good cause. She couldn't put her mother through the nightmare of a trial and the vicious publicity it would bring on them. Mrs. Peale had suffered enough.

She went back into the house. Mrs. Peale was coming out of the bedroom, wrapped in her chenille housecoat, pale and weak. "Could you get me some pineapple juice, sweetheart?" she asked, forcing a smile.

"Of course!" Sassy ran to get it. "Are you all right?" she asked worriedly.

"Just a little sick. That's nothing to worry about, it goes with the treatments. At least I'm through with them for a few weeks." She frowned. "What's wrong? And who was that man you were talking to?"

"Here, back to bed." Sassy went with her, helping her down on the bed and tucking her under the covers with her glass of cold juice. She sat down beside her. "That was the assistant district attorney—or one of them, anyway. A Mr. Addy. He came to talk to me about Mr. Tarleton. He wants to offer him a plea bargain so we don't end up in a messy court case."

Mrs. Peale frowned. "He's guilty of harassing you. He assaulted you. He should pay for it."

"He will. There's jail time and a fine for it," she replied, candy-coating her answer. "He'll have a criminal record. But I won't have to be grilled and humiliated by his attorney on the stand."

Mrs. Peale sipped her juice. She thought about what a trial would be like for Sassy. She'd seen such trials on her soap operas. She sighed. "All right, dear. If you're satisfied, I am, too." She smiled. "Have you heard from John? He was going to bring me some special chocolates when he came back."

Sassy hesitated. She couldn't tell her mother. Not yet. "I haven't heard from him," she said.

"You don't look well…"

"I'm just fine," Sassy said, grinning. "Now you go back to bed. I'm going to reconcile the bank statement and get Selene's clothes ready for school tomorrow."

"All right, dear." She settled back into the pillows. "You're too good to me, Sassy," she added. "Once I get back on my feet, I want you to go a lot of places with John. I'm going to be fine, thanks to him and those doctors in Billings. I can take care of myself and Selene, finally, and you can have a life of your own."

"You stop that," Sassy chided. "I love you. Nothing I do for you, or Selene, is a chore."

"Yes, but you've had a ready-made family up until now," Mrs. Peale said softly. "It's limited your social life."

"My social life is just dandy, thanks."

The older woman grinned. "I'll say! Wait until John gets back. He's got a surprise waiting for you."

"Has he, really?" Sassy wondered if it was the surprise the attorney had just shared with her. She was too sick to care, but she couldn't let on. Her mother was so happy. It would be cruel to dash all her hopes and reveal the truth about the young man Mrs. Peale idolized.

"He has! Don't you stay up too late. You're looking peaked, dear."

"I'm just tired. We've been putting up tons of stock in the feed store," she lied. She smiled. "Good night, Mama."

"Good night, dear. Sleep well."

As if, Sassy thought as she closed the door. She gave up on paperwork a few minutes later and went to bed. She cried herself to sleep.

John walked into the feed store a day later, back from an unwanted but urgent business trip to Colorado. He spotted Sassy at the counter and walked up to it with a beaming smile.

She looked up and saw him, and he knew it was all over by the expression on her face. She was apprehensive, uncomfortable. She fidgeted and could barely meet his intent gaze.

He didn't even bother with preliminary questions. His eyes narrowed angrily. "Who told you?" he asked tersely.

She drew in a breath. He looked scary like that. Now that she knew who he really was, knew the power and fame behind his name, she was intimidated. This man could write his own ticket. He could go anywhere, buy anything, do anything he liked. He was worlds away from Sassy, who lived in a house with a leaky roof. He was like a stranger. The smiling, easygoing cowboy she thought he was had become somebody totally different.

"It was the assistant district attorney," she said in a faint tone. "He came to see me. Mr. Tarleton was going to insinuate that you were jealous of him and forced me to file a complaint…"

He exploded. "I'll get attorneys in here who will put him away for the rest of his miserable life," he said tersely. He looked as if he could do that single-handed.

"No!" She swallowed. "No. Please. Think what it would do to Mama if a whole bunch of reporters came here to cover the story because of…because of who you are," she pleaded. "Stress makes everything so much worse for her."

He looked at her intently. "I hadn't thought about that," he said quietly. "I'm sorry."

"Mr. Addy says that Mr. Tarleton will probably agree to plead guilty or no contest to the sexual assault charge." She sighed. "There's a fine and jail time. He was willing to prosecute on the harder charge, but there would have to be proof that he did more than just kiss me and handle me…"

He frowned. He knew what she meant. A jury would be unlikely to convict for sexual assault and battery on an unwanted kiss and some groping, and how could they prove that Tarleton had intended much more? It made him angry. He wanted the man to go to prison. But Mrs. Peale would pay the price. In her delicate condition, it would probably kill her to have to watch Sassy go through the trial, even if she didn't get to court. John's name would guarantee news interest. Just the same, he was going to have a word with Mr. Addy. Sassy never had to know.

"How is your mother?" he asked.

"She's doing very well," she replied, her tone a little stilted. He did intimidate her now. "The treatments have left her a little anemic and weak, and there's some nausea, but they gave her medicine for that." She didn't add that it was bankrupting her to pay for it. She'd already had to pawn her grandfather's watch and pistol to manage a month's worth. She wasn't admitting that.

"I brought her some chocolates," he told her. He smiled gently. "She likes the Dutch ones."

She was staring at him with wide, curious eyes. "You'll spoil her," she replied.

He shrugged. "So? I'm rich. I can spoil people if I want to."

"Yes, I know, but..."

"If you were rich, and I wasn't," he replied solemnly, "would you hesitate to do anything you could for me, if I was in trouble?"

"Of course not," she assured him.

"Then why should it bother you if I spoil your mother a little? Especially, now, when she's had so much illness."

"It doesn't, really. It's just—" She stopped dead. The color went out of her face as she stared at him and suddenly realized how much he'd done for them.

"What's wrong?" he asked.

"There was no grant to pay for that surgery, and the treatments," she said in a choked tone. "You paid for it! You paid for it all!"

Chapter 10

John grimaced. "Sassy, there was no other way," he said, trying to reason with her. She looked anguished. "Your mother would have died. I checked your company insurance coverage when I had Buck put you on the payroll as assistant manager. It didn't have a major medical option. I told Buck to shop around for a better plan, but your mother's condition went critical before we could find one."

She knew her heart was going to beat her to death. She'd never be able to pay him back, not even the interest on the money he'd spent on her mother. She'd been poor all her life, but she'd never felt it like this. It had never hurt so much.

"You're part of my life now," he said softly. "You and your mother and Selene. Of course I was going to do all I could for you. For God's sake, don't try to reduce what we feel for each other to dollars and cents!"

"I can't pay you back." She groaned.

"Have I asked you to?" he returned.

"But…" she protested, ready for a long battle.

The door opened behind them and Theodore Graves, the police chief, walked in. His lean face was set in hard lines. He nodded at John and approached Sassy.

He pushed his Stetson back over jet-black hair. "That assistant district attorney, Addy, said you agreed to let Tarleton plea bargain to a lesser charge," he said. "He won't discuss the case with me and I can't intimidate him the way I intimidate most people. So I'd like to know why."

She sighed. He made her feel guilty. "It's Mama," she told him. "He—" she indicated John "—is very well-known. If it goes to court, reporters will show up to find out why he's mixed up in a sexual assault case. Mama will get stressed out, the cancer will come back, and we'll bury her."

Graves grimaced. "I hadn't thought about that. About the stress, I mean." He frowned. "What do you mean, he's well-known?" he added, indicating John. "He's a ranch foreman."

"He's not," Sassy said with a long sigh. "He's John Callister."

Graves lifted a thick, dark eyebrow. "Of the Callister ranching empire over in Medicine Ridge?"

John lifted a shoulder. "Afraid so."

"Oh, boy."

"Listen, at least he'll have a police record," Sassy said stubbornly. "Think about it. Do you really want a media circus right here in Hollister? Mr. Tarleton would probably love it," she added miserably.

"He probably would," Graves had to agree. He stuck his hands into his slacks pockets. "Seventy-five years ago, we'd have turned him out into the woods and sent men with guns after him."

"Civilized men don't do things like that," Sassy reminded him. "Especially policemen."

Graves shrugged. "So sue me. I never claimed to be civilized. I'm a throwback." He drew in a long breath. "All right, as long as the polecat gets some serious time in the slammer, I can be generous and put up the rope I just bought."

Sassy wondered how the chief thought Tarleton would get a jail sentence when Mr. Addy had hinted that Tarleton would probably get probation.

"Good of you," John mused.

"Pity he didn't try to escape when we took him up to Billings for the motion hearing," Graves said thoughtfully. "I volunteered to go along with the deputy sheriff who transported him. I even wore my biggest caliber revolver, special, just in case." He pursed his lips and brightened. "Somebody might leave a door open, in the detention center…"

"Don't you dare," John said firmly. "You're not the only one who's disappointed. I was looking forward to the idea of having him spend the next fifteen years or so with one of the inmates who has the most cigarettes. But I'm not willing to see my future mother-in-law die over it."

"Mother-in-law?" Graves gave him a wry look from liquid black eyes in a lean, tanned face.

Sassy blushed. "Now, we have to talk about that," she protested.

"We already did," John said. "You promised to marry me."

"That was before I knew who you were," she shot back belligerently.

He grinned. "That's more like it," he mused. "The deference was wearing a little thin," he explained.

She flushed even more. She had been behaving like a working girl with the boss, instead of an equal. She shifted. She was still uncomfortable thinking about his background and comparing it to her own.

"I like weddings," Graves commented.

John glanced at him. "You do?"

He nodded. "I haven't been to one in years, of course, and I don't own a good suit anymore." He shrugged. "I guess I could buy one, if I got invited to a wedding."

John burst out laughing. "You can come to ours. I'll make sure you get an invitation."

Graves smiled. "That's a deal." He glanced at Sassy, who still looked undecided. "If I lived in a house that looked like yours, and drove a piece of scrap metal like that vehicle you ride around in, I'd say yes when a financially secure man asked me to marry him."

Sassy almost burst trying not to laugh. "Has any financially secure man asked you to marry him lately, Chief?"

He glared at her. "I was making a point."

"Several of them," Sassy returned. "But I do appreciate your interest. I wouldn't mind sending Mr. Tarleton to prison myself, if the cost wasn't so high."

He pursed his lips and his black eyes twinkled. "Now that's a coincidence. I've thought about nothing else except sending Mr. Tarleton to prison for the past few weeks. In fact, it never hurts to recommend a prison to the district attorney," he said pleasantly. "I know one where even the chaplain has to carry a Taser."

"Mr. Addy already said he isn't likely to get jail time, since he's a first offender," Sassy said sadly.

"Now isn't that odd," the chief replied with a wicked

grin. "I spent some quality time on the computer yesterday and I turned up a prior conviction for sexual assault over in Wyoming, where Mr. Tarleton was working two years ago. He got probation for that one. Which makes him a repeat offender." He looked almost angelic. "I just told Addy. He was almost dancing in the street."

Sassy gasped. "Really?"

He chuckled. "I thought you'd like hearing that. I figured that a man with his attitude had to have a conviction somewhere. He didn't have one in Montana, so I started looking in surrounding states. I checked the criminal records in Wyoming, got a hit, and called the district attorney in the court circuit where it was filed. What a story I got from him! So I took it straight to Addy this morning." He gave her a wry look. "But I did want to know why you let him plead down, and Addy wouldn't tell me."

"Now I feel better, about agreeing to the plea bargain," Sassy said. "His record will affect the sentence, won't it?"

"It will, indeed," Graves assured her. "In another interesting bit of irony, the judge hearing his case had to step down on account of a family emergency. The new judge in his case is famous for her stance on sexual assault cases." He leaned forward. "She's a woman."

Sassy's eyes lit up. "Poor Mr. Tarleton."

"Right." John chuckled. "Good of you to bring us the latest news."

Graves smiled at him. "I thought it would be a nice surprise." He glanced at Sassy. "I understand now why you made the decision you did. Your mom's a sweet lady. It's like a miracle that the surgery saved her."

"Yes," Sassy agreed. Her eyes met John's. "It is a miracle."

Graves pulled his wide-brimmed hat low over his eyes. "Don't forget that wedding invitation," he reminded John. "I'll even polish my good boots."

"I won't forget," John assured him.

"Thanks again," she told the chief.

He smiled at her. "I like happy endings."

When he was gone, John turned back to Sassy with a searching glance. "I'm coming to get you after supper," he informed her. "We've got a lot to talk about."

"John, I'm poor," she began.

He leaned across the counter and kissed her warmly. "I'll be poor, if I don't have you," he said softly. He pulled a velvet-covered box out of his pocket and put it in her hands. "Open that after I leave."

"What is it?" she asked dimly.

"Something for us to talk about, of course." He winked at her and smiled broadly. He walked out the door and closed it gently behind him.

Sassy opened the box. It was a gold wedding band with an embossed vine running around it. There was a beautiful diamond ring that was its companion. She stared at them until tears burned her eyes. A man bought a set of rings like this when he meant them to be heirlooms, handed down from generation to generation. She clutched it close to her heart. Despite the differences, she knew what she was going to say.

It took Mrs. Peale several minutes to understand what Sassy was telling her.

"No, dear," she insisted. "John *works* for Mr. Callister. That's what he told us."

"Yes, he did, but he didn't mention that Taggert was his middle name, not his last name," Sassy replied patiently. "He and his brother, Gil, own one of the most famous ranches in the West. Their parents own that sports magazine Daddy always used to read before he left."

The older woman sat back with a rough sigh. "Then what was he doing coming around here?" she asked, and looked hurt.

"Well, that's the interesting part," Sassy replied, blushing. "It seems that he…well, he wants to…that is…" She jerked out the ring box, opened it, and put it in her mother's hands. "He brought that to me this morning."

Mrs. Peale eyed the rings with fascination. "How beautiful," she said softly. She touched the pattern on the wedding band. "He means these to be heirlooms, doesn't he? I had your grandmother's wedding band," she added sadly, "but I had to sell it when you were little and we didn't have the money for a doctor when you got sick." She looked up at her daughter with misty eyes. "He's really serious, isn't he?"

"Yes, I think he is." Sassy sighed. She sat down next to her mother. "I still can't believe it."

"That hospital bill," Mrs. Peale began slowly. "There was no grant, was there?"

Sassy shook her head. "John said that he couldn't stand by and let you die. He's fond of you."

"I'm fond of him, too," she replied. "And he wants to marry my daughter." Her eyes suddenly had a faraway look. "Isn't it funny? Remember what I told you my grandmother said to me, that I'd be poor but my daughter would live like royalty?" She laughed. "My goodness!"

"Maybe she really did know things." Sassy took the rings from her mother's hand and stared at them. It did seem that dreams came true.

* * *

John came for her just at sunset. He took time to kiss Mrs. Peale and Selene and assure them that he wasn't taking Sassy out of the county when they married.

"I'm running this ranch myself," he assured her with a warm smile. "Sassy and I will live here. The house has plenty of room, so you two can move in with us."

Mrs. Peale looked worried. "John, it may not look like much, but I was born in this house. I've lived in it all my life, even after I married."

He bent and kissed her again. "Okay. If you want to stay here, we'll do some fixing up and get you a companion. You can choose her."

Her old eyes brightened. "You'd do that for me?" she exclaimed.

"Nothing is too good for my second mama," he assured her, and he wasn't joking. "Now Sassy and I are going out to talk about all the details. We'll be back later."

She kissed him back. "You're going to be the nicest son-in-law in the whole world."

"You'd better believe it," he replied.

John took her over to the new ranch, where the barn was up, the stable almost finished, and the house completely remodeled. He walked her through the kitchen and smiled at her enthusiasm.

"We can have a cook, if you'd rather," he told her.

She looked back at him, running her hand lovingly over a brand-new stove with all sorts of functions. "Oh, I'd love to work in here myself." She hesitated. "John, about Mama and Selene…"

He moved away from the doorjamb he'd been leaning against and pulled her into his arms. His expression was very serious. "I know you're worried about her. But I was serious about the companion. It's just that she needs to be a nurse. We won't tell your mother that part of it just yet."

"She's not completely well yet. I know a nurse will look out for her, but…"

He smiled. "I like the way you care about people," he said softly. "I know she's not able to stay by herself and she won't admit it. But we're close enough that you can go over there every day and check on her."

She smiled. "Okay. I just worry."

"That's one of the things I most admire about you," he told her. "That big heart."

"You have to travel a lot, to show cattle, don't you?" she asked, recalling something she'd read in a magazine about the Callisters, before she knew who John was.

"I used to," he said. "We have a cattle foreman at the headquarters ranch in Medicine Ridge who's showing Gil's bulls now. I'll put on one here to do the same for us. I don't want to be away from home unless I have to, now."

She beamed. "I don't want you away from home, unless I can go with you."

He chuckled. "Two minds running in the same direction." He shifted his weight a little. "I didn't tell your mother, but I've already interviewed several women who might want the live-in position. I had their backgrounds checked as well," he added, chuckling. "When I knew I was going to marry you, I started thinking about how your mother would cope without you."

"You're just full of surprises," she said, breathless.

He grinned. "Yes, I am. The prospective housemates will start knocking on the door about ten Friday morning. You can tell her when we get home." He sobered.

"She'll be happier in her own home, Sassy. Uprooting her will be as traumatic as the chemo was. You can visit her every day and twice on Sundays. I'll come along, too."

"I think you're right." She looked up at him. "She loves you."

"It's mutual," he replied. He smiled down at her, loving the softness in her green eyes. "We can add some more creature comforts for her, and fix what's wrong with the house."

"There's a lot wrong with it," she said worriedly.

"I'm rich, as you reminded me," he replied easily. "I can afford whatever she, and Selene, need. After all, they're family."

She hugged him warmly and laid her cheek against his chest. "Do you want to have kids?" she asked.

His eyebrows arched and his blue eyes twinkled. "Of course. Do you want to start them right now?" He looked around. "The kitchen table's just a bit short… ouch!"

She withdrew her fist from his stomach. "You know what I mean! Honestly, what am I going to do with you?"

"Want me to coach you?" he offered, and chuckled wickedly when she blushed.

"Look out that window and tell me what you see," she said.

He glanced around. There were people going in and out of the unfinished stable, working on the interior by portable lighting. There were a lot of people going in and out.

"I guarantee if you so much as kiss me, we'll be on every social networking site in the world," she told him. "And not because of who you are."

He laughed out loud. "Okay. We'll wait." He glanced outside again and scowled. "But we are definitely not going to try to honeymoon here in this house!"

She didn't argue.

He tugged her along with him into a dark hallway and pulled her close. "They'll need night vision to see us here," he explained as he bent to kiss her with blatant urgency.

She kissed him back, feeling so explosively hot inside that she thought she might burst. She felt shivery when he kissed her like that, with his mouth and his whole body. His hands smoothed up under her blouse and over her breasts. He felt the hard tips and groaned, kissing her even harder.

She knew nothing about intimacy, but she wanted it suddenly, desperately. She lifted up to him, trying to get even closer. He backed her into the wall and lowered his body against hers, increasing the urgency of the kiss until she groaned out loud and shivered.

The frantic little sound got through his whirling mind. He pushed away from her and stepped back, dragging in deep breaths in an effort to regain the control he'd almost lost.

"You're stopping?" she asked breathlessly.

"Yes, I'm stopping," he replied. He took her hand and pulled her back into the lighted kitchen. There was a flush along his high cheekbones. "Until the wedding, no more time alone," he added huskily. His blue eyes met her green ones. "We're going to have it conventional, all the way. Okay?"

She smiled with her whole heart. "Okay!"

He laughed. "It's just as well," he sighed.

"Why?"

"We don't have a bed. Yet."

Her eyes twinkled. He was so much fun to be with, and when he kissed her, it was like fireworks. They were going to make a great marriage, she was sure of it. She stopped worrying about being poor. When they held each other, nothing mattered less than money.

But the next hurdle was the hardest. He announced a week later that his family was coming up to meet John's future bride. Sassy didn't sleep that night, worrying. What would they think, those fabulously wealthy people, when they saw where Sassy and her mother and Selene lived, how poor they were? Would they think she was only after John's wealth?

She was still worrying when they showed up at her front door late the next afternoon, with John. Sassy stood beside him in her best dress, as they walked up onto the front porch of the Peale homeplace. Her best dress wasn't saying much because it was off the rack and two years old. It was long, beige, and simply cut. Her shoes were older than the dress and scuffed.

But the tall blond man and the slender, dark-haired woman didn't seem to notice or care how she was dressed. The woman, who didn't look much older than Sassy, hugged her warmly.

"I'm Kasie," she introduced herself with a big smile. "He's Gil, my husband." Gil smiled and shook her hand warmly. "And these are our babies…" She motioned to two little blonde girls, one holding the other by the hand. "That's Bess," she said, smiling at the taller of the two, "and that's Jenny. Say hello! This is Uncle John's fiancée!"

Bess came forward and looked up at Sassy with wide, soft eyes. "You going to marry Uncle John? He's very nice."

"Yes, he is," Sassy said, sliding her hand into John's. "I promise I'll take very good care of him," she added with a smile.

"Okay," Bess said with a shy returning smile.

"Come on in," Sassy told them. "I'm sorry, it isn't much to look at..." she added, embarrassed.

"Sassy, we were raised by an uncle who hated material things," Gil told her gently. "We grew up in a place just like this, a rough country house. We like to think it gave us strength of character."

"What he means is, don't apologize," John said in a loud whisper.

She laughed when Gil and Kasie agreed. Later she would learn that Kasie had grown up in even rougher conditions, in a war zone in Africa with missionary parents who were killed there.

Mrs. Peale greeted them with Selene by her side, a little intimidated.

"Stop looking like that," John chided, and hugged her warmly. "This is my future little mother-in-law," he added with a grin, introducing her to his family. "She's the sweetest woman I've ever known, except for Kasie."

"You didn't say I was sweet, too," Sassy said with a mock pout.

"You're not sweet. You're precious," he told her with a warm, affectionate grin.

"Okay, I'll go with that," she laughed. She turned to the others. "Come in and sit down. I could make coffee...?"

"Please, no," Gil groaned. "She pumped me full of it all the way here. We were up last night very late trying to put fences back up after a storm. Kasie had to drive most of the way." He held his stomach. "I don't think I ever want another cup."

"You go out with your men to fix fences?" Mrs. Peale asked, surprised.

"Of course," he said simply. "We always have."

Mrs. Peale relaxed. So did Sassy. These people were nothing like they'd expected. Even Selene warmed to them at once, as shy as she usually was with strangers. It was a wonderful visit.

"Well, what do you think of them?" John asked Sassy much later, as he was getting ready to leave for the ranch.

"They're wonderful," she replied, pressed close against him on the dark porch. "They aren't snobs. I like them already."

"It's as Gil said," he replied. "We were raised by a rough and tumble uncle. He taught us that money wasn't the most important thing in life." He tilted her mouth up and kissed it. "They liked you, too," he added. He smiled. "So, no more hurdles. Now all we have to do is get married."

"But I don't know how to plan a big wedding," she said worriedly.

He grinned. "Not to worry. I know someone who does!"

The wedding was arranged beautifully by a consultant hired by John, out of Colorado. She was young and pretty and sweet, and apparently she was very discreet. Sassy was fascinated by some of the weddings she'd planned for people all over the country. One was that of Sassy's favorite country western singing star.

"You did that wedding?" Sassy exclaimed.

"I did. And nobody knew a thing about it until they were on their honeymoon," she added smugly. "That's why your future husband hired me. I'm the soul of discretion. Now, tell me what colors you like and we'll get to work!"

They ended up with a color scheme of pink and yellow and white. Sassy had planned a simple white gown, until Mary Garnett showed her a couture gown with the three pastels embroidered in silk into the bodice and echoed in the lace over the skirt, and in the veil. It was the most beautiful gown Sassy had ever seen in her life. "But you could buy a house for that!" Sassy exclaimed when she heard the price.

John, walking through the living room at the Peale house, paused in the doorway. "We're only getting married once," he reminded Sassy.

"But it's so expensive," she wailed.

He walked to the sofa and peered over her shoulder at the color photograph of the gown. His breath caught. "Buy it," he told Mary.

Sassy opened her mouth. He bent and kissed it shut. He walked out again.

Mary just grinned.

He had another surprise for her as well, tied up in a small box, as an early wedding present. He'd discovered that she'd had to pawn her grandfather's watch and pistol to pay bills and he'd gotten them out of hock. She cried like a baby. Which meant that he got to kiss the tears away. He was, she thought as she hugged him, the most thoughtful man in the whole world.

Sassy insisted on keeping her job, regardless of John's protests. She wanted to help more with the wedding, and felt guilty that she hadn't, but Mary had everything organized. Invitations were going out, flower arrangements were being made. A minister was engaged. A small orchestra was hired to play at the reception.

The wedding was being held at the family ranch in Medicine Ridge, to ensure privacy. Gil had already said that he was putting on more security for the event than the president of the United States had. Nobody was crashing this wedding. They'd even outfoxed aerial surveillance by putting the entire reception inside and having blinds on every window.

Nobody, he told John and Sassy, was getting in without an invitation and a photo ID.

"Is that really necessary?" Sassy asked John when they were alone.

"You don't know how well-known our parents are." He sighed. "They'll be coming, too, and our father can't keep his mouth shut. He's heard about you from Gil and Kasie, and he's bragging to anybody who'll listen about his newest daughter-in-law."

"Me?" She was stunned. "But I don't have any special skills and I'm not even beautiful."

John smiled down at her. "You have the biggest heart of any woman I've ever known," he said softly. "It isn't what you do or what you have that makes you special, Sassy. It's what you are."

She flushed. "What about your mother?"

He kissed her on the tip of her nose. "She's so happy to have access to her grandchildren, that she never raises a fuss about anything. But she's happy to have somebody in the family who can knit."

"How did you know I can knit?"

"You think I hadn't noticed all the afghans and chair covers and doilies all over your house?"

"Mama could have made them."

"But she didn't. She said you can even knit sweaters. Our mother would love to learn how. She wants you to teach her."

She caught her breath. "But it's easy! Of course, I'll show her. She doesn't mind—neither of them mind—that I'm poor? They don't think I'm marrying you for your money?"

He laughed until his eyes teared up. "Sassy," he said, catching his breath, "you didn't know I had money until after I proposed."

"Oh."

"They know that, too."

She sighed. "Okay, then."

He bent and kissed her. "Only a few more days to go," he murmured. "I can hardly wait."

"Me, too," she said. "It's exciting. But it's a lot of work."

"Mary's doing the work so you don't have to. Well, except for getting the right dresses for your mother and Selene."

"That's not work," she laughed. "They love to shop. I'm so glad Mama's getting over the chemo. She's better every day. I was worried that she'd be too weak to come to the wedding, but she says she wouldn't miss it for anything."

"We'll have a nurse practitioner at the wedding," he assured her. "Just in case. Don't worry."

"I'll do my best," she promised.

"That's my girl."

Finally there was a wedding! Sassy had chewed her nails to the quick worrying about things going wrong. John assured her that it would be smooth as silk, but she couldn't relax. If only she didn't trip over her own train and go headfirst into the minister, or do something else equally clumsy! All those important people were going to be there, and she had stage fright.

But once she was at the door of the big ballroom at the Callister mansion in Medicine Ridge where the wedding was taking place, she was less nervous. The sight of John, in his tuxedo, standing at the altar, calmed her. She waited for the music and then, clutching her bouquet firmly, her veil in place over her face, she walked calmly down the aisle. Her heart raced like crazy as John turned and smiled down at her when she reached him. He was the most handsome man she'd ever seen in her life. And he was going to marry her!

The minister smiled at both of them and began the service. It was routine until he asked if John had the rings. John started fishing in his pockets and couldn't find them. He grimaced, stunned.

"Uncle John! Did you forget?" Jenny muttered at his side, shoving a silken pillow up toward him. "I got the rings, Uncle John!"

The audience chuckled. Sassy hid a smile.

John fumbled the rings loose from the pillow and bent and kissed his little niece on the forehead. "Thanks, squirt," he whispered.

She giggled and went to stand beside her sister, Bess, who was holding a basket full of fresh flower petals in shades of yellow, pink, and white.

The minister finished the ceremony and invited John to kiss his bride. John lifted the beautiful embroidered veil and pushed it back over Sassy's dark hair. His eyes searched hers. He framed her face in his big hands and bent and kissed her so tenderly that tears rolled down her cheeks, and he kissed every one away.

The music played again. Laughing, Sassy took the hand John held out and together they ran down the aisle and out the door. The reception was ready down the hall, in the big formal dining room that had been cleared of furniture for the occasion. As they ate cake and paused for photographs, to the strains of Debussy played by the orchestral ensemble, Sassy noticed movie stars, politicians, and at least two multimillionaires among the guests. She was rubbing elbows with people she'd only seen in magazines. It was fascinating.

"One more little hurdle, Mrs. Callister," John whispered to her, "and then we're going to Cancún for a week!"

"Sun and sand," she began breathlessly.

"And you and me. And a bed." He wiggled his eyebrows.

She laughed, pressing her face against him to hide her blushes.

"Well, it wasn't a bad wedding," came a familiar drawl from behind them.

Chief Graves was wearing a very nice suit, and nicely polished dress boots, holding a piece of cake on a plate. "But I don't like chocolate cake," he pointed out. "And there's no coffee."

"There is so coffee," John chuckled, holding up a cup of it. "I don't go to weddings that don't furnish coffee."

"Where did you get that?" he asked.

John nodded toward the far corner, where a coffee urn was half-hidden behind a bouquet of flowers.

Graves grinned. "I hope you have a long and happy life together."

"Thanks, Chief," Sassy told him.

"Glad you could make it," John seconded.

"I brought you a present," he said unexpectedly. He reached into his pocket and drew out a small package. "Something you young folks might find old-fashioned, but useful."

"Thank you," Sassy said, touched, as she took it from his hand.

He gave John a worldly look, chuckled, and walked off to find coffee.

"What is it, I wonder?" Sassy mused, tearing the paper open.

"Well!" John exclaimed when he saw what was inside.

She peered over his arm and smiled warmly. It was a double set of CDs of romantic music and classical love themes.

They glanced toward the coffee urn. Graves lifted his cup and toasted them. They laughed and waved.

Chapter 11

They stayed on the beach in a hotel shaped like one of the traditional Maya pyramids. Sassy lay in John's strong arms still shivering with her first taste of intimacy, her face flushed, her eyes brilliant as they looked up into his.

"It gets better," he whispered as his mouth moved lightly over her soft lips. "First times are usually difficult."

"Difficult?" She propped up on one elbow. "Are we remembering the same first time? Gosh, I thought I was going to die!"

His blue eyes twinkled. "Forgive me. I naturally assumed from all the moaning and whimpering that you were…stop that!" He laughed when she pinched him.

An enthusiastic bout of wrestling followed.

He kissed her into limp submission. "We really must do this again, so that I can get my perspective back," he suggested. "I'll pay attention this time."

She laughed and kissed his broad shoulder. "See that you do," she replied. She pushed him back into the pillows and followed him down.

"Now don't be rough with me, I'm fragile," he protested. "See here, take your hand off that...I'm not that sort of man!"

"Yes, you are," she chuckled, and put her mouth squarely against his. He was obediently silent for a long time afterward. Except for various involuntary sounds.

They held hands and walked down the beach at sunrise, watching seagulls soar above the incredible shades of blue that were the Gulf of Mexico.

"I never dreamed there were places like this," Sassy said dreamily. "The sand looks just like sugar."

"We'll have to take some postcards back with us. I can't believe I forgot my cell phone in the hotel room." He sighed.

"We can get it later," she suggested. "I have to have at least one picture of you in a bathing suit to put up in our house."

"Turnabout is fair play," he teased.

She laughed. "Okay."

"While we're at it, we'll buy presents for everybody."

"We should get something for Chief Graves."

"What would you suggest?"

"Something musical."

He pursed his lips. "We'll get him one of those wooden kazoos."

"No! Musical."

He drew her close. "Musical it is."

After the honeymoon, they stopped for the weekend at the Callister ranch in Medicine Ridge, where Sassy had time to sit down and get acquainted with John's sister-in-law, Kasie.

"I was so worried about fitting in here," Sassy confessed as they walked around the house, where the flowers were blooming in abundance around the huge swimming pool. "I mean, this is a whole world away from anything I know."

"I know exactly how you feel," Kasie said. "I was born in Africa, where my parents were missionaries," she recalled, going quiet. "They were killed right in front of us, me and my brother, Kantor. We went to live with our aunt in Arizona. Kantor grew up and married and had a little girl. He was doing a courier service by air in Africa when an attack came. He and his family were shot down in his plane and died." She sat down on one of the benches, her eyes far away. "I never expected to end up like this," she said, meeting the other girl's sympathetic gaze. "Gil didn't even like me at first," she added, laughing. "He made my life miserable when I first came to work here."

"He doesn't look like that sort of man," Sassy said. "He seems very nice."

"He can be. But he'd lost his first wife to a riding accident and he didn't ever want to get married again. He said I came up on his blind side. Of course, he thought I was much too young for him."

"Just like John," Sassy sighed. "He thought I was too young for him." She glanced at Kasie and grinned. "And I was sure that he was much too rich for me."

Kasie laughed. "I felt that way, too. But you know, it doesn't have much to do with money. It has to do with feelings and things you have in common." Her eyes had a dreamy, faraway look. "Sometimes Gil and I just sit and talk, for hours at a time. He's my best friend, as well as my husband."

"I feel that way with John," Sassy said. "He just fits in with my family, as if he's always known them."

"Mama Luke took to Gil right away, too." She noted the curious stare. "Oh, she's my mother's sister. She's a nun."

"Heavens!"

"My mother was pregnant with me and Kantor and a mercenary soldier saved her life," she explained. "His name was K.C. Kantor. My twin and I were both named for him."

"I've heard of him," Sassy said hesitantly, not liking to repeat what she'd heard about the reclusive, crusty millionaire.

"Most of what you've heard is probably true," Kasie laughed, seeing the words in her expression. "But I owe my life to him. He's a kind man. He would probably have married Mama Luke, if she hadn't felt called to a religious life."

"Is he married?"

Kasie frowned. "You know, I heard once that he did get married, to some awful woman, and divorced her right afterward. I don't know if it's true. You don't ask him those sort of questions," she added.

"I can understand why."

"Gil's parents like you," Kasie said out of the blue.

"They do?" Sassy was astonished. "But I hardly had time to say ten words to them at the wedding!"

"John said considerably more than ten words." Kasie grinned. "He was singing your praises long before he went back to marry you. Magdalena saw that beautiful shawl you'd packed and John told her you knitted it yourself. She wants to learn how."

"Yes, John said that, but I thought he was kidding!"

"She's not. She'll be in touch, I guarantee. She'll turn up at your ranch one of these days with her knitting gear and you'll have to chase her out with a broom."

Sassy blushed. "I'd never do that. She's so beautiful."

"Yes. She and the boys didn't even speak before I married Gil. I convinced him to meet them on our honeymoon. He was shocked. You see, they were married very young and had children so early, long before they were ready for them. John and Gil's uncle took the boys to raise and sort of shut their parents out of their lives. It was a tragedy. They grew up thinking their parents didn't want them. It wasn't true. They just didn't know how to relate to their children, after all those years."

"I think parents and children need to be together those first few years," Sassy said.

"I agree wholeheartedly," Kasie said. She smiled. "Gil and I want children of our own, but we want the girls to feel secure with us first. There's no rush. We have years and years."

"The girls seem very happy."

Kasie nodded. "They're so much like my own children," she said softly. "I love them very much. I was heartbroken when Gil sent me home from Nassau and told me not to be here when they got home."

"What?"

Kasie laughed self-consciously. "We had a rocky romance. I'll have to tell you all about it one day. But for now, we'd better get back inside. Your husband will get all nervous and insecure if you're where he can't see you."

"He's a very nice husband."

"He's nice, period, like my Gil. We got lucky, for two penniless children, didn't we?" she asked.

Sassy linked her arm into Kasie's. "Yes, we did. But we'd both live in line cabins and sew clothes by hand if they asked us to."

"Isn't that the truth?" Kasie laughed.

"What were you two talking about for so long?" John asked that night, as Sassy lay close in his arms in bed.

"About what wonderful men we married," she said drowsily, reaching up to kiss him. "We did, too."

"Did Kasie tell you about her background?"

"She did. What an amazing story. And she said Gil didn't like her!"

"He didn't," he laughed. "He even fired her. But he realized his mistake in time. She was mysterious and he was determined not to risk his heart again."

"Sort of like you?" she murmured.

He laughed. "Sort of like me." He drew her closer and closed his eyes. "We go home tomorrow. Ready to take on a full-time husband, Mrs. Callister?"

"Ready and willing, Mr. Callister," she murmured, and smiled as she drifted off to sleep.

Several weeks later, Sassy had settled in at the ranch and was making enough knitted and crocheted accessories to make a home of the place. Mrs. Peale had a new companion, a practical nurse named Helen who was middle-aged, sweet, and could cook as well as clean house. She had no family, so Mrs. Peale and Selene filled an empty place in her life. Her charges were very happy with her. Sassy and John found time to visit regularly. They were like lovebirds, though. People rarely saw one without the other. Sassy mused that it was like they were joined at the hip. John grinned and kissed her for that. It was, indeed, he said happily.

One afternoon, John walked in the back door with Chief Graves, who was grinning from ear to ear.

"We have company," John told her, pausing to kiss her warmly and pull her close at his side. "He has news."

"I thought you'd like to know that Mr. Tarleton got five years," he said pleasantly. "They took him away last Friday. He's appealing, of course, but it won't help. He was recorded agreeing to the terms of the plea bargain. I told you that judge hated sexual assault cases."

Sassy nodded. "I'm sorry for him," she said. "I wish he'd learned his lesson the last time, in Wyoming. I guess when you do bad things for a long time, you just keep doing them."

"Repeat offenders repeat, sometimes," Graves replied solemnly. "But he's off the street, where he won't be hurting other young women." He pursed his lips. "I also wanted to thank you for the gift you brought back from Mexico. But I'm curious."

"About what?" she asked.

"How did you know I could play a flute?"

Her eyebrows arched. "You can?" she asked, surprised.

He chuckled. "Maybe she reads minds," he told John. "Better take good care of her. A woman with that rare gift is worth rubies."

"You're telling me," John replied, smiling down at his wife.

"I'll get back to town. Take care."

"You, too," Sassy said.

He sauntered out to his truck. John turned to Sassy with pursed lips. "So you can read minds, can you?" He leaned his forehead down against hers and linked his hands behind her. "Think you can tell me what I'm thinking right now?" he teased.

She reached up and whispered in his ear, grinning.

He laughed, picked her up, and stalked down the hall carrying her. She held on tight. Some men's minds, she thought wickedly, weren't all that difficult to read after all!

* * * * *

FALLING FOR MR. DARK
& DANGEROUS

Donna Alward

Dear Reader,

Why is it that sometimes the thing we want the least is exactly what we need the most?

When I was writing *Hired by the Cowboy* and *Marriage at Circle M* for the Harlequin Romance line, I got to wondering about Mike's cousin, Maggie. Maggie became Mike's foster parent when she wasn't that much older than he was, and I wanted to know what had happened to her. I got to know her, and realized that the strength she displayed in her childhood had been tested in her adult years—so much so that she had resolved never to love again.

I realized she needed a hero who could restore her faith... in herself, in life, in love. And that hero was Nate Griffith, a U.S. marshal sent to Canada on a case. The kind of man she shied away from—young, vibrant, principled and in a profession that carried far more danger than she was comfortable with. The kind of man who could show her that there was more to life than complacency and fear. That living without risk isn't living at all...it's just existing.

I'm thrilled that *Falling for Mr. Dark & Dangerous* is being reprinted in this edition. I had so much fun writing it and my editor remarked afterward that she kept getting hungry while reading it! I've shared some of the recipes featured in the book on my website in the Recipe Corner. hope you'll pop over and have a peek!

You can visit me at my website, www.donnaalward.com, and check out my current releases. Or you can catch up with me on Twitter, @DonnaAlward, or on Facebook as Donna Alward, Romance Author. I'd love to hear from you.

Love,

Donna

Acknowledgments

When I decided I wanted to write a book with a cop hero, I turned to Mark Graham, U.S. marshal, who not only provided me with all the law-enforcement information I needed, but also gave me a glimpse into what it's actually like to do the job that he does. Thank you, Mark, for the info and the laughs. You rock.

Dedication

My paternal grandmother was an avid reader. Even bringing up several children during the Depression and beyond, her attachment to Harlequin romance books is legendary in our family. So much so that at one point or another, we've all been called "Myrtle," after her—my mother, my sisters, even me. Now my own children have taken on that tradition; this summer found my girls on a bunk with a book more often than not. And at one point or another they were dubbed "Myrtle."
Gram passed away when I was seventeen, but I think of her often these days as I'm now writing the stories that she loved so much. I dedicate this book to my gram, for passing on her love for books to all of us, and hope that in some small way I have done her proud. This is for you, Grammie.

Chapter 1

The crunch of tires on snow let Maggie Taylor know he was here. The U.S. marshal. The man who'd thrown a monkey wrench into things before he'd ever even arrived.

She parted the curtains and looked out over the white-capped yard. A late March storm had dropped several centimeters of snow earlier in the week and then the temperature had plunged. Now it looked more like Christmas than impending spring.

Maggie sighed as the black SUV pulled up beside her truck. She'd almost booked a trip to get away from the late surge of winter. She'd always found an excuse not to travel, but now that Jen was away from home, she'd decided to treat herself for once and go somewhere hot, where she'd be catered to instead of doing the catering. In fact, she'd been taking extra time browsing around the travel agent's on a trip to Red Deer when *he* had called, requesting a room for a prolonged stay.

Of course, since she'd been out at the time, Jennifer had taken the call and booked him in without even asking. Not only had it spoiled her plans, but it had caused a huge argument between her and Jennifer. She pressed her thumbs against her index fingers, snapping the knuckles. If it hadn't been about that, it would have been something else. They were always arguing, it seemed. They never saw eye to eye on anything anymore.

As if preordained, Jennifer chose that moment to gallop down the stairs. Maggie stared at the pink plaid flannel that covered her daughter's bottom half, topped by a battered gray sweatshirt that had seen far better days. Maggie felt guilty at the relief she knew she'd feel when Jennifer went back to school after her spring break. These days they got along much better when there were several miles between them.

She dropped the curtain back into place, obscuring her view of the man getting out of the vehicle.

"Honestly, Jen. You're still in your pyjamas and our guest is here." She ran her hands down her navy slacks and straightened the hem of the thick gray sweater she'd put on to ward off the chill.

"I haven't done my laundry yet." Jennifer skirted past her and headed straight for the kitchen.

Maggie sighed. Even though Jen complained that there was *nothing* to do around here, she somehow always left laundry and chores up to Maggie. And Maggie did them rather than frustrate herself with yet another argument. Their relationship was fragile enough.

When Jen had informed her of this particular booking, Maggie had lost her cool instead of thanking her daughter for actually taking some initiative with the business. Instead she'd harped about her ruined vacation plans.

She should just let the resentment go. Mexico wasn't going anywhere. She'd go another time, that was all. And the money from this off-season booking would come in handy come summer, when repairs to the house would need to be undertaken.

The marshal was a guest here and it was her job to make him feel welcome. Even if she had her doubts. A cop, of all people. He was probably rigid and scheduled and had no sense of humor.

Letting out a breath and pasting on her smile, she went to the door and opened it before he had a chance to ring the bell.

"Welcome to Mountain Haven Bed-and-Breakfast," she got out, but the rest of the words of her rehearsed greeting flew out of her head as she stared a long way up into blue-green eyes.

"Thank you." His lips moved above a gray and black parka that was zipped precisely to the top. "I know it's off-season, and I appreciate your willingness to open for me. I hope it hasn't inconvenienced you."

It was a struggle to keep her mouth from dropping open, to keep the welcome smile curving her lips. His introductory speech had locked her gaze on his face and she was staggered. She'd be spending the next three weeks with *this* man? In an otherwise empty bed-and-breakfast? Jennifer would only be here another few days, and then it was back to school. It would be just the two of them.

What had started out as an annoying business necessity was now curled with intimacy. He was, very possibly, the most gorgeous man she'd ever seen. Even bundled in winter gear she sensed his lean, strong build, the way he carried his body. With purpose and intent. His voice was smooth with just a hint of gravel, giving it a rumbling texture; the well-shaped lips unsmiling despite his polite speech. And he had killer eyes...eyes that gleamed brilliantly in contrast to his dark clothing.

"I *am* in the right place, aren't I?" He turned his head and looked at the truck, then back at her, frowning a bit as she remained stupidly silent.

Pull yourself together, she told herself. She stepped back, opening the door wider to welcome him in. "If you're Nathaniel Griffith, you're in the right place."

He smiled finally, a quick upturn of the lips, and exhaled, a cloud forming in the frigid air. "That's a relief. I was afraid I'd gotten lost. And please—" he pulled off his glove and held out his hand "—call me Nate. I only get called Nathaniel when I'm in trouble with my boss or my mother."

She smiled back, genuinely this time, as she shook his hand. It was warm and firm and enveloped her smaller fingers completely. She couldn't imagine him in trouble for *anything*. He looked like Mr. All-American.

"I'm Maggie Taylor, the owner. Please, come in. I'll show you your room and get you familiar with the place."

"I'll just get my bags," he said, stepping back outside the door.

He jogged to the truck, reaching into the backseat for a large black duffel. He leaned across the seat for something else and the back of his jacket slid up, revealing a delicious rear-view clad in faded denim. A dark thrill shot through her at the sight.

"Wow. That's *yum,*" came Jen's voice just behind her shoulder.

Maggie stepped back into the shadows behind the door, feeling the heat rise in her cheeks. "Jennifer! For God's sake, keep your voice down. This is our guest."

Jen took a bite of the toast she'd prepared, looking remarkably unconcerned by either her words or her appearance. "The cop, right? The one I booked? Mom, if the front's anything like the back, it totally beats Mexico."

Nate turned around, bags in hand, and Maggie pressed a hand to her belly. This was silly. It was a visceral, physical reaction, nothing more. He was good-looking. So what? She was his hostess. It wasn't her style to have an attraction to a guest.

It wasn't her style to feel that sort of pull to anyone for that matter, not these days. It was just Jen pointing out his attributes. Maggie wasn't blind, after all.

His booted steps echoed on the veranda and he stomped the snow from his boots before coming in and putting down the bags.

Maggie shut the door behind him. Enough draft had been let in by the exchange and already the foyer was chilly.

"I'm Jen." Jennifer plopped her piece of peanut butter toast back to her plate and held out her hand.

"Nate," he answered, taking her hand and shaking it.

When he pulled back, a smudge of peanut butter stuck to his knuckle.

"My daughter," Maggie said weakly.

"I gathered," he answered, then with an unexpected grin, licked the smudge from his thumb.

Jen beamed up at him, unfazed, while Maggie blushed.

"You took my reservation," he offered, smiling at Jennifer.

Jen nodded. "I'm on spring break."

Maggie held out her hand. "Let me take your coat," she offered politely. "The closet's just here."

He shrugged out of the jacket and Maggie realized how very tall he was. Easily over six feet, he towered over her modest height. He handed her the coat, along with thick gloves. She smiled as she turned to the closet, the weight of the parka heavy in her hands. For a man from the sunny south, he sure knew how to dress for an Alberta winter.

The phone rang, and Jen raced to answer it. Nate's eyes followed her from the room, then fell on Maggie.

"Teenagers and phones." She raised her shoulders as if to say, "What can you do?"

"I remember." He looked around. "She gave great directions. I found you pretty easily."

"You drove, then?" Maggie hadn't had a chance to get a glimpse of his plates. Maybe the SUV was a rental. He could easily have flown into Calgary or Edmonton and picked up a vehicle there.

"The truck's on loan from a friend. He met me at Coutts, and I dropped him off before driving the rest of the way."

Maggie shut the closet door and turned back, getting more comfortable as they settled into polite, if cool, chitchat. This was what she did for a living, after all. There was no need to feel awkward with a guest, despite Jen's innuendoes.

"Where does your friend live?" Maggie asked. Nate gripped the duffel by the short handles. Maggie paused her question. "Would you like some help with your bags?"

"I've got it." He moved purposefully, sliding the pack over his shoulder and gripping the duffel.

Maggie stood nonplussed. His words had been short and clipped, but she'd only been offering a simple courtesy.

Her lack of response stretched out awkwardly while Jennifer's muffled voice sounded from the kitchen. Inconvenience at his arrival was now becoming discomfort. Perhaps she'd been right after all when she'd thought about having a cop underfoot. Terse and aloof. She prided herself on a friendly, comfortable atmosphere, but it took two to accomplish it. By the hard set of his jaw, her work was clearly cut out for her.

Nate spoke, finally breaking the tension.

"I'm sorry. I didn't mean to be rude. I'm just used to looking after myself." He smiled disarmingly. "My mother would flay me alive if I let a woman carry my things."

Maggie wondered what his mother would say if she knew Maggie looked after running the business *and* all the repairs on the large house single-handedly. She was used to being on her own and doing everything from starting a business to repairing a roof to raising a daughter.

"Chivalry isn't dead, I see." Her words came out cooler than she wanted as she moved past him to the stairs.

"No, ma'am." His steps echoed behind her as she started up the staircase.

When they reached the top, she paused. Perhaps because of his job he was naturally suspicious, but she was trying hard not to feel snubbed after his curt words in the foyer. It should have been implicitly understood that whatever was in his bags was his business. She'd never go through a guest's belongings!

"The Mountain Haven Bed-and-Breakfast is exactly that. A haven." She led him to a sturdy white door, opened it. "A place to get away from worries and stress. I hope you'll enjoy your stay here."

He looked down into her eyes, but she couldn't read his expression. It was like he was deliberately keeping it blank. She'd hoped her words would thaw his cool manner just a bit, but he only replied, "I appreciate your discretion."

He went inside, putting his duffel on the floor and the backpack on the wing chair in the corner.

"Local calls are free, long distance go on your bill, unless of course you use a prepaid card." Maggie dismissed the futility of trying to draw him out and gave him the basic rundown instead. "There's no television in your room, but there is a den downstairs that you're welcome to use."

Maggie paused. Nate was waiting patiently for her to finish her spiel. It was very odd, with him being her only guest. Knowing he'd be the *only* guest for the next few weeks. It didn't seem right, telling him mealtimes and rules.

She softened her expression. "Look, normally there's a whole schedule thing with meals and everything, but you're my only guest. I think we can be a little more flexible. I usually serve breakfast between eight and nine, so if that suits you, great. I can work around your plans. Dinner is served at six-thirty. For lunch, things are fluid. I can provide it or not; for a minimum charge on your overall bill. I'm happy to tell you about local areas of interest, and you have dial-up internet access in your room."

Nate tucked his hands into his jeans pockets. "I'm your only guest?"

"That's right. It's not my busiest time right now."

"Then…" His eyes met hers sheepishly. "Look, I'm going to feel awkward eating alone. I don't suppose… we could all eat together."

Nate watched her closely and she felt color creep into her cheeks yet again. Silly Jennifer and her suggestive comments. The front side *was* as attractive as the back and Maggie couldn't help but notice as they stood together in the quiet room. It wasn't how things were usually done. Normally guests ate in the dining room and she ate at the nook or she and Jen at the kitchen table. Yet it would seem odd, serving him all alone in the dining room. It was antisocial, somehow.

She struggled to keep her voice low and even. "Basically your stay should be enjoyable. If you prefer to eat with us, that would be fine. And if there's anything I can do to make your stay more comfortable, let me know."

"Everything here looks great, Ms. Taylor."

"Then I'll leave you to unpack. The bathroom is two doors down, and as my only guest it's yours alone. Jennifer and I each have our own so you won't have to share. I'll be downstairs. Let me know if there's anything you need. Otherwise, I'll see you for dinner."

She courteously shut the door, then leaned against it, closing her eyes. Nate Griffith wasn't an ordinary guest, that much she knew already. She couldn't shake the irrational feeling that he was hiding something. He hadn't said or done anything to really make her think so, beyond being proprietary with his backpack. But something niggled at the back of her mind, something that made her uncomfortable. Given his profession, she should be reassured. Who could be safer than someone in law enforcement? Why would he have any sort of ulterior motive?

His good looks were something she'd simply have to ignore. She'd have to get over her silly awkwardness in a hurry, since they were going to be essentially roommates for the next few weeks. Jen wouldn't be here to run interference much longer, and Maggie would rely on her normal professional, warm persona. Piece of cake.

He was just a man, after all. A man on vacation from a stressful job. A man with an expense account that would make up for her lost plans by helping pay for her next trip.

* * *

Nate heaved out a sigh as the door shut with a firm click. Thank goodness she was gone.

He looked around the room. Very nice. Grant had assured him that the rural location didn't mean substandard lodging, and so far he was right. What he'd seen of the house was clean, warm and welcoming. His room was no different.

The furniture was all of sturdy golden pine; the spread on the bed was thick and looked homemade with its country design in navy, burgundy, deep green and cream. An extra blanket in rich red lay over the foot of the bed. He ran his hand over the footboard. He would have preferred no footboard, so he could stretch out. But it didn't matter. What mattered was that he was here and he had all the amenities he needed. To anyone in the area, he'd be a vacationing guest. To his superiors, he'd be consistently connected through the internet and in liaison with local authorities. Creature comforts were secondary, but not unwelcome. Lord knew he'd stayed in a lot worse places while on assignment.

He unpacked his duffel, laying clothing neatly in the empty dresser drawers. His hand paused on a black sweater. When Grant had mentioned a bed-and-breakfast, Nate had instantly thought of some middle-aged couple. When he'd learned Maggie ran Mountain Haven alone, he'd pictured a woman in her mid-to-late forties who crocheted afghans for the furniture and exchanged recipes for chicken pot pie with her guests. Maggie Taylor didn't fit his profile at all. Neither did Jen. He'd known she was here, but she seemed precocious and typically teenage. Certainly not the kind to get in trouble with the police.

He rested his hips on the curved footboard and frowned. It was hard to discern Maggie's age. Initially he'd thought her maybe a year or two older than himself. But the appearance of her nearly grown daughter had changed that impression. He couldn't tell for sure, but she had to be at least late thirties to have a daughter that age. Yet…her skin was still creamy and unlined, her eyes blue and full-lashed. Her hand had been much smaller than his, and soft.

But it was Maggie's eyes that stuck in his mind. Eyes that smiled warmly with welcome but that held a hint of cool caution in their depths. Eyes that told him whatever her path had been, it probably hadn't been an easy one.

He stood up abruptly and reached for the jeans in his duffel, going to hang them in the closet. He wasn't here to make calf-eyes at the proprietress. That was the last thing he should be thinking about. He had a job to do. That was all. He had information to gather and who better to ask than someone in the know, someone who would take his questions for tourist curiosity? Inviting himself to dinner had put her on the spot, but with the desired results.

The afternoon light was already starting to wane when he dug out his laptop and set it up on the small desk to the left of the bed. Within seconds it was booted up, connected and ready to go. He logged in with his password, checked his email…and waited for everything to download. Once he'd taken care of everything that needed his immediate attention, he quickly composed a few short notes, hitting the send button and waiting what seemed an age for them to leave the Outbox.

"I miss high-speed internet," he muttered, tapping his fingers on the desk, waiting for the dial-up connection to send his messages. Waiting was not something he did well.

But perhaps learning to wait was a life lesson he

needed. He'd been one to act first and think later too many times. Dealing with the aftermath of mistakes had caused him to be put on leave in the first place. He hadn't even been two weeks into his leave when it had been cut short and he'd been given this assignment, and he was glad of it. He wasn't keen on sitting around twiddling his thumbs.

Grant had asked for him personally. As a favor. And this wasn't a job to be rushed. It was a time for watching and waiting.

He frowned at the monitor as the messages finally went through. He didn't want to run up a long distance bill while he was here, but staying in communication was important. For now, his laptop *was* his connection to the outside world. It was a tiny community. The less conspicuous he was, the better.

He realized that his room had grown quite dark, and checked his watch. It was after six already, and Maggie had said dinner was at six-thirty. He didn't want to get things off to a bad start on his first day, so he shut down the computer and put his backpack beneath the empty duffel in the closet.

Maggie heard his footsteps moving around upstairs for a long time, listening to the muffled thump as she mixed dough and browned ground beef for the soup.

Nate Griffith. U.S. Marshal. The name had conjured an image of a flat faced cop when Jennifer had told her about the reservation. Despite the flashes of coolness, he was anything but. He couldn't be more than thirty, thirty-one. And it hadn't taken but a moment to realize he was all legs and broad shoulders, and polite manners.

"Whatcha making?"

Jennifer's voice interrupted and for once Maggie was

glad of it. She'd already spent too long thinking about her latest lodger.

"Pasta e fagioli and foccacia bread."

"Excellent." Jen grabbed a cookie from a beige pottery jar and leaned against the counter, munching.

Maggie watched her. There were some days she really missed the preteen years. Parenting had been so much simpler then. Yet hard as it was, she hated to see Jen leave again.

"Day after tomorrow, huh. Did you book your bus ticket?"

"I booked it return when I came, remember?" She reached in the jar for another cookie.

"You'll spoil your supper," Maggie warned.

Jen simply raised an eyebrow as if to say, *I'm not twelve, Mother.*

"You should be glad I'm leaving. That leaves you alone with Detective Hottie."

Maggie glared.

"Oh, come on, Mom. He's a little old for me, even if he is a fine specimen. But he's just about right for you."

Maggie put the spoon down with more force than she intended. "First of all, keep your voice down. He is a paying guest in this house." She ignored the flutter that skittered through her at Jen's attempt at matchmaking. "He wouldn't be here at all if you'd asked first and booked later."

Jennifer stopped munching. "You're still mad about that, huh."

Maggie sighed, forgetting all about his footsteps. It wasn't all Jen's fault. She did her own share of picking fights. She should be trying to keep Jen close, not pushing her away.

"I just wish…I wish you'd give some thought to things first, instead of racing headlong and then having to backtrack. You took the reservation without even consulting me."

"I was trying to help. I told you I was sorry about it. And they did come through with the cash, so what's the big deal?"

How could Maggie explain that the big deal was that she worried over Jen day and night? She hadn't been blind the last few years. Jen had skated through without getting badly hurt. Yet. But she'd had her share of trouble and Maggie was terrified that one day she'd get a phone call that something truly awful had happened. She wished Jen took it as seriously as she did.

"Let's not argue about it anymore, okay?" Arguing over the reservation was irrelevant now. Maggie had been irritated with Jennifer at the time for not taking a credit card number, but it had ceased to matter. The United States Marshals Service was picking up the tab. All of it. A day after Nate had reserved the room, someone from his office had called and made arrangements for payment, not even blinking when she'd told them the rate, or the cost of extras. And she'd charged them high season rates, just because she'd been so put out at having to put her travel plans on hold.

She pressed dough into two round pans, dimpling the tops with her fingers before putting them under a tea towel to rise. No matter how much she wished she were lying on a beach in Cancún right now, she still derived pleasure from doing what she did best. Cooking for one was a dull, lonely procedure and her spirits lightened as she added ingredients to the large stockpot on the stove. Jen had been home for the last week, but it wasn't the same now that she was nearly adult and spreading her wings. Having guests meant having someone else to do for. It was why she'd chosen a bed-and-breakfast in the first place.

The footsteps halted above her, the house falling completely silent as their argument faltered.

"I didn't mean to pick a fight with you."

"Me, either." Jen shuffled to the kitchen doorway and Maggie longed to mend fences, although she didn't know how.

"Supper in an hour," she called gently, but it went ignored.

Maggie reached across the counter to turn on the radio. She hummed quietly with a recent country hit as she turned her attention to pastry. Her foot tapped along with the beat until she slid everything into the oven, added tiny tubes of pasta to the pot, and cleaned up the cooking mess, the process of cooking and cleaning therapeutic.

At precisely six-twenty, he appeared at the kitchen door.

She turned with the bread pans in her hands, surprised to see him there. Again, she felt a warning thump at his presence. Why in the world was she reacting this way to a complete stranger? It was more than a simple admiration of his good looks. A sliver of danger snuck down her spine. She knew nothing about him. He looked like a normal, nice guy. But how would she know? She didn't even know the reason why he was on a leave of absence. What could have happened to make him need to take extended time off? Suddenly all her misgivings, ones she rarely gave credence to, came bubbling up to the surface. Most of the time she was confident in her abilities to look after herself. Something about Nate Griffith challenged that. And very soon, it would just be the two of them in the house.

"Is something wrong?"

She shook her head, giving a start and putting the

pans down on top of the stove. "No, not at all. You just surprised me."

Maggie took a deep breath, keeping her back to him. "Dinner's not quite ready. It won't be long."

"Is there anything I can do to help?"

He took a few steps into the kitchen. It was her job to make him at ease and feel at home, so why on earth was she finding it so difficult? She forced a smile as she flipped the round loaves out of the pans and on to a cooling rack. "Jen should be down soon. Besides, it's my job to look after you, remember?"

"Well, sure." He leaned easily against the side of the refrigerator. "But I thought we were going to play it a little less formal."

He had her there. She thought for a moment as she got the dishes out of the cupboard. He was only here for a few weeks. What harm could come of being friendly, after all? Her voices of doubt were just being silly; she was making something out of nothing. He'd be gone back to his job and the palm trees before she knew it.

"All right." She held out bread plates and bowls. "Informal it is. We can use the kitchen or the dining room, whichever you prefer. If you could set the table with these, I'll finish up here."

He pushed himself upright with an elbow. "Absolutely." He moved to take the dishes and their fingers brushed. Without thinking, her gaze darted up to his with alarm. For a second she held her breath. But then he turned away to the table as if nothing had connected.

Only she knew it had. And that was bad, bad news.

Chapter 2

He'd set the three places at one end of the table; one at the head and the other two flanking it. There was little chance of her getting away with sitting across from him. He'd be close. Too close. With his long legs, their knees might bump under the table. Her pulse fluttered at the thought and she frowned. It wasn't like her to be so twitchy.

As she watched, he lit the thick candles at the center of the table with the butane lighter.

Maggie paused at the intimacy of the setting and shook it off again, putting the soup tureen on the table. It shouldn't make her feel so threatened, but it did. Even with Jennifer here, a simple dinner had somehow transformed into something more. Maggie simply didn't *do* relationships of any kind. Not even casual ones. It always ended badly with her being left to try to pick up the pieces. After the last time, with Tom, there hadn't been many pieces left to pick up. She had to hold on to every single one. All that she had left was put into raising Jennifer and running her business. She didn't know why he'd go to the bother of setting the atmosphere, and it unsettled her.

"Ms. Taylor?"

Maggie realized she'd been staring at the table. She laughed lightly. "I'm sorry. You were saying?"

"I asked if you ran the Haven alone. I'm afraid I didn't get many details when I booked."

"I do, yes." She brought the basket of bread to the table and invited him to sit with a hand. She was surprised when he waited until she was seated before seating himself. "Jennifer attends school in Edmonton, so she's not around much anymore."

"Which makes you sad."

Maggie smiled, pleasantly surprised by his small, but accurate insight. The house did seem unbearably lonely when Jen was gone. "Despite teenage angst and troubles, yes, it does. I miss having her close by. Speaking of, she should be here by now."

She pushed her chair back and stood, fluttering a hand when he made a similar move out of courtesy. "It's okay. Jen knows to be on time. I'll call her."

Maggie made her way to the bottom of the stairs. What she'd said was true. She did miss having Jen closer, even though at times she was glad Jen was away from here and making new friends. Not all her acquaintances at home were ones Maggie would have chosen. And the last thing Maggie needed was for the marshal to know about Jen's brush with the law.

"Jennifer. Dinner," she called up the stairs.

There was a muffled thump from Jen's room, then she came down, earbuds still stuck in her ears and her MP3 player stuffed in her pocket.

They went to the kitchen together, but when Jen sat and reached for the bread, Maggie shook her head.

"Not at the table, please."

Jen seemed unconcerned as she plucked the buds from her ears. "Hey, Nate," she greeted, snagging the piece of bread as though it were the most natural thing in the world.

Maggie saw Nate try to hide a smile. Honestly, she wondered sometimes if the manners she'd tried to instill had gone in one ear and out the other.

"Hey, Jennifer." Nate politely answered the greeting and broke the awkwardness by starting a conversation. "So…spring break is just about over. You looking forward to getting back to school?"

Maggie relaxed and ladled soup into bowls. Nate apparently had paid good attention to *his* upbringing. Manners and a natural sense of small talk. And for once, Jen didn't seem to mind answering.

"I guess. It's been kind of boring around here. Nothing to do."

"Oh, I don't know. With all this snow…there must be winter sports. Skiing, skating, tobogganing…or are those things uncool these days?"

Maggie grinned behind her water glass. She'd suggested a day of cross-country skiing earlier in the week, only to have the idea vetoed by Jen. The same Jen who a few years ago would have jumped at the chance.

"I dunno," Jen replied.

Nate nodded. "I'm looking forward to spending lots of time outdoors," he said. "No snow where I live. This is a real treat for me."

Maggie pictured him bundled up, his boots strapped into a pair of snowshoes, with his eyes gleaming like sapphire bullets beneath his toque. Her heart thumped heavily. His lean, strong build made the outdoors a natural choice.

"I suppose you're all athletic and stuff." Jennifer paused and tilted her head as if examining him.

"It's part of my job. I have to stay in good shape. Just because I'm not…working, doesn't mean I can ignore the routine." He paused to take a spoonful of soup. "Besides, if I eat your mother's cooking for the next few weeks, I'm really going to have to watch myself." His smile sparkled at Maggie. "This is delicious."

"Thanks," Maggie responded. She was used to receiving polite compliments on her cooking. It made no sense that his praise caused her heart to pitter-patter like a schoolgirl's.

She considered steering the conversation so that Jen didn't monopolize it, but she realized two things. Jen was more animated than she'd been the whole break, and Maggie was learning a whole lot more about Nate by sitting back and listening to their exchange.

"So, Nate…when you're not vacationing, what's your job like? Are you like a regular cop or what?" She popped a spoonful of soup into her mouth while waiting for his answer.

Nate concentrated on adding grated parmesan to the top of his soup. "No, not like a regular cop. I get to do special stuff. A lot of what I do is finding fugitives, people who have committed crimes and are on the run."

"You mean like *America's Most Wanted*?" Jen leaned forward now, her dinner forgotten.

Nate nodded. "Exactly like that. And sometimes I'm sent out on high-profile security details, too."

"Isn't that dangerous?" Maggie's voice intruded. A cop was bad enough, but even she knew that a police officer dealt with a lot of the mundane. This seemed like a whole other level. "Don't you worry about getting killed?"

His eyes were steady on hers. "Yes, but not as much as I worry about getting the job done."

Maggie's chin flattened. Tall, strong and handsome was one thing, but having a target painted on his chest was quite another. She couldn't imagine anyone choosing such a lifestyle.

"Have you ever killed anyone?"

"Jennifer!" Maggie put down her spoon and glared at her daughter for her crassness in asking such a thing. Nate's eyes made the transition to look at Jennifer, the smile disappearing completely.

"Jen, that was beyond inappropriate." Maggie spoke sharply. "Please apologize."

But Nate shook his head. "There's no need. It's a valid question. I get it a lot." He took a drink of water. "I work as part of a team. And our goal is to bring fugitives to justice, or to protect those we are assigned to protect. Of course we prefer to bring them in unharmed. But if we're fired upon, we have to fire back."

Silence fell over the table.

Maggie tried to fill the uncomfortable gap the way a hostess should, yet all she could see was Nate, holding a smoking gun. The thought chilled her considerably.

"That must be very stressful."

Nate nodded. "It can be, yes."

Jen's voice interrupted again. "Is that why you're here?"

Maggie kicked her beneath the table. Jen bit down on her lip but watched him, undeterred.

Nate swallowed. "Part of it, yes. I was directed to take some time off after a...particularly challenging case. A little rest and relaxation is just what the doctor ordered."

He smiled, but it wasn't as warm as before. "In keeping with that, I'd appreciate if you'd keep my presence here low-key. I realize it's a small community, but right now I want to enjoy the outdoors and not worry about speculation."

Maggie aimed a stern look at Jennifer before turning to Nate and answering.

"Of course. You are a guest here, and of course we'll respect your wishes. That's what the Haven is all about." At least she didn't have to worry right now. He was on vacation. What he did for a living had no bearing on anything.

"Thank you," he murmured. He picked up his spoon again and resumed eating, and Jennifer wisely let the subject drop for the rest of the meal.

"Dessert, Mr. Griffith?"

Nate looked up at Maggie as she removed his plate and bowl. The meal had had its uncomfortable moments, but he was actually glad the questions had been asked and answered. He got the feeling that Maggie would have been too polite to ask point-blank what her daughter had. Not only that, but the questions had provided a natural way to introduce his cover. Even if he did feel a bit guilty about the half-lie. He'd deliberately prodded her about some things, like asking if she ran the bed-and-breakfast alone when he knew darn well she did. Still…it was all necessary.

Maggie was waiting, her lips curved pleasantly in what he now realized was her hostess smile. "I shouldn't…but maybe you could tell me what it is first."

Her lips twitched…a good sign, he thought. She'd looked far too serious throughout the rest of the meal. If he could get her to relax a bit, it would go a lot easier toward getting what he needed to know without her feeling like she was being questioned.

"Peach and blueberry tart with ice cream," she answered.

Jennifer clattered around the kitchen, already scooping out servings. "Can't really resist that, now can I," he acquiesced. "So…yes, please. And stop calling me Mr. Griffith. Mr. Griffith is my father or my uncle."

Maggie put on coffee while Jennifer finished doling out servings of the tart, taking hers and escaping to the den and the television. When Maggie placed the dessert before him, the smell alone was enough to remind him of home. Sweets weren't something he indulged in much anymore, but his mother was a fantastic baker and plied him with goodies whenever he visited. Right now the scent of fruit and cinnamon took him back to when things were much simpler. Made him wish this were that simple, instead of him having to work his way through hidden motives. But this was the closest lodging to where he needed to be and the most private. There hadn't been much of a choice, so he had to work with what he'd been given.

"What made you decide to take on a business such as this?" He decided to draw her out by talking about herself. "It has to be a huge job for one person."

Maggie avoided answering by pouring coffee into thick pottery mugs.

"I had this house and a whole lot of empty rooms," she explained. Her pulse quickened as she was drawn back nearly twenty years. "I had a house and a baby and a foster child and needed to support us all."

Nate's fork paused midair. "Children? As in plural?"

Maggie smiled thinly. "Yes, for a while I looked after my cousin, until he grew up and did his own thing. He's thirty-one now."

His fork dipped into a slice of peach but Maggie noticed a pair of creases between his brows. She tried to lighten the mood by cracking a joke. "Now you're doing the math. How old must I be to have an eighteen-year-old daughter and a foster child of thirty-one?"

He swallowed and reached for his water as a snort of mirth bubbled out at her directness, easing the tension. "I guess I am."

"I'll save you the trouble. I'm forty-two. I was twenty-four when Jennifer was born. Mike was thirteen. He came to me when he was eleven—when I was twenty-two."

She passed him the cream and sugar, then resumed her seat. "And now you want to ask the question and don't know how to do it politely."

Her heart fluttered. Talking about it was hard, and no matter how many times she answered, it never seemed to get any easier. But by now she knew that it was best to get it over with, quick and clean.

Nate had given up all pretense of eating and was watching her closely, so she tried her safest smile. "When I was twenty-five, my husband, Jennifer's dad, was killed in a work accident."

"I'm so sorry."

"It was a long time ago."

Conversation halted. Probing the topic further would be presumptuous, which was part of the reason why Maggie tended to get it over with as soon as possible. Once it was out there, most dropped the subject, uncomfortable with the idea of asking how it had happened, or worse, why she hadn't married again. She knew her reasons. That was enough.

Nate put a bite of pastry and ice cream in his mouth. Her answers had been plain at best, and he knew she was skimming the surface, evading deeper responses.

It would be rude to press further. And how much did he *really* want to know? He was here for a short time. It would be best if he stayed out of her way as much as possible, kept her questions to a minimum. Get the answers he needed and no more.

Besides, there were some questions about his life he wouldn't want to answer. If she wanted to keep her life private, that was fine by him. What he needed from her had nothing to do with her private life beyond Jennifer's—and her—involvement.

The candle at the center of the table flickered and he watched the flame dance.

Maggie sipped her coffee and changed the subject. "So what brings you to back roads Alberta? Most would choose a more touristy area. Like Banff, or somewhere south of the border. Montana or Colorado. There's nothing around here besides snow and prairie and a bunch of ranches mixed in with the gas industry."

"If this is your tourism pitch, I can see why your beds are empty," he joked.

"This isn't our big season," she answered. "Like I said, most would head to the mountains for the skiing and richer comforts. We get most of our traffic in the summer."

"I'm surprised you don't vacation in the winter, then," Nate suggested.

When she didn't answer right away, he peered closer at her face and it struck him. "You *do* usually travel, don't you? Is my being here…" He paused, knew he was right by the uncomfortable way her gaze evaded his. "You canceled plans because I was coming." He hadn't thought of that. Hadn't thought of anything beyond doing this assignment, and then dealing with the details.

She shook her head. "It's no bother. I hadn't even booked anything yet."

"But you were going to," he confirmed.

Maggie looked up at him and he was struck again by how young she looked. If he didn't know better, he'd have thought they were close to the same age.

"Mexico isn't going anywhere." She smiled shyly, and their gazes caught.

She tried to cover the moment with her own question. "How long have you been a marshal?"

"Five years. Before that I was in the marines."

"Oh."

He grinned at her. "And now *you're* trying to do the math. I'll save you the trouble. I'm thirty-three."

"And you like it?"

"I couldn't do it otherwise."

Somehow their voices had softened in the candlelight, taking on an intimacy that surprised him, pleasantly. He watched as Maggie bit the inside of her lower lip and released it. She had a beautiful mouth. A mouth made for kissing.

When he lifted his gaze she was watching him, and her expression was fascination mixed with shock that he'd been staring at her lips.

Attraction, he realized. It had been a long time since he'd felt it. But there was definitely a familiar surge in his blood as his eyes locked with Maggie's, blocking out the muted sound of the television coming from the den. Maggie Taylor raised his temperature and he couldn't for the life of him understand why.

It was a complication he didn't need. All he really wanted to do was what he'd been sent here to do. He'd put on a good face; pretended this was just a vacation for some relaxation, but he wouldn't have chosen this for a holiday. His idea of fun wasn't in the middle of some godforsaken Canadian Prairie at a bed-and-breakfast. He certainly hadn't expected to feel whatever it was he was feeling for the proprietress. He wasn't sure if the desire to flirt with her was a detriment or a bonus.

The light from the candles sputtered, throwing shadows on her face. She was as different from his regular type as sun was from rain. Subdued, polite, grounded, yet anything but boring. It took a woman of character and stamina to lose a husband so young and still bring up a family and run a business. How had she done it all alone?

Jen coughed in the den and Maggie looked away as the moment ended. Nate caught his breath as the color bloomed in her cheeks. He hadn't imagined it, then.

"Excuse me, I should clean this up." Her voice was overbright as she scrambled up from the table, knocking over her empty mug.

It crashed to the floor, breaking into three distinct pieces.

"Oh, how clumsy of me!" Without looking at him, she knelt to the floor to pick up the pieces. Nate watched, amused. It had been a long time since he'd met a woman who intrigued him, and even longer since he'd had the power to fluster one the way Maggie seemed to be right now.

"Let me help you," he suggested, pushing out of his chair and squatting down beside her.

"Ow!"

Maggie sat back, one of the pieces of pottery in her left hand and a small shard sticking out of a finger on the opposite hand. A drop of blood formed around the tip.

"Maggie, take a breath." Nate took her hand gently in his. "Are you sure coffee was a good idea?" He chuckled as he concentrated on her finger, pinching the fragment between his thumb and forefinger. "Perhaps decaf next time, hmmm?"

He pulled out the shard, but it had gone deeper than he expected and the drop of blood turned into a substantial streak.

"Do you have a first-aid kit?"

Her voice was subdued. "Of course I do. Under the sink in the bathroom."

He rose and headed for the stairs.

"The one over there. In my living quarters."

He stopped and looked at the closed door leading off the kitchen. She had wrapped a napkin around the finger and stood up, taking the larger pieces of the mug and placing them gently on the table.

"I'll get it," she said.

"No, you sit tight. I will."

Nate changed direction and went through the door, feeling somehow like he was trespassing. This was crazy. Less than six hours here and he was flirting with the owner and wandering around her private living space. He went into the bathroom, surprised by the scent of cinnamon and apples coming from a scented oil dispenser plugged into the wall. Switching on a light, he was bathed in an intimate glow—no blaring bulbs here. Soothing blue and deep red splashes of color accented the ivory decor. Nate felt very much like he was intruding.

He searched the small vanity cupboard until he found a white box with a red cross on the top. He shut off the light and went back to the kitchen, where he found Maggie at the sink, the napkin off her finger as she ran it beneath cold water. She lifted it out of the stream and looked at it closely in the soft light from above the sink.

"I think all of it came out," she explained. "What a klutz I am."

"Not at all." Nate set the kit down on the counter and flipped open the lid. "It's not deep, so you just need a small bandage."

"I can get it, truly."

"You're right handed, aren't you? Putting it on lefty would be awkward. I've got two capable hands."

Maggie looked down at his fingers holding the bandage. Capable indeed. His hands were wide, with long tapering fingers. She swallowed, but held out her finger anyway.

The sound of the paper wrapper tearing off the bandage echoed through the kitchen. Nate stepped closer, anchoring one sticky end and then holding her hand before wrapping the rest around and sticking it to itself. Her heart pounded painfully; she was sure he could hear it as he applied the small wrap.

"All better," he said softly.

"Thank you," she whispered.

He started to pull his hand away, but for a long moment his fingertips stayed on hers. She lifted her eyes to his and found him watching her steadily. Oxygen seemed scarce as she fell entranced by his intense eyes, the shape of his lips. Lips that leaned in ever so slightly.

"You're welcome." And he lifted her finger to his lips and kissed the tip.

Chapter 3

Nate flipped through the channels aimlessly. There really wasn't going to be much to do here in the evenings, especially when the days were still fairly short. At the end of March, this far north, it was full dark early in the evening. Whatever work he did, it would be during the day. It was becoming very clear that after dinner he'd either spend his time here, in the den, or upstairs in his room reading or working online.

He'd rather be upstairs, putting his thoughts together, but on the off-chance that Maggie might come in, he stayed.

He had questions, ones whose answers could get him started in the right direction. Not to mention the fact that he'd enjoyed their little interplay in the kitchen earlier. It had been a long time since he'd indulged in a little harmless flirtation.

Maggie entered with a coffee carafe and mugs on a tray. She put them down on the coffee table. "I thought you might like some coffee," she offered. "I made a fresh pot and promise not to break any more mugs." She smiled tentatively.

The brew smelled wonderful and Nate brushed aside the thought that he'd be up all night if he drank too much of it. He wasn't about to refuse the gesture. If nothing else, it would give him more time with her, and that wasn't a hardship. "That would be wonderful." When she poured the first cup, he nodded to the second. "Are you joining me?"

She smiled. "If you like."

Nate looked up into her eyes. They were warm and friendly with something more. Perhaps a shy invitation, definitely a quiet curiosity. "I would like." He returned her smile. "It's quiet. The company would be nice."

Maggie took her own cup and sat, not on the sofa next to him, but in a nearby chair. Nate was taking up the couch and she was far too aware of him to sit next to him. In the winter months, this room became the family room, and she often snuggled up on the couch with a blanket and a DVD. In season, it was where the guests went to relax.

Normally she didn't socialize with her guests, either. But normally her guests didn't travel alone at the end of winter. She was accustomed to guests traveling in pairs. A romantic getaway, or a stop on the way to somewhere else. Very rarely did she have singles, and when she did, it was nearly always in prime season when they were out exploring the area or the nearby Rockies, or when other guests were present to facilitate conversation.

But Nate was definitely here alone. She'd noticed the absence of a wedding ring at dinner.

"This gives me a chance to pick your brain," he was saying, and she stopped staring at his hands and paid attention. The tingling sensation that he was more than he seemed prickled once more.

"Pick my brain?"

"About things to do while I'm here."

She exhaled slowly. Just tourist information, then. She'd had the uncomfortable feeling after their interchange in the kitchen that he was about to get personal. "Well, there are always day trips into the mountains. I have pamphlets, but there are lots of winter activities there." She crossed her legs, adopting the tour-guide voice she used with guests. "Or a few hours either northeast or south will take you to major cities for shopping, the arts, whatever you want."

"I meant more locally. What I can do with *Mountain Haven* as my base." Nate put down his cup and leaned forward slightly. He wasn't going to let her off the hook, it seemed.

Maggie swallowed. His voice was deep and a little rough; it rumbled with soft seduction through the room. The remembrance of her finger against his lips rippled through her.

"We're…we're usually closed this time of year. I'm afraid I haven't given it much thought."

"I see." He looked down into his cup, frowning, then took a drink.

"But…I have some personal gear I could loan you." His disappointment in her answer was clear and she instantly regretted being so cool. She punctuated the offer with a soft smile.

"Personal gear?"

Maggie hesitated. She knew that out in the shed she'd find Tom's things—cross-country skis, snowshoes, even his old hockey skates. They'd been out there over fifteen years, and she'd never had the heart to throw them away.

But holding on to them didn't make much sense anymore. For the last several years, she'd nearly forgotten they were even there. If Nate could get some use out of them, why shouldn't he?

"My husband's things. Snowshoes, skis, that sort of thing." She took a sip of hot coffee to cover the tiny waver she heard in her own voice.

The television still chattered in the background, but Nate went very still. She heard nothing beyond the quiet resonance of his voice.

"That's not necessary. I can outfit myself, if you can tell me where to shop."

Maggie nodded slightly. "I understand if you're uncomfortable with using Tom's things." What man would truly want the leftovers of a dead man, after all?

"I don't mind at all. I thought maybe *you* were uncomfortable with it, which I completely understand."

Maggie looked up. Nate was watching her calmly, one ankle crossed over his knee. His lips were unsmiling, but not cold. No, never cold, she realized. She was starting to understand that what she'd mistaken for coolness earlier was just him waiting, accepting. Like he understood far more than he should for someone so young.

And he was young. When she thought about the numbers, she realized there was much *behind* her and much *ahead* for him. She'd been married, raised a child, knew what to expect from life and had accepted it. But he had so much yet to discover. She was good at reading people, doing what she did, and unless she missed her guess, Nate had all those things ahead of him.

But when she looked into his eyes like she was now, the numbers faded away into nothingness. Somehow, without knowing each other hardly at all, she got the feeling they were strangely coming from a similar place. Like she recognized something in him though they'd never met before. Something that superseded the difference in their ages.

"It's not doing anyone any good in storage. You are most welcome to it."

"In that case, thanks. I appreciate it, Maggie."

He used her given name again and it felt very personal. Like they'd crossed a threshold moving them from simple guest/proprietor relationship to something more. Which was ridiculous, wasn't it?

Maggie leaned ahead and poured herself more coffee. It was good Nate was going to use the things. Letting go of Tom had taken a long time. But the sense of loss never left her completely. Or the sense of regret. She had a box of small trinkets she kept all the time, mementos of those she'd loved, tucked away in a box in her closet. She had memories and other reminders of Tom; the skis and snowshoes wouldn't be missed. It was a long time ago and in most respects, she'd moved on.

And in the others…that was none of his business.

Jennifer popped in the door, grinning first at Nate and then over at Maggie. "I thought I smelled coffee."

Maggie was glad of the interruption. "You'll have to grab a mug from the kitchen."

With a flashy smile, Jen saluted and disappeared. Maggie couldn't repress the smirk that twisted her lips. Nate looked over at her with raised eyebrows, and Maggie let out a soft laugh. For all of her troubles, Jen was the breath of fresh air that brightened the house when she was home.

"She's got lots of energy," Nate commented dryly, his hand cradled around his mug as he lifted an eyebrow at Maggie.

"That comes from being eighteen."

"You make it sound like you're in your dotage."

She laughed. "Well, I'm a lot closer than I care to admit."

Nate put down his empty cup and rested his elbows on his knees, linking his hands together. "Believe me, Maggie. You're anything but *too old*."

Maggie's pulse leaped as his gaze locked with hers. Too old for what? For him? She couldn't deny the undercurrents that kept running through their conversation, or the way he'd kissed the tip of her finger. The way she'd caught him staring at her lips. Perhaps flirtation came naturally to him. But she was very out of practice.

"I'm old enough to have a grown daughter to worry about."

Jen popped back in the door and headed straight for the coffeepot, oblivious to the tension in the room. As she poured, she gave her mother the update. "Three loads down, one more to go and my term paper is printing as we speak."

"Atta girl." It was a relief for Maggie to turn her attention to Jen and away from Nate's probing glances.

"Hmph." Jen grumbled as she stirred milk and two heaping teaspoons of sugar into her mug. "Break would have been more fun if I could have gone out instead of being cooped up here writing about the War of 1812."

"What exactly do you do for fun around here?" Nate took a sip of coffee.

Maggie looked at Jen. Maggie's idea of going out for fun wasn't quite the same as Jen's. Maggie preferred for Jen to hang out with girls her own age. Maybe go into Sundre to a movie or something. It was one thing about living in a very small community. Maggie remembered it well. Someone would make a liquor run and everyone would converge on an agreed spot. Most of the time it was harmless, but not always. As they both well knew.

"I, uh…" Jen actually faltered, looking at her mother.

Good, thought Maggie. Perhaps Jen was realizing now that what she'd done was serious. And that it definitely wouldn't seem funny to a cop.

"Um, you know, hang out with other kids and stuff. There's not much to do around here. No place to go other than the store."

"The store?"

Maggie answered the question. "The General Store. Unless you go into Sundre or Olds, it's the only place around to pick up what you need." Maggie looked at Jen, who was staring into her coffee cup. "I'm afraid kids tend to be at loose ends a lot of the time. It's good that Jen's going to school in Edmonton. There's more there for her to see and do."

Jen's head lifted in surprise and Maggie offered a warm smile. Sure, in her heart she also knew there was potential for Jen to get into much more trouble, and that worried her. But by the same token, there was more to catch Jen's interest and keep her busy. It was just hard not being there to make sure she was making good choices.

Maggie went to pour more coffee and realized the cream was empty.

"If you'll excuse me, I'll be right back."

Nate watched her leave, then casually leaned back on the couch, crossing an ankle over his knee again.

"I get the feeling you and your mom just had a whole conversation."

Jen looked up, her cheeks pink. "Well…yeah. Maybe. How'd you know?"

Nate chuckled softly, settling back into the cushions. "Ah. I, too, have a mother. One that saw far more than I ever thought she did."

"My mom sees everything."

Nate purposefully kept his pose relaxed, inviting.

It might be his only opportunity. "See now? It sounds like there's a bigger story in there somewhere. You get in some trouble, Jen?"

Her lips thinned and he recognized the stubborn rebellion in her eyes.

"You're a cop. If I did, it would be dumb to tell you, wouldn't it."

Nate nodded. When she got that obstinate jut to her chin, she looked remarkably like her mother. He couldn't help but smile at the thought. "I can see how you'd think that. But you know, I'm not here to bust you for anything. And sometimes an impartial ear comes in handy."

"Why don't you ask my mom?"

"Because I'm asking you. Because maybe I also became a cop to help people."

Again, Jen stared into her cup, avoiding looking him in the eye. "I got into some trouble with the RCMP last year."

"Doing?"

"I got caught with drugs." Her fingers turned her coffee cup around, avoiding him.

"Were you using?" Nate was careful to voice the question gently, without censure.

"No. I mean, I'd tried a joint or two, I guess. Like everyone else. I thought it was gross. I was just...I didn't sell it or anything."

"You weren't using and you weren't selling. Delivery?"

"Yeah, I guess you could say that." Her eyes slid up to his and he knew he'd been right to take it plain and simple. Her fingers stopped fiddling with the mug.

"You were a go-between. And you got caught with it."

She nodded. "Yes. I mean...I know it was wrong, but

it was only pot. My mom was so mad. I was…scared to say much of anything, but in the end she made it okay. She made it so I could come home. And then she sent me away to school. A change of scenery, she said."

But Nate knew that tone of voice. He could tell Jen resented being sent away. But his job wasn't to mend fences between Maggie and Jennifer. He held his breath, listening for any evidence that Maggie was coming back. If only she would stay away another five minutes, he might have what he needed. An ID.

"Jen, who were you doing it for? A boyfriend? Did someone threaten you?"

She shook her head so hard he knew whatever came next would only be a partial truth, if that.

"No. No. Pete was never my boyfriend. He's…he's just the go-to guy, you know? On a Saturday when you can't make it into Sundre to the liquor store, or whatever, you go see Pete, and he sets you up."

Nate gritted his teeth. Small potatoes crime, the kind everyone hated but mostly turned a blind eye to as if it would never affect them. "Booze and recreational drugs?" He forced his voice to remain calm and inviting. Damn. Pete seemed to have changed professions, just like Grant had said. There was no doubt in his mind that the local residents probably considered him the community miscreant, but had no idea of his real past.

If he was indeed the man he'd been sent here to find. More than ever now he had to be sure.

"It started out as something fun, something *exciting,* you know? But then it all changed and I wasn't sure how to get out. And I was scared to talk to Mom. I knew she'd blow her top about it. In one way…" She blushed. "I guess in a way I'm glad I got caught. Because then it was over and done with. I just hate that I disappointed her."

Suddenly Jen's face changed, no longer embarrassed but fearful. "You're not going to say anything, are you? I mean…gosh, I probably said too much…we just sort of got to a place where we're okay, you know? Not fighting about it all the time."

Nate felt guilt spiral through him. He'd actually inspired her trust and now he was indeed going to use what she'd told him. The only thing that made it okay was knowing that in the big picture he was doing the right thing. He had no desire to hurt Jen, or Maggie. On the contrary.

"It's okay, Jen. I wouldn't use what you told me against you."

"You're sure?"

"I'm sure. Like I said, my job is also to help people." *Helping people by getting rid of scum,* he reminded himself. *Helping people by getting the information right.*

"Yeah, and besides, you're from the States. So there's no jurisdiction, right?"

He swallowed. It didn't matter how long he did this, some things simply didn't sit right even when they were necessary. He reminded himself of the bigger purpose and lied. "Yeah, that's right."

"My mom…she was mad, but I think she was more upset that maybe I was in big trouble. I…I don't want to hurt my mom again."

Nate smiled. Jen was a good kid, no matter how much trouble she'd gotten into. He hoped Maggie knew it. It spoke well of her that she was worried about her mom's feelings. But his concern was Pete.

"How old is this Pete? I mean, does he usually use young girls to move his stuff?"

"I dunno. Old. Like in his forties, I guess. He just moved here a few years ago. He, you know. Tries to keep it on the low. He's not really hurting anybody. It's just parties and stuff."

Nate hid another smile at Jen's perspective of "old." At eighteen, he supposed it seemed that way. Yet Maggie fell into that bracket and he wouldn't consider her old at all. He remembered the sound of her breath catching in her throat when he'd kissed the tip of her finger. No, there was nothing old about Maggie.

He heard a door shut down the hall and he realized whatever information he'd received was all he'd get. But it was enough.

"Hey, Jen, you want some friendly advice?"

"I guess."

"Make sure you always learn from your mistakes. I can tell that the experience isn't something you'd care to repeat. Take your lessons learned with you."

Take your own advice, buddy, a voice inside him said.

"You're not going to tell my mom? That I told you?"

"Not unless she asks. And you know, she might be really glad to know what you just said. About not wanting to hurt her. Might be a good way to mend some fences."

"I'll think about it."

When Maggie came back in, she put down the cream and ruffled Jen's hair. "I put your last load in the dryer for you. And hung up your sweater."

"Thanks."

Nate tasted cold coffee and suddenly knew what had been plaguing him for the last few weeks. He was homesick. He was missing someone being there for him when he got in trouble, the way Maggie was there for Jennifer. Someone who cared enough to do the little things, for no reason at all. And despite how complicated the trip was rapidly becoming, he was glad he'd somehow ended up at Mountain Haven.

Maggie breathed on her fingers, fumbled with the key and finally got it shoved in the lock.

It turned hard, stiff from the cold and lack of use, but finally the padlock sprung apart and she opened the shed door with a flourish.

"Enter, if you dare."

She aimed a bright smile up at Nate. He'd been quiet last night after she'd come back in the room, and had excused himself soon after. But this morning he was back to what she assumed was his friendly self. Now he was with her, ready to dig out Tom's things and see if they were fit for use.

He smiled back, his even teeth flashing white in the frosty air. "I think I mentioned that I was also a marine. I'm not afraid of an itty-bitty shed."

"Not even of spiders?"

He laughed. "It's minus a million out here. If they can get through this parka, they deserve a meal."

He ducked into the shed while Maggie waited just outside the door. His sense of humor was a surprise, but it wasn't unwelcome.

"You find anything?" Her breath came out in puffy clouds as she called in after him.

"Yeah. Hang on." A few things rattled and banged as he rearranged articles, pulling things free. Maggie caught a glimpse of his backside as he bent to pick something up from the floor. She stepped away from the door. He was becoming far too alluring and she had to keep her head.

"Incoming!"

She sidestepped quickly as a pair of snowshoes came flying out. When he emerged, cobwebs clung to his coat and hat. She resisted the temptation to reach up and brush them away. Touching him would be a big no-no. She was at least self-aware enough to understand that much.

He proudly held a pair of cross-country skis in one hand and the poles in the other.

"Did you find the boots?"

"Hang on." He pitched the skis in the snow and went back inside, returning with a dusty pair of black boots with square toes. "Size eleven and a half. Should fit all right, even if I double my socks."

"You're crazy to want to go out in this cold." He wouldn't know where he was going and she knew she'd worry in this weather. "With the windchill it's nearly minus thirty."

"Bracing, wouldn't you say?"

"More like frostbite."

"Yes, but then I'll be out of your hair."

Maggie's lips twitched. "Guests at Mountain Haven Bed-and-Breakfast are *never* in the proprietress's hair."

"You say that now, but I'm god-awful when I'm bored. Disposition of a gator."

Maggie laughed and folded her mittened hands as he tried sliding his feet into the snowshoe harnesses. Despite her words, it would be easier for her if he weren't around 24/7. No matter what *should* be, the two of them alone in the house held a certain degree of intimacy. Intimacy she didn't want or understand. It had never happened with a guest before, but she could feel it stirring between them already. Amicability. The feeling that perhaps they were similar sorts of people. And yes, a level of physical attraction that couldn't be ignored.

"I can't seem to get this on right."

Maggie watched him struggle for a minute, then went

to him and knelt in the snow, showing him how to fit his boots into the harness and buckle up the ends.

As she knelt, he bent to see what she was doing and Maggie felt the heat from his body blocking the wind. He was too close. She fumbled with the straps, so took off her mittens to buckle them with her bare hands. Touching him in any way was a mistake. Each time they were together the ridiculous urges grew. He was big and strong and she'd already seen glimpses of compassion and humor. How was she supposed to stay immune to that?

"Try that." She went to get up, and immediately felt the pressure of his hand at her elbow, helping her.

She stepped away.

He took a few steps, gained confidence, picked up the pace, and promptly fell.

Maggie giggled into the wool of her mittens, she couldn't help it. One side of his body, from jeans to the side of his toque, was covered in snow.

"You need some help, tough guy?"

"Not from a scrawny thing like you." He planted his hands and hopped up. "Go ahead and laugh. I bet you couldn't do it."

Maggie's snickers died away as he tried again, the gait awkward but steady. He didn't look back so couldn't see the look on her face, see how his casually tossed out words hurt her.

But the truth was she could do it. She used to snowshoe a lot. First she'd taught Mike when he'd lived with her in Sundre. Then she'd met Tom and she'd gotten pregnant, and they'd married and moved here. That first winter they'd gone on long jaunts with Mike and Jen in a baby backpack.

She turned away, closing the shed door and putting the lock back on it. She hadn't realized what she'd had, and had squandered so much time asking what if. By the time the truth hit her, Tom was gone and she was left alone again. Only this time with the responsibility of a teenage foster child and a baby.

Nate jogged back to her, leaving gigantic bird-shaped tracks behind him in the snow. "Thanks for this. It's going to be fun wandering around."

"You're welcome. You can leave the skis and stuff on the porch, and bring the boots inside."

"Maggie?"

She looked up at him. His green-blue eyes pierced her. "Are you sure you're okay with me using these? You're quiet all of a sudden. I don't want to intrude, really."

"It's not that. They're not doing anyone any good locked up in there. Don't worry about it." She tried to muster a cheerful smile. "I'm going to make a light lunch before I have to take Jen to the bus station."

"You're going to miss her." His voice was quiet in the winter stillness.

"Yeah. I am. Even though we fight like cats and dogs. Still…I think she's better off where she is."

She knew Jen was. The last thing she needed was being back home all the time. She'd get bored and want to go out with friends, and get mixed up with the wrong people again. Maggie had been able to bail her out last time. That wouldn't work again. As lonely as it was without her, she knew she'd made the right decision, getting her into a school there.

"Anyway, she's got to go back so I'm going to do the proper mother thing and ply her with food and a care package." She tried a smile but it fell completely flat.

Nate bent to take off the snowshoes. "You might not think she appreciates it now, but she does. And once she's grown up she might even tell you about it."

Maggie had her doubts. "Are you close with your parents?"

She grabbed the skis and poles while Nate carried the snowshoes and boots and they walked slowly to the house.

"Yes, I am. I have a brother and a sister who chose nice, safe professions, and me, who picked the military and then law enforcement. I know my mom worries. But you know, even when I was overseas, she still sent care packages. The one thing about living in Florida and having them up north is not seeing them as often as I'd like."

"It sounds as though you had a perfect childhood."

"I suppose, although I'd probably just call it normal."

Maggie swallowed. Nate would never understand *her* life. He'd had brothers and sisters and two parents and he still had them. This whole family system in place, even if they were miles apart. The only family she had now was Mike and Jen.

"What about you, Maggie? Where are your parents?"

Maggie climbed the steps to the veranda and leaned the skis against the wall. She put her hand on the doorknob but paused, knowing he was behind her waiting for an answer.

"In a plot next to my husband," she replied tonelessly, before turning the knob and going inside.

Chapter 4

The restaurant was nearly empty, and when Maggie walked in she was surprised to see Nate sitting at a table with Grant Simms. She caught her breath and held it for a moment. Grant wasn't a bad sort, he just *knew* things. Things she would rather Nate not find out.

She wondered briefly why they were together, but then realized it was natural that enforcement types would gravitate to each other. Nate had probably seen Grant come in and looked for some company. Lord knew she wasn't the best conversationalist today.

Nate turned toward the door as she came in and his eyes lit, the intimate look warming her. She smiled back despite her misgivings. There was a magnetism—a pull—that she would never admit aloud but couldn't deny to herself. A feeling so unexpected, unfamiliar in its long absence. She couldn't bring herself to feel sorry about the attraction rising up now. It provided a welcome distraction. The alternative was going home to an empty, quiet house. A reminder of how lonely she was when Jen was gone. A taste of how it would be when Jen moved on with her own life and Maggie would be left alone.

She pulled off her gloves and approached the table. "Jen get off okay?"

"Yes, the bus is gone." His words brought her firmly out of the moment and back to the very real present. She nearly choked on her reply, swallowed against the sudden tightening in her throat as she said the word "gone." Saying goodbye had been emotional to put it lightly. She hated watching Jen go away, hated the helpless feeling that flooded her every time she left. Hated the fear that somehow this could be the last time. In her head she knew it was irrational, but her heart didn't quite get it. Knowing Jen was out of her sight frightened her more than she'd ever admit.

But she said nothing, because Nate didn't need to know, and besides, he wasn't alone. Her eyes skittered to his companion.

His gaze followed hers and he performed introductions. "Maggie, this is Grant Simms."

"Constable Simms." She held out her hand, surprised when the man rose politely and took it.

"Nice to see you, Maggie. Nate tells me you're treating him well."

"Well, as the only guest, I don't have to play favorites, it's true."

"You know each other." Nate looked from one to the other.

"It's a small town, Nate." Grant laughed lightly, but it sounded false to Maggie.

Maggie forced the smile to remain on her lips. In another time she might have liked Grant. He was in his mid-forties, handsome in a crisp, efficient sort of way. But last summer when they'd met it had been in less pleasant circumstances that she'd rather forget. She commented out of politeness only.

"And now you two have met."

"Grant and I attended a conference in Toronto together a few years ago," Nate explained. "We've been catching up."

The two men exchanged a look. Maggie narrowed her eyes. They knew each other before today, then. It was just a crazy coincidence that they'd met up here. How much had Grant told him about her, about Jen? What would Nate think?

Grant Simms was part of the reason why Maggie had been so persistent in Jen going away to school. She knew she should feel gratitude. Things could have been so much worse. But today of all days, it was a bitter reminder of how much she missed the girl she'd known; how far apart she and Jen had grown that it had come to this. Regrets.

A waitress appeared, bearing a coffeepot. "Sit down, Maggie," Nate invited. "Have a coffee."

She didn't see a way to properly refuse, besides, she was suddenly feeling quite raw. She took the chair Nate held out, sat gratefully.

"Cream?"

He held out the saucer containing tiny plastic cups of creamer. She took two, biting her lip as her fingers began to tremble.

The waitress filled her mug while she struggled with the tab on the creamer. It finally peeled back, but by this time her hands were shaking so badly she jostled the cup as she went to pour, sloshing coffee over the edge and on to the table, staining the cloth.

"Oh, how clumsy of me!" She blinked furiously, out of humiliation and sheer emotionalism. Why couldn't this get any easier? It should get better each time. Instead it was always the same. She functioned through goodbye and then fell spectacularly apart later. Why couldn't she have made it another hour so she could do it in private, instead of in front of the two men she'd least want to witness it?

"It's okay, Maggie. I've got it." Nate dabbed at the spilled coffee, making her feel even more foolish.

She tried to catch her breath. It would be fine. Jen's bus would drive into Edmonton and she'd go back to campus and her dorm room and in two months she'd be home for summer break. They'd get back to how things were. They could do it, she knew it in her heart. She'd seen glimpses of it today. Her fears were groundless.

Only they weren't. Silly, perhaps, but not groundless. Life could change on a dime.

"Are you okay?"

Nate's voice murmured into her ear, low enough that no one could hear. His warm breath tickled the hair behind her earlobe and she focused on inhaling and exhaling. When she opened her eyes, Grant had gone to see the waitress about a towel and fresh coffee.

Maggie looked at Simms's retreating back and then up into Nate's concerned eyes. She wished he didn't see so much, it made her feel naked. "I'm fine. I just want to go home, if that's all right with you."

Nate dug in his wallet and dropped a bill on the table as Grant came back with a tea towel in his hand. "Grant, I think we're going to be off. It was nice to see you again." He held out his hand and the other officer shook it.

"Give me a call while you're around, Nate. We should shoot some pool or something."

"Will do. See you later."

"Nice to see you, Maggie."

He was friendly looking and polite but there was something in the other man's eyes she didn't quite trust. He knew. Had he shared that information with Nate after all?

Her response came out frosty. "You, too." She could feel Nate's hand, warm and reassuring against her back. She tipped her lips up in a perfunctory smile.

"Let's go then."

They were almost to the truck when Nate's rough voice stopped her progress. "Hey, Maggie? Why don't you let me drive back?"

She stopped and turned. He'd pulled his collar up in an attempt to keep some warmth close to his ears, but they turned pink in the frigid air. She wished again that she didn't find him so attractive, especially now when she knew she was raw and vulnerable. His clipped hair, straight bearing and sheer size didn't intimidate her, not at all. She was drawn to it. It was the oddest thing. She'd never gone for the clean-cut, military type before. There was something about them she didn't trust. Whether it was because of past history or simply knowing how dangerous their lives were, Maggie had never gravitated toward that type of man.

But with Nate, even after a few short hours, there was a constant curiosity that took her by surprise. Knowing there was much more to him than met the eye and wondering what it could be; wanting to dig below the surface to find out what mattered to Nate Griffith.

"You want to drive my old beater? Why?"

He laughed, the masculine sound turning her knees to jelly. He had a strong, rich laugh, one that rippled. "I'd hardly call it a beater. But…sorry, it's a guy thing. I feel kind of weird having you chauffeur me around."

"It's okay. Consider it part of the vacation treatment." It was tempting to let him drive. Her hands were still shaking and she was thankful he'd gotten her out of the restaurant so quickly. But over the years she'd handled everything thrown her way on her own. Knew she could. It was the one thing she was sure of. The last thing she needed was to let him see how fragile she was. "I can drive."

He stopped her at the driver's side door. "Please, Maggie. You were trembling in there." His hands turned her gently so she was facing him, blocked from the wind by his massive body. "Saying goodbye to Jennifer didn't go well, did it?"

He was hard to resist when he looked down at her with obvious concern. When was the last time anyone had been concerned about her? The relief of it was almost enough to make her want to sag against his body and let him carry a little of the burden. But that was ridiculous. He was a virtual stranger.

"It never does. It's just a parent's worry."

"Worry to the point of shaking, and turning white as a sheet?"

She swallowed. She hadn't realized it was that obvious. Somehow saying goodbye set off a reaction every time, but she hadn't realized it showed so very much. She got the feeling he'd keep up the inquisition, and she tried a plain answer, hoping it would stop him from prying more.

"I've lost a lot of people in my life, Nate. Sometimes it hits even though it's been a long time. Saying goodbye…" She took a big breath. Met his eyes and said it all at once. "Saying goodbye triggers a lot of those old feelings of panic. It'll pass. It always does."

"Then you worry about decompressing and I'll worry about the road. This once." He held out his hand, unsmiling, simply waiting.

She took the keys from her pocket and placed them

into his hand. He was steady, she already got that. His warm fingers closed over hers.

"Maggie, she'll be fine. She's a good kid."

Grant must have kept quiet then. Nate wouldn't have said such a thing if he knew about her arrest last year. A tiny sliver of relief threaded through her.

They got in the truck and he started the ignition. Maggie reached over and cranked up the heater, trying to halt the chills that wouldn't seem to stop shaking her body.

"You want to talk about it, Maggie?" He pulled out of the parking lot, watching her from the corner of his eye.

Her smile wavered a little. Did she? Perhaps. Maybe it would be nice to talk to someone who didn't know everything, who didn't look at her like *that widow that never remarried.* Too many people here knew her past. But she'd kept it all inside for so long she wasn't comfortable delving too deeply.

"I'm fine. It's just…" Her eyes held his as he waited before putting the truck in gear. "I can't protect her when she's away. But she's eighteen. It's right for her to be where she is."

"All moms worry. It's part of the job description." Nate smiled again and she felt it spread over her. He turned on to the highway, leaning back in the seat and resting a hand comfortably on the steering wheel. "But I get the feeling there's more to it than that."

Maggie stared out the window. Her relationship with Jen was so complicated. It had been easier when Jennifer had been small, and life had been simple. But Jen had grown up, wanted her independence. Didn't understand Maggie's need to keep her sheltered and fought her every step of the way. Without Nate understanding that, she didn't think he could understand how much a simple hug of farewell and "I love you" meant. She didn't have anyone to talk to about it and appreciated the impartial ear.

"Jen and I don't often see eye to eye. But today... today was different."

"How so?"

"I didn't get the level of hostility I normally do. We talked about summer vacation. It was...nice. But it felt..."

The sense of panic settled in her gut again and she pursed her lips.

"It felt?"

She was glad his eyes were on the road so he didn't see the tears flickering on her lashes. "It felt like good-bye. Like making peace. And it scared the hell out of me."

She sighed when he didn't answer. "I know. It's a fatalistic approach and it sucks."

He laughed. "Well, you're very self-aware."

Tension drained out of her at the sound of his chuckle. Telling him had been good. She'd stopped confiding in her friends long ago. The last thing she wanted to do was bore them to tears about the fears that never quite went away. She'd picked up her life and made something of it. She had a successful business, was a mother. It didn't make sense to most of them that she still had issues. Besides, she wanted people to forget about Jen's troubles, and talking about it wouldn't help at all. But Nate was safe. In the overall scheme of things, it would be forgotten soon enough, when he was gone.

"I'm hungry. Let's stop at the store."

"The store?"

"Up here." She pointed to the turnoff. "I'll pick up something special for dinner."

"You got it." He followed her directions, pulling into a parking space and killing the engine.

Nate hopped out of the cab and trotted over to her side before she could blink. He opened her door and she slid out, self-conscious at his solicitude.

They stood there for long seconds. Nate's heart thudded erratically at the continued closeness, the same feeling he'd had this morning when she'd kneeled to strap on the snowshoes. She'd trusted him today, and lately trust had been in short supply. The more he talked with her the more he realized it couldn't have been easy. Not for a self-sufficient woman like her. As the pieces started to come together, he could understand how putting her kid on a bus today was a big event.

"Nate, I..." She paused, looking up at him. Her eyes were blue, the color of the Atlantic on a clear day, and her lips were parted as she paused, seeming to search for words. For a fleeting second he thought about putting his lips against hers just to see what would happen. If the need he felt stirring for her was real or imagined. If the warmth of her mouth would take away some of his own misgivings, as well as appease some of her own.

But that would hardly be fair, so he waited for her to finish what she was saying.

The silence drew out, until he prompted her with "You..."

She blinked slowly. He wasn't imagining it, then. There *was* some sort of a connection between them. It hadn't just been the candlelight at dinner last night.

She cleared her throat. "I was just going to ask if you'd like to rent a movie after. There's a video store in Sundre. It's not far."

If he were home he'd work out or read, or flip through TV channels much as he had last night. It was different now. They would need something to fill the time. To keep him from thinking about how pretty she looked or how she kept him from feeling lonely. They would be alone together. It would be getting dark, there would be dinner with just the two of them and a long evening stretching before them. They'd only be fooling themselves now, insisting it was a hostess-guest relationship. Something more had been forged between them today. A movie would be just the thing to quell the silly urge to spend the evening with her in his arms.

"That might be nice."

She let out a breath, the air forming a cloud above her head. She had to move soon or he'd reconsider kissing her. Which would be a huge mistake, especially in front of the only store in the community with everyone watching. Even he understood about gossip in small towns. More than she realized. He'd pretended to be surprised she knew Grant, but he wasn't, not at all. He knew all about their past association. How could he, in all conscience, kiss a woman he'd lied to less than an hour before?

"Maggie?"

"Yes?" She shoved her hands into her pockets.

"What's for dinner?"

She smiled at him then and he suddenly realized he'd been waiting for it. Maggie smiling sucked all the bitterness out of the cold air and replaced it with something else. He felt better than he had in a long time, and rather than analyze it to death, shoulds or shouldn'ts, he simply enjoyed it.

"Come inside and we'll find out," she suggested impishly, darting for the door, her dark hair streaming out behind her in the wind.

Movie be damned. Nate was starting to realize it would take more than a DVD to keep him from thinking about Maggie Taylor.

Nate followed her into the store, more intrigued than

he remembered being in a long time. He'd sensed a lot of things about Maggie since arriving, but a sense of fun wasn't one of them. Especially this afternoon when she'd nearly come undone in front of Grant. Yet watching her eyes twinkle at him as she flicked her hair out of her face, he realized there was more to Maggie than met the eye. Much more. He was beginning to regret not kissing her when he'd had the chance.

"Hey, Nate, you helping here or what?"

He straightened, pinning a smile on his face. "Helping with what?"

"Dinner. You pick it, I cook it."

She was standing at the meat counter. He went up beside her and noticed she was quite serious about choosing choice cuts. "Steak?"

"Yeah." The corners of her lips flickered in teasing. "You caveman. Like red meat, yah?"

He couldn't stop the snort, surprising both of them. "Yah, red meat good."

"T-bones or rib eyes?"

The very thought had his mouth watering. He was used to cooking for himself, pointless as it seemed. It had been a long time since any woman had taken care making him a meal. To be given the choice…

"Rib eyes. And mushrooms."

She ordered the steaks, adding in a good-size portion of stewing beef for another meal.

"Any other requests?"

She turned with the paper packages in her hands and he swallowed. She was making an effort, he realized. To dispel the gloom from the start of the afternoon and replace it with something bright and shiny.

"I trust your culinary judgment completely. Surprise me."

She started down another aisle, but turned her head at the last moment. "I just might, Nate. I just might."

He had no doubt about it.

Chapter 5

It seemed changed somehow.

The house actually felt different with Jen gone. Her presence had been a barrier between Maggie and Nate in one way, and brought them together in another. Now, with just the two of them at Mountain Haven, the opposite was true. Her absence was forcing them together physically, but propriety reared its head again and Maggie tried to keep things how they were supposed to be. She'd said enough this afternoon, when Nate had invited her confidence. It really wouldn't be wise to smudge the lines any further. No matter how empty the house felt with Jen gone. No matter how tempting Nate's company could be.

She opened the oven and pulled out the cookie sheet, placing it on the stove and turning the roasted potatoes so they'd brown evenly. She was a hostess cooking dinner for a paying guest. That was all.

Then why, oh why, did it feel like a date, for heaven's sake?

She paused, the spatula frozen midturn. *Because after only two days she'd allowed him in.* She'd broken her own personal rule about becoming friends with guests and had told him personal things that had been incredibly painful to verbalize. It had felt good to talk, and she'd needed it, but Maggie knew it couldn't happen again. She couldn't let herself become vulnerable to him. To anyone.

She slid the pan back in the oven and turned her attention to the Caesar salad. Cooking soothed her, warmed her soul. It was more than nourishment, always had been. She'd learned to cook at her mother's elbow at a young age, and when she'd been orphaned, it had been the one task that gave her any sense of comfort, of connection. It still did.

Nate came to the door and she wondered, in a moment of sheer fantasy, what it would be like if he came up behind her and slid his arms around her waist. To feel the comfort tangibly from his touch, more than the pressure of his hand on hers as he took her keys, like this afternoon. He looked like he'd perhaps taken advantage of the time to have a nap. His cotton shirt was wrinkled and his hair was slightly mussed. There was definitely something to be said for the rumpled look, she thought as her mouth went dry.

"Smells good."

She reached into a jug, pulling out her favorite salad utensils, using dinner preparations as a refuge. Talking out of turn while she was raw and upset was one thing, but she'd had time to pull herself together. It was up to her to set the tone where it ought to be.

"Thanks. I thought we'd eat in the dining room tonight." She held out the salad bowl. "The steaks are almost done, but if you could take this in, I'll be there in a minute."

When she entered the dining room, she was struck yet again by the sense of intimacy. It was the custom for her guests to eat here, but she'd never experienced a feeling of "specialness" to the room before. Now, with Nate present, it looked—felt—changed somehow. Richer, darker, smaller.

It would have been an out-and-out lie to think that the extra effort she put into the meal was completely platonic. She'd wanted to impress him, to do something special. Perhaps because of how nice he'd been to Jen, or because he'd put up with her episode this afternoon and had listened to her troubles. Perhaps because she was tired of being lonely, of going through the motions, and he was a willing ear.

She put down the tray and unloaded the serving bowls. Nate stood at the corner of the table, pouring the merlot she'd uncorked.

"Thank you." She took the glass from his hand when he held it out.

"No, thank you," he murmured. A candle hissed and sputtered before finding its flame once more. "You've outdone yourself, I can tell."

"Nonsense."

He waited until she was seated before taking his own, and she glowed inwardly at the presence of manners.

"This looks wonderful, Maggie." She handed him the platter, steaks surrounded by herbed and browned potatoes, and he helped himself.

"All in the line of duty." She brushed it off with a glib comment.

His hand paused, then put down the platter. He seemed to think for a moment, his lips pursing in a thin line. "I get the feeling you've been doing things in the line of duty for a really long time. Especially after what you told me this afternoon."

She looked away. Was she that transparent? She'd told him little about her life in the greater scheme of things. Just the basic facts. But what he said was true. She'd shut away so much of life, had focused on what she did and bringing up Jen. It was easier than letting her heart get involved again.

"I enjoy what I do." She put him off. Talking about the bed-and-breakfast was a nice, safe topic.

"When was the last time you did something purely selfish? Just for yourself?"

She couldn't remember, and she was disconcerted that he'd been able to read between the lines so easily.

She made her hands busy by filling his salad bowl. "I love my job, you know. I couldn't do it otherwise. It makes me happy."

"I don't mean your job."

He put his hand over hers, stopping her from fiddling with the salad. "Maggie."

She stalled, caught by the simple touch.

"Whether or not it's your job…thank you. For making me feel at home here."

Maggie looked up. His eyes were completely earnest, caught somewhere between that blue and hazely-green color.

"You're welcome."

His gaze held her captive in the flickering candle-light as he held her hand. "And for trusting me this afternoon. I'd like to think—maybe—that we're becoming friends."

She pulled back. "I don't usually befriend my guests, Nate."

He thought for a moment, then a smile brightened

his face, as if he knew that was exactly what she was supposed to say. "Yes, well, I'm special."

She couldn't help the quiver of her lips at his teasing. How was she to answer that? She got the feeling that he was, indeed, special. Different. But to say so wasn't wise.

"Don't let it go to your head. And thank you. For being so kind today. I'm sorry I was all over the map. I don't usually fall apart in front of my patrons."

"You're welcome." He pulled back, buttered his bread and broke it into crusty pieces as they enjoyed the meal she'd prepared.

"So, anything else I should know about Maggie Taylor?"

She'd hoped that thanking him would put an end to the personal talk, but that wish fluttered away. She wondered if it was the cop in him, the need to ask so many questions. She focused on spearing a lettuce leaf. "I told you anything that's interesting. I'm really very boring."

He laughed, cutting into his steak. "Yeah, right, Maggie. The last word I'd use to describe you is dull."

She picked up her wine and drank to hide her face. Was he serious? Dull is exactly how she'd put it. She'd had the same life for the last decade and a half. Running this business and raising a daughter. Watching middle age creep up on her. Nothing exciting in that.

"What do you want to know, then? How much starch I put in my pillowcases? Do I grow my own herbs?" She tried to make a joke of it.

"Sure, if that's what's important to you."

A smile teased her lips before she straightened once more, the picture of propriety. "I sprinkle, not starch and I grow some of my own herbs, but not all."

"Did that hurt?"

"No, I guess it didn't."

They ate in silence for a few more minutes and then Nate spoke again. "I'm more interested in how you became the person you are now. How you grew up and what made you choose this as your livelihood."

The crisp romaine leaves wilted in her mouth. She swallowed. Damn him. "The life story of Maggie Taylor? Only if you're having trouble sleeping."

"Why do you do that?" Nate pushed away his plate and cradled his goblet. "Why do you diminish who you are, what you do? I wouldn't have asked, Maggie, if I didn't think it was worth knowing."

She flushed. She had no wish to unearth the pain and disappointment she tried to keep buried every day. Or go into the sad and lonely reasons why she'd chosen to open a bed-and-breakfast. What she'd revealed earlier was all he was getting today. It was time to put a stop to this line of questioning right now, because she was beginning to feel like this was an interrogation, not a heart-to-heart. Like he wanted her to tell him things she shouldn't. She stood, piling his plate on top of hers. "Do you want dessert? There's pumpkin cake with caramel sauce."

His eyes assessed her; she could feel them burning into her as she cleared the dishes.

"I'm sorry, I'm prying. It's unfair of me."

"Yes, it is. I appreciate your listening to me this afternoon when I was upset. But the details of my life are personal. And I know you will respect that."

"I like you, Maggie. I was simply curious."

She couldn't seem to come up with a response. He stood and gathered what was left of the dirty dishes and followed her into the kitchen, putting them on the empty counter.

"Maggie?"

"What." She put down the dishes and turned to face

him. She couldn't do this. Being stuck with someone every hour of the day was, for some reason, very difficult. Most who came to Mountain Haven were interested in the area, in *their* lives—not hers. Trouble was, she wanted to tell him. To unload all the pain she'd held inside for so many years. She didn't understand it. Couldn't fathom *why* he was different. She'd never felt such a compulsion before.

He didn't say anything. He stood not five feet in front of her, but nothing came out of his mouth. She saw the muscles bunch beneath his shirt and she wondered what it would be like to run her fingers over the skin of his arms, of his broad shoulders.

"What," she whispered again, shocked when she heard her voice come out warm and husky, like the caramel sauce she'd made for the cake.

Without warning, he took two steps forward, curled his hand around her head and kissed her.

His lips were warm and tasted faintly of the acidic richness of the merlot. Taken by surprise, and on the heels of her own thoughts, she didn't push away. Her lashes fluttered down as his arm came around her, tucking her close to his hard body as his lips opened wider, taking the kiss deeper.

And oh, he felt marvelous. Strong and patient and thorough. Her heart pounded, sending the blood rushing through her veins, awakening her. He was vibrant and young and mysterious and so very, very real. Her hands slid over his shoulder blades, down, down, until they encountered the back pockets of his jeans.

He broke the kiss off in stages: gentle, fluttering tiny kisses on the corners of her mouth, making her weak in the knees and wanting more, not less. She chased him with her lips, and he caught her bottom one in his teeth before letting go and putting a few inches between them.

She looked up, frightened by the intensity of his gaze, more frightened that perhaps her own mirrored it so blatantly. It was a shock to realize that she wanted him. Wanted a man she hardly knew. Wanted him in the most basic way a woman could want a man.

Right now she'd crawl into his skin if he'd let her.

She pushed away blindly, stopping only when her backside hit the counter. Her breaths were shallow, ripe with arousal. All from a single kiss, a few fleeting moments where their bodies touched.

"I've wanted to do that all day."

And the words, huskily spoken in the muted light, sent a rush of desire flooding through her.

Shame reddened her cheeks. This was wrong. He was patiently waiting for her reaction and all she could do was feel embarrassed that he'd affected her so strongly. She'd pushed away her sexual being for so long she'd all but forgotten it existed. Had settled for a dim appreciation of a man's looks on occasion. But she'd never, not since Tom, behaved in such a wanton way.

"I...you...pumpkin cake," she stammered and wanted to slide through the floor into oblivion. Any pretense of dignity was gone.

"Not right now."

"C...c...coffee?"

"Maggie. Should I apologize?" His words were soft, with that hint of gravel rumbling through, and her pulse leaped at the intimacy of it. "I don't want to."

I don't want you to, either. She raised her chin as best she could. She had to put some distance between them somehow. "It would be appropriate."

Who was she kidding? It wasn't like she hadn't participated willingly. He might have initiated it but she'd been right there, keeping up.

"I'm sorry." His voice was husky-soft in the dim light filtering in from the dining room. "I'm sorry you're so damn pretty I had to kiss you."

Holy hell.

She couldn't do this. Couldn't. "Yes, well, I've known you two days. You're a guest in my house. A paying guest. Perhaps you should remember that."

It might have worked if her voice hadn't trembled at the end. She gathered what little bit of pride she had left around her and swept from the room.

He wasn't the only one that needed reminding.

Sunlight filtered through the window of the bedroom as Nate stirred. He squinted against the bright light, checking his watch. Eight-fifteen. He never slept this late.

He usually didn't lie awake until the wee hours thinking, either. But he had last night.

He rose, pulling on the clothes he'd laid out. Thermals beneath heavy gray-toned camouflaged pants. Thick socks and a long-sleeved undershirt under a crew necked cotton pullover. He'd layer today and adjust. Took the backpack out of the bottom of the closet, left in it what he'd need and stowed the rest in the bottom of his duffel.

A day out of the house was definitely in order.

He'd been foolish to kiss Maggie last night. Problem was, he'd been thinking of it all afternoon and through dinner. He enjoyed seeing her flustered, enjoyed the moments of banter between them. But then, seeing her vulnerable, knowing how difficult she found it watching her daughter leave, brought out his protective side.

It was something he'd inherited. He couldn't do what he did without it.

He put the pack on the bed, seeing her sad eyes in his mind. It wasn't all about justice. Most people thought so, and for some it was true. But not for him.

Sometimes it wasn't about punishing the guilty, but protecting the innocent.

He padded down the stairs in his stocking feet and wandered into the kitchen. It was quiet; not a dish or crumb in sight. The appliances gleamed and floor shone. He smiled to himself. He was beginning to recognize her penchant for order, especially when she was preoccupied. Had his kiss done that? Or had it simply been because of Jen?

He frowned as his early morning thoughts trickled back. Had she put all that extra effort into the meal, had she kissed him back, simply as a substitute? To keep herself from thinking about her daughter's absence? Had he been a distraction?

And wouldn't that be a good thing? A harmless flirtation was far more desirable than something complicated. Yet…the thought of him being a stand in chafed, good idea or not.

Nate wondered if Maggie had had the same trouble sleeping and was making up for it now. Quietly he filled the coffeemaker and started the brew filtering. There was no sense dwelling on it. A more important question was whether or not she had a thermos on hand for him to take with him today.

The side door opened and Maggie appeared, completely dressed, pulling her hair back into a sensible ponytail.

When she looked up at him, his heart gave a solid thump. Where had that come from? It was difficult enough being here under the present circumstances.

Attraction, kissing…they weren't on the agenda. He couldn't afford to be distracted. And she certainly wouldn't understand if she found out the truth. He offered his best, polite-only smile.

"Good morning."

"Good morning," he answered back. Silence fell, awkward. So the kiss wasn't forgotten, nor forgiven. The smile faded from his face. "I started the coffee. I hope that's all right."

"I'm sorry I wasn't up to see to it."

Great. Now they were speaking—and standing— like wooden statues.

"Maggie, I *am* sorry about last night. I was out of line. Your business is yours. I had no right to pry."

He sensed her relief as the clouds cleared from her eyes. "Thank you, I appreciate that." She offered a small smile and he watched her go to the cupboard and dig out ingredients. Perhaps his greatest transgression hadn't been the kiss then, but the intimate questions.

"I like you, Nate. You're a nice guy." He winced. A nice guy? Hardly. Her words were hollow as she spoke from within the cabinet. "It's understandable that things…progressed, I suppose. But I'm not comfortable with it. It can't happen again."

"I know that."

She turned around, flour bin in hand, her smile a little easier. "I'm glad. And I hope you like pancakes."

She couldn't know. Couldn't possibly know how much he wanted to tell her everything. To tell her why he was really there, how it would help her, and Jen. But he couldn't. It was what it was. It was pancakes and pleasantries and half-truths.

"Pancakes are good." He thought of the day ahead. "With a couple of eggs would be even better."

"Eggs I can do. How do you like them?"

"However you fix them will be fine." He offered her the first truly genuine smile of the day. "I'm used to eating them in all forms, believe me."

She beat the batter in the bowl as the griddle heated. "I suppose you have, with your past history. What's your favorite?"

He grinned at her back. "Over easy."

"Then that's what you'll have. What are your plans for the rest of the day?"

The tension had dispelled with apologies and talks of breakfast. "The temperature's gone up a bit, so I thought I'd give those snowshoes a workout." He went to the counter and took the plates and cutlery she was laying out as the first pancakes sizzled on the pan. "I've been two days without physical activity. Add that with home cooking…"

He put the plates at the kitchen table, turning back as she put the pancakes on the warming tray and cracked eggs into a fry pan.

"There's syrup and juice in the fridge," she called out, pouring two more perfectly round circles on the greased griddle.

It was something he missed, more than he'd realized. Everyday chatter over meal preparations, having someone to sit with at the table. Now it only happened when he was home in Philadelphia for holidays, with his brother and sisters around. Mom cooked for everyone, and ribbing and teasing were the order of the day. He was surprised to find it so far away from his ordinary life.

When the eggs were done, she filled his plate. "Sit down, Nate, I'll bring you some coffee."

The pancakes were light and fluffy and he poured syrup—real maple syrup, not the table version—over the top. Two eggs, done to fragile perfection, sat alongside. He'd heard before that the way to a man's heart was through his stomach. As his own rumbled, he thought that just might be true.

"Hey, Maggie?"

"Hmmm?"

"You wouldn't happen to have a thermos, would you? I'd love to take some coffee along this morning."

"I've got one around here somewhere."

She took her place across from him. "How long are you planning on being out?"

"Most of the day, I think."

"Then you'll need a lunch."

"You don't have to…"

"Don't worry about it. It's all part of the 'extras' I quoted your boss."

The pancakes went dry in his mouth. Of course. The tentative friendship they'd forged was punctuated with reminders that he was a client. It was as she'd said all along. This was her job. She was being paid to see to his needs. Food and comfortable shelter.

"Thank you, then."

He sliced through his pancake. He'd asked for the coffee, but had planned on a few protein bars keeping him going throughout the day. If the USMS was footing the bill, there was no reason for him not to take the lunch. Maggie had reverted to her pleasant, professional self. It was like the emotions of yesterday hadn't happened. It was for the best.

He pushed out his chair. "Thanks for breakfast. I'll go upstairs and get my pack."

In his room he reconsidered his clothing and stripped off his cotton shirt, putting his bulletproof vest beneath it. He wasn't anticipating any trouble, but there was no harm in being cautious. Taking care, an ounce of prevention and all that. He checked his pack one last time and went back downstairs.

"Your lunch."

Maggie appeared in the foyer with an insulated pack and a silver thermos. "Sandwiches and fruit. And a slice of the cake you missed last night. I hope that's okay"

"It's perfect." He took them from her and tucked them carefully into his bag, withdrawing his GPS at the same time and tucking it in his parka.

"Are you sure you know where you're going?"

He nodded. "I have a map of the roads right here." He held up the unit. "As long as I stay within the grid, there's no way I'll get lost."

"I'll see you at dinner then."

He pulled his toque over his ears. "Yes, ma'am."

Outside, he squinted in the sunlight and put on his sunglasses. He strapped on the snowshoes bare-handed and pulled on his gloves. It was cold, but not the frigid bitterness of yesterday.

He started off over the lawn, his gait gaining rhythm as he caught his stride. According to his information, a little over two miles southwest from here he could set up, dig in and enjoy more of her coffee as he watched. And waited.

Chapter 6

Maggie watched him go, heaving a sigh of relief when he crossed through the grove of trees at the edge of her property. She closed her eyes, breathing deeply, willing her body to relax.

This morning had been nothing more than an acting job, and one she wasn't sure she could keep up.

His apology had gone a long way, but as soon as she'd seen him standing there, looking large and dangerous and undeniably sexy, she'd wanted nothing more than to kiss him again and see if it had really been as good as she remembered.

Something had changed. At first it had been a simple appreciation for a good-looking man, full stop. The last person she'd ever be interested in was someone in law enforcement. Maybe the problem was that he wasn't here in any official capacity. He didn't wear a uniform, or a badge, or carry a weapon. It made it easy to forget. Until something intruded to remind her. Like seeing him with Grant Simms. Or the way he questioned her last night.

And then she forgot all over again when he kissed her and turned her knees to jelly.

She went back to the kitchen and began to tidy the mess. Jen had put the idea in her head, but it hadn't taken much to keep it there. And now Jen was gone and Nate wasn't and it wasn't right that she should have such feelings. Maybe she'd been wrong not to date all this time, because it felt suspiciously like slaking a thirst. Nate was younger and energetic and she found that irresistible. And it was foolish to think she could relive her youth through a man who was just passing through.

This morning was a new day and she'd awakened knowing that keeping distance from Nate was the best thing for everyone. The emotional pitch from yesterday had dissipated and she was left with a clearer head. Nate was leaving within a few weeks and she couldn't get attached to him. Anything that happened between them was temporary. They both knew it, and also knew further episodes like last night's would be pointless. After that kiss…even flirting was a dimension best left unexplored. These weeks at Mountain Haven weren't real. What was real was his life back in the States, the one where he was a marshal who spent his days apprehending criminals.

She spent the morning cleaning, discovering with great interest that Nate was a neat lodger. He'd already made up his bed, and his laptop was closed, the mouse pad and cordless mouse sitting on top of the cover. There were no clothes lying about. In fact, except for the laptop on the desk, she could hardly tell anyone was even staying in the room.

For some odd reason, she didn't find that knowledge very comforting.

She curled up with a book in the afternoon. The sun sliding through the south facing window of her personal "parlor" warmed her, making her drowsy. She hadn't slept until nearly 2:00 a.m., and after the emotional roller coaster of yesterday, the six-plus hours she did get hadn't seemed to have alleviated all her exhaustion.

When she woke, it was after four, dinner wasn't started and Nate wasn't back, despite the darkening shadows of fading daylight. She'd been dreaming, odd dreams with Nate and Jen and Grant. Nothing that made sense. Jen, in handcuffs, with Nate holding her wrists. Grant coming forward and pinning some sort of medal on Nate's chest.

She stood up, rolling her shoulders and dismissing it. It was silly, that was all. She could puzzle it out easy enough. It was worrying that Nate would find out about Jen, and after seeing Grant and saying goodbye yesterday, it was probably natural.

A niggle of concern skittered down her arms as she realized another hour and he'd be out of daylight. Where could he have gone that would have taken him all day? He had to be exhausted. Had he gotten lost despite his assurances to the contrary?

He'd definitely cooled off when she'd mentioned his boss, too. Knowing she was behind schedule, she put chicken breasts in the microwave to thaw, the sound of the appliance filling the empty house. He hadn't appreciated the work reminder. As soon as she'd brought up the fact that his bill was paid, he'd gone cold and distant. She wondered why that was. Wondered why he'd chosen to come here, of all places. What had forced him to take a leave of absence?

As she kept her hands busy, her mind kept pace. She could understand the leave being paid, but it still didn't quite sit right that his vacation was being paid by the Marshal Service. Not if it were a personal trip.

The sound of his boots on the porch coincided with a sudden thought. She couldn't believe she hadn't thought of it before.

The bill, the location, his contact with Constable Simms.

He was here on a job. It was the only thing that made sense, and an icy spear shot through her body as the door opened.

He stomped inside, cheeks flushed and boots in hand, putting them on the mat so that no snow fell on her floor.

"Sorry I'm late."

Maggie didn't know what to say. She was still reeling from the possibility that had zoomed through her head. What if he had been lying to her all along? What had he really been doing today? How was he connected to the very same constable responsible for Jen's arrest?

And how in the world did she go about getting the truth? Did she even want to know? Really? She took a step backward.

"Maggie, are you okay?" He was across the foyer and in the hall in a flash. "Is it Jen?"

Oh Lord. She was horrible at poker faces. She'd really have to do better, because if her suspicions were correct, he was a heck of a player.

"No, Jen's fine. I fell asleep this afternoon and I think I'm still waking up." She gave a light laugh, then frowned when it came out with a false ring.

"I'm going to go change. Fell down a few times and got wet." He started for the stairs.

"Nate?"

He paused with his hand on the banister.

The words she wanted didn't come. She wasn't sure

she was wily enough to trick him into answering, and was afraid of asking point-blank. What if he were here on a job? Would it change anything? Certainly not between them. There *was* no them.

"Nate, I…"

His fingers gripped the railing tighter and she closed her eyes briefly, taking a fortifying breath.

"I had a lot of time to think today and I was wondering what happened that made you need a leave of absence."

She blurted it out in one rapid sentence before she could think of taking it back.

"Well. That's blunt."

His eyes cooled as he pressed his lips together. He didn't want to talk about it. Either that or he was hiding something. Whatever the reason, she found she suddenly wanted to hear the answer very much.

"Perhaps my reasons are private." He turned to go back up the stairs but she persisted.

"But the Service is paying all your expenses, and the first time you go into town I find you talking to local authorities."

Nate stared at her. She was way too close to hitting on the truth. Yesterday he'd thought maybe she'd ask questions after seeing him with Grant, but he realized now she'd merely been wrapped up with Jen. Now that she'd had time to think, not everything added up nice and neat. The way she was looking at him now, it was as though she knew. But on the off-chance she didn't, he kept his expression carefully neutral.

He took his hand off of the banister and stepped off the landing, putting less distance between them. He remembered how she'd felt against him last night. Had thought about it a lot today when the job got boring. There was a chance, a slim one, that he could divert her now.

"You want to know why I had to take time off, is that it?" He made sure he worded it carefully—the reason for his leave, not the reason for being at Mountain Haven. He didn't want to have to out-and-out lie again. He'd rather angle the truth.

Even he knew it was a flimsy distinction.

"I...I do." She folded her hands in front of her. "I know I'm prying. And I told myself I wasn't going to ask. But I'm asking anyway."

"Funny. I asked you about *your* life last night and you closed up tighter than a clam." He'd been tempted to tell her the truth earlier this morning, seeing her warm from her bed, remembering how she'd felt in his arms last night. Thankfully he'd been smart enough not to. Because he was beginning to get the picture that she didn't like cops. First the way she acted around Grant yesterday and the cold way she was looking at him now. He let his gaze drop to her lips. "At least at first."

She blushed at the innuendo but persisted. "I know. But you're a guest in *my* house."

"And when I arrived, you assured me that privacy for your guests was of the utmost importance."

Perhaps if he pushed the topic off track enough she'd take the bait and move on.

"Perhaps concern for my own safety trumps that."

Dear God, what *had* run through her mind today? He wondered briefly if she'd gone through his things, but to ask would only confirm her suspicions and somehow he knew she wouldn't have done that. No, she'd be honest and ask like she was doing right now. And he had no idea what to give her for an answer.

"Where *did* you go today, Nate?"

She wasn't going to let it go. And he knew the only

way to appease her was to give her the one story he was allowed to give. Even if he absolutely hated retelling it.

"All right. Let me get changed into dry clothes and I promise I'll tell you."

He jogged up the stairs, avoiding her probing gaze. He had to get out of his gear first. The last thing he needed was for Maggie to discover there was more than skin beneath his street clothes.

When he came back down, she was emptying dishes out of the dishwasher.

"Your things," he said quietly, holding out the thermos and bag.

"Thank you."

She put them down and simply waited, her eyes pinning him to the spot.

"Is this about yesterday, Maggie? Because if it is, we can keep this business only. I admitted I crossed a line. We can stop this right here."

Her cheeks flushed slightly. "It's that bad, then. Bad enough you'd try changing the subject a hundred times before talking about it." She turned back to her dirty dishes.

She had him to rights there. There was no pleasure rehashing the past. He'd failed, and it ate at him. Almost as much as being forced to go on leave. He didn't need vacation. He needed to focus.

If he didn't feel the strong need to protect her so much, he'd come out with the truth and be done with it. He hated lies.

"It was a month ago." The words sounded strangled to his ears so he cleared his throat and started again. "It was a month ago and a case of bad intel. We were on assignment. My team. To bring in a sex offender. We knew he had firearms on the premises…that much was correct. So we were…armed accordingly."

He paused and swallowed. How much should he tell her? Enough to appease her, he supposed. And not so much as to give away his reason for being there. Maggie closed the dishwasher door and gave him her full attention. He didn't know what to do with his hands, so he hooked his thumbs in the belt loops of his jeans.

"The plan was to go in after him. When we gather information, it's pretty complete, so we can make the best tactical plan possible. It was all organized, everyone had their job. Only somehow he must have known we were coming. I don't know whether he was tipped or saw us or what, but he met us at the door."

He looked at her briefly. She couldn't know how hard this was for him, to admit his worst moment. As he faced her, the images came back. The ones that had forced his break from work to begin with. Sounds of gunfire, everything moving in slow motion when in reality it all went down in a matter of seconds. The prolonged moment when he saw the results, the picture branded on his memory.

"He fired. We fired back. You have to understand. All our intel said that he was home alone, we had no reason not to trust it. But he wasn't. There was a woman. His daughter. She took a round and was killed."

It all came out like an official report. He looked away. "So now you know."

"Did you shoot her?"

He licked his lips. "Me personally? No."

"Then why do you carry the burden?"

Wasn't it enough that she had the truth? Why did she have to keep asking questions? It didn't matter who had pulled the trigger. It had been a fatal error.

"It was my team, Maggie. I was in charge."

"It was a mistake, a tragic mistake."

His hands pulled away from the loops and his fingers tightened. "You don't get it. I can't make mistakes. Would you say the same thing if it had been Jen in her shoes? If it had been your daughter who'd been killed?"

Nate turned and escaped out the door on to the veranda, into the blessed coolness of winter air. Telling Maggie had only made him angry again. He should have foreseen. There simply wasn't room for that kind of error in his job. Worrying about killing someone, the wrong person, or losing a member of the team far outweighed the feeling of personal danger.

His boss had made the leave nonnegotiable, even though all Nate wanted to do was get back in the field. He needed work, not time off to think of all the things he'd done wrong.

Then, the leave had become part of his cover and he resented it. It was over and done with. He'd learned from his mistake. Now he wanted to move on. He sure as hell didn't like—or want—the look of sympathy he'd seen on Maggie's face.

Maggie came out behind him, pulling a shawl over her shoulders. She put a hand on his arm and he pulled away.

"Nate, I'm sorry. I shouldn't have pried."

"Now you know and can stop asking."

She took a step backward at his harsh tone and he hated himself more for hurting her, too. This was exactly why he wished he could just tell her why he was here and forget all the secrecy.

He didn't like lying to Maggie. He could argue with himself and say he hadn't lied, that he'd stretched the truth, but it was the same thing. And the last thing he needed was her pity. But he couldn't tell her his assignment and protect her, too. He knew which was more important.

"Thank you for telling me." Her voice was quietly

apologetic. At least his answers seemed to have satisfied her. As she turned and went back inside, he shook off the guilt at smudging the lines of truth. She'd accepted his story completely, and he'd done his job. As much as he hated it, the truth of his "leave" had satisfied her.

He swallowed, not knowing how to patch things up, knowing they should or else the next several days were going to be torture. He followed her as far as the doorway.

"You've got to understand something, Maggie. This is what I do. I'm a marshal and I do my job and if there are consequences to that, I deal with them."

She turned and faced him for a moment, and the warmth from before vanished. "That's very clear," she murmured. And she walked away from him.

His hand smacked the pillar of the porch in frustration. He hated dishonesty. With a passion. Yet this wasn't about being honest. It was about protection. Protection for her, for himself, for the whole community if it came to that. It was a big picture thing. Shifting the truth shouldn't be a big deal. Maggie was temporary in his life. There wasn't room for feelings.

But as he remembered how her lips had clung to his last night, he felt guilt crawl through him anyway.

Guilt because she was, in a sense, part of the job and all he wanted to do was pull her into his arms again.

Right now the best thing to do was keep his distance.

Maggie hefted the grocery bags in her arms, balancing them carefully so she could still use her keys to get in the house. It was midafternoon; she'd still have time to make the steak and Guinness pie she had planned for dinner. Mealtimes were the only times she saw Nate now. He ate in the morning, took a bagged lunch and spent the whole day outside. The weather was warming, hovering just below zero, and soon the snow would melt enough that he wouldn't be able to use snowshoes or cross-country skis anymore. He came back tired, ate his dinner and spent evenings in his room. The few times she'd spoken to him after 7:00 p.m., he'd either been reading or sitting at his laptop.

She'd been wrong to push. She knew it now, had known it as soon as she'd touched his arm and he'd pulled away.

It was good that he was keeping his distance. Because the more she saw him, the more confused she became.

How could the one thing she disliked about him also be the one thing that seemed to attract her? She shook her head even though no one was there to see her. The last thing she wanted was to be involved with someone in law enforcement. Then why did she find it so unbearably sexy? It was just as well their flirting had stopped.

Her key turned easily in the lock; the door was open. She frowned. She was sure she'd locked the dead bolt when she left.

She put the bags down on the porch and eased inside. The first thing she noticed were Nate's big boots on the mat by the door. She exhaled, relieved. It was only Nate, then.

He appeared around the corner and she tried a smile, hoping eventually he'd thaw out and treat her as one of his own and they could reach some level of comfort. "You're back early," she said easily. "So…how did you get in? I suppose doing what you do, you know all the tricks, right? What was it? Credit card? File and pick?"

He held up a hand. "Spare key. You really shouldn't leave it in so obvious a place."

There was something off. She sensed it. He didn't smile, but there wasn't a tone of chastisement in his voice, either. It wasn't about where she'd put her key. It was something else.

She shut the door, forgetting the groceries sitting outside. "What is it?"

He came forward and her heart started beating faster, a thread of apprehension skimming over her limbs. Whatever it was didn't look good; his face was tight and drawn.

"Jen called."

It seemed as though her heart tripped over itself as her breath caught and held, strangling her.

"There was a stabbing on campus."

The life went out of Maggie's limbs. She felt the floor coming up to meet her when Nate's arms caught her full weight.

"God, Maggie!"

Her head spun, dizzy. Jen. Jen. Jen.

"Maggie. Snap out of it."

His voice came from far away, swimming in the back of her brain.

"Maggie!"

He gave her a shake and she met his gaze, not quite seeing. "Maggie! She's fine. She's fine."

Maggie nodded dumbly.

"Look at me."

He was on his knees, holding her on his thighs, bracing her with an arm. His free hand cupped her chin, forcing her to look upward. His eyes, darkened with worry, anchored her. She clung to them as she tried hard to make sense of his words.

"Maggie. Clear your mind," he ordered. Her gaze dropped to his lips. "Think. If she weren't okay, she couldn't have called."

It got through. She nodded, letting out her breath and willing some of the panic to release its grip.

Jen was okay.

"I'm sorry. It was a stupid reaction," she stammered.

"I understand. I didn't mean to scare you." He held her with firm hands, taking her weight.

She became aware of the hardness of his legs beneath her, the tight grip of his hands on her arms. She should pull away but she still felt so shaky she didn't trust herself to get up. It felt too right, letting him carry the weight for a while. So long since she'd allowed herself to lean on anyone.

He pulled her close, tucking her head beneath his chin and stroking her back soothingly. "I never thought of how you'd react. I should have, knowing your history. I should have said she was fine first. God, Maggie, you dropped like a rock."

"I feel stupid." His hand was warm and she let herself absorb it, drawing strength from it.

"Don't."

And then she felt it. A smile that she could picture creasing his face, moving against her hair. She closed her eyes, relief sluicing through her, ridiculously happy that he wasn't angry with her anymore. "I thought you were mad at me." He'd hardly spoken to her since the night she'd pried into his past.

"Not at you. Maybe just…angry in general." He kissed her hair lightly and her eyes sprung open. He pushed her away slightly. "Are you all right now?"

She nodded. "I think so."

"I'd meant to tell you that she called because she didn't want you to see it on the news and worry. But you didn't give me a chance."

She pushed out of his arms and stood up, feeling at once the loss of the security found in his arms. "I don't know why I did that."

He hopped up from his crouched position. The last

thing she expected from him was gentleness, not after the way things had been strained for several days. His fingers touched her cheek, stroking softly.

"I think you know exactly why it happened. You said yourself, you've suffered a lot of loss. Do you want to talk about it?"

She looked up into his eyes. He'd passed an olive branch and it was up to her whether or not to accept it But she didn't talk about her past. No one wanted to hear about it. "Let's face it, Nate. My story's a bit of a downer. It's no big deal."

Another smile tugged at the corner of his lips. "You know, that sounds vaguely familiar."

"Touché."

He let her go, but she felt more connected to him than she ever had before, even more than being held in his arms or kissed. "I'll think about it. For right now, I'm going to bring the bags inside and call Jennifer."

"She's a good kid, Maggie. She knows how much you care and worry. If she didn't, she wouldn't have thought to call you."

Tears stung her eyes. How he seemed to know what she needed to hear was uncanny. "Thanks, Nate. That means a lot."

"Anytime."

She turned her back to him so he couldn't see the naked yearning on her face. Jennifer's welfare was such a hot button for her. The best thing she could do now was leave before she bawled all over him, so she started toward the stairs. He had no idea how tempted she was to take him up on his offer.

Chapter 7

"Maggie. Wait."

"Just leave me alone, Nate. Please. I'm fine." She stopped at the bottom of the stairs, blinking back tears. She wasn't. She was embarrassed, vulnerable, feeling like a fool. Nate kept seeing her falling apart and he kept picking up the pieces. It was becoming a disturbing trend, and one she needed to put to an end. He was, by trade, a protector. He wasn't *her* protector.

She hadn't realized he'd come up behind her until his hand, wide and warm, fell on her shoulder, kneading gently. "I'm the one that saw your face. The one that caught you as you collapsed. You're not okay. You might as well tell me and get it out."

She tried to exhale but the air came out in shaky jolts, the very sound tearing her apart a little more with each breath. She was so tired. Tired of being afraid, tired of pretending. All it did was exhaust her. He put his other hand on her right shoulder, both hands now massaging gently.

The caring touch ripped away any shred of control she had left, and she dropped her head, two tears splashing over her lashes and down her cheeks. She tried to sniff them away, but failed miserably.

"Please don't be kind. I can't bear it."

"Why?"

The question was what she needed, something to shift the focus from his hands on her shoulders. She turned to face him, straightening her shoulders. "You want reasons? Let's start with the fact that you're here for a few weeks and then gone again. You're just passing through, Nate, and we both know it. And then... well, there's the whole cop thing. You're a marshal first and foremost, as you so eloquently pointed out the other day. Not to mention you're..." She paused, her cheeks flushed as she blurted out, "You're nearly a decade younger than I am!"

The words echoed in the hall. She lowered her voice. "And that's the last thing I need. Or want."

"Did I imply that this was something more?"

She huffed. "Imply? Constantly! Starting with the first night when you kissed my finger!"

She gaped when a smile curled his lips and he leaned against the banister.

"Ah, yes. When you grew so flustered you dropped your cup. And you should know I couldn't care less about your age. It's just a damned number." He slid a few inches closer and she instinctively backed up.

"Don't flirt with me, Nate. We're both past that."

His smile faded. "I only wanted to help you and you're making this my fault. Perhaps you can explain that."

How on earth could she explain that being with him made her feel more vulnerable than she could ever remember being? His profession threatened her. And her attraction for him was equally as frightening. Because she was undeniably attracted to all those things that scared the daylights out of her.

And those fears blended with the hurts of the past and the result was a woman who was incapable of making sense of it all and threatened to be overwhelmed. Above all, the urge to let him help was so strong.

"I can't do this. I can't cry all over a guest. And that's what you are, though I seem to keep forgetting it. Please…just let me be."

But he ignored her plea. He captured her hand and pulled. "I think we both know that I'm not just a guest. Not anymore." He tugged again, pulling her into the strong circle of his arms.

Oh, the warmth of him, the smell…her own laundry soap blended with his aftershave and that little bit of something that was just him. She couldn't fight him any longer. Emotions that had been building ever since Jennifer's arrest last year snapped and let go. Defeated, Maggie turned her head against his chest and let the tears come. Nate's shoulders relaxed and he tucked her against him, holding her while she finally let everything spill out.

Maggie knew it was wrong, but it felt right. Why now, after all this time, did she finally feel connected to someone? There were so many reasons why he was wrong for her. He was a man who lived for his work, and thought nothing of putting himself in danger. He had his life ahead of him. They didn't even live in the same country.

And in a very short time, he'd be gone. She was shocked to find, in the circle of his arms, that she would miss him when he was gone.

But she had right now, and she burrowed deeper into his chest, letting the clean scent of him surround her.

Letting his body form a cocoon as the slightest bit of healing trickled into her body.

The tears abated and she became aware of his hand running up and down her back, slowly, firm and sure. She needed him on so many levels. Desire filled the raw, aching hole and she was tempted to channel everything into a physical manifestation. But that would be wrong.

His lips touched her ear and she turned toward them. He spoke instead.

"Trust me, Maggie," he whispered, and she shivered. "You need to talk to someone. And I'm here."

She wanted to trust him. It was part of the problem.

Maggie made herself pull away and look up into his face. *He's beautiful,* she thought, stunned. Not just his body, not just the color of his eyes, the strong line of his lips or the cleft in his chin. But beautiful on the inside. Strong, yes, and stubborn. But principled and caring and compassionate. She wanted to share everything with him. Needed to. She'd pushed it down, pretended that the past didn't exist to everyone but herself. She couldn't do it anymore.

"What do you want to know?"

His lips curved ever so slightly. "Whatever you want to tell me. I want to know how Maggie Taylor ended up here. I want…"

He stopped and swallowed. Maggie's heart held a moment, waiting for what he'd say next. When he answered, it was as if he were touching her even though they were separated by inches.

"I want to know everything about you."

Maggie chafed her arms, already missing the warmth of his body. She was so tired. Tired of being governed by fear. She needed this.

"Then I'll tell you. Let's get a drink and start a fire. You might want to settle in for the duration."

He smiled. "One fire coming up."

Maggie got glasses and a bottle of rye whiskey from the cupboard. When she went into the living room, flames were licking warmly in the gas fireplace and Nate was sitting on the sofa, his elbows braced on his knees, staring into the orange blaze.

"Here. Hold these."

He held the glasses while she poured a small amount in the bottom of each one, then put the bottle down on the coffee table. She took a seat next to him, sipping the liquor. It warmed a path to her stomach and she closed her eyes and sighed.

"Why don't you start at the beginning, Maggie. I know you lost your parents and your husband, but that really only scratches the surface." Nate's voice touched her and she opened her eyes. He held her gaze so she couldn't back away. "There's clearly more. Like why it still hurts so much. How it's shaped you into who you are, how you got to be owner of a bed-and-breakfast in the middle of nowhere, looking after everyone else instead of yourself."

Maggie tucked her left foot under her leg, leaning back against the cushions. She had told herself that telling him, no matter how close they seemed to get, would be crossing a line. But they'd already crossed several lines with the kiss and with her sobbing all over him. Perhaps if he knew…really knew…who she was, it would actually have the opposite effect. Part of her wished it would be so. That perhaps the details would be sufficient to keep him at arm's length. What man wanted a woman still grieving for her loss and paralyzed by fear? It would be easier for her to resist him if he resisted her first.

And the other part of her yearned for him to listen, to understand, to accept.

"The beginning? Things were pretty normal for me growing up, until my parents died when I was a teenager and I had to look after myself." She took another fortifying sip of the rye. It sounded cut-and-dried now, but her whole world had been ripped apart, changing everything. She was no longer someone's daughter. She'd become Maggie, the orphan, trying to find her way.

"How did they die?"

"In a car accident."

His free hand dropped to her knee, stayed there. "I'm sorry. That must have been horrible for you."

"Thank you."

"Didn't you have anywhere to go?"

She smiled sadly. "Not really. And seeing I was the age of majority, I looked after myself. Got a job. Tried to make some sense of things."

"And then?"

She looked down at the sight of his hand on her leg, wished fleetingly it didn't feel quite so good. She didn't feel like she was burdening him with prolonged grief. Nate didn't know her family, her friends. Knowing she could speak freely without the guilt she often felt when talking to others was a relief, and the words came easier with every breath.

She lifted her head and their eyes met. There was no pity on his face. She wouldn't have been able to take that. But there was compassion and patience and she was grateful for it. The tension abated in her neck.

"Then I met Mike. He is my second cousin, the son of a cousin who had a baby far too young and made really bad choices, which resulted in Mike being put in foster care." She looked away from his hand and up into his eyes. "When I met him, I was twenty-two and he was eleven, still being bounced from home to home. And I suppose I thought, here is someone who is my flesh and blood, someone who knows what lonely means. It was the only hint of family I had and I needed to cling to it. Hadn't realized it until he was standing there in front of me."

"You needed him as much as he needed you."

Maggie nodded. She had. Mike had given her purpose. She doubted he knew to this day how much.

"I was working steadily, had an apartment in Sundre. I petitioned the court for guardianship and I got it. I don't know who was more surprised, me or Mike."

"You became each other's family."

"Yes, I suppose we did. Mike was a good kid, he was just scared. Didn't trust people much and I couldn't blame him. I did the best I could, but heck, I was young, too, and still raw from all I'd been through. I met Tom. Mike was a teenager when we got married and had Jen. I suppose he felt in the way after that, although he never said anything about it. Mike never talked about things like that much." She smiled at Nate. "Sounds like someone else I know. Anyway, by the time he graduated, he was rodeoing in season and working odd jobs in the off-times."

Her smile turned wistful. "I didn't think he'd ever find anyone to trust his heart to, but he did."

"Like you did with Tom?"

Maggie suddenly realized that she'd been talking, really talking, more than she'd planned. Maybe it was the fire, or the liquor, or the fact that Nate was safe and comfortable. Regardless, this afternoon they had turned a corner. Somewhere in the mess of confusion she'd made the decision to stop fighting and it shocked her to realize how quickly she'd dropped her guard.

But now Nate had turned the subject to Tom and it was different than talking about Mike. She wasn't sure she could go on. Certainly not as easily as she'd talked about her cousin. Tom had done for her what Grace had done for Mike. Given her a place to put her heart for safekeeping. Or so she'd thought.

Losing him had been the most devastating thing she'd ever been through, and it had taken every ounce of her strength to put her life back together. Even now, pieces were missing and it was incredibly painful. A memory flashed through her mind, not of Tom, but of Nate kissing her in the kitchen. The sheer beauty of it had scared her to death. It couldn't happen again. She couldn't feel like that again. The last time she'd had that depth of feeling, she'd ended up being crushed beneath it. It was an odd position to be in, trusting Nate yet needing to push him away.

Surely talking about one's dead husband would make any man put on the brakes.

"Yes. I did trust my heart to Tom."

"And then he died and you were left with Jen."

Her throat closed up a bit and she nodded.

"Come here."

Nate took her glass away and deposited it on the table with his own. Shifting, he leaned back against the arm of the sofa, running one leg along the inside edge. She knew she should keep her distance, but he felt too good. Unresisting, she let him pull her back until she was cradled in the lee of his legs, his arms around her loosely, his fingers lightly circling her wrists.

"Oh, Nate." She sighed, staring into the dancing flames. Why did he have to be so perfect? Why was it that after all this time, Nate Griffith could make her feel things she hadn't felt in years? Including the need to spill about her past?

She paused for so long he squeezed her wrist. "You're thinking too much. Forget the reasons why and just let it out, Maggie. It's been in there a long time, hasn't it?"

She nodded.

He stroked her wrist bone with his thumb. "Can you tell me about him?"

Her throat thickened and she swallowed. "I don't know," she whispered, her voice thin in the rich air.

"I'd like to hear about it, if you want to tell me." He touched his forehead to her hair.

"You have to understand that I really don't talk about Tom. To anyone. Talking about him now…doesn't come easily."

Nate waited.

Maggie closed her eyes and absorbed the warmth and strength of his body into her soul. Why not tell him and be free of it? He'd be going back to his job in a few weeks and they'd never meet again. He'd forget all about her and her dead husband, after all. What would be the benefit of a quick fling? Because after the way he'd kissed her, she knew that was a distinct possibility. He'd leave her behind and she'd be left hurt, all over again. Because she didn't do casual, or temporary. And she didn't do serious relationships, either.

He was alive, breathing, real. And if she weren't careful, she'd set herself up for hurt. It would be foolish to do that when it could easily be avoided. Maybe telling them would bring them closer in one way, but it should certainly cool the jets on any attraction between them.

"I was waitressing and Tom was working the patch." At Nate's pause, she amended, "The oil patch. He was doing security at a refinery north of town and used to come in for breakfast and pie in the mornings. The first time we met, I teased him about eating pie at 6:00 a.m."

An image flirted with her, Tom, young and energetic, blond and teasing dimples. She realized she'd been sitting for a few moments with a smile of remembrance on her lips. "Sorry."

"Don't be. Go on."

"I was trying to raise Mike, and working a couple of jobs to make ends meet. Tom was a breath of fresh air. For our first date, he packed a picnic and waited on me, since, he said, I was always waiting on him. I was twenty-three."

Color crept into her cheeks. "I hadn't planned on life changing so quickly, but I fell hard and fast. I was starved for love and he was everything I could have imagined wanting. We got married three months later. Seven months after that Jen was born."

"And you moved here?"

She nodded. She remembered quite clearly the day he'd brought her here, late in the fall with Jen in a blanket in her arms. She'd been so angry with him when she'd found out he'd already bought it without consulting her. It was stupid, she realized later. Fighting over something so silly, when the truth was she'd adored the place as soon as she'd crossed the threshold. Drafty corners and all.

"Yes, we came here. He was making good money in the patch, and we could have the house and I could stay home and be with Jen. Maybe even have a few more."

Nate lifted his right hand from her arm, stroking her hair. "You wanted more children."

"I did then. He…" She stopped, unsure of how to go on. She did that a lot. She was unused to saying personal things aloud, but it seemed like it was *all* she'd been doing since Nate arrived. "He fixed something in me that had been broken when I lost my family."

"Only then he died, too."

"Yeah. And I think that day I realized that it didn't matter what I did, the people I loved were going to leave me. I only had Jen left."

"And that's why you worry about her so much. You're waiting for something to happen to her, too."

He understood.

Maggie felt all the panic and tension drain out of her body in one long, flowing river. The fact that it made sense to someone other than herself was liberating. "Yes."

Nate closed his eyes and cupped her head in his hand. All the resistance he'd felt vibrating through her body had melted away and she lay against his chest. Trusting, empty.

She'd been hurt so much. He really hadn't had any idea of how deep her hurt had gone. Maybe he should have, after today. The truth was he had wanted to know, to feel close to her. He cared about her, and he was shocked to realize it had only taken a few short days for his feelings to be involved.

But she'd given in easily, told him more than he'd ever expected and he wasn't sure what to do with it.

The one thing he knew for sure, now more than ever, was that he couldn't be responsible for hurting her again. Maggie Taylor was too precious to be trifled with. He'd never met a woman with more pain, yet so strong. He couldn't imagine anyone picking up the pieces of their life in the way she had, with a baby and a foster child and a need to make a living. He knew for damned sure he couldn't be the one to turn that upside down.

Which made it insanely difficult, because he wanted her more than ever.

She'd trusted him today and he'd thought it was what he wanted. Now he knew that was a mistake. If she were to find out why he was really here, all that trust would be broken. No, it would have to be done clean.

And when he left, it would be with a smile and warm memories of what they'd shared. How they'd helped each other. He felt the sting of irony that the truth would only tarnish the fleeting relationship they'd built.

It was how it had to be.

Long moments passed and he simply held her in his arms, felt her breathing, felt their connection growing and expanding. Never before had he felt so comfortable with a woman.

He looked around the room over the top of her head. Comfortable, welcoming, cozy. Like her. Yet…a blazing fire, a sparkling glass bottle of dark liquid, splashes of color…vibrant. Also like her. A woman who made her living caring for others but one who knew how to stand on her own two feet. A survivor.

A woman he wanted. Completely.

But he couldn't have her. Not after all that had happened today. It would be completely unfair to her, in every way. He felt guilty enough about misleading her about his work. He knew for damn sure he wouldn't take advantage of her when she was stripped bare. Because he knew she hadn't told him every detail. He wondered how Tom had died. She hadn't told him about the troubles she'd had since, or Jen's brush with the law last year. And he wondered if she'd ever trust him enough to let him in completely.

So he held her in his arms as the afternoon wore on, wondering how the hell he was going to get through the next week.

Chapter 8

Cooking. He watched her from the doorway, his arms folded over his chest as he leaned against the woodwork. He realized now it was what she did when she was particularly bothered or upset. After the events of the afternoon, he guessed they'd have a fine meal tonight.

She turned a beef mixture into a casserole as her brows pulled together in a frown. She lifted a fragile square of pastry and laid it over the top of the beef, pricking it with a fork. But he heard the deep sigh that seemed to come from her very toes.

"Penny for your thoughts."

She spun, her hand flying to her chest in surprise. He smiled. At least he could still surprise her.

"Only a penny?" She tried to joke, but her attempt at a jaunty grin wobbled. It appeared she hadn't bounced back as well as she was trying to portray.

"Maggie, are you sure you're okay?" He dropped his arms and started into the room.

She took a deep breath and squared her shoulders. "Of course I am."

She slid the dish into the oven. Turned and faced him, pasting on a smile that he understood was clearly for his benefit. She wiped her hands on her apron.

"It's chinooking. Which means tomorrow you'll be slogging it out in the muck."

He pushed away the urge to simply cross the floor and kiss her. He'd been thinking of it ever since she'd lain in his arms. But she was too raw, he could see that. "Chinooking?"

Maggie took a dishcloth and began wiping down the counter. "It's a wind that comes over the mountains, and it'll melt all the snow that's left. Some days it seems to blow and blow, but when it's done, it'll feel like spring around here."

Great. Warmer weather meant walking, and walking in muck. He'd actually hoped the cool weather would prevail a little longer. He frowned. Wished Maggie had an ATV he could borrow. Only then she'd ask why, and where he was going…dammit. Things were growing more complicated by the second.

"You don't have a headache, do you?" She took a few steps forward. "A lot of people get them, especially if they're not used to the pressure change. If your head is bothering you, I have painkillers in the cabinet."

She was the fragile one here and she was worried about his headache? The only headache he had wasn't from the pressure change, but from finding ways to keep his reasons for being here private without telling bald-faced lies. How to remain focused on his job without thinking about her every waking minute.

He was starting to fall for her, he realized. His head really did start to ache.

"My head is fine."

"Oh."

The short, quiet word told him he'd been too harsh and he tried to soften his expression. He hadn't meant to snap at her. "But thanks for asking." He pushed his thoughts away and tried a smile. "How long until dinner?"

"About an hour."

Her reply was cool and he guessed she wasn't quite ready to forgive him for his snappishness. "I guess I'll go read or something, then."

"Nate?"

He paused. Lord, but she was beautiful. She'd wiped away any trace of her earlier tears and her eyes shone the most perfect shade of blue, like his grandmother's china bowl on his mom's cabinet, the one he was never allowed to touch as a boy. Blue Willow, he remembered now. Timeless and beautiful, like Maggie. Her lips were slightly puffed and he wanted to kiss them until they both ran out of breath. His chest tightened, strangling. He wanted to carry her upstairs, undress her, run his fingers over her creamy skin. Make love to her on the homemade quilt until the shadows grew long and disappeared. He wanted to tell her the truth and be free of it. He couldn't do any of those things.

She was watching him as though she could read his mind and he shuddered.

"What, Maggie?" It came out almost a whisper and the line of tension crackled between them.

She broke eye contact first, and half turned, breaking the spell. "Let's go for a walk while dinner's cooking. I'll show you what a Chinook arch looks like."

Getting outside was probably a really, really good idea. Otherwise he'd do something foolish that he couldn't take back. Like kiss her again. Like tell her how he was feeling. Ridiculous.

They pulled on boots and jackets, leaving their hats behind and putting their hands in their pockets.

Once outside, Maggie led him down the driveway to the road. It was paved, but barely. Narrow with no lines printed on it. Just a country road leading to the only place she'd called home in almost twenty years. He was a city boy, born and bred. The wide-open space, the simplicity of it, was a revelation. He breathed deeply, the sharp wind buffeting his chest. Felt a little of the tension slip away.

"See that?" She lifted her finger and pointed to the white sweep of clouds in the west. "That's a Chinook arch. Like a horizontal rainbow of cloud front. I've seen it warm over ten degrees Celsius in less than an hour. I've seen snow melt so quickly that you'd swear by the sound of the drips that it was raining."

"You love it here." He shook off the feeling of guilt from prying again, torn between caring for her and wanting to see the whole picture. It was like she was trying to forget all about their earlier conversation, and pretend it had never happened.

She kept walking, and he listened as her footsteps squeaked on the melting snow of the shoulder of the road.

"I've never been anywhere else. This is home."

"It's very different from where I'm from."

"Florida?"

He laughed. He'd only been in Florida for the last few years, although he loved it there and considered it his home base. "I was brought up in Philadelphia. Where my parents are. But yes, Florida, too. Have you ever been?"

She shook her head. "I've been to Vancouver. Once."

They walked on, Maggie's hair blown back by the force of the westerly wind. "I always had Jen, and she had school. And during breaks, I always had guests. I've never had the chance to travel."

His chin flattened. "Until a few weeks ago, and you got saddled with me instead. I'm sorry about that."

He loved how she smiled back. It was free of agenda, unfettered by awkwardness and with a hint of growing trust at the corners. Had he inspired that?

"I'm starting to not regret that quite as much as I did at first." She tried tucking her hair behind her ears. "You've been everywhere, I suppose," she commented.

"I've been around. The Middle East, Europe with the marines. All over North America with the Marshal Service. But…"

Maggie turned her head to look up at him, a strand of hair whipping around her face and catching in her mouth. She plucked it out with a finger. He reached out and tucked it back, his finger lingering by her earlobe.

"But…"

He dropped his hand. He doubted she could really comprehend the places he'd been or the things he'd seen. "But there's no place like home. Other than my mom's place, here with you, at Mountain Haven, is as close as it gets."

"What about your place in Florida?" The moment suspended as the wind howled around them.

What about it? It was empty and functional and a place for him to sleep and eat. Had been for several months.

"My house there doesn't really feel like a home."

He could tell by the look in her eyes she wanted to ask more but didn't. Instead she placed a hand on his forearm, unaware of how the simple gesture touched him.

"Then I'm glad you're happy here."

That was it. He was surprised. Any woman he knew

would have asked long ago if there was a wife or girl-friend in the wings. But not Maggie. He understood now that she'd learned long ago to simply accept. He almost wanted her to ask, just so he could tell her there was no one. No one with a claim on his heart.

Maggie turned to keep walking and he clasped her hand in his. She smiled softly, squeezing his fingers.

"Thank you, Nate, again. For being there today. It helped. More than you know."

Their hands swung gently between them as they am-bled along rough pavement. It hit him as being a bit sur-real, walking down a country road, holding hands with a beautiful woman. "Something's happening between us, Maggie, we both know it."

"I…I'm not prepared for that."

"I know."

His low words were almost lost in the power of the Chinook, but she heard them. He looked over at her, saw her swallow, look down at her feet as their steps slowed.

"Maggie, don't run, okay? We've both been dancing around it until neither of us knows how to act or what to say. So I'm just going to get it out of the way. I'm at-tracted to you. More than I thought possible."

Her mouth opened and shut a few times before she could speak. "I know. And I've started to trust you, Nate, and it scares me to death. I don't have it in me to start anything. There are so many reasons not to."

His lip curled at the thought of trust. The one bugbear in all of this was that he knew she trusted him more with each passing day. And he knew she shouldn't. Knew that she'd be more hurt if she knew he'd been keep-ing secrets all this time. He wondered again whether it would be better to just tell her.

Then he remembered the look in her eyes today when she'd thought Jen was hurt, when she'd told him about all the loss she'd suffered. He couldn't tell her and walk out the door each day that was left, knowing how she'd worry. She didn't need that. She had enough to worry about. Not only that, if he told her, he'd lose any hope of finding out what it was he already suspected. That Maggie knew a hell of a lot more than she was saying.

He felt her eyes on him and he turned his head, his face softening slightly. "Sorry. I didn't mean to disappear." He took her other hand in his, stopping their progress in the middle of the road, running his fingers over her soft knuckles.

He leaned forward, just a little, and touched his lips to her forehead, catching a strand of her hair in his mouth as the wind whipped it around. He pulled it out with a finger.

Their time together was growing short. He wouldn't have to worry about seeing her every day, knowing he was keeping secrets from her. Another week was all that was left in his stay and they would probably never see each other again.

It was crazy how empty the thought of that made him feel.

Her hair whipped around and he reached out, threading his fingers through the long strands, pushing them back so her pale face was framed by the darker skin of his hands. It was wrong to feel this way and he knew it. But in the end the pull to her was too strong to fight.

"I'm sorry, Maggie. I have to."

He pulled gently with his hands, drawing her closer and up, dipping his head until he touched her lips with his.

She was sweet, so very sweet, and a little salty from her earlier tears. His eyes slammed shut and he focused on the feel of her, real and alive and responsive. Despite her earlier protests, despite all the reasons why she couldn't, her mouth opened beneath his and he squared his feet, planting his weight, taking it as deep and as dark as she'd let him.

The wind howled around them, warm and wild, swirling up dust. He lowered one hand, pressing it to the small of her back, pulling her closer so that their bodies were meshed as closely as their outerwear would allow. Her arms reached up, circled his neck as she adjusted the angle of her head to better fit his and his blood sang. He gripped her hair, tugging to tilt her head back, and he ripped his mouth from hers, sliding his tongue up her neck.

She whimpered, and he felt the vibration on his lips.

He froze. God, here he was doing the very thing he'd promised himself he wouldn't, not today. This was what going for a walk had been meant to avoid. Breathing heavily, he gently released her and backed away.

"You're stopping." Her cheeks flamed red but she met his eyes bravely.

"You're too vulnerable, Maggie. We both know it."

"I think I'm old enough to know what I want." She lifted her chin.

He couldn't stop the surge at her words. She wanted him. That was clear. Her response had told him plainly she wanted him as much as he wanted her.

Maggie held his gaze, trying to seem stronger than he knew she felt. She wasn't the kind to take something to a physical level and be cavalier about it. He took a step backward. "But I'm not sure you'd see it the same way tomorrow, and I don't want to take advantage. And the last thing I want to do is hurt you in any way." He tried slow, steadying breaths. "Besides, we're in the middle of the road."

Maggie looked left and right while the only sound

was the Chinook and dripping water from melting snow. Then she snorted, a tiny, ladylike bubble of noise.

"Oh goodness, we are, aren't we?"

"Yeah."

Things seemed back to normal for a few minutes. They turned back in the direction they'd come and the wind was at their backs, buffeting them along. Maggie tried tucking her hair behind her ears, but it wouldn't stay. It blew wildly around her head.

It was good they'd stopped when they had.

When they reached the lane up to the house, she stopped suddenly. He looked at her, then at the house. It seemed to be waiting for them to go in.

"So what do we do now?"

Nate knew what he wanted to do, but it would cause more problems than it would solve. He sighed.

"Damned if I know, Maggie. Damned if I know."

Maggie hummed as she folded the clothes in her basket, laying them in two piles on her bed; one for her, one for Nate. He'd offered to do his own laundry if she'd let him use her facilities, but she didn't mind doing it for him. When she'd offered, there'd been a slightly tense moment as she'd worried he'd think she was just after billing the service.

Truth be told, it was nice to have someone to do for. Washing his clothing was nothing at all. She'd merely made the comment that she could throw it in with her own and the awkward moment had passed.

She smoothed her hand over a pair of his jeans, rubbing out the creases from the dryer. Her fingers lingered over the denim, picturing how the fabric molded to his frame. Not in many, many years had she felt such a need for a man, such desire. Not only that, but she'd never expected that she'd find those things that made him a cop—the haircut, the penchant for neatness, the physicality—so alluring.

When he was gone on his ramblings during the day, she couldn't believe how wantonly she'd behaved during their walk. In the middle of the road, of all things. But the moment his arms went around her and he kissed her, she forgot everything beyond the feel and taste of him. For those few moments, she forgot the fear. When she was in his embrace, she forgot all the reasons why he was wrong for her. He made her feel young and alive and the novelty was intoxicating.

They'd walked back to the house and she'd wondered how on earth they were going to coexist in the same house for the next several days. Wanting him to kiss her again, knowing it was inadvisable. Wanting much more from him, yet afraid to take that giant step into being intimate with a man. She didn't take those things lightly.

But she needn't have worried at all. Nate had reverted to his pleasant, normal self. Full stop. No more long looks, intimate smiles, toe-curling kisses. None.

And she missed him.

The laundry finished, she put her own clothes away and stacked his, along with the guest towels, back in the basket to take upstairs to his room. Maybe he'd put on the brakes because she'd never given him a reason to move forward. And yes, he was only here for a short time. But he understood her. That much she knew. She'd trusted him with her past and that was a subject she rarely talked about. And he'd made the first move each time they'd kissed, touched.

What if he was waiting for her to make a move now?

Maggie swallowed as saliva pooled in her mouth. After seventeen years of celibacy, she was afraid. Afraid of looking silly. Afraid of the intensity. Afraid of another man seeing her body. She wasn't twenty anymore.

She'd had a child. She'd aged. And his body was youthful and perfect.

"Maggie?"

Nate called as he came in the door and she couldn't stop the flood of welcome that rushed through her. When had she started truly looking forward to his return every day?

"I'm in here."

She let out a slow breath. This was silly. He was only a man. This was only a crazy reaction to having him so close; to being alone together.

She hefted the laundry basket, settling it on her hip. It wasn't in her to make the next move. No matter how much she wanted to.

She turned the corner into the kitchen, the basket sliding off her hip to the floor as she saw his face.

"Have you got bandages, Maggie?"

His voice was calm, reasonable, but all Maggie saw was blood streaming from a gash that ran down his forehead to just below his eyebrow.

"Maggie. Bandages."

She sprang into action, the sight of the cut always before her eyes as she ran to the bathroom for the first-aid kit.

When she came back, he'd pulled out a kitchen chair and sat in it. Maggie grabbed an ivory hand towel from the spilled basket and immediately pressed it to the cut, staunching the blood as it seeped darkly through the cotton. "Hold this for a minute."

She opened the kit and saw her fingers trembling. He was fine, it was just a cut, she reassured herself. But seeing the blood, the open gash, had sent pins and needles through her extremities. What if he had a concussion, or needed stitches?

She looked up, gauze and scissors in her hand, and watched as Nate's face paled and he weaved slightly.

She dropped the items to the floor and knelt before him, pressing one hand to the towel and the other to the back of his head, pushing him forward.

"Put your head between your knees," she commanded, hoping to God he didn't pass out or get sick. Either one might mean concussion.

He obeyed, saying nothing.

"Take slow, deep breaths, Nate."

She moved to the side a bit, still holding the towel to the wound and rubbing a hand over his shoulders. The movement gave her time to find her own bearings, and she realized something shocking.

In the instant she'd seen his blood, known he was injured, her only thoughts had been for him. Not of Tom. Not of Jen. Not of fear born from years of loss and anxiety. But for *him*.

It was more than lust, more than feeding a hunger. It was Nate, the man, and he inspired feelings Maggie had thought long extinct. For her, it had suddenly become much deeper and meaningful. And complicated.

"I'm okay now."

His voice came through, deep and rough, and she blinked back tears at the mere sound of it.

"Sit up slowly, that's it." She helped guide him up until he was upright in the chair once more. Once he was stable, she put his hand on the towel and moved quickly to grab a chair so she could sit facing him.

"I'm going to pull the towel away now," she murmured, gently pulling the cotton from his head. She swallowed at the amount of blood staining the ivory. With light fingers, she held his forehead and examined the cut. "You should have stitches."

"I'll be fine, just bandage it up."

"Nate, it's huge. Even with stitches, you'll likely have a scar. You can guarantee it if I patch you up. Not to mention it'll take longer for it to heal."

"There's steritape in my bag. I'll get it."

"Tell me where it is and I'll get it for you."

"No. I mean, I'm feeling much better."

"Don't be stupid. You asked for my help, let me give it."

"The bleeding's nearly stopped. I'll get the tape and let you do it, all right?"

She sat back at his sharp tone. She wasn't sure why she'd been so worried, if he were going to be this stubborn. Men. Why was it that admitting they needed help was so difficult?

He got up from his chair and made his way to the stairs.

She took the towel and threw it in the trash; there was no saving it. What on earth had happened to him, and how long had he walked before getting to the house?

"Maggie."

Her head snapped up. Nate's voice was weak and thready. She rushed toward the stairs. Why hadn't he let her go after the supplies rather than playing the tough guy?

"Oh my stars, Nate."

He was halfway down the stairs, clinging to the banister and holding a small kit in his hands.

She went up half a dozen steps and slid beneath his right arm, bolstering his weight. "You big ninny. Trying to do this yourself. From now on, you're doing exactly what I tell you."

"Yes, ma'am."

Carefully they made their way to the bottom of the stairs and she helped him back to the chair. He sat heavily, closed his eyes while she took the kit from his hands.

"This isn't my forte, just so you know. You really should see a doctor."

"No doctors. It's just a scratch."

"Don't be stupid."

A muscle in his jaw ticked. "I just don't like doctors, okay? I've had worse wounds, trust me. I've been patched up by medics, by colleagues and even by a tribal leader in Africa."

"You are so stubborn." Maggie held the first strip of tape. "Take a breath. Now let it out. Slowly."

As he exhaled, she pushed the edges of the wound together and applied the tape.

His eyes opened, the blue-green of the sun through a bottle. They focused on her face. "Thank you for doing this."

She caught the tip of her tongue in her teeth as she applied the next strip.

"I want it noted that I thought you should see a professional."

His gaze never wavered, and her stomach tumbled, both from the first-aid and from his intense focus.

"You can charge for services rendered. I'll speak up for you."

Her lips twitched. "So you're not *that* badly injured, if you're cracking jokes."

"It's a scratch," he repeated. "I've got scars much worse."

Her hand halted, another strip of tape stuck to her index finger. She wondered where he had scars; what they looked like. Her body heated as she imagined touching him, kissing all the places where they marked his skin.

And just as quickly, she cooled. She couldn't forget that the very presence of the scars were a real reminder of the life he led. And the danger he represented.

"What happened, anyway?"

He cleared his throat. "I was walking the creek. Don't know exactly what happened, but I must have slipped in some mud. Hit my head on a rock, I guess. And got my bell rung pretty good."

Maggie reached for a swab, cleaned the bottom of the cut and reached for the gauze. It made sense, she supposed. The creek bank could be slick this time of year, and a stripe of dried mud ran up his leg.

"And you walked all the way back here with your head bleeding."

He nodded slightly, wincing. "Yeah. Used a mitten to control the bleeding—it's a write-off by the way—and hit for home."

She sat back, packing the kit again. "You're patched up, for what it's worth. I still think you're probably concussed."

"Then you'll have to keep an eye on me, won't you?"

He smiled his most charming smile, and suddenly the life went out of her legs.

She sat heavily. She hated the sight of blood, but her immediate concern for his health had overridden it. Now that he was attended to, the aversion came back heavy and strong. The smell of blood was the smell of death. She would have taken him to the hospital out of sheer worry, but she didn't like hospitals any more than he apparently did. Hospitals were always a reminder of what she'd lost.

"You need tea, Maggie. Now you're pale."

She nodded. "I'll make some. I think we could both use it. I've got to keep my eye on you for the next while."

She would have moved to get up but he stayed her with a hand on her knee. "I don't know how to thank you. You've always gone above and beyond, but today... that's different. I owe you, Maggie."

She rose, his hand sliding off her leg. "It's fine. It's the smell of the blood, that's all."

She forced herself to smile. He couldn't know, and she didn't want him to. For all he was aware, Tom had been killed on the job. And he had been. But it hadn't been an accident. No indeed. Tom had been shot. And by the time she'd reached the hospital he was in a coma. He'd never regained consciousness. All she had for parting memories were the sights and smells of his blood.

Too late she realized she was trembling. Nate lifted his hand and cupped her jaw with his fingers, steadying her. It was the most natural thing in the world to put her arms around him, try to gain strength from his.

He pulled her close and she linked her hands behind his back.

That's when she felt it beneath her fingers, hard and cold.

She pushed out of his arms.

"You're carrying a gun."

Chapter 9

Maggie stepped back, away from him. She could still feel the cold lump of the steel, the shape of it, tucked into the waistband of his jeans.

He was in her house, carrying a weapon. He had to have brought it with him, she realized. He'd had it all along. Her blood ran cold at the thought. In those moments all of Maggie's old feelings reared up, making her next words strangled and raw.

"You're carrying a gun."

The words echoed through the room. For long seconds Nate simply stared at her, as if determining what would be the best thing to say. She drew in a shaky breath. Tom had carried a handgun during his duties. To her recollection, he'd never fired it.

Not until the night he'd had to protect himself. Not until the night he'd come face-to-face with another weapon and he'd fired back. The end result was that he'd lived long enough to make it to hospital and the other man hadn't. And because the trespasser—a so-called activist—had also died, it didn't matter that Tom had died defending himself. His name had been sullied by the press, bandied about in the news like some political trick. One side placing the blame on him, the other side blaming the other man. Maggie had been caught in the middle, trying to grieve and defend him while being left alone with an infant daughter and a teenage cousin.

The very thought of Nate carrying a gun and being so calm about it made her sick to her stomach. She'd trusted him. He'd told her about his leave of absence and she'd believed him. Now she realized it was all a lie. The day it had hit her—he was on assignment—she'd known. And she'd let him divert her from the truth. But a man on a leave of absence, on vacation, didn't carry a gun.

Maggie folded her hands, keeping them from fidgeting and twisting by sheer willpower. He'd more than misrepresented himself to her. He'd insinuated a place for himself at Mountain Haven. With her.

She swallowed against the bile in her throat. He'd known all along and yet he'd let things grow between them. The sting of betrayal was made worse by her acute embarrassment at her actions. She'd kissed him. Wanted him. She'd started to care for him, deeply. Had considered taking it further, knowing he was leaving. Thank goodness she hadn't articulated her feelings. She clenched her fingers, turning the tips white. But she refused to turn away. Gathering all her strength, she squared her chin.

"Get out."

Nate froze. "You want me to leave?" He picked his words carefully, keeping his voice neutral.

"Do you or do you not have a gun tucked into the back of your jeans?"

She already knew the answer even as he sighed. At his brief silence, she raised an eyebrow.

"Yes, Maggie. I'm carrying a weapon."

She folded her arms, putting even more distance between them. "Why would that be, Nate? Am *I* some kind of threat to you?"

"I'm a marshal, Maggie. I don't go anywhere without a weapon. Ever."

Instead of reassuring her, her lips thinned. She'd accepted him at face value and it had been a terrible mistake on her part. She'd believed everything he'd said, had wanted to help him. Had wanted to nurture him. Knowing she'd been duped stung her pride, her self-judgment. She asked the question simply to clarify what she already knew.

"You mean you've had a gun on you the whole time you were here?"

"Yes, Maggie."

She swallowed. She had to know all of it. Know how blind she'd been to what was going on around her. There was no turning back now. "When we went to Olds?"

"Yes." His eyes settled on hers steadily. She wanted him to look guilty, but he didn't. She wrinkled her brow. If she didn't know better, she'd almost think he looked relieved.

"When you went snowshoeing?"

"Yes."

"And walking each day?"

She wished he'd show some emotion, rather than standing tall, unflinching before her. His eyes were honest but unreadable, a look she realized he probably used in his job every day.

"Yes."

Maggie paused, her eyes widened. "The day we went walking in the Chinook?"

She waited for his answer, her heart in her throat. That day she'd been vulnerable, and that day she'd made the choice to trust him with much of herself. He'd held her as she'd cried in his arms, listened as she'd told him about Tom. She couldn't have been so wrong, could she?

"Yeah. That day, too." His eyes searched hers, like he was asking her to understand. But she didn't understand anything. He hadn't really told her anything. How could he have held her and kissed her and been kind all the while having a handgun tucked in his jeans?

She turned away and he bent a little, trying to explain.

"Maggie, listen, what I said is true. I don't go *anywhere* without a gun." He stepped forward, holding out a hand but she backed away. If he was asking her to say it was all right, to understand why he'd done it, he could forget it. She'd been honest with him. He obviously didn't think he needed to reciprocate.

"It's a part of who I am," he continued. "You shouldn't take it personally."

"Not take it personally?" Maggie raised her voice, and she laughed a little at the end, the sound sharp and dry with disbelief. How could he possibly think she wouldn't take it personally? He'd come into her home. He'd brought guns into her home. And he hadn't told her. What else hadn't he told her? Was his whole story a fabrication?

She pointed to the door. "I want you to leave, Nate. You can get in your truck and drive into Olds and find a room at a motel. I'm sure your superiors will pay for it."

"I can't do that."

His reply was strong and definite, like he was giving an order, she thought. It would be much easier if he'd look away, or at least have the grace to look uncomfortable. But he kept her pinned with his eyes, begging her to understand. To accept. She'd done enough accepting. She'd accepted the death of her parents, leaving her orphaned. She'd accepted Tom's death, accepted the findings of the RCMP in their official report. She'd accepted Jen's troubles and had taken them on herself, done what she could to minimize the damage. She'd let Nate into her house and accepted his story about the girl as his reason for being here.

But she was done. She refused to turn away from him. He had to know she meant what she said. She leveled her gaze. "You're not welcome here. Not with your weapons."

"Maggie, you have to listen to me." He implored her with an outstretched hand, but she took another step backward. "I have to be here. *I have to.*"

"Why? Why here? And tell me the truth. I think I've earned it."

"Because I've been put here. I wish I could tell you more. But I can't. It's for your own protection."

She half turned, refusing his reply. It wasn't enough. Her heart pounded. All the little feelings she'd had but dismissed over the past few weeks bubbled up again. Tiny things that hadn't added up but that now made sense. "You're not on leave, are you?"

"No, I'm not."

Those three words took the starch out of her knees. She reached out and gripped the back of a chair. *His* chair, the one he sat at during meals and with his morning coffee.

She looked away, staring past him toward the kitchen window. Outside she could see her grass, working hard to grow and turn green, and the dark earth of the garden, yet to be planted. This was her world. The one that had been her mainstay for years. Her safe place. Right now she wished she could get it back, that sense of normalcy. Wished she could forget all the long forgotten things Nate had made her feel. That extraordinary world, with him, wasn't real. Knowing he'd deceived her made her long to return to normal more than anything.

At her drawn-out silence, he added quietly, "If it's worth anything, I didn't like it. Didn't like having to pretend."

"It's not worth much. It was all a lie then," she affirmed. She walked over to the counter and braced her hands on the top. The first time she'd considered truly moving on, doing something adventurous, out of her normal pattern, and this was what came of it. She'd thought she was safe with him. How could her judgment have been so off? She felt like a complete fool.

"Not all of it." He finally moved, going to stand behind her, yet keeping a subtle distance. He was close enough she could just feel the warmth of his breath on her neck. It made her remember how he tasted, how his arms felt, strong and sure around her. She had to stop thinking about it. It had been nothing more than momentary weakness. A flaw she wouldn't repeat.

"I was put on leave. The story I told you was one hundred percent true. But I was called back to work before it was over."

"And you're here on assignment." Everything she thought she knew melted away, leaving a dry, empty space.

"I'm sorry, Maggie."

Nate wanted to go to her, pull her into his arms and beg her to understand, but he wouldn't do that to her. He'd already done enough. He could see that as she spun to face him, her eyes wide with shock at the turn of the afternoon. He shoved his hands into his pockets to keep from reaching out. This was exactly what he hadn't wanted to happen. But his earlier encounter changed everything.

"What sort of assignment brings you to the middle of nowhere, Alberta? I don't understand. How do you even have jurisdiction here?"

He wished he could tell her everything, but he couldn't, not yet. Not without clearing it first. "I can't tell you the specifics."

She snorted. "Of course not. I'm just supposed to accept what you've told me and be a good girl and not question, right? I'm sorry, I can't do that."

Nate's frustration bubbled over. "Don't you think I wanted to tell you? Every time I looked into your eyes? Every time I kissed you, or you told me a little more about yourself? I hated having to lie to you, Maggie! But there's bigger issues at stake here!"

The outburst cost him. His head pained sharply and he exhaled slowly, trying to will it away. Yelling at her wouldn't solve anything.

"How on earth could I know that?" Her shout echoed through the kitchen.

This was why he'd kept the plan from her. Knowing what he knew about Peter Harding had made it clearer than ever that he had to keep her from harm. The more people that knew, the more danger they would all be in. If Peter found out who he was and where he was staying they could lose their opportunity. Or worse. No, it was necessary they keep it on a need to know basis. He reminded himself of that, drawing on all his strength to try to make her see reason.

"I know. And that's part of why I didn't say anything. You'd naturally have questions. Worries. I wanted to tell you, I did. I have reasons why I didn't."

"I don't care about your reasons." She tried to slide past him but he caught her with a hand on her wrist.

"Maggie, don't. Let me give you what I can. Sit down and we'll talk."

Nate kept the pressure on her wrist. He looked down at his fingers circling the pale skin of her arm. Why did he care? His cover was blown. Maggie knew who he was. How long before she put the rest together? But that wasn't all. He'd known all along he wasn't being honest and he'd gotten close to her anyway. And more than trying to find out information. He'd started to get involved with her personally. He couldn't begin to count the mistakes he'd made.

He should let her walk away and get on with the job, get it finished and get out. But he couldn't. Couldn't let her think everything between them had been a lie. Because it hadn't been. It had been, perhaps, the most real thing he'd experienced in a long time.

He cared about her. And not just the physical attraction, although there was that. He cared about Maggie, her hurts, her fears. Wanted to protect her. Wanted… damn. He wanted to love her, if it came to that.

"It wasn't all a lie," he began. But stopped, looking away for a moment. What was he trying to do? Get her to butt out or make her understand how deep his feelings really went? Trying to argue semantics wasn't the right strategy.

Maggie was glaring at him like he was the villain, for God's sake. The horrible thing was, he *felt* like a villain. All because he hadn't been able to be honest with her all along. And because he still couldn't. Not about the case, not about his feelings for her. Grant had been specific in keeping Maggie out of the loop until they knew for sure; to protest he cared about her would only come across as a diversion.

"Don't try to justify it now, just because you're caught."

"I won't."

She'd asked earlier if she were a threat, and she'd been sarcastic. But the answer that had jumped into his brain at the time had been *more than you know.* It was true in more ways than one. In the back of his mind he remembered what Grant had told him that day at the coffee shop. His gut said he could trust her. But what if he was wrong? After what had happened before his leave he wasn't sure he trusted his instincts anymore. What if Grant's suspicions were true and Nate let personal feelings get in the way? It would ruin everything. There was no way he could put people in danger based on a feeling. It was too much of a risk.

Right now he had to decide exactly how much to tell her. Enough to ease her mind and not enough to compromise things. Smooth things over. Get her to let him stay long enough to finish the job. He couldn't let his growing feelings for her cloud the priority. He pushed away the need to pull her into his arms, kiss away the hurt marking her face right now. He wasn't foolish enough to think she was only angry at him. She was hurt, too, and she had every right to be. What a mess.

He released her wrist and forced himself to relax, one muscle at a time, to make his body and expression as normal as possible. As he did it, her response mirrored his, until they both were more at ease.

"I'm asking you, please. Give me a chance to explain."

She hesitated long enough that he could take the opportunity to press his case. "I owe you an explanation. Let me give it."

She nodded and led the way back to the kitchen table. His head was aching now that the adrenaline had burned off but he forced it to the back of his mind. He could take something for the pain later.

He sat heavily, turning the chair to the side so he was facing her. "You know that Grant and I met at a conference in Toronto a few years ago. When this case came up, it was a natural fit for me to work with him on it. It was all set up before I had a chance to think."

"So you're working with Grant." She crossed her right leg over her left.

"He's the local liaison, yes. And it's true, I was on a leave of absence and they brought me back. At the time it seemed the logical cover. It's a small town, Maggie. What would people say if they knew I was here? I had to keep under the radar. It was much easier to come under the ruse of a vacation. Only…only I met you and I hated lying to you from the beginning."

"He says conveniently."

She was going to be a hard sell, especially without the details she seemed so intent on getting. Right now she was sitting in her chair, legs crossed and arms folded close to her body. Defensive to cover the pain. Unwilling to listen. But he knew it was there. Her eyes evaded his as he attempted to make contact. She had every reason to be hurt. He'd let himself become personally involved with her under false pretenses. He knew better.

"I still don't understand how someone from the States gets to come up here. Isn't there a whole jurisdiction issue?"

This was the one part Nate knew he could explain easily. "There's a Memorandum of Understanding between the U.S. authorities and Canadian. I liaise with a local department or contact, and here I am."

"So when you met Grant, it wasn't about catching up."

"No. We were information sharing."

"And you'd deliberately come along that day. When I took Jen to the bus station." Her arms crossed tighter.

Her blue eyes flashed, accusing. She deserved an honest answer. He wished he could give her one, prevent her from building a wall around herself. He didn't want her to shut him out. Even if what Grant thought was true, the more he could keep Maggie out of it now, the better. He could at least give her some kind of protection.

"I did. We met to discuss…details."

"Who could you possibly be looking for?"

Nate sat back in the chair. This was the one question he couldn't answer right now. How could he tell her? She was more wrapped up in it than she knew. It wasn't only the proximity that made her the perfect choice. And how on earth could he ask her what he needed to know? Grant had aired his suspicions and Nate admitted to himself that they weren't groundless. The problem was, he'd lost his objectivity. The evidence on paper didn't fit the person sitting before him now. There was more at stake than just the two of them. He had to be cautious.

"I can't tell you that."

"Again, convenient." She pushed her chair back but he put both hands on her thighs, keeping her seated.

"It's for your protection, Maggie, can't you see that?"

"Frankly, I can't."

The pounding in his head was increasing. It didn't matter that he'd been hit today. They had to move and move now. If he ruined this case there'd be no leave of absence. Two mistakes in a row wouldn't go over well. But it was more than that. Maggie was at the center of it, whether she knew it or not. Things would escalate from this moment forward. He had to take the time to explain things the best he could. For now. Then he'd deal with her innocence. He knew in his heart that whatever Maggie had done, it had been unwittingly. Had to have been.

They should have had more time to make their move

against Harding. But Nate had been distracted, he'd gotten careless. He'd ventured in closer to the farm and was on his way back out again when Pete had driven up in his truck. Nate had stopped, intending to see what was in the back of the vehicle when he'd frightened a flock of geese. The resulting flapping of wings and honking had sent up the alarm and he saw the rifle. And it hadn't been pointed at the birds.

He'd made himself a moving target, but Pete was a good shot. A graze was lucky.

He couldn't blame her for being scared. And she was under the impression that he'd only taken a fall.

The silence drew out as they stared at each other.

It was like they were holding a conversation without saying any words. When she finally spoke, he understood exactly what she was asking.

"When?"

Nate stood, walked a few feet and hooked his thumbs in his belt loops. Maggie looked away. He understood why. And hated it. It would be unfair of him to ask her for more.

"Tomorrow morning, best guess."

"So soon." The words were strangled.

"We need to move fast, before he takes off again."

"He?"

The name sat on his tongue and he debated. What would she do if he told her? And had Harding found out where he was staying yet?

Lord, he'd gotten careless and had put her in danger anyway. They had to strike first before Harding had a chance to regroup. He looked into Maggie's ashen face. And ignored the evidence for once. She was as innocent in all this as Jen had been. He'd stake his life on it. "I promise I'll tell you. Tonight."

"Nate, you'll be in danger," she repeated.

"I know." He ignored the searing pain in his head and squared his shoulders. "But this is what I'm trained for, Maggie. It's what I do, and I do it well."

"And afterward?"

She had to know how this was all going to end. There could be no other way. "Afterward Grant and I transport him back to the U.S. to stand trial."

This would be his last night at Mountain Haven. They both knew it. What Nate wanted and what he knew was possible were two very different things. He wanted to be with her. To love her. To take away that beautiful memory. Instead he'd be planning an op. Working to keep her safe. The thought left him hollow.

"This person is wanted. A *fugitive,* Maggie. It's what I do. I bring in criminals who are running from the law. Do you think we go after the small-time shoplifters? Do you?"

To his relief she stayed put in her chair. Her face paled further and her eyes widened. He hadn't wanted to frighten her but perhaps now it was the only way. To make her see why he'd felt the need for keeping her in the dark.

"The people I bring in are armed robbers, murderers, rapists, child predators. What do you think could happen if someone like that knew I was here to find them, knew you were involved?"

"If you're trying to scare me, it's working."

"Good. Because that's how important this is. It's the reason—the *only* reason—I had to keep quiet."

She looked away. "It doesn't change that you…"

He swallowed. She was right. He'd put his feelings for her above his duty. It was the first time he'd ever done that and he knew it had been a mistake. It served no purpose save to hurt both of them.

"No, it doesn't. I let myself become personally involved with you and I had no right. If you'd been any-one else…"

"You'd what?"

His breath caught as she turned liquid blue eyes on him. It was a day of truths. All too soon he'd be gone and perhaps if she knew, she'd accept his partial silence a little easier.

"I'd never have started to fall for you."

Calmly she rose from her chair. "You deceived me, used me. There is no excuse for that. You blew it, Nate."

I sure did, he thought, watching her walk away.

"Maggie."

She stopped at the doorway, refusing to turn around and face him.

"Can I stay, Maggie?"

Her words came, brittle. "I honor my commitments. I accepted your reservation and your bill is paid."

On the contrary, he knew he'd be paying for this for a long time to come. A day wouldn't go by that he wouldn't think of her. The scent of vanilla and cinna-mon, the sound of her laugh or howl of the westerly wind.

Maggie disappeared into her living quarters and Nate sighed. There was a lot to be done and a limited amount of time. He'd have to sort things out with her later. Right now he had a phone call to make.

They couldn't let Pete slip through their fingers again. He had to call Grant, assemble the team and prepare to go in. And add attempted murder to the list of charges.

Because he knew he'd gotten lucky. And he couldn't count on his luck to hold.

Maggie held it all in until she was in her living quar-ters. She shut the door with a firm click, then went and sat in the chair by the window, staring outside but seeing nothing.

Had he really fallen for her? Or was that his way of trying to smooth things over?

She didn't know what to believe anymore. She only knew that for the first time since Tom's death, after all those long, lonely years, she'd finally let someone in. She'd finally started to care. It had gone beyond simple flirtation and the physical. She'd *fallen.* She'd fallen for the man she thought he was. Kind, caring, strong, trustworthy.

Now she felt like a complete fool.

In the isolation of her room she let the tears come. Tears for all she'd lost, tears of humiliation. She hated her weakness, for allowing herself to fancy he was truly interested in her. She'd spent the majority of her life seeing things exactly as they were.

And where they were right now was that she was a forty-two-year-old widow with a teenage daughter and a bed-and-breakfast. Full stop. After years of protecting her heart, she'd let down her guard and had become vulnerable, trusting. She'd cautioned herself not to let herself get hurt again but she'd done it anyway. She'd let herself be seduced by the magic and romance of the situation, conveniently forgetting that reality would come crashing through.

She'd been stupid to believe he'd wanted her. She'd been naive. He was staying now, but not for her. For the job.

She should have done *her* job and put a stop to any personal connections they'd made. She'd been foolish and fanciful and…weak. The tears were bitter and cold and she resented them nearly as much as she resented Nate right now. Damn him for making her feel this way…hopeless and vulnerable. She hadn't cried often since Tom's death, and not once had it been over a man. Until now.

She swiped her hands roughly over her cheeks, brushing away the moisture. She'd indulged enough. She went to the bathroom and washed her face, covered the redness with makeup and vowed she'd never cry over a man ever again.

He was gone from the kitchen when she entered it again. The remnants of her first-aid treatment had disappeared, too, except for a bottle of painkillers that remained on the counter beside an empty glass. She should have realized his head would be hurting after the bump he'd taken.

The house was deathly silent. If he were concussed, he shouldn't be sleeping. Or if he did, she should at least wake him frequently. Just because she was angry and hurt didn't mean she wanted anything to happen to him.

She went upstairs, her feet creaking on the old steps, sounding louder than normal in the awkward silence that seemed to envelop the house. She should have insisted he see a doctor.

His door was open a crack and she tapped gently, pushing it open a few inches.

"Come in, Maggie."

Her body trembled at the sound of his soft, sure voice. In her anger it had been easy to believe he'd felt nothing for her, had used her. But as she pushed the door open with a squeak, and faced his eyes as they looked at her, she knew there was something between them. Something tenuous and tender, and now tainted with mistruths.

He was different, even if it was only her own perception that made him so. He wasn't Nate Griffith, reevaluating, but Nate Griffith, U.S. Marshal, back on the job.

"You're awake. I was worried."

He was sitting in the straight-back chair, and the laptop was open in front of him. He spun so that he was facing the door, but he didn't get up. As much as she hated the lies, as much as she hated the guns…something about him made her feel safe. It had always been that way; hating what he did while still feeling proud and protected.

His flak jacket lay on the bed in plain sight. There was no point in hiding it from her now. She could say she didn't care about him all she wanted. The surge of relief she felt knowing he'd at least had a vest on told the truth.

"I didn't mean to worry you. Believe me, Maggie. I wanted to save you more worry. You've had your fair share."

"I saw the pills downstairs. Does it hurt much?"

Automatically his fingers found the bandage on his forehead and he winced. She fought back the urge to go to him and examine the wound.

"It's paining a bit yet. Nothing I can't handle."

"You shouldn't sleep for long periods of time. I'm pretty sure you probably have a concussion." Her fingers curled on the doorknob. Her first instinct was to care for him. But things were too tenuous between them. She didn't want him to think all was forgiven just because she was concerned about his medical well-being.

"Me, too. That's why I'm…" He paused, then unsmiling, treated her with the truth. "That's why I'm working."

Her muscles stiffened. "Working."

He nodded. "The investigation is moving forward quickly now. We need to speak about that."

Her head spun as all the possibilities ricocheted in her mind. She couldn't imagine an empty house again, without him to cook for, talk to, laugh with. How could that be, knowing what she knew now?

He'd be going away. But before that, she supposed he'd get what he'd come for. And that wasn't her, even as a tiny voice inside her wanted it to be. And after what he'd said…there would be risks.

She kept her hand on the knob of the door. Better she know now. Other than Jen and Mike, it had seemed like everyone she'd cared about in her life had met a tragic ending. And even Jen could have been in more trouble if Maggie hadn't worked hard to change things. It would be better all around if she kept her distance from Nate.

"What do I have to do with it?"

He glanced at the laptop and her eyes followed. It seemed to be some sort of mapping diagram. She knew without him saying that it was a plan.

"Grant Simms will be here within the hour. Two at most."

Maggie's lip curled. Grant Simms again. He'd been at the local detachment for probably five years and he had a way of looking at Maggie like he *knew* things. When she'd pleaded Jen's case, she hadn't liked the way he'd watched her. Assessing. Like he was trying to figure her out, when her only motive had been to minimize the damage to her daughter. Jen had made a mistake. Maggie didn't think it should follow her around indefinitely. She realized now that Grant had probably told Nate everything about last summer and he'd never mentioned it. More secrets.

"You trust Grant."

"Of course I do."

She pulled back a little. It felt too much like choosing sides and she needed to distance herself again. Being close to him made it too easy to forget the many ways he had wronged her.

She would rather they met somewhere else. But it was hardly fair to ask that of him when he was already popping pills for his headache. She'd do it, knowing that it would make things move faster, letting her get her life back in order sooner. Then she could put this all behind her, once and for all.

"I'll put some coffee on."

She left the room, but turned to pull the door closed behind her. Before it was latched, she saw Nate already facing the computer again, his hand on the mouse.

He was a cop, a fugitive hunter, focused on the job. There was no room in his life for her. It was just as well she knew now before something happened she'd truly regret.

Chapter 10

It was probably good Grant was coming. At this rate, the deep freeze would be full and she'd have to send a care package to Jen. Maggie stared at the pile of dirty dishes on the counter and the cooling racks full of baked goods on the table. She was more upset than she'd initially realized.

Baking meant she could avoid Nate. She could distract herself from thinking about how he'd lied to her, how he was putting himself in danger again, how in danger *she* felt when he kissed her and touched her, lighting her body on fire.

Only the distracting wasn't working so well this time.

She was sliding another batch of muffins out of the oven when the doorbell rang. She put the muffin tins on top of the oven and pulled off her oven mitt as she went to the door.

Grant Simms was on the other side, dressed in plainclothes but with his issue pistol in plain sight.

"Good evening, Maggie."

"Constable Simms."

She knew she sounded frosty and didn't care. She stepped back, holding the door open, the only invitation to come in that she offered. He stepped into the breach.

With Jen behind him.

"Jennifer!"

For a moment she wondered if Jen were in trouble again, but dismissed it. She had no doubt that Jen had learned her lesson. Still, what was she doing here?

"Constable Simms sent for me this afternoon. He wanted me to answer some questions about Peter Harding."

Peter Harding?

"Hey, Grant."

Nate's voice came from the stairs and the three of them turned to look up.

He was fully dressed, in jeans and a dark longsleeved T-shirt that accented the breadth of his chest and the curved muscles in his arms. "U.S. MARSHAL" was emblazoned down the sleeve. He'd shaved, changed the gauze and tape on the bandage. For the first time since arriving, he had on a holster and his handgun was in it. All pretenses were officially gone. Maggie blinked. Everything was upside down. What was now reality seemed surreal to her.

When Nate got to the bottom, he and Grant shook hands, the grip strong as their eyes met. And Maggie knew that despite her personal feelings, Nate and Grant were a team. They were cut from the same cloth, and she was oddly reassured.

"Hell of a thing, you getting trimmed."

Maggie's face blanched as the words seemed to

bounce around. All the blood drained from her head, leaving her spinning as Jen's and Nate's faces blurred. Nate frowned at Grant. The bandage glared white on the corner of his head.

"You didn't tell her?" Grant's voice echoed in her head. She knew what trimmed meant. She knew it meant he hadn't fallen and hit his head on a rock. Trimmed meant he'd been grazed by a bullet.

She heard Nate's voice, it sounded far away. "No. I didn't want to worry her."

She closed her eyes, willing away the shock and numbing fear. Nate put his hands on her shoulders. She wanted to lean back against his strength but resisted. He'd lied to her over and over again. When would she learn?

"You were shot." She shook off his hands, knowing being touched by him made her vulnerable. She wanted to escape but didn't know how. He was blocking the door and Grant and Jen were watching it all. There was nowhere safe in the house. Yet how could she deal with this?

"Give us a minute, Grant. Jen, if you wouldn't mind waiting in your room, we'll call you when we're ready." Nate took charge, gripping her arm and leading her down the hall to the kitchen. Once there he squeezed her arms and bent his knees so he was looking in her eyes. "I was grazed, that's all."

"You were shot." She shook her head wildly, stopping when his grip tightened. "A man fired a gun at you with intent…the fact that he was slightly off the mark is irrelevant. And you wouldn't even go to the hospital!"

"I know a flesh wound when I see one, Maggie. And there wasn't time for a trip to the emergency room."

She'd had his blood on her hands.

"No time," she echoed. What did that mean? She

pulled away but stopped by the kitchen table, standing next to the first chair. The one he'd sat in while insisting that she bandage the wound.

"I don't know what to say. I didn't want you to panic. And we can talk about this, but not now. There isn't time for it."

She nodded. This couldn't be happening. It was all becoming a big blur that she didn't understand. Things were moving too fast. She'd barely begun to assimilate that he was actually on the job. Now everything else came crashing around her. Grant was here. Jen was here, of all things. Maybe Nate cared, maybe he didn't. But the one thing that was clear was that he'd used her. Used her to get to this particular moment in time.

"Maggie, is there coffee?" Nate's voice was efficient but calm, and it grounded her. She turned her head, focused on his face. The truth had changed him. He was taller, somehow. More commanding. There was a force about him that was magnetic. He was a man to be reckoned with; a man who would protect what was right. She should hate him for it but couldn't help but admire it.

"Yes, and fresh muffins."

"That would be great. We'd like it very much if you'd join us."

"What do you need me for?"

"It'll all make sense, Maggie."

Grant had only ever been coolly polite to her, and now they were asking, no demanding, that she accommodate their meeting.

Lord, she had so many mixed feelings over the matter she felt like making more muffins. Why couldn't they go back to the way it was before? It had seemed complicated, but it was simple compared to this. Before, it had been new and foreign. Now Nate was putting his life on the line and nothing she could say would make any difference.

Nate put his hand on hers as she retrieved a plate. The firm warmth of it heated her cold fingers.

"Thank you, Maggie. I know this isn't easy for you."

"No, it's not." She avoided his face, focusing instead on arranging the muffins on the plate.

"And I don't mean to make it any harder…so I'm going to ask you something in private."

Her hands stilled over the butter dish. There was more? How much more could she possibly take today?

"What could you possibly want to ask of me now?"

Surprise held her still when he took both her hands in his own. She risked a look up; his eyes held apology and understanding.

"You shared things with me these last weeks. Things about your life. And we…we developed an attachment. Yet…" He paused, looked at his toes, then looked up again.

"Just ask what you want to ask, Nate. We're too far along for niceties now."

"I find it hard to believe you haven't been involved with anyone since Tom."

Maggie's brows drew together. She couldn't read his face; he'd switched back into cop mode. What did her sex life, or lack of it, have to do with anything?

"What does it matter?"

The pressure on her fingers tightened. "Damn, I wanted to wait to ask you this at a better time. Maggie, have you been involved with anyone? Say, last summer?"

Last summer? She looked up into his face, her eyes widening with confusion. "You're asking me if I've had a boyfriend since Tom. Specifically about a year ago."

"That's what I'm asking."

"I don't see what business it is of yours, but no."

She pulled her hands away and resumed arranging the tray. What reason could he possibly have for delving into *her* past? It was dry as dust. There hadn't been anyone since Tom. Not even close, until…

Until Nate. It always came back to Nate.

"You weren't involved with Peter Harding?"

Peter Harding? This was what this was about? It was the second time she'd heard his name tonight and Maggie's stomach dropped. Why in the world would he think she was involved with Pete? How could anyone? She had very real reasons to hate the man, not have an affair with him. Her fingers tightened on the edges of the tray.

She looked up at Nate, surprised to find him serious. "I have no use for Peter Harding. None whatsoever. He's despicable."

The relief on his face was so profound that suddenly it all fit together. Pete was Nate's assignment. Pete, the man responsible for Jen's arrest, had shot Nate today. The thought made her knees go weak but she stood her ground. "He's who you're here for, isn't he?"

Had he thought she was involved all this time? She took a step back.

"Did you seriously think that I had an affair with a man like that?" And suspecting it, had he seduced her anyway? Or had he tried to get close to her so she'd betray Pete? The very idea turned her stomach.

"I believe you when you say you didn't," he conceded. "Once I got to know you, I knew it couldn't be true. But I had feelings that I recognized might be clouding my judgment." His voice grew stronger. "But Grant is going to ask you and I wanted to give you the heads-up. I thought it might be easier for you if it came from me first."

Grant, of course. She wondered if that was why he always looked at her with that cold, assessing glare. At least Nate had judged her correctly. She stared down the hall at the entrance to the den, her distrust growing. He'd let Jen go, but he hadn't been pleasant about it. Now he'd dragged her into this mess once again, when it would be best if it were all forgotten. She simply wanted to go on as if Peter Harding had never existed!

"What has Pete done?" She collected herself and put the plate of muffins in the center of the tray. "After all you've put me through, you can at least tell me that."

"Bring in the coffee, Maggie. We'll talk."

She put the carafe on the tray and Nate took it from her hands. This was all happening so quickly. Only this afternoon she'd been humming and folding Nate's laundry and now she had the RCMP sitting in her den, talking about bringing in fugitives over coffee and muffins.

Nate put the tray down on the coffee table and Maggie poured three mugs of the steaming brew. She sat on the couch, surprised when Nate sat down beside her instead of in the chair closest to Grant, almost as if he were choosing her side. She stared at his thigh, lean and muscled even through the denim. She put down her spoon in time to see Nate meet Grant's gaze and give a small shake of his head. Grant shifted in his seat.

"Maggie," Grant began, "first of all I want to apologize for putting you in the middle of this. It was my idea completely. I certainly didn't mean to cause any upset."

She wasn't sure whether to believe him or not. Yet something in his tone rang genuine, something she hadn't heard before.

"You're after Pete Harding." She took a sip of the coffee, trying hard to appear calmer than she felt.

"Yes, we are." Nate broke in. "Your place was the natural fit. You're geographically close by, I could stay here legitimately and your known connection to him helped."

"My connection," she echoed, lost. "I already told Nate I wasn't involved with him."

"Through Jennifer," Grant said gently.

Maggie turned and looked at Nate. "You did know." Her heart sank. She'd been aware from the first what he did for a job and she'd wanted to spare him the details of Jen's arrest. But he'd known all along. Of course he had.

He nodded. "I did. But it didn't matter. Jen told me about it anyway before she left to go back to school. She felt very sorry about putting you through so much trouble."

Maggie's eyes stung. Pete Harding was a waste of space in her opinion. Bootlegging and selling pot, petty stuff to most but she knew how it could cause lasting damage. Jen had been quiet when the whole arrest happened, unwilling to share much information at all, and it had scared Maggie to death. She'd wanted Pete pulled in but she'd been informed at the beginning that there wasn't enough to warrant his arrest, so she'd focused on what was best for Jen. For months she'd lived in the same community resenting his presence and his above-the-law attitude.

She was glad Jen seemed to be on the other side of her troubles now. And yet here was Pete again, front and center in Maggie's life. She huffed out a breath.

Grant spoke into the breach. "I'm glad to hear there was nothing going on with you."

Maggie turned her attention to Grant. "Why on earth would you have suspected such a thing? How could you? All I did was try to protect my daughter!"

Grant rested his elbows on his knees. "You're about the same age, you've been a widow for a lot of years. And you were very persistent in dropping the matter last summer when Jennifer was arrested. It looked like you were protecting him. We couldn't take chances. When we found out who he really was…we had to act."

Maggie put down her cup. "My only concern was minimizing the damage to Jennifer, and I was as much as told that there wasn't enough on Pete to charge him with anything. You haven't been here long, Grant, but if you'd talked to anyone in the community they would have told you point-blank that I'd never have anything to do with someone like Pete Harding."

"The only thing we had on file for you was Tom, and the questions brought up from his death…on paper it was very plausible."

Maggie looked at Nate. The eyebrow not hindered by gauze was wrinkled; like he was confused about something.

"Paper isn't enough." She turned her attention to her coffee cup.

"I know. Please accept my apologies, Maggie."

His words, his tone, his expression, were all earnest. Maggie looked at Nate again. He'd been thoughtful enough to ask her about it in private. Perhaps it made no sense in light of recent truths, but if Nate trusted Grant, it was good enough for her.

"Let's just move on, shall we?"

Nate angled himself on the sofa. "If you have anything you know about Pete that you'd like to share, that would be helpful."

Maggie couldn't think of a thing. "I only know he operates off his property. Booze and drugs. Wouldn't surprise me to find a grow operation on the property somewhere."

Nate grinned suddenly, the expression lighting up his face. "Oh, we found it. Thanks for the snowshoes, by the way. I don't think there's going to be much of a crop this year."

So he hadn't been going for walks, either. He'd been haunting the fields. "You were staking him out."

Nate nodded. "I took what I needed in my backpack and made do."

His backpack. Maggie now understood that he'd not only carried his lunch but very likely firearms and ammunition as well as surveillance gear. She fought against the sense of the surreal, tried to remain in the moment. It didn't seem possible that this was happening in her house.

Who was this man? The more she discovered, the more he seemed a mystery. How could he be the same man she'd kissed? The same man she'd told secrets to, the one who'd inspired feelings in her that no man had since she'd been married to Tom?

"You don't know anything more?"

She shook herself out of her thoughts in time to register the question.

"No, nothing."

"Then I think it's time to bring Jen in. If there's anything she can share that she didn't last fall, it could be helpful."

Grant went out and returned a moment later with Jen, who kept her eyes downcast and picked at a fingernail.

"Jen, honey, Constable Simms and…and Nate—" she still couldn't seem to bring herself to call him a marshal "—just want to ask you a few questions about Pete Harding. You're not in any trouble. Right?" She aimed the last at Nate, giving him a warning eyebrow.

Nate nodded. "That's right. You haven't done anything wrong. Why don't you sit down, and we can see if you remember anything that might be important."

Jen sat on the sofa beside Grant and met her mother's gaze with red-rimmed eyes.

"I'm sorry, Mama," she said, swallowing.

Maggie's eyes misted. Jen hadn't called her Mama for several years and it took her back to those uncomplicated days of her childhood.

"You're forgiven."

Why it had taken nearly a year for them each to say those important words, Maggie didn't know, but as soon as they were spoken, everything changed. Her daughter was back. Really back. The relief hit her square in the chest.

"Jennifer," Grant began, "last summer you didn't give us a lot of details and we think that you may have been afraid to say much of anything. I want you to forget that fear now. Nate is here, and I'm here, to take Peter Harding in for good. He can't hurt you, Jen. But you can help us so he doesn't hurt anyone else."

"What do you want to know?"

Jen's face was pale but somehow strong, and Maggie realized what a treasure she was. She met Jen's eyes and nodded.

"Did Pete ever threaten you?"

"He said that if I ever ratted him out I'd be sorry."

"Anything more specific? Did he use several girls to run his product?"

Jen shook her head. "Not that I know of. At first... at first he was kind of cool, you know? Then he got a little scary. I felt weird around him but by that time I was afraid to walk away. Then he..."

She stopped, turned away and Maggie's heart stopped.

"Then he what, Jen." She tried to keep the shake out of her voice but failed.

"He showed me a trapdoor in the barn. It was where

he hid his stuff. And he said if I did anything to cause trouble he'd hide me there, too."

Maggie's stomach tumbled clear to her toes as the ramifications covered her in waves.

Nate's mouth fell open and Grant's face turned red.

"Why in God's name didn't you tell me this last summer?" Grant's elbows came off his knees and his fingers flexed tightly as he raised his voice.

Jen sniffled. "I was too afraid! I figured if I kept on the low it would go away and it would be okay."

Maggie stood, crossed the room and pulled Jen into her arms. "Oh, baby," she whispered, holding her daughter close as she sobbed. "You should have told me. We could have stopped him months ago."

"You were so mad, I didn't want to upset you anymore. And then you sent me away and I thought that…"

The childlike plea in Jen's voice touched her. In all this time, she hadn't considered that Jen might have felt turned away. She'd only considered her daughter's wellbeing. The backs of her eyelids burned.

"You thought what? That I didn't want you anymore?" Maggie put her hands on either side of Jen's face and looked her dead in the eyes. "Oh, honey, I hated being without you. You're all I've got. But I wanted to keep you safe. To get you away from your troubles. I could never stop loving you! I certainly wouldn't ever punish you by sending you away!"

Jen's arms tightened around Maggie's neck and Maggie closed her eyes, feeling the tears trickle on her cheeks and not caring that Nate and Grant stood by watching. She'd sent Jen off to school somewhere else, tried to pretend none of it had happened and all the while her baby girl had felt the sting of rejection. Had thought she wasn't wanted, which couldn't be farther from the truth.

Grant's voice interrupted quietly. "Jen, if there's anything else you have to tell us, now's the time. I wish you'd said something last summer."

Jen's voice came out in a hoarse whisper. "He said if I told anyone he'd lock me in there. I didn't think the cops would take it seriously, they'd think he'd only said it to scare me. But I saw the look in his eyes. I believed him."

Nate ground out an earthy curse, then the den fell eerily silent.

Whatever Pete had done, it had been enough that the U.S. government had seen fit to send Nate up to get him. And they didn't do that for simple bootleggers. Maggie's body felt like stone; she couldn't move. Implications of what might have happened to Jen fell on her, heavy and cold. And for the first time, she was glad that it was Nate with her. Glad he was on the job. Grateful and...proud. Her arm tightened on Jen's shoulder as they faced the men together.

"I'm sorry," she whispered. "I have to know. What is it he's done? What's he charged with?"

After a moment's silence, Nate answered. His tone was clear, strong and the words sent an icy chill up the backs of her legs.

"He's charged with three counts of kidnapping and sexual assault, and one count of murder."

A cry escaped her throat as she crumpled, sliding away from Jen. Nate's arm reached out, supporting her as shock rippled through her body.

Harding's threats didn't seem so harmless now. Delayed fear pulsed through her veins at what she could have lost. She'd lost everyone else. She couldn't have borne losing her baby girl, too. And she'd come closer than she'd thought possible.

Nate ignored Grant. Instead he put a finger under

her chin and lifted it. When she looked up into his face, ashamed of what she'd done, frightened of what she'd just heard, what she saw in his eyes warmed her soul.

He would do whatever it took to make things right. He would protect her. He would protect Jen. She knew it in her heart. How could she hate him now for hiding the truth? Now that she knew all of it, she understood.

"It will be over soon, Maggie, I promise. Peter Harding will be gone from your life forever. You won't have to be afraid. Jen won't have to be afraid."

She closed her eyes briefly. "Thank you."

He pressed his lips to her forehead and she let herself lean into it, just for a moment, gathering a little strength.

After a few minutes, she squared her shoulders. Nate had said that things were moving fast. That meant he and Grant had to be planning how to make the arrest. Her heart beat erratically, nerves bubbling over. Nate would be in danger. The best thing she could do now to help was make sure they had the time and space to plan, to prepare. To ensure there would be no mistakes.

"We'll leave you to talk now. You must have things to discuss."

"Maggie?" Grant's voice interrupted. "Jen isn't staying. I want her away from here, and safe. I have an officer ready to take her back to Edmonton as soon as we're finished here. I'm sorry."

"But…" Maggie looked up at Nate, then back to Grant. It would sound silly, insisting that she'd only just gotten Jen back. But now that she knew everything, she didn't want to let her go.

"Can't I stay here, with Mom?"

Nate's hand squeezed Maggie's and he looked down into her eyes. "It would be useless to ask *you* to leave, I know that. But we can keep Jen away from it. It would be one less thing for us to worry about."

Maggie knew that right now it was more important to keep Nate focused on his job. She looked up at Jen, raised an eyebrow. Jen looked stronger now, less frightened. Nate had a way of doing that and she loved him for it.

Jen wrapped her arms around herself. "It's okay, Mom. Once it's over I'll come home. I promise."

Maggie rose, her thigh tingling as Nate's free hand lingered over the fabric of her trousers. "I'll come and get you myself." She held out her hand and Jen took it. Maggie's knees trembled but she made herself take one step, then another, to the door. She avoided Grant's gaze as she left the room with Jen, closing the door behind her.

She leaned back against it. Yes, Peter Harding would be gone for good. But so would Nate.

And the thought of being without him made her very lonely indeed. She hated it almost as much as she hated the fact he'd be putting himself in danger.

A half hour later, after a quick cup of tea and a restorative, albeit brief conversation with her daughter, Maggie heard voices in the hall; heard Nate say "that's it then." Maggie put down her teacup and held Jen's hand as she went to see Grant—and her daughter—away. She'd been remiss in her manners earlier, but she saw things differently now.

Very differently. Knowing what Pete had done, knowing how much trouble Jennifer could have been in…Grant deserved her gratitude and respect, certainly not the curtness she'd treated him to on his arrival.

When she walked toward the front door, Grant's eyes seemed to smile at her. She was no longer intimidated by his size, his bearing. Instead she was oddly reassured that he'd do everything in his power to make sure things turned out the right way. The animosity she'd felt for him all these months evaporated.

"Thank you, Maggie, for the hospitality—and for the information."

"You're welcome," she said, meaning it. She caught Jen in a quick hug. "Love you. Call when you get in. And I'll see you soon."

Grant lifted a hand in farewell and jumped the two steps off the porch, Jen following behind.

"Constable Simms?"

He stopped. Maggie sensed Nate behind her and knew what she was about to say was as much for him as it was for Grant. "Be careful."

He smiled at her, a genuine, wide smile. She hadn't known his face could change that much. He looked ten years younger. "I'm always careful." His smile faded as he looked up at Nate, standing just behind her. "Nate... I'll see you at the staging area at five. Get some sleep, will ya?"

Nate nodded. "I'll be there with bells on."

He reached over and squeezed Maggie's hand. "I've got things to do. I'll see you later."

He left her on the cold porch, shivering in the frosty spring air and watching Grant and Jen drive away. More than ever, she had no idea what it was she wanted. She only knew she wanted it over.

By midnight she was sufficiently worried. She'd heard nothing out of Nate since Grant's departure, not a whisper of him moving around upstairs. The vision of his cut loomed before her eyes. He'd held it together during Grant's visit, but she'd seen the gray pallor beneath his usual healthy color. She'd kept hoping he'd stir, perhaps come down to the kitchen for a snack. She'd bathed and changed into a pair of sleep pants and a

T-shirt, but nothing. Her conscience nagged at her, telling her to forget her hurt feelings and check on him. The few hours of frenetic activity had subsided. And she was left feeling raw and open. It brought back so many memories she'd tried to bury.

She hated to wake him. He had to be up early and needed his rest. Yet…she was pretty sure he'd suffered some sort of a concussion.

She crept upstairs, although she couldn't figure out why. She was going wake him anyway, so why was she worried about making noise? Perhaps it was simply that now they were forced to tiptoe around each other. Hold a fragile balance. She didn't feel prepared to tip the scales in favor of the anger or the hurt she felt. The betrayal at his lies and the fear of the danger he was putting himself in, all mixed together with gratitude that he was there in the first place. None of her emotions matched up and she was completely off balance.

She opened his door. It was dark inside and he was in bed, sprawled beneath the covers. One ankle curved outside the quilt, the skin of his foot pale in the muted moonlight pouring through his window. His lips were slightly open in sleep, the white bandage on his head a stark reminder of all that had transpired that afternoon.

She didn't want to touch him. Not now. It would do nothing but stir up memories and futile longings.

"Nate." She whispered it, willing him to wake. But he never moved, his chest barely rising and falling.

"Nate." She put a little more force behind it, to no avail.

Heart pounding, she sat tentatively on the edge of the bed. One of his arms was spread wide, his forearm sprinkled with dark hair visible under the edge of the blanket. She touched it lightly, the warm skin tingling on her fingertips. She'd never met a man like him. He was strong and deliberate, even in sleep.

"Nathaniel," she whispered, her throat tight.

His lashes fluttered up as he opened his eyes. The turquoise color glowed darkly in the shadows, focusing on her face.

"Maggie," he murmured, the soft sound an endearment.

Her body warmed. Lies or not, the undercurrent of desire hadn't abated. She'd had time to think since the events of the afternoon, and even knowing there was no future for them, she understood his reasoning for secrets. He'd done it to protect her, to protect everyone, and had put himself in danger in the process. She didn't like it but she understood it. He'd only done what he'd needed to do.

What she didn't understand was why he'd let things progress between *them*. Why he hadn't kept his distance. If he was here on business, why hadn't he kept it as business?

But was that what she really wanted? Then she would have missed out on the last few weeks, and despite the pain, both from dredging up the past and from learning about his deception, she couldn't bring herself to be sorry any of it had happened. She wasn't sorry that he'd made her feel more alive than she had in years. She'd never be sorry he'd kissed her and held her.

"I'll go," she murmured. "I wanted to make sure you were awake. You shouldn't sleep for long periods at once."

"Stay."

He hadn't moved. His foot curled around the blankets at the end of the bed, his arm stayed beneath the covers. But his eyes, and that one word, held her there.

"Don't," she whispered. She swallowed. Hadn't there

been enough pretense today? He didn't need to act like there was still something between them. The truth was out, and it was bigger than both of them.

"Not everything about my being here was a lie, Maggie."

"How can you say that," she whispered furiously. "It was a cover from the moment you called and gave your reservation to Jen." She turned away from his gaze. "Your interest in me was a cover."

She didn't want him. But even knowing it, her heart begged him to dispute it.

The arm shifted. His fingers reached up until they touched the skin of her face and it was all she could do to not close her eyes at the tender touch. She couldn't seem to move off the side of the bed, anchored there by the gentle graze of his fingertips and the intensity burning in his eyes.

"I lied about the professional side, because I had to, and now you know why." The backs of his fingers caressed her jaw. "But everything…personal between us was the truth. It was not part of the plan. I wasn't anticipating *you.*"

"Why should I believe you?" She jerked her head away from his hand. She couldn't think, couldn't remain objective when he touched her this way.

"Because if you don't it means you were wrong." He didn't let her get away. His fingers curled over her ear and beneath her hair as he rose up on the opposite elbow. "Wrong when you felt this *thing* building between us. Wrong when you touched me and I touched you. Wrong when you trusted me."

His lips curled ever so slightly into a smile. "You weren't wrong, Maggie. Those feelings—they're real."

She wanted desperately to believe him as his soft words wooed her. To believe that everything that had

342 Falling for Mr. Dark & Dangerous

transpired…their confidences, the little touches, the way her heart soared when he kissed her…had been true. But she couldn't escape the memory of the cold steel tucked beneath his shirt today. Or the way she'd had his blood on her hands. She hated guns. Hated them with a passion. Even knowing he was a cop hadn't meant that much to her. He'd been on holiday, and for the brief time he was at Mountain Haven she'd chosen to ignore the fact when it suited her. He hadn't been on duty. He'd been someone else.

"I'm sorry about the gun," he whispered, as if he could read her mind. "You have to know I'd never hurt you. You have to know I'd do anything—*anything*—to protect you. Even lie."

"I feel used," she admitted, amazed that she still felt she could confide her feelings. How could she be so angry and yet feel so close to him? Yet they'd always seemed able to talk. She remembered how he'd held her in the den earlier when she realized the depth of the danger Pete Harding represented. He had told her the truth when he could.

Perhaps in an odd way, that was the one thing that had been truthful between them. The ability to talk when it was necessary. He had a way of bringing out her secrets. Most of them, anyway. She still held a few close to her heart. She didn't want to see pity on his face. And without telling him, he'd never understand why she had reacted as she had to discovering his gun, or knowing he could have been killed.

His eyes searched hers. "I know you do, and I'm so sorry. And I did want to tell you. I even mentioned it to Grant, but he thought it would be better if I didn't."

He tugged with his hand. She was sitting on one hip and lost her balance, falling slightly to lie over his chest.

"Nate, I…"

He stopped her words with his mouth. First lifting and seeking her lips, and once finding them, pushing up and twisting so that she fell beneath him.

It was different from the other times. This time it went beyond the sexual and hit her straight in her heart, and she didn't fight it. Maybe it was the freedom of the truth that changed it, maybe it was knowing it was all coming to an end, but despite everything he still had the power to do this; to make her feel like a desirable, loved woman. It was more than knowing he was younger, or the fitness of his firm body. It was in the way he touched her, like he couldn't help himself. Like she was something treasured.

But he was leaving tomorrow, and she wanted to absorb the feeling and keep it locked inside for safekeeping. To be able to look back and remember it when he was gone, to cherish it like she did the items she kept in her special box. For once, she stopped analyzing the pros and cons and let herself *feel*.

In the dark, on a rumpled bed, they were horizontal with his weight pressing her into the mattress. Her hands lifted, only to find the warm, bare skin of his shoulder, curved and dipped with hard muscle. Her fingers drifted lower, over his shoulders and back, stopping at a rough wrinkle. One of the scars he'd mentioned? She couldn't tell in the dark.

"This isn't a lie." His lips hovered over her ear before trailing down her neck. His weight pushed her deeper into the mattress. "What you do to me isn't a lie."

His mouth claimed hers again and she met it eagerly. She'd let fear stand in her way for too long. Now his time at Mountain Haven was drawing shorter with each fleeting moment. She'd been waiting for someone. Someone she could feel safe with. It shocked her to realize she still felt Nate was that man. Even after everything that had been revealed today.

He shifted slightly, his hand slipping over her T-shirt. He cupped her in his palm and her body surged from the contact, long-lost desire settling in her core. She arched, pressing herself more firmly into his hand, glorying in the feeling she'd nearly forgotten in her long abstinence.

He lowered his head until she felt his moist breath through the cotton.

A moan ripped from her throat and she gripped his hair with her hands.

And he stilled, his muffled cry of pain vibrating just below her heart. In the heat of the moment, she'd forgotten about his head and the gash that had unraveled everything.

"I'm sorry," she whispered. She was sorry she had hurt him. She was sorry they'd stopped, because being with him made her feel alive.

But it was madness and nothing good could come of it, no matter how much she craved him. He would still be leaving. He would still put himself in harm's way every day. She'd already been through it once. She couldn't deal with it again.

Nate didn't move. He simply dropped his head, resting it for a moment on the softness of her diaphragm. She closed her eyes and imprinted the feeling of him there on her soul.

"It's all right." His voice grated in the darkness. "We should stop. I promised myself I wouldn't do this."

Maggie suddenly felt very exposed, though she remained completely clothed. She put her hands on the bed, pushing herself upward a few inches. The fantasy was over, reality firmly back in its place. The need to protect herself overrode the longing to be with him one last time before he left.

Nate rolled to the side, propped up on an elbow. "I promised myself I wouldn't let this go too far. I can't make love to you, Maggie. No matter how much I want to."

His explanation fell flat. He didn't really want her and she'd been foolish to indulge in rolling around on the bed with him. Things were far too complicated. He probably thought she'd come up here with this very purpose in mind. Her cheeks burned at the thought.

"I don't recall asking you to."

Her icy words cooled the room considerably.

"No, you didn't."

She pulled away, stood beside the bed glaring down at him, angry at herself for falling under his spell yet again. He'd been the one to tug her down and kiss her first. To what purpose? Surely he didn't feel like he had to pretend anymore.

"What were you trying to do, anyway? Distract me from the fact that you've been pretending all this time? Or just smooth things over to soothe my hurt feelings? I assure you, I'm over it."

His nostrils flared but he didn't move from his position. "That's not it at all. I wanted to show you that despite everything, *this* much was real." His lip curled with the bite of sarcasm. "At least it was for *me*."

How dare he. He'd been the one to lie and pretend and she'd done nothing but be honest with him. Brutally honest, she remembered, her cheeks burning. Now he was accusing her of using him? Declaring his intentions to be pure while challenging that hers were anything but? And then pushing her away in the end anyway.

"When will you be wrapping this thing up?"

Nate pushed up off his elbow, sitting up in the bed. His brows pulled together in the middle.

"Tomorrow, then if it goes as planned, transport the day after. Why?"

Maggie smiled coldly. "Then I only have one more day of doubting every word that comes out of your mouth."

She instantly regretted her statement, but gathering every last shred of pride she had left, she swept from the room, shutting the door behind her.

Chapter 11

The coffee was brewed, but Maggie stared out the kitchen window, seeing little in the predawn hours. She'd slept fitfully, waking every few minutes, worrying, thinking too much. Finally at four she'd risen, dressed and put on coffee. She'd sleep later. She'd have lots of time for sleep.

Nothing made sense. She'd been mad about the lies; she wasn't anymore. She was proud of who he was, but it scared her to death. She cared about him, more each day, but she wanted him gone. Wanted this over.

Wanted to come out of it unhurt, and the longer it went on, the more she was sure that was impossible.

Her head tilted as she heard sounds echoing through the upstairs. Nate was up. He was packing his things to walk away, leaving forever. She should be glad things hadn't gone further than they had. In her head she knew that was true. But all her heart felt was an aching loss at an opportunity missed; a return to a life that was lackluster and plain. Most of all she was sorry she'd lashed out at him last night. He had enough to worry about without her throwing around accusations. It didn't solve anything.

She couldn't stand the thought of sitting here, waiting for news throughout the day. Listening for his footsteps when he came back…or didn't. No, it would be better if they said their goodbyes now.

He'd be down soon. Maggie took out a frying pan and got eggs from the fridge. The last thing she could do for him was make him a decent breakfast. It had nothing to do with any service she was being paid for; nothing to do with him being a guest in her home. It was, simply, the last caring act she could give him.

The eggs were delicately done when his steps echoed on the stairs. Maggie turned off the burner and went to the cupboard to fetch a plate. When she spun back around, she froze.

He was magnificent.

There was no other word for it and it frightened her almost as much as it exhilarated her. There was no hiding who he was from her this morning. He stood in the breach between hallway and kitchen, dressed in his customary jeans. But everything else seemed different. A long-sleeved shirt hugged the muscles of his chest and arms, and for the first time she caught sight of his USMS badge. It hung from a silver chain around his neck, a plain star within a circle with the words "United States Marshal" engraved in the perimeter. In his hands he carried more gear—a vest with several pockets, and two holsters. They made him seem so very large, imposing. Only she couldn't help but notice the dark circles beneath his eyes and a stab of worry went through her. He needed to be alert this morning. Was it her fault he wasn't rested?

"I made you breakfast."

It was all she could think to say. Anything more would open a door she didn't want to walk through today. They both knew what he was going to do. They both knew that he was leaving. There was nothing more to say without bringing up recriminations and regrets.

He put his gear on an empty chair and sat down as she placed the plate at *his* place. "Are you joining me?"

Food was the last thing on her mind and she didn't think she could stomach it anyway. "I'll just have some coffee," she murmured.

Gone was the easy banter they'd shared over mealtimes. Gone was the subtle flirting, the friendly smiles and eye contact. The sound of his knife and fork were amplified through the kitchen and each clink was torture. She got up from the table and refilled his coffee cup.

"Maggie, I'm sorry about everything I've put you through. I've been incredibly unfair."

The emptiness crawled in again. His job came first and that was how it should be, she realized. And she didn't want anything permanent from him, so why did it hurt so much?

"Don't say anything. We both know it's what you do. We knew all along that this moment would come."

"This isn't easy for me, Maggie," he said quietly. "I wasn't counting on finding you."

Her fingers tightened on the back of a chair. He didn't understand how she felt the need to pull back. To save herself from more pain. Seeing him hurt was bad enough. Finding out he'd been shot was another story. A fresh bandage shone on his forehead, a bright reminder of the consequences of his job. It was too close, too fresh. Even after all these years. She couldn't handle the danger. She knew it as surely as she was breathing.

"Maggie, please. Talk to me."

She lifted her head, her vision blurred with angry tears. "And say what, Nate? You could have been killed! And don't shrug it off, because I know what it's like, okay? You're not the only one keeping secrets!"

His lips dropped open as her voice rose.

"I don't know what you mean. What secrets?"

She snorted, looking away for a moment. "What am I thinking. It was probably all in the background check you did."

"What on earth are you talking about?" He came forward, placing his hand on the countertop. "You're not making any sense!"

She put her hands on her hips. "Tell me you don't know, then. Tell me you don't have a clue that my husband died because he was shot on the job!"

The words came out so quickly she had no chance to hold them back. She'd never hidden the fact that Tom had died, but she'd also never let on he'd been shot.

His body stiffened. "He what? I swear to God, Maggie, I didn't know."

"How could you not know? Stop lying to me!"

The outburst rang through the silence. "Maggie, I'm telling you truthfully. I didn't know about your husband. I only knew you were a widow. I promise. Grant didn't tell me anything more." He came forward, reached out to touch her. "It explains so much. Why you held back. Why you were so upset about the gun and the shooting. What Grant said last night about the file. I never knew. How did it happen?"

Maggie remembered the look of confusion on Nate's face the previous evening when Grant had mentioned Tom's death. Perhaps he hadn't known after all.

But talking about it still hurt. It still brought back all the bitter memories of that night and she had to swallow the bile that had risen in her throat thinking about what she'd been put through.

"He was a security guard for one of the oil companies. An activist didn't look kindly on their policies. Tom paid the price for that. We paid the price, too, living with the inquiry, living without him."

"I'm so sorry, Maggie. Such a senseless way to lose a husband and a father."

She warned him off with a raised hand, blinking furiously. "Don't. Please, don't be kind. I can't handle any more."

The last thing she needed now was sympathy. Her eyes darted up to the clock, ticking along steadily as if they had all the time in the world. But they didn't. He had to go, and soon.

"You'd better finish your breakfast."

Her cold tone put an end to further conversation. Nate sat. Maggie didn't know how he could eat, her own stomach was tied in knots over the whole thing. She supposed this was an ordinary day for him. Perhaps it was routine for him. Get up, get dressed, eat and go to work. For her, this would never be normal.

Finally it was over. Nate rose from the table and brought his plate to the sink.

"Thank you, Maggie."

The words were deep and hushed in the quiet. Maggie closed her eyes, wanting to get goodbye over with and yet desperate to cling to every second she had with him.

"You're welcome."

Her throat thickened so that it was difficult to swallow. It was silly, she told herself, that she'd come to care so much about someone in a few short weeks. Someone who had misrepresented himself and lied to her. But she was smart enough to realize it wasn't that easy. Without intending to, Nate had broken through so many barriers she'd erected since Tom's death. She'd started to feel again—to want, to need. For a few glorious moments, it had been bliss.

But in the end it wasn't worth the thud and she knew it.

"Nate, I…"

She turned but he was gone.

She found him near the front door. He'd shrugged into his vest and she could do nothing but stare. Never in her life had she been so glad to see Kevlar and she prayed it would keep him safe. Each pocket contained some piece of equipment he would need. The marshals crest appeared again on a flap that lay over his heart. As she watched, he propped his foot on a stair step and fastened a holster over his thigh, his movements practiced and efficient.

From his pack he took a handgun, placed it in the holster and straightened. When he did he spied her watching him and their eyes clashed, held.

"You look so different," she whispered. He was a stranger yet not. He was the man she was attracted to, but so much more.

"This is who I am, Maggie."

"You're more than that, Nate. Don't think I don't know it."

Her lower lip quivered, she bit down to stop it.

Five more minutes. That was all she had to get through.

"I want you to take it all, Nate. When you leave this morning that has to be it."

His gaze fell on something by the front closet and she turned her head. His duffel waited, already packed.

It was what she wanted. It was. That didn't mean seeing him walk away wasn't going to hurt.

She met his gaze. He waited, strong and steady. How she wished she were brave enough to take a step forward, to tell him what it had meant to her, knowing him. To feel his arms around her one more time, to breathe in his scent.

"I've got to go, Maggie."

"I know."

They were whispering now. He shouldered his pack and picked up his duffel. Put his hand on the doorknob. And paused.

Maggie's body trembled. How could this be it? How could he walk out with nothing more than a goodbye? Yet to say more would take more than she could give.

The bags slid to the floor and he reached out, pulling her close and pressing his mouth to hers.

Her heart leaped as she wrapped her arms around his neck, pressing as closely as she could though the thickness of his vest held them apart. The hard metal of the gun on his leg dug into her thigh; she didn't care. She just wanted to tell him at last how much he meant to her despite the complications.

"Oh God, did you sleep at all?" she wailed, pulling back and cradling his jaws in her hands, her thumbs touching the shadowed half-moons beneath his eyes.

"I couldn't. I could only think of you, Maggie." He crushed his mouth to hers again. When they finally came up for air, his voice was raw. "I wish you'd never left my room last night."

Her heart thundered. She'd started to wish it, too, even knowing it was wrong. How was it that she could be so afraid for him this way—wrapped in Kevlar and strapped with weapons—and yet be so fatally attracted?

"I'm sorry, Nate. I'm not mad anymore, I promise." She gulped in air, trying to control the urge to cry.

She couldn't go through this again. His lips touched

her eyelids gently and his hands cupped her face. She knew this had to be goodbye. He needed to go, to get what he'd come for and finish it. There was no sense in going over again what couldn't be changed.

"I've got to go," he repeated. "I just couldn't leave without you knowing…" He lowered his forehead to hers. "Damn, Maggie. This wasn't just some assignment and we both know it. I'm sorry I hurt you. More sorry than you know."

"How can I be angry with you?" She tried to smile but it faltered. Soon his touch would be gone for good. "You did what you had to, Nate, I understand that."

"It wasn't just the job."

His breath warmed her cheek and she closed her eyes, swallowing. Oh Lord, this was turning into the farewell she'd craved and dreaded all at once.

"I wanted to protect you, you and Jen. I see every day what men like Pete can do. I'd die before I let him hurt either of you more than he already has."

Her blood chilled. The danger was real and imminent. Yet she was proud. "Do you know how rare you are?" At the shake of his head, she persisted. "You are. You take responsibility for *right* when most of us shy away."

"But…you want me to walk away."

"And it's the only thing to do." His thumb grazed her cheek and she fought back tears. "Now go. Grant will be waiting."

He picked the bags up again and opened the door. And just as quickly dropped them again.

And faced her, looking as serious as she'd ever seen him.

"I love you, Maggie."

The words stopped her cold.

He loved her? Maggie stepped away. No, no. They'd

said all that they needed to say. He didn't mean it. He was supposed to be going to meet Grant. They were supposed to have their goodbye and she'd put her life back together. It was all supposed to be temporary.

But in a moment he changed everything with those three little words. This was different. *Love* was different. Love hurt. She didn't have room for love.

She turned her back. "You're just reacting to today, that's all. What you need to do, what happens next. You can't love me…you've only known me a few weeks. You're just getting caught up in the moment."

"No, I don't think so."

Maggie faced him. This wasn't happening. He couldn't love her. It was supposed to be a beautiful goodbye, that was all.

"Nate, don't do this. I can't love you. You live thousands of miles away. And my life is here, with Jen."

"I know that." He took a step closer, unwilling to let her get away. "It's confusing, but it doesn't change how I feel. Or that I had to tell you."

Something inside her broke, a quiet snap that pierced the dam of denial. She'd told herself for so long that no one would ever love her again, but she'd been wrong. Nate loved her. It would never work, but simply knowing it filled her with a warmth she'd long forgotten.

She pushed it aside, that lovely joy, and replaced it with the stark reality of what he did for a living.

"What is it you want, Nate?"

He came closer still until Maggie felt the cool wood of the banister pressing against her back.

"I want you. I want all of you, Maggie. I don't know how, but I can't let you go."

"You're talking about a future beyond today."

He was so compelling. His weight was balanced squarely over both feet, a pillar of strength and fortitude. He was everything a woman could ever want, so why was she determined to run in the opposite direction?

Because she knew what happened to people she loved, and Nate already faced enough risk every day. She wouldn't survive going through that again.

"Marry me, Maggie Taylor."

Her mouth dropped open for the briefest of seconds before she forced it shut again. Everything in her felt like weeping, only she couldn't. She couldn't fall apart now.

"Oh, Nate, you know I can't." She turned away.

"Why not?" He grabbed her wrist and turned her back around.

Maggie set her lips, looking from his fingers circling her wrist up into his oh-so-earnest eyes. "First of all, my business and home are here."

"Sell it and start a new one. I can sell my house and we'll buy a new place on the water."

She shook her head. "Jen goes to school here."

"Bring her along. She can transfer her credits. Or she can go to school here and fly to Florida on holidays. Most kids would kill for spring break in the Sunshine State."

He was tearing down her arguments one by one and panic threaded through her veins. Why had he ever come here? She'd learned how to live her life her own way and he waltzed in changing everything. She couldn't handle that. Didn't know how to do it.

And the fact remained that she was a forty-plus widow with a grown daughter and he was nearly a decade younger, just embarking on that phase of his life. It wouldn't be fair to either of them.

"What about children?"

Nate paused and Maggie knew she'd hit a spot. She

grabbed at it, persisted. "Don't you want children, Nate? I already have Jen. I'm forty-two years old. And look at you. You're in your prime. Thirty-three and ready to start a family. And I don't want any more babies, not at my age. I'm sure of that."

"You're playing the age card. And that's not fair. I don't give a damn that you're older than I am. I never have, and you know it."

But she shook her head, stopping him. "No, I'm thinking ahead. It wouldn't be fair to you."

She skirted past him and into the den. It was true. She didn't want to have kids in her forties. Didn't want to be sixty and going through the teenage years, or trying to pay for college as she was retiring. But she couldn't blame Nate for wanting a family. It was another in a long list of reasons why it would be better to walk away. Perhaps one he could actually relate to.

"I don't want kids."

He followed her into the den. Maggie reached out and picked up a knickknack, turning it over and over in her hands. "You say that now, but…"

"No, Maggie. I don't want kids." His voice was firm, definite. "I've seen too many who weren't loved. I have nieces and nephews and I love them, but I've never wanted any of my own. I'd rather put my energies into helping ones who need someone to care. I'd hate to do that and not have energy for my own at home. That wouldn't be fair. So I'm okay with not having children."

He closed the gap between them. "Do you have any other roadblocks you'd like to erect? Because none of it changes the fact that I love you."

She could throw out the fact that he was asking her to uproot her life while his remained unchanged, but she knew she could never ask him to change who he was. Perhaps he'd change jobs, but he'd always be in law enforcement. There was no point even bringing it up. Not when she knew the real issue was that she never wanted to love and lose like she already had too many times in her life. Today had shown her that losing Nate would hurt. How much more would that be magnified after months, or even years of marriage? How could she stand waiting at home every day, wondering if he was all right, wondering if this would be the day he wouldn't come home? How could she stand to have her heart broken a second time?

There was only one way. And in her heart she silently apologized for it before she opened her mouth, knowing that while it hurt him, having to tell it was tearing her apart.

"I will never love anyone the way I loved Tom. I'm sorry, Nate."

He stopped cold and her heart wept as the light went out of his eyes.

"That's it then. I can't compete with a ghost."

"What did you expect me to say?" she whispered. "You know me better than anyone has known me in a long time. You had to know I wouldn't pick up and leave my life behind. Not for…"

The pause said more than the words ever could have.

She couldn't love and lose so horribly. Not again.

"Please, Nate, don't make this harder than it already is." Everything in her longed to reach out and touch him but she couldn't afford the moment of weakness. "I can't love you the way you want me to."

"I can't argue with that." He ran a hand over his short hair, leaving little bits in spikes. "I can argue with logistics. I can't make you feel something you don't. I misread."

He shrugged his shoulders, inhaled. "That's it then.

After we pick up Pete I'll be spending the night in town. In the morning I'll be leaving with Grant."

His eyes, dark with disappointment, caught hers one last time. "I know it's not nearly enough, but thank you, Maggie. For everything."

He turned and walked out the door, and she let him go, wishing he'd do it quickly now instead of prolonging the pain.

He stepped off the porch and toward the SUV that would take him away from her.

"Nate?" She couldn't help calling out to him as he lifted the tailgate and put his gear inside.

"Be safe."

He raised a hand in farewell and slid behind the wheel. Maggie closed the door and walked numbly back to the kitchen, putting his dirty dishes in the dishwasher for the last time.

She'd thought that once he was gone the tears would come, but they were locked deep inside, too deep for her to give them license. She sat at the empty kitchen table, closing her eyes.

After a time she rose and went to do the morning chores, anything to keep herself occupied. Returning to his room was another reminder of how close they'd come to making love last night and Maggie regretted how she'd acted. She wished now she had that beautiful memory to carry her through, but she hadn't been able to let down the wall she'd built around herself. When he'd stopped them, she'd convinced herself he was rejecting her.

But what she'd really been afraid of was herself. And now she'd hurt him without intending to.

But Nate had broken through her barriers anyway. She finished making his bed and turned, only to find the St. Christopher medallion he always wore, twined around the base of the bedside lamp. She sat on the edge of the bed where she'd lain with him, holding the heavy pewter in her fingers. Fighting the feeling of superstition that he should be without his good luck charm today of all days.

And when she realized how long she'd been sitting there, she fastened it around her neck. Tomorrow she'd put it in the trinket box she kept of reminders from those she'd loved. For that's what he'd done to her.

For the first time in fifteen years, she was in love.

And he was in love with her.

And now he was gone. Even knowing he wasn't coming back, she wouldn't rest until it was over and she knew he was safe.

Chapter 12

When the car door slammed, she leaped up in anticipation.

But it wasn't Nate's SUV. Instead it was Grant's cruiser and he walked, alone, toward Maggie's front door.

"No," she breathed, a hand lifting to cover her mouth. Everything in her body went icily cold. She shook her head, backing away from the door. *Not again*.

Grant took off his cap and tucked it under his arm before ringing the doorbell.

She couldn't answer it. She pressed both her hands to her face, refusing to touch the doorknob. She couldn't listen to him say the words that she knew would come next. Oh God, she'd done that once before and it had blown her whole world apart. Tears seared the backs of her eyelids as she remembered the officer telling her Tom had been killed. And this morning...

The doorbell rang again. "Maggie?"

A single sob escaped. This morning Nate had told

her he loved her and she'd told him that she wouldn't love anyone the way she'd loved Tom. She'd cast him off and sent him into a dangerous situation believing she didn't love him at all.

But she did. She loved him so much she refused to believe in a world where he didn't exist.

"Maggie, for God's sake, open the door!" Grant shouted now and for some reason the command jolted her to action and she turned the knob, pulling the door open. And saw the smear of blood on his shirt.

He took one look at her face and his own gentled. "You're pale. Come sit down."

She shook her head. "Just say it, Grant. Please, just say it and get it over with."

His eyes were kind, so kind, and she hated him for it.

"He's not dead, if that's what you're thinking."

Her breath came out in a rush. "I think I'll sit down now."

She made it to the first chair on the veranda and her knees gave out.

Grant knelt before her, chafing the sides of her thighs with his hands. The connection gave her something to focus on.

"Thanks to you, and to Jen, we found a stash of drugs, money and weapons beneath the barn. And we were right in bringing him in, and none too soon. We found the cell. There were restraints. We're checking it now for DNA evidence."

The thought that it could have been Jen in there momentarily made Maggie's heart stop.

"But that's not all, Maggie. I'm just going to tell it to you straight, okay?" He squeezed her hand and met her gaze squarely. "I came alone because Nate was shot and he's been taken to hospital."

"How bad is it?" She pulled away, twisting her pale

fingers together, trying to hold it together and absorb everything Grant was telling her. Trying not to panic. Trying not to act like her whole world was crumbling around her.

"He's alive, but beyond that I really don't know."

Dread and fear froze her.

"I…" She halted; this was Grant whom she barely knew, yet she had to say it. "I turned him away this morning. I was wrong to do that, Grant." Her words came out childlike and contrite.

"I can take you to the hospital. Grab what you need and I'll wait."

Maggie nodded dumbly. Her only thought now was seeing Nate and telling him she loved him before it was too late. He couldn't leave her, not when the lie was there between them. Not before she had a chance to make it right. She got to her feet woodenly, stopping only to grab her purse and lock the door.

Grant opened the door to his cruiser and helped her inside. He got in the driver's side and called something in on his radio before reversing and pulling out of the lane.

He didn't spare speed and she was glad of it as they hit the main road. A call came back on the radio and Maggie tried to interpret it, but she couldn't seem to make sense of the words.

Grant answered back. Then turned to Maggie.

"Nate's stable for the moment, but they're airlifting him to Edmonton."

Maggie didn't move; it was simply another layer of shock. He was ill enough that he had to be transferred to a bigger hospital. He had to hold on until she got there, he simply had to. Flashes hit behind her eyes, of arriving at the hospital and finding Tom in a coma. All the things she wanted to say to him were meaningless. And then he'd been gone.

Nate had to hold on. He had to.

"I'm going to take you there, Maggie. Pete's in custody and not going anywhere. And odd as it seems... Nate's my partner. We'll go together."

Maggie sat back in the seat, surprised when Grant turned on his lights but not the siren, taking the highway north to the capital city. She didn't know what to say to him...her normal ability for small talk had evaporated.

But Grant suddenly seemed able to fill the gap.

"Maggie, I looked into what happened with Tom. It wasn't as simple as him just being shot. And a thing like that...I can see how it would change a person. I know you got to the hospital too late. And the investigation was no picnic...especially on top of all the grief you must have been feeling."

His clear eyes were unrelenting as he turned his head to look at her, like he could see her thoughts. The notion didn't unsettle her now, not like it used to.

"It's normal to be scared. And there are no guarantees. But...for what it's worth...I think it would be a crying shame to walk away from something, from *someone* who loves you as much as Nate does because you were afraid. You'd miss out on something wonderful, don't you think?"

Maggie tried to swallow around the lump in her throat. He made it sound so easy. Nothing about loving Nate Griffith was easy. When she'd said she couldn't love him like she had Tom, it hadn't been a complete truth. She did love him and it scared her to death. She loved him so much that she couldn't imagine losing him. That was what she'd meant and she'd deliberately let him draw his own conclusion as to her meaning.

"It can be damned lonely being a cop. Sometimes

it's family that keeps us grounded. Wives put up with a lot, but…"

He kept his eyes on the road, smoothly passing a tractor-trailer and moving back into the right lane again. "Sometimes having that anchor keeps us going." He cleared his throat and looked back at her. "Think about it," Grant concluded.

There were so many questions. She had the bed-and-breakfast and a daughter and nearly crippling fears about being involved with such a man.

How badly had he been hurt?

And how could she let him do this alone?

At the hospital, Grant sidestepped a news crew, which had already arrived. An officer being shot was news and Maggie had no desire to be captured on camera. As Grant snuck them through, Maggie stared at the TV crew openmouthed, the lingering sense of déjà vu pervading again. A nurse directed them to the Intensive Care Unit and from there to a waiting room outside the closed, quiet doors.

When the time came, Grant went in first. Maggie tried to straighten her hair, make herself look presentable. But Grant was back within a few minutes, unsmiling.

"He's still unconscious."

"I want to see him."

Grant nodded. "The doctor says it's all right. I'll take you to him."

Once inside Nate's room, Maggie forgot all about Grant. Nate, her Nate, lay pale and prone on the bed. Tubes ran from his nose and more from his arm. His lashes were still on his gray cheeks, and as she watched, one finger twitched against the blanket.

But that was all.

"He lost a lot of blood," a nurse whispered, padding into the room softly and deftly adding a bag to his IV stand. "It's perfectly okay that he's not awake."

Maggie's shoulders slumped as she pulled up a chair to the bed, as quietly as she could. "Thank you. Is it all right if I wait?"

"We usually only let visitors in for a few minutes."

"I just want to sit with him. I don't want him to wake up alone."

The nurse looked at Maggie a long time, then at Grant, still in uniform, still with the stripe of dried blood.

"As long as you sit quietly."

Maggie nodded.

Grant stepped forward. "I'm going to get us some coffee."

She nodded dumbly; coffee was the last thing she wanted but didn't have it in her to argue.

And then the room was quiet, except for the soft beep of a monitor.

She looked at Nate's slumbering form. It was clear from the position and bandaging that the shot had hit his leg. A thousand questions flooded her brain…how bad was it, would he be permanently injured, did his head injury of yesterday affect his health now, did they get the bullet out, did it hit the artery…but all of them were subverted by a single thought: *Please don't leave me.*

Grant brought coffee; stayed awhile, but in the end he had to return home. There was paperwork to be done and arrangements to be made now that Nate would not be transporting Harding himself. With a promise to come back as soon as he could, Grant left and it was only the two of them. Maggie chafed Nate's hand between hers.

"Hold on, Nate. Please hold on."

* * *

The haze was white, then gray, and then blurry shapes came into focus.

Nate swallowed—his mouth was bone-dry—and realized that the beeping sound he heard wasn't his alarm clock, but a monitor that was attached to somewhere on his body.

He was in the hospital, and in that moment, he remembered exactly what had happened. The sound of the shot and the explosion of pain, and he instinctively stiffened. Only tensing brought the pain back and he forced himself to relax.

And when he did, he realized there was a mop of dark hair on the bed beside his hip.

Maggie.

He turned his head a half inch and tried to whisper her name, but nothing came out. He sighed and laid his head back against the pillow, closing his eyes, marveling that she was there, sleeping on his hospital bed.

He was a marshal, he knew that. He also knew that never in his life had he felt as strong a connection as he did to Maggie. He loved her, and it was different than anything he'd experienced before. Nothing about Maggie was easy. Perhaps that was why she was so perfect for him.

Why in the world couldn't she see that?

He sighed, knowing he couldn't place one iota of blame on her. Not after today. Before today he could have insisted that he wouldn't get hurt. He could have told her about all the cases he'd been on where he'd come out without a scratch.

But after today…there was no denying it. What he did had risks. And after the way her husband had died, hell, he couldn't blame her for not taking that on again.

He moved a hand until it could touch the soft silk of

her hair and he rubbed a few strands between his fingers. She had said this morning that she couldn't love anyone as she'd loved her husband. But that wasn't what had made him walk away.

He had sensed her desperation and panic, and he knew he couldn't pressure her into taking the chance. It wasn't fair to ask that of her, not after all she'd been through already. She'd already risked and lost everything. She'd fought him so hard this morning that he had known he couldn't hurt her more than she'd already been hurt.

Yet here she was. Waiting for him in a hospital room. He couldn't imagine how difficult this must be for her. He licked his lips.

"Maggie," he managed this time, his voice a rough croak.

She lifted her head slowly, one cheek red from being pressed against the blanket, her hair untidy and she began to tuck it behind her ears by what he knew now was force of habit.

"Nate."

As soon as she said his name, her eyes welled with tears and a few slid past her lashes and down her cheeks. To Nate, she'd never looked more beautiful. Her voice was soft and musical like he remembered. He'd heard it enough times in his head. Played it over and over like a favorite song, only he never tired of it.

He raised his hand, cupped her cheek and closed his eyes.

Home.

This was how it felt then. Everything he had known was missing came down to this very moment. Home wasn't his place in Florida or the Haven or a place at all. It was Maggie. Maggie was the home he'd been looking for.

He looked at her tearstained face, drawn with worry and anxiety, and he knew he'd been wrong to propose. Every argument she'd put up had been justified but easily disputed. Until the end. Maggie would never intentionally hurt anyone, so for her to say what she had, told him exactly how frightened she was. As much as he loved her, he knew that her feelings for him only caused her pain. The kindest thing he could do was accept her words and let her go.

"What are you doing here?"

Maggie linked her fingers with his. "Grant brought me. You're in Edmonton. You were shot."

His eyes widened. She'd said the last without flinching at all.

"I remember. Pete?"

"Is in custody. Grant was here... he brought me... but he left several hours ago to look after things. He's coming back in the morning."

Nate nodded. "I'm sorry I worried you. I'll be fine, though. You don't have to stay."

"Just try to get rid of me and see what happens."

Nate's mouth dropped open and for the first time, Maggie smiled.

It made him hope, even as pain shot from his leg into his gut. But hope was all he had, and he didn't want to squander a second of it. "I'll take you for as long as you'll let me."

"How does forever sound?"

Maggie laughed at the expression on his face. He hadn't been expecting that. But she'd had a good long time to think, and cry, and worry, and pray. And every single time she came up with the same answer: Any time with Nate was better than no time at all.

He winced and she stood up, glancing at the IV bags.

"I'll call the nurse. You are nearly due for pain medication, I think."

He stopped her. "No, not yet. They'll put me to sleep. And right now I want to see you."

Her body warmed. All day she'd had images of what he was doing and they blended with the memories of the night Tom was killed. And then her fears had come true. And with them, truth—she loved him. But she hadn't known what to do with it.

Only hours spent at his bedside had shown her what was real, and right.

"Let me get you some water, at least," Maggie chided. "You need fluids. The doctor said so."

She wanted to kiss him but wasn't sure if it was the right thing or not. In the end she waited so long she just smiled and scooted from the room.

She was coming back from the ice machine when she spied Jen, curled up in a chair in the waiting room.

"Honey?"

Jen came awake instantly, standing up and tucking her hair in the same way her mother often did. "How's Nate? Is he all right?"

Maggie nodded, going into the room and sitting down next to Jen. "He just woke up. He's okay. In a lot of pain, but fine."

Jen's shoulders relaxed and Maggie's brows pinched together.

"I didn't expect to see you quite this soon. How long have you been here, waiting?"

"A few hours. Constable Simms called me at the dorm and told me what happened. Said maybe you'd like some company. But when I got here and peeked into Nate's room, you were asleep. So I came out here to wait." She reached over and took Maggie's hand in hers. "How are you holding up?"

"Me?"

Jen nodded. "Yeah. You. This couldn't have been easy for you, Mom. Not after Dad."

Maggie wiped her lashes; how many times was she going to cry today anyway? "When did you grow up so fast?"

"I dunno." Her old grin was back, impish. "Fast enough to see that you're in love with him."

Maggie's head snapped back to stare at her daughter. Jen's dark ponytail bobbed as she nodded her head. "You are. I knew when I came home there'd been something between you. You were different. And the way he held you last night…"

Maggie's heart thumped hard as she looked into Jen's eyes, ones so like her father's.

"How would you feel about that?" She posed the question carefully.

"Dang, Mom, you've been alone too long. And Nate's cool, you know? He's one of the good guys." Her cheeks pinked. "He took care of Pete, didn't he?"

"Yes, yes, he did," Maggie murmured.

"Well, then, I think you'd be a fool to let him get away."

Maggie couldn't help but laugh a little. "You do, do you?"

"I do. Now, do you think it'd be okay if I said hi to Nate and then went home? I have a nine-thirty class in the morning."

"I think that would be fine."

They went into the room together, Maggie holding the plastic cup of ice chips and Jen with her hands in her pockets. But when she saw Nate, she went over to the bed, leaned over and kissed his cheek. "Thank you," she said quietly. "Thank you for helping me. For helping us." She threw a quick glance at her mother.

"You're welcome," he whispered, his voice too hoarse for anything stronger. "And we owe you, too, Jen. I'm proud of you."

Jen squeezed his hand. "I'm going to leave you two alone, but I'll come back after class tomorrow. Do you want anything? The only thing worse than dorm food is hospital food. I can sneak it in."

Maggie swallowed thickly. It was so much like a family. Yet she'd turned Nate away just hours ago. Would he believe her now, when she was ready to tell the truth?

"Chocolate pudding," he murmured. "I love chocolate pudding."

Jen laughed. "Talk to you soon," she said in farewell, before closing the door behind her, leaving them alone in the dim light.

He patted the bed beside him. "Come here," he commanded, his voice still weak but warm.

She put the cup of chips on the table beside the bed and perched on the mattress gently, trying to disturb as little as possible.

He took her hand in his. The hospital band chafed at her a bit, but his other hand was connected to the IV.

"Let's go back. Why don't you tell me what you meant about the forever bit. Because this morning you were prepared to never see me again."

It had hurt her to hurt him. And during the long day, waiting for news, she'd looked around her. What did she have at Mountain Haven? Nothing more than a list of excuses. A house, a home. A garden and a roof that needed repairs. She'd considered it her safe place but now knew she'd only been hiding.

She had a daughter who was already moving away, embarking on a new stage in her life. And what had Maggie done? She'd let her fears dictate her actions, letting her grief have control. She'd been so afraid of what might happen that she'd pushed away the one true thing.

Only Grant had shown up and had told her Nate was hurt, and none of it mattered anymore. Saying goodbye had done nothing to quell her feelings, or her worry. She knew in that moment that she wanted to stand by him *through* it, not pretend it didn't exist.

"You left, and I waited. It was awful, not knowing. But not near as awful as seeing your blood on Grant's uniform. Or hearing him say you'd been shot."

"I'm sorry I put you through that. I realized this morning that I had asked too much of you. It's never easy being married to a cop, for anyone. And after what you've already been through…I should have realized."

Maggie's heart skipped. "Are you saying you don't want to marry me?"

His eyes met hers, the blue-green glittering darkly in the pale light. "That's not the issue. The truth is, I should have been more sensitive. I knew all along how you felt and I pressured you anyway."

"Maybe I needed it." She straightened her shoulders. After all she'd been through today, it wasn't as hard being brave as she thought it would be.

"I love you, Nate."

Saying the words, finally saying them, filled her with something so surprising she didn't know what to do with it. It was like everything in her expanded, awakened. There was power in it, beautiful power she hadn't expected.

She ignored the trembling in her hands and gripped his fingers. She longed to touch him, wished he weren't hooked up to monitors and medication. Instead she had to make do with their tenuous connection.

"It's true. I do love you, and I'm sorry I let my fear dictate how I acted. I think I need to explain," she murmured, her voice shaking a little. He'd opened his heart to her that morning, now it was her turn. And she wanted to do it. It didn't mean it was easy.

"Losing Tom was the hardest thing I ever did," she began. "Not only was he shot, but he killed a man in the process and he was made out to be both hero and villain. Like my parents, I'd loved him and counted on him and he was suddenly gone. I had Jen and Mike to look after and I had to do it alone. I swore from that point that I would never give myself over to that sort of hope again. It hurt too much to lose. That's what I meant. I couldn't love like that again, not because I didn't love you but because the need to protect myself was too strong to give in to it."

"I knew that."

"You did?"

"All the other arguments were logical and easily remedied. But that one…I could see how afraid you were. And I knew you were too precious to hurt that way again. So I walked away, knowing at least I wouldn't be the one to cause you that sort of pain."

Tears flooded her eyes. "You knew."

"Of course I knew. Did you think I didn't get it? We got to know each other over the last weeks. I fell in love with you."

"When Grant said you were hurt, I knew without a doubt. I had to tell you that I had been afraid to love you. Afraid of what it meant to change my life for you. Afraid to live."

"Oh, Maggie."

"I want to live, Nate. I didn't realize I wasn't…didn't realize I could…until you came along. You changed everything. None of it matters without you."

"But I'm still a marshal. Look at me. I was really

hurt today. I still have a job to do. And I'm not sure I'd be happy doing anything else."

"I'd never ask you to."

"What about being afraid? You were so angry when you discovered who I was. When you thought Jen might be hurt and when you found out I'd been shot."

"And I'll still worry. But I'll worry whether we're together or not. Grant said something to me today. He said that sometimes family is the glue that holds you together. I want to be that for you. Don't you see, Nate?" Her lip quivered but she kept on. "You always put yourself in danger. I want to be your safe place. The way that you've become mine. I always thought I was safer in my little corner. But I was so wrong."

"I love you, Maggie. And I'd do anything to be able to hold you right now."

Six inches lay between his body and the edge of the bed, but Maggie didn't care. She stretched out, aligning herself with his good side, her cheek resting against his shoulder. "Will this do?"

His voice rumbled, slow and sexy in her ear. "For now."

He was warm and strong and for the first time in nearly half her life she felt exactly where she belonged. Now, safe in his arms, the relief flooded her, and she finally let the tears come as she wept against his shoulder.

"Don't cry, Maggie. Please don't."

His voice, that smooth baritone with the hint of grit, rumbled from his chest against her cheek. She shook her head against the cotton of his shirt. "I was sure of how I felt. But I also knew I might be too late. I was so afraid I'd be too late to tell you…"

"You're not."

He caught sight of the chain around her neck and the medal hanging from it. "You found my St. Christopher."

She nodded. "I was going to put it in my special box of memories. Only it's not a memory. I'm not ready to give up on the future yet."

He squeezed her. "Oh, Maggie. I'm so glad." He released her and she lifted her chin so she could gaze into his eyes. Those beautiful, turquoise eyes that had somehow seen her from the very beginning.

"Is this a good time to ask you again?"

Her heart tripped over itself.

"Will you marry me, Maggie? We can figure the rest out later. Just say yes."

"Yes." And she shifted a little, pushing herself up on the bed so she could kiss him properly.

When she pulled away, she stayed propped up on an elbow. "Is your house big enough for one more? Maybe two?"

"You mean in Florida? You'd move there to be with me?"

A tiny smile worked its way up her cheek. "I would. I can sell Mountain Haven. And find a job there, or open a business. I think I might become very partial to palm trees."

"You would really give up your life here?"

"I would."

"What about Jen?"

"Didn't you already solve these arguments this morning?" She teased him. "Jen's finding her own way. In another few years she'll be on her own completely. She's becoming an adult and making her own decisions. I'll leave it up to her what she wants to do."

He closed his eyes and Maggie was shocked to see a tear gather at the corner of his eye. "Nate? What is it? Should I get the doctor?"

He shook his head. "No…it's just…" He opened his eyes again, struggling with emotion. "This morning when I was shot I thought I was going to die. And now here you are. It doesn't seem possible. I lied to you, Maggie, and led you on and did nothing but confuse your life. And here you are ready to give up everything for me. It doesn't seem right. It should be me making the sacrifices."

"No, Nate. You changed everything for me. Why should you give up your life? I'm not giving up anything, not really. Because I wasn't really living. I was only existing. You did that. Only you."

"You actually mean that?"

"I do. I want to be with you. I know a part of me will always be afraid you're not coming back. But I can't sacrifice all the good stuff. Living without you isn't living at all. It's just putting myself in a box and hoping I'll never get hurt. And it's not what I want anymore."

"I want to touch you, do all the right things," he whispered in the semidarkness. "I don't have a ring for your finger, but if you'll say yes I'll rectify that problem as soon as I get out of this bed."

"I don't need a ring to know what's true. All I need is you."

He traced a finger down her cheek with his free hand. "This sounds odd considering where I am. But there are things I can promise and things I can't. And you know that, Maggie. But I can promise you that when you're my wife I'll do my best to come home to you every night, to love you and protect you. Those things will never change."

"That's all the guarantee I need," she whispered, pressing her lips to his once more. "It's more than enough."

* * * * *

**Enjoy this sneak peak from Susan Meier's upcoming book,
SINGLE DAD'S CHRISTMAS MIRACLE.**

*Clark Beaumont is trying to make it through the holidays
for the sake of his kids. Is Althea Johnson the Christmas
miracle he's been searching for?*

After a quick supper of salads made from things they found in
the refrigerator, Althea cleaned the kitchen, then joined Clark
and his kids in the living room for TV. Shopping, pizza and
making salads as a family had gotten Clark past his nerves and
had turned Jack chatty.

But the day had been too much for Teagan and she fell asleep
on Clark's lap. Gently cradling her, he rose from the sofa.

Althea rose, too, to help put the little girl to bed, but he stopped
her with a wave of his hand. "I'll get her. You and Jack relax."

He returned in ten minutes, telling Althea that he hadn't
bathed her, simply slid her out of her clothes and into pajamas.
She nodded.

He smiled at her.

And her stomach plummeted. She couldn't describe the look
in his eyes, the way his smile affected her, but she knew that—in
her entire life—nobody had ever looked at her quite like that.

She turned her attention back to the television, her nerves
tingling.

Ten minutes later, Jack yawned and stretched. "I'm tired, too."

As he walked past Clark, Clark grabbed his hand and

squeezed. "Too much time walking outside."

Jack sniffed a laugh. "It was still fun."

"Yeah. It was."

Jack grinned, happier than Althea had ever seen him. "Good night."

She and Clark said, "Good night," and Jack left the den.

Althea turned her attention back to the TV. Out of the corner of her eye, she noticed Clark shifted on the sofa, bringing his knee up to the cushion so he could see her.

That's when it hit her that they were totally alone.

"I'm sort of tired, too."

She squelched a sigh of relief. She'd probably imagined he was looking at her differently. She faced him with a smile. "Good night, then." She pointed at the TV. "I'll turn everything off."

He smiled and nodded, but didn't get up from the sofa. Instead, he leaned toward her, caught her shoulders and pulled her to him. His lips met hers softly.

Her heart knocked against her ribs and she pulled back slightly, but he kept her where she was, moving his lips across hers again.

Warmth exploded inside her. Her breath shivered out. She wanted to wrap her arms around his neck, pull him to her and lose herself in him and the kiss that was so gentle and sweet.

But he pulled away. Smiled again. "Good night."

Then he left the room and she sat staring at the door.

Hadn't they decided they weren't going to pursue this?

SINGLE DAD'S CHRISTMAS MIRACLE
by Susan Meier
is available October 2013 only in Harlequin® Romance.

HARLEQUIN®
Romance

Save $1.00 on the purchase of

SINGLE DAD'S CHRISTMAS MIRACLE

by Susan Meier,

available October 1, 2013,
or on any other Harlequin® Romance book.

Available wherever books are sold, including most bookstores,
supermarkets, drugstores and discount stores.

Save $1.00

on the purchase of
SINGLE DAD'S CHRISTMAS MIRACLE
by Susan Meier,
available October 1, 2013,
or on any other Harlequin® Romance book.

Coupon valid until June 30, 2013. Redeemable at participating retail outlets
in the U.S. and Canada only. Limit one coupon per customer.

52610963

Canadian Retailers: Harlequin Enterprises Limited will pay the face value of this coupon plus 10.25¢ if submitted by customer for this product only. Any other use constitutes fraud. Coupon is nonassignable. Void if taxed, prohibited or restricted by law. Consumer must pay any government taxes. Void if copied. Nielsen Clearing House ("NCH") customers submit coupons and proof of sales to Harlequin Enterprises Limited, P.O. Box 3000, Saint John, NB E2L 4L3, Canada. Non-NCH retailer—for reimbursement submit coupons and proof of sales directly to Harlequin Enterprises Limited, Retail Marketing Department, 225 Duncan Mill Rd., Don Mills, ON M3B 3K9, Canada.

U.S. Retailers: Harlequin Enterprises Limited will pay the face value of this coupon plus 8¢ if submitted by customer for this product only. Any other use constitutes fraud. Coupon is nonassignable. Void if taxed, prohibited or restricted by law. Consumer must pay any government taxes. Void if copied. For reimbursement submit coupons and proof of sales directly to Harlequin Enterprises Limited, P.O. Box 880478, El Paso, TX 88588-0478, U.S.A. Cash value 1/100 cents.

5 65373 00076 2 (8100)0 11864

® and TM are trademarks owned and used by the trademark owner and/or its licensee.
© 2013 Harlequin Enterprises Limited

REQUEST YOUR
FREE BOOKS!

2 FREE NOVELS
FROM THE ROMANCE COLLECTION
PLUS 2 FREE GIFTS!

YES! Please send me 2 FREE novels from the Romance Collection and my 2 FREE gifts (gifts are worth about $10). After receiving them, if I don't wish to receive any more books, I can return the shipping statement marked "cancel." If I don't cancel, I will receive 4 brand-new novels every month and be billed just $6.24 per book in the U.S. or $6.74 per book in Canada. That's a savings of at least 22% off the cover price. It's quite a bargain! Shipping and handling is just 50¢ per book in the U.S. and 75¢ per book in Canada.* I understand that accepting the 2 free books and gifts places me under no obligation to buy anything. I can always return a shipment and cancel at any time. Even if I never buy another book, the two free books and gifts are mine to keep forever.

194/394 MDN F4XY

Name _____ (PLEASE PRINT) _____

Address _____ Apt. # _____

City _____ State/Prov. _____ Zip/Postal Code _____

Signature (if under 18, a parent or guardian must sign)

Mail to the Harlequin® Reader Service:
IN U.S.A.: P.O. Box 1867, Buffalo, NY 14240-1867
IN CANADA: P.O. Box 609, Fort Erie, Ontario L2A 5X3

**Want to try two free books from another line?
Call 1-800-873-8635 or visit www.ReaderService.com.**

* Terms and prices subject to change without notice. Prices do not include applicable taxes. Sales tax applicable in N.Y. Canadian residents will be charged applicable taxes. Offer not valid in Quebec. This offer is limited to one order per household. Not valid for current subscribers to the Romance Collection or the Romance/Suspense Collection. All orders subject to credit approval. Credit or debit balances in a customer's account(s) may be offset by any other outstanding balance owed by or to the customer. Please allow 4 to 6 weeks for delivery. Offer available while quantities last.

Your Privacy—The Harlequin® Reader Service is committed to protecting your privacy. Our Privacy Policy is available online at www.ReaderService.com or upon request from the Harlequin Reader Service.

We make a portion of our mailing list available to reputable third parties that offer products we believe may interest you. If you prefer that we not exchange your name with third parties, or if you wish to clarify or modify your communication preferences, please visit us at www.ReaderService.com/consumerschoice or write to us at Harlequin Reader Service Preference Service, P.O. Box 9062, Buffalo, NY 14269. Include your complete name and address.

ROM13R